PHONIC INTERWOVEN

The Ongoing Rebuke of Raw Skiffle

Grant E. Mitchell

A Churly Murpheus Bronze Jaunt

SCENE: In the filthy, dirty, Dusty Southwest
TIME: In the year of our Lured, Nineteen Hundred and Ninety-Eight, a fourteen year old Harris Wittels critiques one of Louis CK's jokes from a live stand up performance, right to his face. At the same time in the streets of Tokyo, fried butterflies are served on sticks to hungry pedestrians with promises of good fortune and a protein kick for whatever the day may bring. And in Paris, Fraunch, someone is feeling way too satisfied for having stomached a bit of dank pungent cheese

Chuck Mafia Bricks

London   Sydney   PDX   Tempe   New Orleans

This work is a book of fiction. Apart from actual historical events, all of the names, characters, and incidents are products of the author's imagination or are used fictitiously. All song lyrics used with permission. Any omissions will be corrected in subsequent editions.

Reference note: "LtAWS" is pronounced "El-tawz"

Listen to Raw Skiffle at www.phonicinterwoven.com

Copyright © 2015 by Grant E. Mitchell. All Rights Reserved

Predatory Facelift Professional Loggerhead

Not so long ago, and relatively near this very spot, there was not a castle sitting atop a hill. There was no daring prince or beautiful captive maiden. There were no dragons lying in wait beneath cavernous mountains, ready to terrorize the villagers of a kingdom that was also non-existent.

These pages do not contain whimsical tales of gallantry and grandeur, nor magical secret potions that wake the soul to life. Still the thirsting spirit may seek satisfaction. Juice the succulent, supple symphony of survival. Inside the cast of candied pulp, rings the subtle truth of sweet sensation.

Outside civilization…

Table of Contents

Chapter the One

January 23, 1998

Some America was about to go down. Disparage us the chivalrous. For the day after tomorrow was the Super Bowl. The Broncos were eleven point underdogs to the defending champion Green Bay Packers. We were southbound on the 491, three quarters of an hour out of Cortez, Colorado. In possession of one ticket to the game and a stash of cash in the back, tank full of gas. Deep in thought, ten toes across the bow on an evening sail. The gas station counter clerk had smiled politely when offering the receipt for the root beer, fuel and jerky. She was young and adrenal, the clerk. Her recollection would entertain long into the night. The slight curve at a decline pitched gravity off and to the starboard side for a fraction of a view into the nothing, northwesterly.

Straightening out, we were running strong. Revolutions per revolutions: Pure resolution to continue. It's cold and I'm just starting to sweat. Spinning wheels. Raid a pony's pantry. Words, phrases, and collected energies. Sounds and silence lived in my walls and decorated my skin. It can be lonesome when it often seems your time has passed. Eras and decades that have come and gone. And come again, and gone again. Eyes look at you differently when you don't belong. Whispers tisk much more sinister if your look is deemed as other. You think about possibility. You factor in probability. You love the idea of potential and the journey. At the very least you can muster half a smile. At worst you can't, and it's sad for a few minutes or lifetimes. It all really does come around. No matter if it's by the riverside or on a stretch of gravel like this narrow highway. Drop your troubles, must calm down. ‖ You try to break away the habits diminishing health. Corrosive acids on your brain steams, rust. Lucille Ball in the clouds with Desi Arnaz, Pop used to say. I don't know why.

5

High tide was upon us. Tossed in the wind leaping out from hill and tree. Aiming for a turn-off that had been spoken of once around a fire circle near Omaha, Nebraska. He has now slowed in several places. I used to roll up Tobacco Road down around near North Cackalack to Knoxville. Plus up to Norfolk and east ways to neck deep in the Atlantic. You ride the trails long enough and sure as summer shore will stop or show. You will hit the sea or dock and build a life. Two days before I knew freedom, I knew oppression dark and heavy laid. I was a shell of my former self. Shadows of glorious days that were purely memories shared.

Izzy bought me for seven hundred seventy-seven dollars and seventy-seven cents. We immediately went out for a drive and received a honk and two peace signs before I was left in a garage to gather dust and cobwebs. I was broke down and no longer in service. It would be years until attention could be spent on rejuvenation. Certain days, Izzy would climb inside and sit on my bench seat, imagining where in the world he was parked. Out the bay window he could almost see the jungle's edge, the beach, the English countryside or a futuristic dystopian hellscape. Palm fronds which he'll push away to reveal drama and the Delta blue. His thoughts brought faces of folks from elsewhere, the sounds and breezes that played about the cab. Serenely. It was shades of a ghetto grave, if you will it to be so. Navigating consciousness, one at a time.

January 24, 1998: Zero-nothing and some change

Feedback. "Boring, man. Luigi board of soopavizas! What're you looking at? What? Are you seeing?" More feedback. The small bar technically qualified as a venue. The mob of audience was one CPA above a bunch of bums. There was a prevailing current of dark apprehension. The unfocused evil drenched the nodding heads. Drops of sweat and glandular activity at full operating capacity. Two men stood on stage behind their microphones, guitars loosely slung and dangling free. A third gargoyle sat hunkered down behind the drums. The trio had already played nonstop for twenty minutes, with seamless transitions between the songs in the first half of the set list. No one cared. Now they were drinking from bottles of beer and tweaking their business before they would kick back into high gear to bring their part of the show to a close.

"This next one is called Body Bag," said the lead guitarist slash singer. "Parenthesis No Sensei. Parenthesis Dojo Does It. End parenthesis." The drummer cracked down with both sticks on the snare and the room hung empty, echoed as calamity and all hell fell down the sound erupted into steady rhythmic chaos. Molten vibrations. The horde's legs and arms pounded the floor and air, irreverently. Faces and body blows show the signs of redlined violence. On some level all is nothing and death and sex linger close. Momentum increases.

"Fear. Does not exist. In this dojo does it?" A wave of voices in the rabble holler back, "No Sensei!"[1]

Attentive, the thick throng starts to swirl and stampede. Their mass spins about in the tightly cordoned area. The heat of stage lights blasting sheer the lifted sphere on which the triumvirate stand, allowed to amplify and reveal these spirits' motivation, shared inspiration to dare. The room was in general agreement. The men and women watched and wanted one thing and everything all and never. Baby please. Baby, please don't. Baby don't please. Baby don't please no bass drop. The bass player's head bopped, arm extended down his vibrating strings pumping low end frequencies through his rumbling subwoofers, and out amongst the ears and souls of the witnesses.

Alyssa rose from obscurity, from a seat on the floor where her back had been up against a cold brick wall. She wasn't tall but the sound waves didn't discriminate. The crowd was totally blocking her view of the musicians on stage. This club, this town was foreign to her. Though really she was the outsider. She was the tag-a-long who came with Roxy, who was in with the band but seemed distracted and uninterested. Standing, Alyssa leaned deep into the wall and could see the tattooed arm of the bass player, his muscles twitching on his right forearm. She felt the thrill of the music and saw some of the crowd chanting in sync with the voice singing out over the house speakers. Roxy told her the singer was Sonny. The banner hanging crooked behind the drummer read: Dystopian Squalor Syndicate.

There was a cluster of miscreants around the bar, partially blocking the path from the tables in the back to the stage and open floor in the front. A high shadowed ceiling bounced the aggressive snare hits down into the mob below. The guitar cut out, leaving the pulse of low throbbing bass oozing through the seams in time.

"Pain. Does not exist. In this dojo does it? No sensei! Get him a body bag."[1a]

Sonny's band, also known just as the Syndicate, was finishing up a loosely managed tour with two other groups in similar positions. Meaning everyone was desperately trying anything to make some kind of splash in the industry. They had been out on the road for six weeks, hitting most parts of the western United States, the mid-West, the east coast and certain spots in the South. Outside in the alley behind the show, the muffled music from the band coated dumpsters and the transitory in town for the evening's entertainment. Figures appeared from the darkness, pale with winter's breath.

8

Alyssa wandered off into the dense crowd and unleashed a holler to contribute to the energy flowing through the building. It would be cold if she stood outside. Posting up in a corner near a pool table, she was a few steps from an exit and felt the chilled air claw inside whenever the door was opened. Most folks were dressed in shades of pitch black. Faces and hands were the only visible skin, save for the few who had shed layers in an attempt to remain free and unbound. No doubt knives were hidden in boots and tucked under belts. Anger and aggression acted as fuel. Lust for the blood rush drove distant stares with a bitten lip. Vicious souls battled hyperawareness in a sulfuric stew. A sacred rite left over a burning flame; simmer for eternity or three and a half hours.

The night's audience had completely coalesced inside the juke-ing joint, an ill-reputing point of least returns. Fierce rug burns. Bodies crept forth and back, into and out of view. Most were mainly stationary, though did shake intermittently or rampage for stretches before crashing into some greater force, or wall. Thuds and thwacks. Roxy and Alyssa Rose mixed in with all the hats and coats. They made the drive from their homestead in a neighboring town. It was January in northern Arizona.

Dystopian Squalor Syndicate was a three-piece bit of heavy that had been playing shows all around the United States since forming in 1994. They were focused on the Southwestern states, but did also venture into the Northwest, Middle America and the East Coast. Boonz (bass) and Truck (drums) found Sonny back when he was still hitting up blues open mic nights and jamming on a street corner with his old Squire pumping through a Danelectro HoneyTone mini-amp, running off a single nine-volt battery. Just played until it cut out, like a boom box or any other bit of electronics.

There was an unsustainable hunger that fueled the group's rapid development and evolving sound. The environment created proved contagious and alluring. It had been over a year since the Syndicate had been through this specific hamlet of Show Low. Word had spread, and the necessary amount of enthusiasm showed up. The moment had arrived for a

9

monumental rise, while the adrenaline pulsed and repulsed again. Blood alcohol levels were up, and most everybody was down. A song ended and the lights went dim. There began movements on stage as the figures and their shiny things hovered about. A sense of tension was created, anticipation and promises of retribution for non-silence. Now the Syndicate stood motionless. A crunchy guitar riff chunked twice, followed by feedback and the kick drum and snare quipped quickly in two triplets. The drums exploded and the whole lot of 'em brought it down with a thunderous groove. Some beast from a corner let loose a guttural yell. Other animals hooted and screamed in response.

This was a woodsy locale, but fresh and lively in its patron's support of real good noise. Roxy and Alyssa pushed out into the dense amalgam of human flesh. Away from the safety of the wall, the two began the navigation of the seething dance floor. The stage lights came ablaze and once more the riot slammed the audience into high gear. There was no discernable movement apart from the sweeping and slashing of the drummer's wildly active limbs. The racket was pleasing and driven with passion and incredible fervor. It was a complex expression of the minds that listened to the music. The pit and the vacuous wilderness in between its boundaries were teeming with vigor. It's got dang Rock N Roll.

Alyssa Rose was not tied down. She drew in the sounds' waves as they were tossed around. With her hand outstretched and gripping the back of Roxy's jacket, they both wedged full on ahead through the sonic undead, to a spot with a better view. Stopping right in the heart of the monstrous crowd, Roxy crouched and sprung up and jumped and pumped with swinging fists she launched head first into the harmony; again and repeatedly. Alyssa remained still and was protected by the space that the monkey girl was making.

"This song is you."

"What?" Alyssa said.

"This bong is blue." Roxy repeated, eyes on the stage.

"What now?" Alyssa shouted.

"This song is true!"

The guitar wailing sanctuary, still more sorrow came, then stop please surrender kind stranger. "Baby don't please no bass drop," and the bottom fell out while the snare fired automatic at the poor remnants of the shining ones who had entered for this death and rebirth twelve times over from the music's full release. Roxy came to a halt and swung her neck down to her friend and said, "Tis an honest groove."

"Yeah-yeah, crazy lady." Alyssa, for all her love of what Roxy represented and the example she set, sometimes wondered if there wasn't some role she was playing as that of the noble and righteous feminine enforcer. It's better than the alternative.

Sonny cried, "Original!" He strummed twice massively on his Gibson SG, "For the masses- talk to me!" The three men of Dystopian Squalor Syndicate drew up a wild clatter, dark matter style increased, riffs ripping on a backbeat, syncopated heart sweet rhythm it arrives on a cloud, sailing. "Come a, train smokin'- chain gang chokin' mouth full of coal. It don't, change nothin'- 'cept say sump'n 'bout truth." It echoed off. Building concrete sandals and the band handles notes on a scandal to push oblivion rushed into the breakers, one two shakers on the earth Quakers squash abdicators staunch fabrication. Factors in the harassed detractors.

Bass guitar. Pounding and pounding and come on, drop to the rolling tidal waves sound brigades real solid. Beat squalid, streets come calling, rumble and rumblin' on. Bodies all upon contact feet kicking raunch that heat get gutter all up on a fleet of freedom and crass continuity. Deep into the set, the marionettes were tangled and hungry, desperate for connection to never end. Though man is mortal when happy and fed and drunk and high on tunes and timbre. Not much longer and the Syndicate would give them closure and contentment. Soul thy reinvent spent energies.

"Let's get," said Roxy.

"They're still playing," said Alyssa.

"Yeah, it's their last song."

"How do you know?"

"I told you, I know people. I know," Roxy added in finality. The two women stepped back through the edges of rushing rowdies and people planted whose eyes remained focused hard on the stage still erupting with auditory orgasms.

"Where are we going now?" Alyssa asked.

"Hookah bar, kind of; somebody's house. I told you, it's where we'll meet up with Sonny and a few others," said Roxy.

"Right. If that's what you say."

"We're moving when we hit outside. So cover up your pretty little head."

"Go screw," said Alyssa, spouting strident liberalization.

Chapter Three • Of a Kind Midnight Calm

Outside civilization, far from the centralized forms of societal life, the sun is not shy to shine full the love that feeds the uninhibited country. Unabashed it beams pure on the righteous land left untamed by the ambitious growth of progress. Amidst this heaven, veins of travel often surge under the footprint of the few who traverse across and through the dirt and diamonds. Callous and determined, noble and pure, even the aimless transient finds comfort and compassion in the constancy of the blessed road beneath their feet.

Along one unremarkable stretch of highway, barely worthy of regard among the great thoroughfares and parkways of proper culture, there had begun a commotion among the trees and the midnight calm.

"What is this noisy man doing to his stubborn machine?" asked a particularly bothered fir tree.

"It is unfortunate," answered the midnight calm with reassuring tranquility. "But surely he will pass as all wandering creatures have done before him."

"Yes, but what have we done to deserve this unbearable hindrance upon our peace? Perhaps I should fall and give him a scare, or we could sick our friend the bear on him."

Many of the other trees agreed that sicking the bear on the man would be most fun and extremely to the point. The rocks cresting the ridge proposed that they hurl themselves down upon the intruder, no doubt as equally sufficient an idea as a falling fir tree. The pebbles and stones added that in their recollection, it had been quite some time since there had been a good "bear sicking" on anyone at all. Still the midnight calm resolved to spare the bear, giving this trespasser a while longer to either come to agreement with his vehicle, or join with the rocks and trees in their observance of rest.

"Come on man, low expectations, just..." The traveler pleaded, as he tried to will the engine to come alive. There was a weak pulsing flutter but nothing more. "The heart of the wounded warrior, but not the spirit," the man sighed, letting his forehead fall to repose on the steering wheel of the old

Volkswagen camper. There was no one around to curse, nothing to blame but the flow of energy in accordance with the whims of the great magnet.[2] "Great indeed," reflected the man, now stranded in this darkest night, in an altogether unknown territory.

However unpleasant the stop had first seemed, the scenes surrounding this portrait could not have been more serene. The witching hour lay bare with scented airs before the pines cast silky shadows upon the hillside path below. It was a kind, humble valley located somewhere between Here and There. Though more closer to There, as the wearisome duo had conquered many miles since last passing through any populace of even the slightest esteem. They now sat in commune with Mother Nature herself, settled in the fact that this would be their nest for the night and the coming morning.

The rocks and trees, the midnight calm, all of Mother Nature witnessed the steady soothing effect that realization and acceptance had on this poor being. Abandoned by the world, he was driven away across the land, and deposited here at their small cleft of earth. Perhaps when the midnight calm becomes the peaceful morning, their new neighbor might climb up to visit the rocks on the ridge, or sit beneath the trees and enjoy their shade. And of course, whispered the pebbles and stones, there still may be hope of sicking the bear on him. For as all tenants of the forest know, sicking the bear on man is indeed the most divine of all amusements, and extremely to the point.

• • • • • • •

The peaceful morning arrived as expected, waiting patiently for the man to resume his labors. Crouching down directly behind the vehicle, he peered deep inside its soul in attempt to diagnose and in turn remedy his old friend. Twice or thrice, he would dash up to the front, after which the injured van would make weak replies proving the efforts feeble if not utterly worthless. This stirring began to wake the trees, as the great sun's soft breath bled warmth down through their branches. There was upon the place a pleasant breeze,

14

encouraging and fresh. The pebbles and stones were content without the bear, as the man had now taken to tossing them all about. They would fall at the feet of the majestic trees, or fly high up the hill, cascading lazily down to new resting spots for the coming day. The proud rocks on the ridge were even paid a visit, when their perch was scaled and settled upon for what seemed to them a wondrous eternity. It was rumored that the man had spoken a single word, "Extraordinary," after standing to survey the entire scope of his surroundings. Everyone was pleased, though the trees were somewhat saddened that this explorer had not climbed to their splendid heights. Still he was commended by all, as one to be admired and respected for having a true appreciation of their landscape's natural wonder.

The man returned to the road and seemed to be contemplating a course of action. The peaceful morning took notice as the pleasant breeze began to rustle with word of movement from not far off. For a moment, the whole congregation wondered aloud what horror it would be if the bear were to come around. Had he been sicked after all? The rocks above scolded the pebbles and stones below, though no one came forward and all were in consensus that the bear would be most unnecessary, and extremely *not* to the point. All the scandalous chatter was put to rest, when another vehicle was seen coming around the hill from up the road. The man had also noticed the car appear in the distance, and was positioning himself near his idle friend so as not to be missed. Leaning on the horn for a moment, he began to wave as the other travelers drew near.

"Ay oh river!"[3] He hollered as they began to slow.

The Cherokee was colored a dim shade of yellow, brushed hazy by the mist of dust kicked up from the tires. Two casually bohemian women could be seen looking on inquisitively at the man signaling peaceful greetings at their approach. Smiles were exchanged, as they pulled to a stop alongside the van.

"Trouble?" asked the woman behind the wheel. She reached forward, turning down the stereo oozing something spiritual and real. A bare and tattooed arm rested half-out the window, dark sunglasses slowly lowering to offer an uncompromised view of the stranger she was considering.

"Trouble? Me? No ma'am. The bus? Definitely. Payson is just up ahead right?"

"Yeah, like twenty miles. I'm Roxy and that's Alyssa. Anything we can help with?"

After satisfying her initial curiosity, Roxy pushed her shades back on full, moving again to make some vital adjustment to the music. Beside her, the girl called Alyssa smiled politely across at the man on the road. She let her eyes drift along the length of the old relic run aground on the shores of the highway. She seemed to peek through some spectral filter, giving her alone true understanding of such an endearing sight.

"There's a chance I could get back on the road with a jump, if you don't mind?"

"As long as we're talking about the bus and not you; sure, no problem. You must be a free spirit then, right? What's your name?"

"Izzy, Israel. More like a captive spirit. Bound to this spot in paradise since last night." He watched as the girl in the passenger seat leaned her head back to rest, letting her eyes gently close. His had not been a paradise. Surely the only such existence lay hidden among the secluded imagination of the one that now filled his vision.

"Well, I say hey man, even the most devoted gotta get off the river sometimes, right?"

With that, Roxy pulled up behind the dormant VW and Izzy went to grab his starter cables from the cab. After propping up the Jeep's hood, the cables were attached and the customary nods were given to proceed. Izzy hopped in behind the wheel, and with a brief petition to a higher power, turned the key. There was a promising sound much livelier than the faint heartbeats of last night, but still no dice. He turned the car off, paused for a beat, and again engaged the ignition, hearing the engine fire and roar to life, marvelous and majestic. A moment to rejoice, he revved the beast boldly, drawing power and nourishment to where it had been lacking.

From behind, he could hear the Jeep's stereo erupt with a pulse of primal rhythms. Proud of his accomplice's rejuvenated spirit, Izzy nearly flipped back triumphantly to detach the cables and close up shop for the time being. Roxy was singing as he returned to express his gratitude. *"Original, verve. Hit a conceptual, nerve,"* she crooned simple and percussive, then killed the music and looked up with a curious glance.

"You good?" she asked.

"Yeah, I should be fine to get into town. What is that you all are listening to?"

"The Lo-fi 45 Phonic Interwoven," the driver recited with sudden flare. Beside her, Alyssa reached for the volume, turning the song back up to an unassuming presence.

"That's a mouthful, isn't it?" said Izzy.

"No sir, *that's* an earful," Roxy quipped.

"Well Roxy, Miss Alyssa," and he tipped the imaginary brim of his imaginary cap in the direction of the women. "I thank you all so much for stopping to help."

"Sure thing man, it was nothing," Roxy said putting her Cherokee in gear.

"No, really," Izzy paused, wanting to convey his deepest sincerity. "Not nothing, it was everything." He let go his kindness to them both, feeling truly blessed for this brief meeting. He turned to the passenger once more, feeling the subtle urge to bow before her.

"Me-yow," Alyssa's dulcet tone sailed softly into the morning peaceful, precisely to the point. Through the music's pulsing warmth, she gave an inaudible laugh, melted into the shadow of a smile, and was gone. Izzy's rescuers drove off holding up a peace sign, leaving a small cloud of dust from the tires of such a peculiar shade of redemption. He stood for a moment, wondering where women like these were most likely grown. Who instilled in them the grace and ease which carried them off on the pleasant breeze? What morning is not peaceful, nor midnight calm, when such altruistic souls share in making the collective whole? *Great indeed.*

17

January 24, 1998

Twenty miles to Payson, through pines and the hilly terrain, running streams and perpetual life hiding just out of sight of the path cut around the unchecked growth. The evolution of the wood was evident only in the sacred scars of time, the lush green and pristine. Rarely were the storms of man able to leave even a trace of occupancy. Theirs were fleeting ventures, shacked up under the stars in piety with their surroundings, the burnt offering of the collected branch. The old ones, it was said, would hunt the animals and splay the carcass over the fire before devouring their kill, as does the carnivore.

All this moved through Izzy's mind, and in a corner of his thoughts, he held constant watch over his cohort's progress and condition. The city sundials shone one as he pulled into town, and made his way about looking for an auto shop. Low water in the battery cells, an amateur mistake. He cursed himself for not checking that out back in Colorado. Content that his vehicle was strong once again, he snagged a small can of sustenance from his pantry, and sat down on the cab floor to indulge his appetite. The modest streets were quiet. A truck drove by sporting fresh mud, and in the distance a woman could be seen walking with a child. Inspiration struck, and he bagged and stored the remaining can of food, setting off on foot to see what he could.

No matter where he walked, he was always within sight of the great trees both near and far, the backdrop of the mountains, a blue sky their canvas. This was not civilization. This was only a scattered few. Tiny huts politely nestled in amongst the wild. The buck would be as natural a sight as the man and his footsteps upon the paths around town. Israel imagined himself as a proud stag, looking on at this strange human habitat, keeping out the vigilant eye for their brazen vessels that sped angrily down the country roads. So he was not surprised to see a familiar yellow vessel emerge from a cloud of dust just up the path.

His meandering as the stag had brought him to an area with only a few lodges in sight in any direction. The Jeep had come from out of the trees, most likely a residence tucked back off the trail. Now as it hurried towards him, he saw Roxy driving alone, windows down, her music both frightening and enlightening the air in among the pines. She was so entranced that she didn't spot Izzy until right upon him. He saw in her a recollection twitch. In a second split she hit the brakes, skidding to a stop some distance past where he stood.

"Trouble!" He heard her shout as the Cherokee backed up hard, and by the time Izzy took three steps, Roxy stopped flat with her rear Michelin inches from his right pinky toe. Light coat of snow. She gave something resembling a smile.

"You must own this town," said Izzy.

"Lease, man. It's magic. Do you believe?"

Izzy took a second to consider the existence of mystically charged communities.

"I seen a peanut stand, I heard a rubber band, I seen a needle that winked its eye."

"Come on, is for real. If it's alive it must be proclaimed," she said.

"So what it's like pick a side? Hatfields or McCoys, Greasers or Socs, Sharks or Jets? I claim no allegiance but to the Father," Izzy said.

"Alright then. But it's more like permission to dream. Where you walking to?"

"Just taking in the day. I have over six hours of driving ahead of me."

"Stop in at my place. Another half mile up ahead, turn down the path with the sign marked Didney World West slash Grangerfords."

"I don't mean to put anybody out."

"Oh yes," Roxy said sarcastically. "We would be *extremely* put out."

Izzy was excited about the prospect of seeing Alyssa again. It was late winter when Northern Arizona's air is less wicked against the skin. Still it chilled the lungs. Israel made quick time on his trek and eventually came to a flat piece of wood nailed to a stake in the ground, a few feet from the edge of the road. In white paint there were brushed the words "Didney World West," and "Grangerfords" right below that. He began down the narrow path and soon spotted the spoken of structure from a ways off. At first it only appeared as a shadowy mass between the towering pines. The stag slowed his gate, looking all around to fully take in the natural corridor provided by the trees.

The forest was breathing. In the surrounding everywhere the land was living. He felt out of place but welcome, walking into the green. Roxy only said to stop in, but gave no idea who or what would be waiting when he arrived. A warm greeting was desired. Close your eyes and listen to the gentle crunch of footsteps on the trail. How long until you doubt your aim and want to look and correct course, but close them tighter. Trust in feeling and symmetry. Then kick a stone, and open to see your destination has a covered porch running across the length of its front, with a rocking chair there, just as it should.

· · · · · · ·

In the lower leftish portion of the second largest wood in the Northeastern quarter of this particular terrestrial spot, there sat a den of the human kind. A dwelling most sufficient to keep its occupants dry or warm when called upon for either. From the outside it had the look of a fortress, in the log cabin style but with the modern lines of a ruggedly perfected domicile. Still the thick, round lengths of timber, which took its witnesses back in time a century or two, dominated its features. Below it, earth and further down, rock and the foundations of humanity. There were trees in every direction. Maybe you could see another place if they were to light up or make some commotion.

Izzy approached in supplication. He mounted the two steps up onto the porch and glided over the deck to face the door. Pressing the doorbell, he stepped back and heard a double ding-dong echo followed by two short yips from a small sounding animal. Thought he heard a piano. A voice from the other side shouted, "Yeah?"

"Roxy said to stop by," Izzy answered.

"Yeah?" Then came footsteps and a pause. The handle turned and was slightly pushed, the door creaked open several inches followed by a, "Come on in then."

The room was lit with sun through the pane glass and lamps placed all about the large parlor. Izzy stepped inside and onto an old rag carpet. A table stood off to the side under a simple oilcloth next to a kitchenette. A variety of rustic chairs were strewn about it. A levy of couches broke the space into sections. A drum set sat in the far corner next to an upright piano. Rich vein in the membrane, from the window to the hall, wood floors and a picture wall. The man with the voice who allowed Izzy entry said 'Hey,' and that his name was Les. With that, he sauntered over towards the piano and sat down sideways on its bench. He laid a hand on the keys and stuck an ear on his fingers. Izzy stood now silent and still in the middle of the salon. A fireplace was centered on the back wall. On the drum set side of the cabin there was an extended hallway and a loft over that wing. It was the same on the kitchen side, except that it had a heavy wooden staircase leading up to another loft with furniture and random things of belonging.

Izzy saw no one else and could not see any creatures that go yip. Staring off, Les dropped an elbow on a cluster of keys, lightly pounded some and said, "Where'd you get found?" Another pause, and this time he slightly turned his head and suggested that Izzy should, "Sit down, man." He fell onto the levy, leaning backwards into its grasp. He'd attempt to acclimate and see what happened. The front window was to his right and the piano was to his left. Behind him were the picture wall and bedrooms. Across the parlor hung the loft, next to the kitchen and dining table. Les kept slowly tapping low tones with sporadic offbeat high notes. Was the girl here?

• • • • • • •

21

That boy was here. He was downstairs and this wasn't supposed to be happening. But it was. What do you do? What do you say? Why do you care, and do I climb down immediately, or stay up in the loft until the next movement is made? Roxy barely left but a few minutes back. Nobody knew the busman, was the general consensus. So what, he drives up to our doorstep, just like that out of the clear blue? I didn't hear anything pull up outside and Les doesn't seem to care about it for nothing.

"Me-yow," Alyssa purred softly from her hiding place in the cleft of the loft.

"Yes?" Said Izzy, glancing over at the piano.

"Didn't say anything, man." Les said blankly. "Could've been the dog."

The dog, Izzy thought. Where is the dog? And it really sounded like a me-yow as opposed to a dog's bark. Why am I here? Is it for the girl? He surmised that the call came from Alyssa. She must be up on that sofa just out of view. Izzy walked the line in his head of encouraging playmate versus detached, mysterious shiny toy. One should be real in any event. To the entire room Izzy asked, "What are you all up to on a Saturday afternoon?" Les started padding the tune from Jaws on the upright's lower end.

"Basic afternoonin'," said Les.

Alyssa bit her lip and tried to restrain herself, as one waits before jumping up at a surprise party. She crouched down low behind the sofa back, strategizing. This didn't feel like just any ordinary adventure on a simple sunny day. It cannot stay like this. There were small pillows tucked about the couch she lay upon. She grabbed one and mimed pulling the pin, as if it were a grenade. They don't call them throw pillows for nothing. In an instant, she flung the explosive over her head and ducked back down into the bunker. She listened closely for impact. The pillow landed at Izzy's left shoe. Minimal damage. No way did it come from anywhere but the opposite loft. Les saw nothing, heard nothing. "Is your dog into flinging pillows?" Izzy asked. A "Me-yow," came again from the parlor walls.

"Yeah, man. It's a merry old land," said Les.

Now this was just too much fun, thought the girl. She wanted to explore an exchange, but dummy Les is camped out on the piano, very unlikely to go anywhere anytime soon. For even an ounce of privacy we need to be going outside. If the man's van is here we could perhaps move there. It was settled, her next movements she made with purpose and intent. She deftly stepped towards the descending stairs.

Israel saw her appear above and make quick time to ground level, where she paused and grabbed a coat off a rack by the door. "Come outside with me," she said. To which Izzy smiled and gave a nod. He walked to the door, opened it and followed Alyssa onto the porch. There was the sun in the sky. The coat that she had pulled on wasn't as much a necessity, but just something to have and hold. She stood with arms folded, and a slight lean against the thick wooden railing fastened beneath the awning. Izzy moved to her side and heard her ask about the bus.

"It's in town. I was walking around and ran into Roxy on the road."

"Where are you going?"

"San Diego. I have a ticket to the Super Bowl."

"That's nice. When is that happening?"

"Tomorrow. Just about twenty-four hours from right now."

"Still got quite a drive ahead of you then."

"Figure about seven hours, based on I can make Phoenix in ninety minutes."

"Starting from now?"

"Starting from whenever I get on out of here."

"Right."

There was only the wind speaking for a good long moment. Nothing was being said by either. Neither was brave enough to speak in truths, or see what the other was actually thinking. Tension was increasing. This was temporary, and could vanish faster than it had materialized. They both wanted to put a good foot forward. Izzy sat down in a rocking chair across from Alyssa. Slowly a creak squirmed unevenly through the porch's foundation. No one spoke. She looked out at the trees. He looked over at her. Creak, creak, creak and the song bird sings.

23

Creak, creak, heavy brush fire burns, reborn. Creak, willow runs aslant a creek— garden's groan. Why is no one speaking words? A subtle entitled tease.

"Why are you all alone?" she said.

"But I have my bus and a bit of family back in Colorado. I'm not alone." Izzy thought about the game, the raucous chorus of cheers and a chance at victory. He looked at the girl, thought about holding her hand.

"How long have you been in Arizona?" Izzy asked.

"I came down from the Northwest three winter's ago. I met Roxy at a candle shop in Sedona. I spent a while down in the valley, but most of my time has been here at the house. I've also been to Flagstaff," said Alyssa.

"Where is home—sorry, that's a dumb question."

"Home is here, is the way I see it. Not dumb."

"Right."

"Have you ever lived in your Volkswagen?" she asked.

"Yes, a lot of vacations and various road trips. After the game tomorrow, I'm planning on making camp at a beach in San Diego, or somewheres a bit further up north."

"Hmmm, the beach. The sands are in my hair and the waters in my ears. The wind as it rushes in between my toes, so lovely. Sharks though," Alyssa said, making him chuckle and she smiled wide inside.

Silence.

"Wow. It's like you're on a mission. That's fantastic."

"Thanks. Yes, things are okay for me. I may appear sad or seem down, but don't believe it. Not for one damn second."

"You're welcome. You don't seem sad. Looks, they can be deceiving. And so on and so forth, and yada yada yada."

"Yeah—I could ever only be slumber party pissed at most things anyway. It doesn't make sense to get all riled and upset. It is the way it is," said he.

"Eh, but I'm not so sure it is anymore; or doesn't have to be that way. But it sounds good. What do you do with all this stability?" she said half-jestingly.

"I ponder."

"What do you ponder?" she challenged.

24

"Creativity, vision, input and output. You and me we all got demons. Some are just on longer leashes and can nip you. Take a chunk right off of you. Leave a hole; pain."

"Man, well alright, but don't tell me about holes unless it's in a doughnut."

No laughs from anyone. Sometimes solid material just doesn't land. Alyssa sighed, she chalked it up to must be a bagel crowd.

"Don't be too cute, Miss Alyssa."

"Whatever. I am only ever the exact right amount."

Izzy forgot where he was. It was three in the afternoon, which put his ETA close to eleven this evening. This was fine. He wondered how long he could stay with the girl before having to set a time for a hard out, cut and run. That wasn't important now. These thoughts were in the way. Is this what Roxy had wanted? Then also, what is to want and to have? "I've hardly done anything resembling a meaningful life experience," Izzy thought. "I fixed a machine and maybe I can spell a few twelve dollar words."

"Never mind. You should come with us down to the valley for Rox and Les and them's show. Unless you need to leave right away," Alyssa said. He didn't have to leave right away. Didn't want to. Had no kind of desire to cut out so soon.

So they both just remained.

A ways across town, Roxy was figuring how to knock out about seven birds with a single pebble; time was getting short. She was working a plan to have Israel play an integral role in the transportation of six full-grown humans and their band's gear down to Phoenix in something like three hours. Her guitar player, Twig, had a Chevy Tahoe that usually handled most of the load, but was currently out of service. Roxy hoped that Alyssa would inspire the man with the van to stick around and make the trip with them. She had after all saved his ass earlier this morning on the road.

Twig's Pop, Catfish, was the opening act tonight at the blues club where they'd all been booked to fill out the Saturday evening entertainment. Also on the bill was a touring band from the Los Angeles area. They all agreed to arrive at 1830 for sound check, before the doors open at about 1930. Catfish went on at 2030, followed by the Cali band at 2130. Then Dream Demonical, comprised of Roxy, Twig, Les and their drummer Moe, would take the stage at 2230 for two hour-long sets until the club closed.

Roxy wanted to give Izzy and Alyssa more time to get acquainted. The way she saw it, his route was probably taking him through Phoenix on Interstate 10. It didn't seem a crazy big ask. She felt good about her chances. Most of the band equipment was in the parlor back home, while the rest was with Catfish and Twig at their place on the other side of town. Moe, who would show up at the cabin at 1700 to load his drums, was already set and so she needn't worry about him. Roxanne relit an extinguished joint, and drew carefully in as the heat from the ember approached her fingertips. She was parked out back of a burger shop with a half-drank vanilla milkshake. Freaking wondrous weather for late-January.

Meanwhile, back at the ranch. Les had a raunchy saloon vibe cooking and the empty cabin could not appreciate the nuance of his performance. With a heavy left hand he pounded stride bass lines, and tinkled trickling melodies with his right. Moe would be arriving soon. Hopefully he'll be early, so they could get a jam session in without Roxy's bass or Twig's guitar. The girl and the boy were still outside and there was something there but it wasn't any of his business. Rox taught the girl how to handle most men, and how to stay away from those who couldn't or wouldn't allow themselves to be handled. At one point, Les saw things developing between himself and Alyssa Rose. It never was to be, though she had a pleasant energy to be around. Who knows what this stranger has going for him that he seems to know Roxy, and somehow found favor with the flower of a girl from another dimension?

Anyhow, you can only play the Entertainer and Basin Street Blues so many times before the crowd will catch onto your limited repertoire; a little Thelonious perhaps. He started in on Blue Monk, harmonizing in thirds and slowly, sparingly dropped in lonesome bass notes in the spaces. Outside, Izzy and Alyssa poked verbally and stoked the fire slowly growing in the souls and hearts of these two locked in civil warring of the wits and senses. Stirring in each other a warm aggression and furtive glow. The porch roof and nearby trees, the setting to ensconce the coupled warriors exchanging blows. Blew them kisses, sweet caresses, blissful wind and bellows wildly passionate below.

From his own pad, good ole Moe Prallums kick started his motorcycle, revving it slightly to let it warm. He shouted behind him, "I'm gone." This signaled his departure to his lady friend inside. He had told Les he'd stop by prior to loading, to go over some starts and finishes of several songs on the set list that night. As well as some middles too.

· · · · · · ·

"Are you heading home to Colorado after you're all through with San Diego and the coast?" Alyssa asked Izzy.

"Possibly. I really just want to go somewhere and write."

"Write what?"

"A some wrawngz," giving it an extra stylish delivery.

"I guess that's more clever than funny. Perhaps a little of both."

"Yes, more clever. A bit of a slow burn, double delay."

"Well, I'm sure I can't wait for that to happen. So yeah, but like I said, Roxy and Les, the piano guy inside, are in a band. They're playing a show tonight in Phoenix at The Rhythm Room. I go to most of their gigs. I can even lift Roxy's speaker cabinet. That's not nothing you know."

"Kudos. I imagine that there's lifting and then there's carrying."

"Man, I ain't no six foot twenty, eight hundred pounds," Alyssa said.

"I said kudos. That's great though, about the music. Sometimes happens songs are words first. Other times words is music without notes," said Izzy

"Hallelujah," exclaimed Alyssa.

"Amen." Israel Dufrene was hooked. Double sigh, triple spry, quadruple scoople of cherries jubilee.

He rose from the weather worn rocking chair. His movement gave Alyssa a start and she looked quickly side-to-side before regaining focus on the man before her. Before him, all was clear when you met a person for they would show you signs of their soul. For the good or the bad, it would appear in gleams of an eye, in a tonal flit of their voice, or in the way they would put themselves together. This man said nothing except for when he spoke. Alyssa felt anxious to coerce more of the banter they'd been sharing. What would speak for him if he would not for himself? Surely his quaint bus might share a tale or two. He appeared just as you'd expect a traveler to look. His clothes said little but comfort, shoes loosely laced and worn around the edges. He stood now, propped up by leaning against one of the support beams connecting the deck to the overhang above. He didn't seem to want or need anything to be able to remain calmly in this present scene, with this mostly present woman. From inside, they both heard

28

several abrupt cantankerous clumps of noise followed by a long howl. Alyssa wondered what Izzy's camper van might say or show if she was allowed access to its secrets. She thought about what she might do with what was basically a house on wheels at her disposal. She took two steps down to the earthen floor and curiously looked back at Mr. Dufrene.

"Can you come with us to the concert tonight?" Alyssa was unaware of Roxy's own machinations. "I won't say it's not a possibility." Izzy paused and instead thought inwardly what he almost spoke aloud. "As long as I'm leaving Phoenix Sunday by 10 a.m., it's really all the same." While even further inside, where words and thoughts aren't found, he couldn't stop but pleading against all logic not to leave this girl without holding her like something real and tangible. Holding strong and deeply and telling her that he could not, would not, and did not want to let go; stupid dumb, wild, and crazy impulses.

From deep down a rumble quaked among the pines, like the approaching of a B-52 bomber nearing its target and finding its range. But nothing soared overhead, as Alyssa ominously turned to Israel and announced, "The drummer." The roaring grew louder and soon up the dirt drive there came a dingy green army motorcycle, complete with sidecar rambling and squirrels scrambling away in terror. The cabin door blew open and the piano player dashed quickly across the porch, jumped down the steps and walked up to the bike as it rolled to a stop in the area in front of Roxy's pad.

"Moe!" Simple and percussive Les rejoiced and something was happening, as the biker gunned the throttle and cut the engine as the bottom fell out of the shaken forest air.

Les planted a hand on the sidecar's edge, and leaped up high and slid down into the seat, landing snugly tucked behind the short windscreen. "No no no. Go go go!" Les excitedly badgered his friend, knowing full well there would be no rides to be had. Though it was always fun to pester the drummer for some off-road tree dodging action.

"Game time is it?" Moe put out to all, mainly aimed directly at Les who was now swerving hard left and right, back and forth through the imaginary trees, whipped in the face by the branches and flashes of shrubbery.

"Showtime, go time, it's yo time," with eight etceteras. They both dismounted the motorbike as the attention stopped briefly on the boy and the girl who seemed somewhere else.

"Rox told this guy to come by. What's your friend's name?" Les said to Alyssa.

"It's Izzy, and he's all our friend," Alyssa replied. Moe walked over the gravel and up onto the porch, stuck out his hand in an offering of acquaintance. Izzy shook the man's hand and that made it official. He was known.

"That's a nice bike, man; sounds real good," said Izzy.

"Thanks. She's strong for her age," Moe said. He looked at Les who was now crouched down over the bike itself and giving the shocks a work out up and down.

"Them nat-zees is a gainin' on us!" Les shouted out glancing backwards over his shoulder.

"Battle stations Leslie, man the pumps," Moe hollered.

With that, Les hit the ground running and followed the rest of the rhythm section inside.

"Watch it with that Leslie garbage," Izzy heard Les tell Moe as the door closed behind them.

Chapter Six • Tea Nine Westfalia

Back in town, Roxy pulled up beside a dumpster tossing in the empty milkshake cup, nothing but the bottom of the trash bin. She turned out onto the road, hoping that at least her drummer was making his way to the band house. Flying through the backwoods towards home, Roxy had to think of a good way to propose to her guest that they all truck it down to their show that night in Phoenix. In the most virginal way she prayed that Alyssa had been greasing the wheel, so to speak. If Izzy's bus wasn't an option, there were very few avenues left to pursue; few as in zero. Zero as in none. She would have to call and cancel the gig. Fat chance they would ever get another show at that venue, which was a classy joint, a gateway to larger opportunities.

In the cabin, Moe and Les were thick into a groove. Izzy and Alyssa paced easily through the thickets behind the cabin, savoring the shared silence and mustering politely probing inquisitions that gave little away but gathered minuscule insights into one another. Alyssa questioned her own tact and if and how much tact was even necessary. You must keep cautious and aware of inhibitions. There was much she wished to say and know, but nothing she'd rather do than walk the woods together in peaceful reflection.

Roxy reached her turn and pulling into the driveway spotted Moe's bike. Immediately a weight was lifted and a chore checked off. At the porch steps she heard a dramatically loose snare roll and a rim shot cracked, filled out into a beat as a hand slammed palm flat onto the keys, and everything could still possibly be alright. The front door opened, in she stepped feud free and feeling rich as the music played. The kick, tap, and keys relax a minute, breathing a brief relief. Repose. Suppose. She could shower if it happened now and was over in three minutes, barely worth getting wet. Crossing the room, she passed the embanked couchments catching Moe's eyes and punched Les in the back of his left shoulder. He quit playing, turning around to see Rox nod at Moe.

"Where's uh, is somebody else here?" said Roxy.

31

Moe let off a quick triplet three times on the kick drum, floor and middle toms.

"Alyssa and a guy that said he knew you are outside," said Les.

"I didn't see nothin' but your bike out there." She took two steps aside and sat against the high sofa back behind her.

"Those two took off then if they aren't out front," Moe said.

"No shit, but did they head towards town or just around?" Roxy said.

"Those two started and didn't stop since he got here. She didn't ever say anything about 'Hey, tell Rox I'm going into town', so yeah. Just take it easy," Les said.

Alternating snare and kick drum doubles came from the drummer. Roxy and Moe looked at Les accusingly. But then heads shook and such it was.

"Yeah Roxannabye, no need to worry," added Moe.

"Take it easy?" she asked. "Take it easy?" with emphasis. "Take it easy?" she paused. "No need to worry? Seriously?"

"Breathe," said Moe.

"Do you even *want* to play the fuckin' show?" Roxy made several attempts at long inhales, then threw her arms up and tilted back, back slowly back and fell onto the cushions of the sofa. Moe and Les watched her feet fly up and disappear with the rest of their bandleader. Everyone stayed put and half-a-minute passed in silence. Some skirmishing from the busted levy and Roxy slowly propped up on the sofa back, rested her chin on folded hands. She stared off into space, concentrating. Was able to breathe.

"Well yall two are coming outside with me to look for 'em," said Roxy.

As they filed out the cabin door, right off they spotted Izzy standing near the Jeep. Alyssa was seated in the vehicle gripping the steering wheel, reminiscent of a 007. Chances were she was barreling along through some secluded alcove below the coastal cliffs, quite certain that death was near and likely if one wasn't focused and aware. Roxy approached them and the rhythm section retreated back inside, anxious to resume the jelly, the jam.

"How's it going?" Roxy asked.

"It's going good," said Alyssa.

"Glad to see you stuck around," Roxy said to Izzy.

"Of course. This is a great setup you've got."

"Hey Rox, can you get Izzy in if he came down to the show tonight?" asked Alyssa.

"Is that right? You're thinking about checking us out?" said Roxy.

"Yeah, I got time," Izzy said.

"Well, what would you say to maybe loading up some bodies and gear in your van and helping us all get over to the venue? If your bus is back up and running?" Roxy asked.

"Sure, sure. Yeah, it was just a battery issue, all straight. Plus, that's the least I could do seeing as how you got me going this morning," said Izzy.

"Sweet. I really appreciate it. Let me grab my keys and we can go pick up your bus, get back here and start to load."

The bassist for Dream Demonical was in and back out of the house as Alyssa climbed into the backseat of the Jeep Cherokee. Izzy got in the front passenger seat, while Roxy jumped behind the wheel, started the vehicle and set it to moving in reverse, then speeding towards the main road, basically on track to pull this thing off. In no time they pulled up beside Izzy's VW bus. He climbed in and was preparing to engage the ignition. He heard a knock-knock to his right. Alyssa Rose stood waving, wanting to go for some kind of ride on a fantastic voyage.

"Slide-slide, slippity slide, hit switches on the block in a sixty-five," Izzy sang, pushing open the passenger door as Alyssa smiled and asked, "What'd you just say?"

"Nothing really, just singing a song."

"I can't wait for you to hear Roxy and the boys' music."

The bus fired up and the girl began to survey the van's interior. It had the two front bucket seats, then a single box seat directly behind the driver and facing to the rear. There was only the one bench seat in the back. The center cab had a type of laminate flooring like your standard kitchen variety. There was a small closet just inside the sliding door. Pale blue curtains were around all of the side and back windows.

"Did you say what year this is from?" Alyssa asked.

"1969 Westfalia camper, with a pop top. I got a good deal on her from an old hippy because the engine was shot. He was basically using it as a guest room there in Colorado."

"That's where you're from?"

"Most immediately from I guess. I was born up over in Oregon, but raised mostly in Cortez right there in Southwest Colorado," said Izzy.

"Don't you love the forest? Mountains. Gigantic pine trees. It's like it all fuzzes out the hard edges of society. Green everywhere. Like what I imagine heaven is, right?"

"Exactly. Minus the golden condos and the pearly gates, Lions of Judah. If I- were king- of the forest!" Izzy sang.

"No, that's totally different," Alyssa laughed.

Once the engine was warm, they pulled out and took up a spot following Roxy in her Jeep. They were passing through a residential area, and if he stayed on this route the woods would thicken, and then they would hit the road that led to the turn off marked Didney World West slash Grangerfords. It was nearing 1700 hours. Roxy didn't mention much about a time frame. Twenty-four hours ago, Izzy had been pulling out of his driveway expecting to speed straightaway to Qualcomm Stadium in San Diego. He was still mostly on track, though admittedly a bit behind schedule. One major change was his interaction with the Rose now on the seat beside him. Once more on the dirt road he had found as the stag, then the turnoff and another minute as they pulled in and he parked next to Roxy's Jeep. There was a pile of instruments and amplifiers starting to build on the porch of the Casa de Roxy. Les and Moe had already begun the loading process.

"We got ninety minutes until sound check, which means we need to be on the road like five minutes ago," Roxy announced within earshot of everyone. The cogs were set in motion. Alyssa was reminding Izzy about how she could lift a speaker cabinet. Walking up next to the porch steps, Izzy asked if there was another vehicle showing up.

"Nobody but us. But we should just be able to fit all persons and equipment if we work it right," Roxy said.

"How many people are coming?" said Izzy.

"Us four, plus we'll be picking up Twig and his Pops on the way," said Roxy

Towards the vehicles, Izzy heard Alyssa call out, "What'd I tell you Izzy?" The not-substantially sized girl stood by his van's open sliding door, lifting up what must've been a four by ten inch speaker cabinet. For a second he thought she would dip down and raise the speaker box high overhead, but instead she just slid it inside the bus and bounced back up to the house for more gear. They all worked to and fro in this fashion until the drums, keyboard, bass guitar and all their accessories were securely inside the Cherokee and VW bus.

"Alright, double check boys," Roxy addressing Moe and Les. "Stick bag, stool, cables, stands, cymbals, semi-positive attitudes."

It seemed all was set and so no time was wasted. Roxy turned to her band mates. "Les, you're in the Jeep. Moe, you'll have to find room in the bus."

Alyssa returned from the house and shouted, "Shot gun."

She sprinted past Moe, who had just finished securing a tarp over his motorcycle and was making his way towards the Volkswagen. Roxy kilt the lights in her cabin, closed the door, and the next second the engines were firing up. The vehicles made a few maneuvers, heading out on the old dirt access road with Roxy in the lead. After several turns they were in town. After several more they pulled to a stop in front of a small cottage, where Roxy laid on her horn with a heavy hand. She hopped out of the Jeep and came back to tell Izzy they wouldn't be long, but he could cut his motor if he wanted. Izzy let it run as he'd filled the gas tank earlier in the day. It was under a hundred miles to Phoenix, so he'd let his engine stay warm. At the front door of the house an old man backed his way out, with a suitcase in one hand, and a small combo amplifier in the other.

"Catfish!" Alyssa hollered as she popped out of the bus, and ran to help the man as he turned to face the minimalist convoy that set before him.

"Well, Miss Alyssa, how you been?"

"Just great. Look, come ride with me in the bus. It's a 1969 Westfalia. With a pop top," she said, politely taking the amp from his grip, freeing him up a bit. It was a much more reasonably sized single speaker setup, appearing now like a handbag compared to the gear she'd helped lug around back at Roxy's.

"Thank you. Sure, if you think there's room for me," Catfish said.

"You can sit up front. It's the best view for the trip," she told him.

"That'll be just fine, thanks," said Catfish, handing his suitcase up to Alyssa who had already stepped into the open van. She tucked the case and amp in snugly, taking the spot right behind Izzy and the driver's seat. Moe was by himself on the bench seat with an arm around his floor tom, set beside him, a true companion. Catfish peered inside the open front passenger door and saw Israel Dufrene nod a subtle greeting, to which the old man nodded in return. Elijah "Catfish" Frye took a seat in the front, making a few adjustments to get comfortable.

"This is Izzy. We found him this morning on the side of the road," said Alyssa.

"Ah, well that's a good catch then," Catfish said, reaching his hand across the front cab as Izzy took hold of the offered palm. They both gave a good firm shake.

"Nice to meet you, sir," said Izzy.

"Yes, yes. Glad to hear you got found," Catfish replied.

Back at the door from where the old man had exited, a body stood with a guitar in case slung over his shoulder and the last amplifier they had to load. He walked over towards the Jeep, with a suspicious eye on the unfamiliar van and its completely unknown driver. Roxy motioned to the back seat of the Cherokee where Les was sitting. The one called Twig set down his amp, took the guitar off and handed it in to the keyboard player, who placed it safely in the vehicle. He kept looking at the bus and shook his head, which Roxy didn't appreciate at all.

"So what's the hook?" Twig asked Roxy.

"What're you talking about? He's repaying a favor is all," she said.

"So that's it. The ride is the hook. Fuckin' hippy trash. Are we supposed to be impressed?" Twig had chosen his side.

"Whatever, man. Get your amp in the back and get in. Please," Roxy pleaded. "What—Do you want to miss the gig? Tell your Pops too bad? Is something going on with you all or what?"

"No, nothing." Twig moving his focus to Roxy. Catfish recognized the feud and walked with a purpose up to speak to his boy.

"Son, just let this man help. Everything will be alright."

There were a few beats and Twig glanced off and away. He wasn't even sure why he had any type of problem with this. He had especially worked this show so that his Pops could play out again. He was going to play guitar for Catfish, who would be playing his harmonicas and singing a set of damn near authentic blues that he'd been performing for basically his whole life. This night was supposed to be a big deal, but his Tahoe was dead and they just got a call from his older brother. His Pops hadn't relayed anything about what was said, or if there was even a problem at all. He was more bothered that whatever the conversation was, it just wasn't his business and so it could all be for nothing and change. He would stop fussing for his Pops. Twig lifted his amp head up and into the Jeep's rear cargo area, setting it beside his cabinet.

"Thank you, Twig." Catfish said. He turned back to the bus and then he and Twig climbed into their respective seats, as the two doors slammed one after the other. The two vehicles cast off, once more taken by the breeze, deer friends in the rear view mirror.

January 24, 1998

One hundred and eight miles Northwest of Payson, a shambly Ford Econoline van sped west on I-40 spitting gray exhaust all in between Flagstaff to Kingman. The travelers would take US-93 north to the Hoover Dam and on through to Vegas. Sonny drove, Truck sat shotgun, Boonz was on a beanbag chair in the back with the gear. After their Friday night gig in Show Low, our villains three had crashed with an acquaintance in nearby Snowflake. A slacking Saturday passed languid, listless and indifferent. The Syndicate continued on towards a Super Bowl Sunday show the next day at a large sports bar just off the Strip in Las Vegas, Nevada. Once fin in the city of sin, they would travel to Los Angeles to connect with a nationally touring festival that would mob around the country for the whole of February and March. It had been over two years since they released their second studio album, Strategic Social Dissent. They were in deliberations about getting off the road to write and rehearse new material. There was only so much you can create playing electric instruments acoustic while simultaneously crossing vast territories, cities, states and cultures. The closest thing they had to management was Boonz's girlfriend, who handled booking and various promotional tasks, phone calls and polite correspondence. As for now, rule of law in the brown box on wheels was mainly non-existent.

"Man, no way Sonny. That's straight bullpuckey," said Truck.

They were deep in discussion; Sonny had just recounted a long story about something he saw sometime in a backroom sankhole.

"Bullshit's older than the Bible, and twice as long," Sonny said.

"Twice as—schlong," added Truck.

"Good one," replied Sonny. He checked his mirrors, and with his speed at seventy-three it'd still be close to three hours until they reached the alluring lights. Dystopian Squalor had played Vegas shows before. Once even at the Hard Rock. But this Super Bowl Sunday show was a big paycheck, never mind that it was at 1530, smack in the middle of the afternoon. Be always on guard for the vampires. There still remained a bit of daylight left, both visors were down as they drove into the setting sun. Boonz in the back had been silent for a while after pounding out bass lines acoustic for the first twenty-five minutes out of Flagstaff.

"Which ain't to say that I wouldn't be indisposed to hypothesizing about a certain said somebody smelling like busted ass," Sonny said.

"I'm awake," said Boonz. "That wasn't even a proper put down."

"Social commentary," said Truck.

Ninety-seven seconds of no one saying nothing.

"That odor's probably your last night lady friend's patchouli." Boonz taking a swipe at Truck who had spent much of the prior evening with a dreadlocked flower girl attached to his arm and neck and lips and, and—

"Whoa, Mr. Claypool acting like he didn't go to the bridge early on Shady Fruit, again." Truck shot back at the bassist.

"I was tired. We all were tired," Boonz said.

"You were stoned, and lying on your back as I recall," Truck said.

"Doin' the Paul Shaffer," Sonny broke in with emphasis.

"Doin' the Paul Shaffer," Boonz repeated.

Settling back into silence, some eyes closed and some looked out at the blurry tree line. Others saw visions crying out for mercy and just one easy day before all the abuse sent everybody spiraling off in opposite directions. They each had a wish to feel the highway's lovin' charms. Communication began to break down back around when the head gasket first started leaking. Fluid now requiring almost daily attention on long trips and soon it will become a numbers game.

"From under the raw torn asunder the rubber and asphalt erodes, at a pace unbecoming evolved folk like we. Exposed to the public and live for your viewing joytainments. Dystopian Squalor— direct from the halls of Valhalla! Featuring Mack Truck- Laraine Newman- Tim Meadows. Plus Boonz Shaffer and the DSS orchestra!" Sonny finished his opening introduction.

"Good one," Boonz said from the back.

"Get 'em!" Truck said enthusiastically.

"Bill Murray—Norm MacDonald."

"Nackrully."

"Julia Sweeney—Mark McKinney."

"Chris Rock."

"Ub course."

"A. Whitney Brown."

"Nurse."

This usually continued on for a good ten or fifteen minutes. With names of film actors and athletes interspersed with political figures, comic book characters, and people you knew from high school. All in that SNL Don Pardo announcer voice. Aftershocks of this exercise could be responsible for someone hours later in a diner yelling out "Harry Shearer," or the occasional shout of "Lenny Pickett," if the timing was absolutely perfect. You do what you can to pass the time. Often it's almost like prison rules or boot camp where it's meal to meal or you'll bury your head in a pocket Bible just to put another day down and behind you. Maybe you hone in on the soft face of a nice girl you saw once in a crowd from the stage, the one you've chosen as your dream girl of choice. You put her smile on repeat against the backdrop of the mountain peaks off in the distance. The chance that tomorrow might be amazing or life affirming, or at least it's not today with a backache and short rest.

Sonny had switched on the van's headlights when they pulled out of their fuel and food stop in Flagstaff. Now the night came on slowly until they could only see the road as far as the lights allowed. The occasional mile markers flickered like ghosts pointing lasers for just a quick flash in their eyes' peripheral. They'd made this trip before and a topped off tank should do it, but just in case they had a full two gallon gas can (because responsible folks do things like that). The van was a 1975 Ford Econoline Truck had found three years ago. They put some money into the stereo system and not much else. It wasn't so bad. Keep an eye on the oil consumption and maybe we can put some six-by-nines or a subwoofer in the rear, or repair the CB radio to talk to the frequencies. The back was mostly cleared out with a bench seat opposite the side door, the only rear windows being the two tinted squares on the back double doors. It was an unspoken rule that the front passenger seat occupant stays awake at night to zing whoever was driving or fetch food or drink or just say 'Hey' or 'How's it' every-so-often, taking over for the driver if ever necessary. Boonz drove last night and today from Snowflake to Flagstaff, which was like two hours but he took over for Truck so he deserved some time without bother. Sonny usually gets behind the wheel when dark hits, and goes until he can't, which means he goes the distance ninety-seven percent of the time.

"If we had permits, do you think we could mount a shotgun on this side window or one of those drop-it-in-the-top grenade launchers?" Truck said dead serious. "For hunting purposes."

Sonny waited a beat: "Well as long as it's for hunting purposes."

"You know the A-Team never got pulled over by the cops talking about, 'Hey you guys can't mount guns and shit on your DIY monster mayhem machine'," said Truck.

"Yeah, I don't remember grenade launchers or a shotgun. And they actually had the Army after 'em so cops weren't a concern. Plus, they fought bad guys and not a twelve point buck," Sonny said.

"For sure they had missile launchers man, machine guns and flamethrowers. Cops never said nothing," Truck said.

"Well they usually worked with cops and vigilante justice seekers, right?" said Sonny.

"Soldiers of fortune, son. Wanted by the government." Truck defiantly. This soaked into the ether. Sonny thought

41

about the line soldiers of fortune.   Would be Soldiers of Misfortune if you put the metal twist on it.

"New band name," said Sonny. "Soldiers of Misfortune."

"Eh, let me see," said Truck and he cleared his throat. "In a world—ruled by My Little Pony and parachute pants—a crack commando unit was sent to prison by the gub'ment. The Man slammed his hand down on the band on the run for a crime they didn't commit. Looking for an antidote for the emptiness of existence?   Searching for salvation for the crimes of humanity? Seeking sanctuary within the respite of redemption? If you have a problem—if no one else can help—and if you can find them, maybe you can hire: Soldiers of Misfortune!" Truck pounded his fist against his chest in a show of solidarity.

"What does their drummer sound like?" asked Sonny.

Truck took two beats to think: "I never kilt nobody. But I saw somebody died."

"Look there Truck," Sonny pointed ahead. "There's the turnoff for Hackberry. That's like a few miles left until the 93 picks up and fifteen minutes to Kingman. Straight shot to the Hoover Dam and the Nevada state line."

The sooner they get to Vegas and find a back lot to park in, the sooner they can all get to sleep and be better set to massacre at the show tomorrow. They were guaranteed twelve hundred dollars cash for the gig. Very rarely did they ever get a four-digit payday.   Boonz had been beating the idea of professionalism into anyone who would listen, and more often those who would not. It wasn't that Truck and Sonny didn't take pride in their music, they were just very confident that once they got on stage, instruments in hand, the rest would take care of itself.   Be undeniably good.[4] Besides, they were traveling the day prior to the show, so there wouldn't be any drama or rushing to make sound check, or all that other bullshit involved in making happen the magic.

In the back, on the blue beanbag cushion Boonz was propped up awkward but sleeping and still. Bass guitar in his lap, his right paw twitched like a puppy lost in a dream. In his mind he stepped up to bat with an antique upright bass resting upon his shoulder, in preparation for the pitch. He took two massive practice cuts as the umpire hollered, 'Play ball!' He turned his head left to face down the pitcher standing in opposition. There was black soot instead of dirt and the infield grass was a filthy-snow gray. On the raised mound stood a dark figure with a ball cap pulled low, shading icy gleaming eyes and holding a glowing red orb trained on his line of sight, focused and in the ready position. Around Boonz's psyche's self a crowd deafly cheered deathly cries of blood-lusty anticipation. Nothing else was within view as the pitcher leaned back on his heels, and then shifted forward, his right arm lifted tall making one slow clockwise circle followed by another quick rotation as he released the fiery sphere underhand and thunder struck overhead with rolling flames spinning towards the plate. Boonz cocked his left leg up, stepped into the pitch swinging the upright bass through the zone making contact bat to ball and crack-smack turned his body into it with all he had and saw the lit meteor trail off into the dark sky. He held his pose for a moment, whipped his stick back and flipped it away, beginning his trot around the bases.

The cheers turned to white noise. Boonz watched the fireball continue to rise as he rounded the bag and saw the heavens catch ablaze like torches; the snowy grass sizzled near his feet. Each step he took kicked up clouds of black and the field fogged up thick. There was sky burning above, dark nothing below as he stomped on second. The molten display increased with crackling campfire snaps drowning out all other sounds. He felt tired and winded and was panting approaching third. Finally, making the turn towards home he saw the mutant pitcher standing over the plate holding the charred upright high at the neck with his left hand. Boonz slowed to a walk and the thunder-fire died down and halfway home the pitcher spun the wooden bass with his right hand, slapping the body several times like you would a basketball balanced on your finger. Stopping right at home base, Boonz reached his foot forward cautiously tapping his toe on the corner of the plate and heard somebody say to, "Watch out for my base."

"Watch out for thy bass, man." Truck repeated, half turned towards the rear cab.

"I'm awake," Boonz mumbled back in no direction.

"Your bass, man." Truck repeated.

"I'm the bass man," Boonz said, deliriously fading away. Half asleep he clawed at the Fender Precision bass across his lap. It seemed more secure and so Truck sat back straight in his seat.

"Awake we dream with sight we seldom see," said Sonny. "In dreams we sleep and find what freedoms be," to the back of the windshield warmly and with weight.

Reaching for the volume knob, Truck spun the stereo up to way louder than was ultimately required, but right about where he was used to it being. Sonny felt around and picked up something from the stained carpet in between the front seats. He handed the object over to Truck and told him to, "Get out that new Tool." The drummer opened and flipped through a swollen CD case for a few seconds, slid out a disc and inserted it into the stereo face, which bit and swallowed. The first track came on and it sounded like a body was clanking rhythmically on steel drums with a light ball peen hammer. Heavy guitar dropped in with thick pulses crunchily back and forth and Sonny settled his attention on the developing groove as they drove steadily on out into Arizona Bay. Rolling down the driver's window he inhaled deeply the cold air, hanging his left arm outside grabbing large palmfuls of winter chill. He stretched his ocular cavities, clenching his whole body then released and brought his arm in, resting both hands on the inside bottom curve of the wheel. The van's heat was on and pumping warmth into the cab to combat the frigid draft rushing in the open porthole. The music kicked very aggressively, roared and rippled thudding drum lines underneath the calculated build of guitar. Whispers encouraging the defilement of normal and the accepted societal slosh. Then the anger fell away and hope floated momentarily on a flourishing cloud of unholy virtue and cymbals. The Syndicate had wore out their copy of Ænima since Truck spent fourteen bucks at the record shop to get it brand new like the week it came out back in late '96. Dystopian Squalor covered Tool's 'Sober,' which was off of Undertow, their first studio album from 1993.

There were several popular songs they kept a medium polish on for those two or three hour sets when the band's original material wasn't enough to fill the time. In the early years, they had experimented with fifteen minute extended improvisational pieces to pad long sets. The guys moved away from that but retained a call sign, a secret code word of 'Diplomat,' which meant that whatever song was being played turned into a drum and bass jam. Then Sonny would come in on guitar once the dust had settled and a workable feel was established. Shit would inevitably build and get crazy again, at which point Truck takes over and either breaks into all-out calamity or picks a beat, playing on until he's satisfied. Ninety-nine percent of the time, Sonny has to come up with an ending or the cows just ain't ever coming home. Worst case you give the kill sign, many slices through the neck, and that's an eight count hard out after the next occurring down beat or count one, it's usually quite obvious. The sports bar in Vegas was only a fifty-minute set, which translated roughly to twelvish songs. They were meant to cover the final hour leading up to kick off for the Super Bowl. Maybe they would do a couple covers, but the majority would be original songs from the Syndicate's own repertoire. Passing by Kingman, Truck took a look at the few lights visible from his perch inside the Ford van. Sonny rolled up his window to the relief of the other passengers, though you'd never hear them complain.

"Ninety minutes to the Vegas city limits," said Sonny.

"We goin' out when we get there?" Truck asked.

"Maybe just to get snacks or something to sip on. We can drive down the Strip, but I don't plan on parking anywhere near there," Sonny said.

"Yeah, yeah. Just for the effect you know. To get that feel," Truck told him.

"Man, we can yell and scream at all of the women and drunk folks well and proper if that's what it takes to do you up right," Sonny totem back.

It was something to look forward to, the yelling and screaming at the women and drunk folks. Divine like donuts.

45

Darn yam jams keep an ear to the grindstone. Bully on the head phones a graph of all distortion in the plans too brutal a sacred price. A caustic bard games sunk floor toms to calm unknotted proof with liquor urge hymn unashamed. A worrier cries a fray with mushed ate fits of fist. Awry the brittle want buy beadings thin. Contusions. One time the squeaky wheel behind the bar's substantial feat. A lone misgiving turns a port and the stabboard leans. Precaution air he tells lament the combing whales of toe tap's room. Strike a vinaigrette, folk scum lift and rotten—mowing some blinds and no dregs. Start and whole on the foreground in a vile of comet, fast passed the mellow hit meat and the motions soar and wise on the pouring pain. Something you've herd the grime before and chance pure fleeting coarse complains of vulgar whims.

Ill nautical waves purge forth the striped release of danger-sewn relieves the muse it purrs like cancer cored and curious. Thick backwards time repeats a call to arms and spatial resonance. The residence sublime prays whispers sprung attack lampoon the hills of Bixbee, sigh the waters blood with reeds. Near four score scared forlorn equipped reborn the minuets. Circus saturates the globe. Sound mines fan bodies glisten true the war crimes cast beside still potter's claim. Try trumpets sentry routes the cattle fry bestow the page of turnips row. Turned up too blue three heavens. On glory mound Victrola bound most Everest tale and loudly.

Peace free reigns.

Sonny cracked his window, sipping the frigid and fresh air once more. Truck slunk down in his seat placing his feet above the glove box in an uncomfortable looking posture. Boonz was not awake. Behind the veil of resting consciousness a wandering imagination peaked out through crudely cut eyeholes at a lusty crowd below. Wearing a heavily cursed cloth hood of dark color, Boonz was aware of attentive faces focused on him from all sides. Standing on a raised wooden platform, he peered down and saw his garb to be a gray cloak covered in matted crud and soaked in shining spotted mud. Before him lay a square slab of a stone bench the length of a body and about thigh high. To his right stood several familiar countenances on hunched and sickly frames. On his left within reach a table was laid out with sharp and serrated blades, various polished hammers and tools, and a stringless black bass guitar wound tightly with thin rope high around its neck.

Boonz felt the sun's heat surround him and a kind breeze blew across the solemn scenario seen by the many. The growing crowd with hushed tones and loud murmurs raised a collective finger directed at those standing next to him on the dais. A sorrowful void enveloped Boonz upon realization that he was altogether unknown. He felt a strong desire to move and began to wrestle with the covering over his face. The movement momentarily blacked out his vision and he let out a blind moan. Far off a church bell tolled. Inquisitions arose, shouts for blood as he rearranged his mask so that his sight would improve. Shuffles came from behind his back and high above a voice called out, "Bring forth the living." Grunts began from stage right. Boonz saw a body led before him being seated facing away, on the rock slab looking out upon the captive audience. Again the bell from off in the distance, the unattended soul on the bench swung their legs up and lay down staring above into the open sky. Boonz felt a forceful shove from behind and heard savage encouragement from the raucous crowd in front. Once more the bell, to his left there were clanking noises from the implements on the table. He gazed over and saw a blade offered to him for the taking. Again the bell, once more the grunting, the blade was pressed against his arm. Looking in the direction of the cold steel his eyes fell on the stringless fretless bass. Was it an Ibanez? Reaching down he grabbed the roped handle and dragged its carcass across the table of tools. Once more the bell, again the shove accompanied by an even more aggressive grumbling. A booming voice cried, "Finish him. Extinguish this evil heathen for his treacheries." Inspired, in one quick motion Boonz lifted the bass two-handed over his head, swinging hard and guiding the instrument earthbound and down, crushing the offering's skull with a crackling mush. The people cheered, and when he looked out to them he witnessed eyes and attention trained gloriously at his own self and existence. In an instant the bell clanged repeatedly and the jackpot sounded as he raised the bludgeon now dripping blood, stuck with chunks of flesh and brain matter. Desperate hands grabbed at the mess hungrily pulling it off the bench and into the belly of the ravenous mob. Boonz saw arms, organs, and legs flee in every direction as trophies, food, and trinkets of a life that had been set free.

After a time the audience was soothed, though now even hungrier. In the distance the bell rang and behind him a grunt and sharp shove in his back. A voice boomed out, "A loss, a gain, a sacred price was paid." A rustling from stage right and the citizenry gazed in awe at the being being led to the altar. Boonz wished he might be next so that he would be loved, lauded, and shared, his limbs taken home as souvenirs. He mourned his masked identity and felt ashamed for doing his deeds behind his cloak and cowardice. The second offering sat down on the bench facing out at the adoring fans that were longing for a piece of their meat-body.

"Begin," spoke the judiciary. Boonz thought he might not be able to take this life. He feared the throngs of people would not like him if he did not harm the soul now laying prostrate to the heaven's atmospheric. A voice said lovingly in his ear, "Do this and you will always be remembered." In unison the crowd began to chant, "Begin, begin, begin." Reluctantly and unsure of his motivation, Boonz lifted up the battle-axe over head and the audience went silent. In slow motion he brought the bass's blunt edge down and hurt and felt the wind's resistance against the lowering hammer. The hushed masses on their tiptoes watched and waited for impact. The next second, the Ibanez GSR caught the crest of the skull, busting bone it continued further through the cerebral forceps and into the cavernous mind, contacting the bench and bouncing off. Boonz dropped to a knee while the rabble roared madly and sung out in ecstasy the executioner's song. He was nothing

48

and invisible. Then he recognized the joyous laugh of a child and looked up to see a youth jumping up and down victoriously on the dead man's chest. The child spun wildly around and Boonz tried hard to smile, though all in vain for the covering over his face. A hand reached up from the crowd and gripped the corpse's twitching leg, pulling the destroyed body off the platform and the mutilation began. The child remained watching hands and feet set off in every direction, entrails passed out among the famished. The youth danced ever vigilantly atop the altar, beginning to garner attention from those in the audience without flesh in their pockets or charms around their necks.

Boonz kept smiling and all his energy went into trying to capture the eye of the little one trampling blissfully in the puddles of scarlet rose. He glanced quickly to his right and there was no one else there. It occurred to him that perhaps it was his own turn to lie down and be received by the adoring fanatics. There was no bell, no shove, and no secretive voice whispering sweet everythings into his ear. The bass guitar he now held by the rope handle at his side near order arms. Without any prompting, Boonz experienced an intimidating uncertainty at what he should do next. The child began to skank. The audience started a rhythmic clapping at an ever slightly increasing pace. Needing and wanting some sort of approval he reached out his empty right hand palm up towards the prancing youth. Unnoticed by all he began to grunt, taking a step towards the child but to no avail. Desiring resolution he proceeded to tap her on the shoulder lightly enough to only register his presence. Abruptly coming to a halt, the angel turned her beaming face to gaze up at the masked man on the platform. The crowd was immediately silenced, as the little one's movement had been what stoked their shouts and cheers. The creature motioned to the bloody bass, reached out her hand as if asking could she see it. Boonz's spirit leaped at the thought that he might have something to offer this precious sprite. Without a second thought he lifted the bass with his left hand, presenting it graciously to the child before him. She peered up, in her eyes was hopeful anticipation as she gripped

49

the neck below the rope, Boonz relinquished control. Surely this was good. Surely this was right. All attention now acutely lay on the two forms standing at the altar. Earth angel spun fast to the right, the Ibanez whirling after her briefly pointing out over the people and then came around smashing hard into the right side of Boonz's head. Dazed, he fell onto the table of instruments, which tumbled down all pieces crashing to the stage floor. Now they would tear him apart, carrying him off into the mist where he would live nobly in the hearts and minds of his fellow man. This did not happen. Yes, there was cheering though it was not for him, as was his view askew from the floor he saw the child carried away as victorious conqueror. The crowd dispersed leaving Boonz injured and alone. And in the distance the bell tolled, though it was not for him that it rang.

Back to reality and Arizona Bay, Boonz felt sick and squinted up front towards his quiet travel companions. Sonny and Truck rode on in silence, if you didn't count the tasty victuals pulsing out of the front speakers.

"You awake?" Truck said.

"No, why?" said Boonz.

"Hoover Dam. The end times are nigh."

"Good. My third eye is putting it on me tonight," Boonz said.

"There's no genius position on the off switch," said Sonny.

Because there isn't.

Roxy and the rest of the caravan had arrived safely and without damage at the world famous Rhythm Room in Phoenix, Arizona. Dream Demonical unloaded their gear directly onto the stage and began to setup for sound check. Catfish and Alyssa Rose sat together on one side of the large vacant room with Izzy nearby dividing his attention between the commotion on stage and the conversation of his new friends. Alyssa also chatted with Catfish for most of the trip down from Payson. Izzy had watched the road and manned the stereo, with Moe crammed silently in the back.

The Rhythm Room was a blues and concert hall located just east of downtown Phoenix. A medium sized venue, it hosted national touring acts as well as weekly blues nights and other legitimate talent showcases year-round. There was a raised stage centered on the front wall, with a dance floor directly below, and tables and chairs on each side of this space. The hall was divided by a waist-high partition with openings in the middle and at both ends to allow patrons to move between the lengthy bar and the showroom. The backstage entrance let out towards the street where the musicians would load in. The main entryway was in the back with easy access from the parking side of the building. From the outside the club was an unassuming lot nestled quietly away from the central hub of the metropolitan area's business district. It was in the vicinity of a Veteran's Hospital, a large pawnshop, and a Mexican buffet.

The only current activity was Roxy and them milling about on stage. An engineer sat in the dimly lit sound booth in the back corner; a couple of staff members would appear and then vanish into the hidden kitchen area. Most of the club was dark. Izzy, Catfish, and Alyssa sat on a padded bench running along the side of the room opposite the main entrance of the establishment. The boy, girl, and the old man had been watching and commenting on Roxy and the boys who were

51

playing an instrumental jam as the sound tech placed microphones all over the stage.

"It has been a *long* time comin', me being here with you all tonight," Catfish said, pronouncing it with an extra long 'long.'

"How's that?" asked Alyssa.

"I'm *old*." Catfish said with a lengthy drawn out 'old.'

"Sure, but you'll tell them all what's what here soon enough," she said.

"I will give it my best," said Catfish.

"Do you know what you'll start off with?" said Alyssa.

"Smokestack Lightning and Mellow Down Easy," Catfish said.

"Man, that's that good Chicago blues," said Izzy.

"By way of the Mississippi Delta, yes it is," said Catfish.

"Rocking chairs and knife fights, and everything's gonna be alrights, if my memory serves me," Izzy said.

"I'm sure there's more to it than that. I was a kid there in Illinois. Then on up into a young man," Catfish said.

"You know anything about Bronko Nagurski?" Izzy asked.

The old man looked physically jolted and turned from watching the stage over to focus on the face of Israel Dufrene. "Son, whatchu don't know 'bout no Bronko Nagurski? I seen him in forty-three right before his last championship game there at Wrigley Field. He made the go-ahead touchdown run, second quarter, set it all in motion. Heard that bit live on the radio and my Pap was all up and riled more than ever. Same year I first snuck in town and heard Big Bill Broonzy and Sonny Boy One at "The Gates" in South Chicago on the west side and that was, I believe, even before Mr. Muddy Waters had plugged into the electricity."

That sat for a minute and Catfish looked back at the stage. Izzy looked over at Alyssa who looked fine with her legs crossed, arm's hands laying about her heart stance. Art glance. Dope dance; smoke glands, odds given no chance that hope bands. Gator in the moat, ants high upon a hill but she don't prance. Won't can't, slow, trance. Show, answers come and they go, maybe so sands. Off time and they reap what they grow plants. Soft prime and repeat cantaloupe tans. Sew grand. Bode jack's life nigh Natchitoches. Pro haps, folk swag. Top range crest sky wit the snowcaps, both froze chaps. Post up on a rock hearin' goat blats, 'coat snatch.' Pop snout to the snide matador jams. Coke bans cloak cans, survive when to drive Fiero stands: nineteen eighty-five in a broke van, six-nine double-you in the homeland.

"Anyone want to go have a smoke, man?" Izzy asked.

"I would not be one to turn down such an offer," said Catfish.

The two men looked to Alyssa Rose who slapped her hands together and began rubbing them steadily, creating warmth and welcoming the excitement soon ahead.

"Yup," she said and rocked forward into a standing position stretching up on tiptoes letting out a precocious vocal howl. Catfish and Izzy rose also. The three headed out into the early evening through the backstage exit.

Out in the lot, the bus was parked nose facing the building not far from the back entrance. Izzy opened the side sliding door as Alyssa hopped in and Catfish reached his arms out above his body, tilting back his head gazing off into the night. Izzy climbed in the van taking the spot next to the girl on the bench seat.

"Stars look much better up there in the woods," Catfish said, climbing in the cab.

Izzy leaned forward grabbing the inside door handle, pulling it smoothly shut. Glints of light from the street lamps above poked through the curtains covering the windows. Izzy stuck his hand into the space between the roof metal and the fibrous camper top above. He pulled out a small tin box, and from it retrieved a single joint. A lighter appeared and lit the magic stick Izzy held with his mouth. He inhaled once quickly. The flame pulsed and fed the animal its ambition. It was then offered to Alyssa.

"Ladies—" Izzy said. The 'first' was silent but understood.

"Aww, thanks." She took the joint between finger and thumb, hit it good and handed it over to Catfish.

"Thank you kindly." The ritual continued circling the triune as they sampled the herb for several minutes, hidden away from the world in a matte almond Volkswagen, into obscurity. Two feet flat on the floor, hands resting on his knees, Catfish set back, sighed and said, "It's been too long a while since I tasted any of that. Makes me want to get up and go somewhere, do somethin'."

"Well, that fits because you *are* somewhere about to do something," Alyssa said.

"Yes, you are right. I really am," Catfish replied.

He placed his hand down into his coat pocket and slid out a chrome piece that flashed in the light. He cupped the instrument up to his mouth, drawing in over the reeds he ripped across the low end and bended hard on the second hole. Straightening out he was releasing tone from the steady waving of his right hand throwing blasts of sound that filled the bus with a full and powerful presence. Catfish gave it two big chops with his busy hand and there was a slight echo as he bit the note off with a flutter of action from his chopping work on the harp. Alyssa let out a, "hmm," meaning an exclamation of feeling and glory amen holy sugar cookies and crumb cake. But it was real yall. The three of them each lowered their eyes in the slightest of bows. All of them were quiet for nearly five minutes.

Catfish thought back on the many years he fought addiction and all the booze he'd put away but made it through still getting at it. His sons were much closer to him now. At least to the point he had some idea where everybody was. It was comforting. His youngest here tonight, setting up with his group to play along with an old man who very well knew the blessing he was receiving; took it none for granted. Time was happening.

The girl, Alyssa, rose to the plane of consciousness in Izzy's mind upon which the two had shared many lives and breaths, births and deaths. Still she was a flower on a mountain temple stepping stone, closer to the heaven shone free. Dumb luck; let it be. Crazy what you find out in the world when you move between the lines, in the spaces—in betwixt. Her eyes fixed on Izzy's hand on the seat next to hers. But worse, care for what you wish, it's bliss.

54

The energy in the van was numinous, varied and voluminous. Pockets full of miracles, pocket full of spells. Izzy felt the stranger taken under and unsure in his own home base. The bus was a wasteland of dreams in realization. In less than a day's span plans took a change grand future rearranged plus a big bag of biscuits, gravy on the side. King, queen, lord of the stars oft born far apart then collide.

"Man, can I sure emphasize with yall two," Catfish said.

The boy and girl snapped out of their daze. Alyssa smiled over at the old man, whilst Izzy watched the glowing pure spirit shine across the cabin.

"How do you mean?" asked Alyssa.

"Look, I'm just settin' here. Feeling what seems a mighty powerful heat, unspoken but only growing heavier with each bit that passes among you both. How often really is it that the right buttons get pushed and then so many that a body couldn't help but be moved?" said Catfish.

"Wool," Alyssa paused. "I'm sure I wouldn't even know how to start on something like that. But I can say you're probably too high for most everybody's good."

"There's no genies in a rusty flashlight, Miss Alyssa. Like there ain't no break in the day, ain't no holdin' a body that's already out the door," Catfish said.

"Hey now. Buddha say—wise man many time speak of temperance," said Izzy.

One beat two and Catfish replied—"Buddha say it's a mean old world, try livin' by yourself. Come on Rosie, just checkin' up on my baybeh. Findin' out what she puttin' down. So many nights and days—she have been out of town. Listen down child, and bye bye bird." There came a rap on the window, the door slid open and Roxy stood there pointing at the stoned harmonica player.

"We on. Sound check," said Roxy.

"Yes we is," Catfish said. He jumped up with a spry hop down to the ground, with a skip to his step he was soon inside.

Once in the venue, Elijah Frye, who was also called Catfish, had his thoughts flying—eagle's wings. Spread

55

throughout works regal things and bloodline's noble veins. Rich man slow hand, poor and simple ways count re-band stand jammin' on the one and two and. Three on the backbeat all's gettin' in wit the Twig man rockin' the microphone.

"A roadhouse resides down that path—it's at that spot I often stay," Twig sang soulful. Catfish grabbed his case of harmonicas and managed the steps onto the stage settling behind a microphone placed before a folding chair that would be his haunt. He sat down, putting his case on the floor to his left, unlatched and flipped it open to display over a dozen blues harps keyed in every note of the chromatic scale, backups for C, A, G, and D; plus low F and low C. They were all diatonic, mostly Hohner Blues. He picked up the B-flat harp for F in cross, and raised it cupped in his hands, letting off a tragic wail. The noise bounced back through the monitor on the edge of the stage.

"I have not returned to that place—in almost one hundred and sixty-five days," Twig finished the phrase and stepped back up off the mic to begin a lead riff, as his father was in the middle of a raggedy rattling shake drawing over holes four and five. The old man laid a slow bend on the tones as the line fell off almost completely. He echoed after with three quick syncopated chords, the whole harmonica was nearly halfway down his gullet.

Desean, who was also called Twig, was hanging on a whale of a wicked whip jerked up hard on the guitar neck, hammered on between the open A-string and the third fret. Roxy had her bass on and was laying out slow walking steps underneath it all as Moe kept a solid two and four on the snare. Les added rhythmic features higher up on the lighter side of his keyboard.

"Just one damn minute 'fore we resume," Twig said back up at the mic. "The bank man is saying I'm poor." A burst of sorrow erupted from the harmonica, as Catfish spoke of pain that came through and pushed forward. "Hold your got dang hound dog Darrell," came the next line. "Say my bank man is saying I'm poe." Twig cut the last lyric short and percussive like the sound of Moe's name. Then the whole group winded up gaining momentum for the resolution, to push on through to the solo section. "I possess a dark despotic sensation. Won't be hittin' that casino no mo'." This time just exactly like Moe. All occupants of the stage sitting back for a ride as the shuffle slammed right into the major fifth, jive and straight on 'til morning midnight drive with the reborn blues kid from Louisiana.

It was a twelve-bar pattern, they ran once through the changes, and Roxy stepped up and spoke something through her own mic to the soundman. She raised her right hand and shaded the hot lights as she peered deep into the room and noticed the soundman signaling towards Catfish. "Have him sing something," came the engineer's voice from the stage front monitors. Roxy strolled over near the harp player; leaning in she politely hollered words in the vicinity of his ear. Elijah nodded and kept blowing the blues harp while he waited for the top to come around. He'd take over the last verse of the song. The tune was based off of Red House, which he taught both his boys when they started out on guitar way back when. Their mother was a sweet gal, and then that thought was gone.

"I will come around this way eventually—" Catfish sang and started stomping on every quarter note. "Down this road we're put upon." The bass and Twig's guitar mirrored the vocal figure. "Way go back, near on around this way," with fierce pride. "Down this road we all put upon." The keyboard took a turn swooning curves in, out, and around about the web of sounds. This was all in anticipation of the hard out that came next following the delivery of the last line. "Zif I can't ever catch me nah breaks," it hung in suspense for two beats. "Guess I just," quick drum fill, "Get along." While the end wound up and came barreling through, Catfish blew a high tone then fell down low landing fat on the downbeat as Roxy raised her bass pointing skyward, her eyes on the whole band and she slashed in one motion towards the ground. The group held out a lengthy sustained chord. Twig and Catfish danced for a second with flourishes over the ending while Roxy lifted her arms even higher and chopped off the last note, the reverberations trailing away into the shadowy recesses of the club.

"What else you need?" Roxy asked of the sound tech.

"Old-timer, could you hear yourself up there alright?" said the soundman.

"Everything sounds fine to me, thank you much," Catfish replied.

"Anybody not want the harmonica in their monitor?" the soundman asked.

No hands went up. "Great. Then if you could just give me one more that should do it," came back from the sound booth.

"Sigourney Weaver!" yelled Roxy. This set the members of Dream Demonical into their respective preparations for that particular song.

"Still got—somethin' to offer up—" sang out acapella then a bass line swoled as the pronouncement was repeated. "Still got—somethin' to offer up—" and a tic tic swirl of a swoosh arm twirl and the rhythm, the rhythm, flow forth given, beats of a wish once made, the power completes. One, two, three "Sigourney Weaver." Pounding in unison, guitar, bass, keys start a rumble in a real nice way.

"Mommy always said there were no monsters.[5] A thing, a construct, the new model droid."[6] More business down low then it began to rise, first slow then faster-faster. The pulse, the run hit top and they bom-bom. Warm love, she was wrapped in a tauntaun. Slither rinse repeat, got power when it gets down rattle and hum, hitting back, forth and up down, destructively. This was one of the newer additions to their set list, hadn't had a chance to work it over much or put it down in a studio. It included several quotes from the Alien film franchise built around the chorus sung in a full-bodied spiritual chant-like figure. Roxy repeated, "Still got—somethin' to offer up—" Called what it is for the OG Weaver, "a chick thing—Lacerta plague, like a fuckin' square-dance," stinger.[6a]

Dream Demonical cut the tune after just the second chorus, as Roxy saw the third act start to stir just off stage. She set things up so that the other band could share Moe's drum set, which would eliminate a lot of the 'moving shit around' mess in between Demonical and the group in from Cali.

SuperheroManz was slated to play after Catfish's blues set, then Roxy and her gang taking things from 2230 to closing.

It was past 1900 hours, getting very close to doors at 1930. SuperheroManz was milling about the stage flipping power switches and plugging instruments into amplifiers. They were a five-piece from the L.A. area with drum, bass, rhythm and lead guitar, and a singer who had pulled out a trombone and was playing something sounding very similar to Zeppelin's Black Dog. Roxy, Twig and them headed to the bar to see what kind of tab they had, if any, for the evening ahead. They procured bottles of beer; Moe ordered a Jack and Coke, while Les asked politely for a bottle of water, straight. They sat down. Roxy spun around on a barstool, then stopped facing the stage, leaning an elbow back against the bar, which was spotless for the time being.

"Anybody know anything about these guys?" asked Moe.

"Les said he found their album at the Indie record shop," said Roxy.

"How was it? What'd it sound like?" Moe put to Les.

"Spoonful of Fishbone. Bit of ska and reggae, can get pretty heavy," said Les.

"Supposably—" Twig said. On stage the trombone started doubling the guitar on the opening of 'Voodoo Chile', in the style of Jimi Hendrix's slight return. Beneath a 'tssk' on the hi-hat the drum's toms tapping gained force, built a current in the pocket set back, hotter and hotter then they dropped down into the One. Long. Jam. Until you get to the mountain next.

• • • • • • •

In the bus, Izzy and Alyssa sat calm on the outside, tried to appear pristine on the inside, ideologues. Real folks have broke cogs. Steel spokes on logs. Feel jolts, speak quotes, and repeat oaths of lauve. Speaking words that hold weight and great significance. To believe in people and worth, and how some of them it have. Being knowned as high-toned with upper angel arms. Mini-melodramatic, static in a space-time fabric, little black book and the answer was magic, a tragic lie.

59

Marked on a page, bass bled out the brick wall backstage. Crack. One wrinkle in time, but what's in the moment: foment the non-recalcitrant chosen.

Supple legs, subtly begs, and nobody wants to hurt no one, but hug and affect. Shun never not now, totally surrender and one with a dot, ciao! Back in the beyond, slow pumping heart strong, olive gators in the swamp song. Understand there's many approaches to laundry, really now. Some days 'just okay' is damn good enough. Though boring is basically always morally reprehensible. Connective, the collective is subjected to a gentle blush. Touch, more and much real lust doesn't suffer fools gladly, if even at all. Happiness is a roof over your head, wheels beneath your feet, skin to the meeting of the minds plus two in the bind. Blessed be, yes, release.

"Can you take me there?" Alyssa asked softly.

He took her there, fully and divine, free from all divide.

Ain't that the truce, rocket surgery. They will say God is not real. What do you believe in? Karma. Well? Yeah, a karma well with wisdom and gold and again and hold. Tighter. Lighten the soul; lengthen the fold, the fallen. It was, it was whole—sometimes to create one must destroy a peaceful notable silence of some sane length.

"How was Arizona?" she asked, softer.

"Very lovely and sweet," said Izzy.

Now in close she curled her lips in pleasure.

"What've you gotten so smiley about?" asked Izzy.

"Stuff," said Alyssa like killer cute. "The night is young and neither are you."

"That cuts me to my core, I will have you know," Izzy said.

Inside Alyssa rose up a thing she wanted to say but shouldn't, and wouldn't, so didn't. She couldn't—go there— can't begin—such is the fate of adrenaline's whim. Even still they were fair, full and content, savoring the quiet. Soon this now would be gone, and all would be back as it was, 'which', (she noted) had been steadily improving in the recent past, culminating in her present state in this bus next to this present him.

People had begun arriving for the show. Inside the Rhythm Room, Roots and Blues music was playing over the house system. Across the parking lot, in sparse intervals, vehicles could be heard pulling in, doors shut and footsteps walked towards the main entrance on the club's southside opposite the street. Izzy and Alyssa remained low on the floor of the cab, entangled and worn out from the friction. They both straightened out their chonies, sitting up and leaned their backs against the base of the bench seat, still half-heaving breathily in the early stages of realization and recovery.

Nobody knew what had happened.

January 24, 1998

To the Northwest, Sonny, Truck and Boonz entered Las Vegas city limits on the 515, taking exit 68 onto Tropicana Avenue heading west. Sonny turned the van north on Paradise Road; Truck saw the UNLV campus on the right side of the street. The Hard Rock Hotel and Casino was next on the left side of Paradise Road. The two musicians in the front seats looked out satisfied that they'd made it to their destination safely. They continued north until they hit Sahara, turning westward to Las Vegas Boulevard. After performing one more ninety-degree maneuver, the brown Ford van headed south towards the Strip to get a view of the infamous whirled and wired spectacular.

"You sure you don't want to stop and walk about a bit?" said Truck.

"Naw man, that's not the plan. Just get an eyeful and you can take it all in tomorrow before and after the show," Sonny replied.

Truck was bummed out. There came a rustling from the back. Boonz peeked up and around for a good look at the action and lights, he thought, 'Where's my camera?' Driving slow their eyes fell to women, the shine, and the drunken stumbling citizenry. Sonny kept his vision mainly on the road and surrounding traffic. He had learned his lesson a few summers back when he was too busy rubbernecking and blew out a front tire on the curb of the middle median that just jumped up out of nowhere. He bent the rim and spent a whole Sunday tracking down a tire repairman who could pound out the wheel. He couldn't make the long trip home on the small spare donut he put on in place of the blow out. Sonny noticed quite a few Broncos and Packers jerseys, it made him almost feel a part of something. Too often it seemed that him and his were always at least once removed from everything that was happening. He wasn't mad about it, just fully aware that where he was wasn't ideally the place that he wanted to be. That place being the streets of the French Quarter, Jackson Square, the Saint Louis Cathedral, and all over Canal Street, New Or Lense, Louisiana.

Sonny spent some good years growing up in Algiers Point, just across the river from the city's downtown. He'd take the ferry over from the west bank of the Mississippi to where it let everyone off near the Riverwalk, just a few minutes hike from Jackson Square. You could watch and listen to the street musicians perform on the sidewalks all around the Quarter. For a while, Sonny and his Pops had a spot next to the large steps directly opposite Jackson Square, most Saturday and Sunday mornings until 1300. This went on all summer when he was twelve. His younger brother was still up in Illinois with their mother, it was a time deeply engrained in his consciousness. Music was a truly magnanimous gift that connected him to his family, and made things feel meaningful and worthwhile. Sonny remembered setting down his open acoustic guitar case, encouraging contributions while his Pops hopped around blowing harmonica, singing "My feet can't fail me now," and "Jesus on the mainline," Mississippi mud gonna let it shine. The brass bands would march on by, souls high-stepping on the second line. Then the evening falls and the people change, the pace shifts to a new and righteous feel. Smiling white ladies and twenty-dollar bills.

"Whoa!" Truck shouted, turning away from the window. "Old lady puke, purple hair!" An Elvis Presley posed off in the distance, camera flashes caught in action, mid-Thank you very much. "Does somebody got a wet wipe?" sung a stranger.

"Look for a place with donuts, Sonny," Boonz dropped in his two pennies.

The background blurred and it was like driving through a Christmas tree in Satan's holiday dominion. Getting rid of all obstacles, 'Hey hun, how you be?' A meerkat's graffiti source code debauchery, second the mode of self-indulgent damnable disregard. Crooked art, off the wall, a cancer threat in the bathroom stall. Johnny rocket science imperative on a back porch swung. Wrong. Swamp song, the deed of demoralization of what and who? Mankind. Be. For the mood rises in mad rude disguises and shows itself unto the sun. Day comes eventually to obliterate the veil.

Raw nerve, boo bird; succotash suffering the flat-Earth's curvature; soft word ease only too pure. But now a thing or two about breathin': If your mama was a saint, then your daddy was a heathen and a half in a hell bag, oersters on the shelf rag, entry in dimension alfresco. Chuckin' Parmesan. Witch blame cursed, the stricken or the plague? Fun bubble burst, missed a flush straight pair of dimes, street perusal of dames.

The boys made it back down to Tropicana Avenue. Sonny turned right heading west past the I-15 to locate a place to park and spend the night. They rarely wasted money on motels. In a few minutes, the dirt brown Ford van pulled into a convenience store lot. The three fellows evacuated their vehicle, mobbing inside the flourescently charged shop that was decorated on the outside glass with neon adverts for alcohol. Boonz found donuts which were small sleeved and off brand. Some pastries is just different on the inside, it's narc ring personnel. Others discovered Cheetos, jerky, Starburst and vittles wit flavors galore. Truck was debating hot pork rinds, though deep down he did not want to be that guy, again. Sonny also grabbed a gallon of water and a quart of 10w30 from the automotive section. They paid the clerk and Truck kept on at Sonny about how early it was, and could he drop him off somewhere with naked ladies or something other than to just call it a night? They knew Boonz would want to go sleep, but Truck gave it a decent run at swaying the general opinion.

"We hole up, eat these snacks, maybe talk about the gig, and crash," Sonny said.

Back on the road, they went another mile and spotted a suitable dark and dead parking lot, spread lightly with automobiles. Sonny rolled in among the metal and cut the engine, removing the keys, stowing them away. Boonz was in the rear, starting in on his pack of donuts. Sonny popped open slash busted into his bag of Cheetos.

"Man, I really wanted to see all the stuff this time," Truck moaned.

"You can't see *all* the stuff. It's just not possible," Sonny replied.

"Yeah, no shit. Not with us sitting here away from everything," Truck said.

"Pick out the big things. Set your sights on what are the real prime targets. Then you might have a chance at an amazing experience," Sonny said.

"Maybe so, I guess if I aim for the best stuff, that guarantees me definitely seeing something. But what about the little things, that even by themselves have potentially mind-blowing capabilities? Mom and Pop shops and whop nops. Nuance," said Truck.

Sonny thought for a bit eating Cheetos, his fingers beginning to orange. "Well now, if you're talking about nuance, that changes things. I thought you said you were just after *stuff*."

"Really? So we can go back out?" Truck asked hopefully.

"No man. But don't let me stop you from seeing all the stuff. If it's in your heart go grab it. But you'll have to hoof it tonight," said Sonny.

Truck nodded satisfactorily. Suddenly he felt enormous regret for passing on those spicy pork rinds. A spicy pork rind is nuance if he ever even knew what nuance was. Boonz back there on the blue beanbag chair crumpled his donut's empty cellophane sleeve loudly, a crispy crinkle.

"Let me get at them Cheetos, Son," Boonz called out.

"Sorry, gotta save some for breakfast," Sonny said.

"Ah, well let me get at that jerky then," from Boonz.

"That's my lunch," said Sonny at which Boonz pshawed. Then Vincent, they call him Sonny, threw the jerky pouch back at his bass player and with a smack it sounded like he got him in the face. Bull's eye; extremely to the point seven six two millimeter; full metal jacket.

"Thanks," said Boonz.

"Just save some for the wolves," Sonny warned and then took out the keys, turning the ignition one click over, activating the stereo. He fetched a CD from the case, slid it in the deck face, a spinning circle, jumped to track fourteen, and he inhaled in every possible sense of the words, disorder and disarray. Just a rancid taste of a couple tunes, before the power goes off. Soon to sleep they'd fall in the land of the debts and deserted, while visions of strippers pole-danced in their heads.

The Rhythm Room had been filling up. Some of it was the regular crowd; some were just out after the juices. Others made the trip specifically for one or all of the acts on the lineup that night. Deference stokes the flame in a nice fashion towards the success of all involved. Master of the storm sleeps standing in the wind. Zen, sitting still stuck to the same spot on the bar; Roxy and the gang hadn't budged. The doors opened and people filtered in filling the spaces around Dream Demonical, like molecules in the cytoplasm of the juke joint. Hyper chasm jump boogie boomed overhead pumping woogie out and seeping upon the crowd. Hats, cats in a rousing chorus of Straighten Up and Fly Right, real loosely chock full of grit and gravel. A blizzard took the Marquis for a romp in the air, then apparently the Marquis got some crazy notion and things went south. Chill up people don't let flow your stop, sang Roxy. Things were off balance for a minute, while Catfish was about on one leg and wobbly. Twig had made it known he didn't much appreciate "that van guy" getting his Pops high.

"Don't act like he's never played a little sideways before," Roxy was forever keeping the peace. Peacing the bar keep who was emerging from the kitchen holding a food basket smothered in yellow. Catfish rose up on his toes and shouted, "Them's mine!"

Roxy intercepted the tortilla chip cheese boat. "These," she said pausing and wielding a mighty finger wag, "are nachos. They mine."

"Hippy fuck," Twig mumbled fully pissed.

"Yeah he do," Catfish chuckled and Roxy had to be quick.

"These," she didn't exactly have a plan, "are the times that try men's souls."

No argument there. Twig was steamed. Catfish only wanted his nachos stating, "Lady, my cheese is getting cold."

"These," working the room immediately before her, "are the days of our lives." Ten minutes until show time to get Catfish steady and have the rest of her band ready for downbeat.

"These," she still had zero parts of a plan, "are the voyages of the Starship Enterprise." A whoop came from further down the bar. A voice called out, "Spock rules!"

"These are the breaks?" Moe said more like a question.

"Yes. Damn straight. See guys, Moe gets it," said Roxy.

Les sat up and raised his had offering, "These are the colors of the rainbow?" Boos sounded from several directions, causing Les to shrink back down.

"These aren't the droids you're looking for," Moe said with greater confidence.

"Amen, hallelujah." Roxy could maybe see a light ahead. She looked at Twig and Catfish, took their temperature.

Twig was battling something. He forced out, "These are the cries of the carrots."

"A little obscure, but yeah man. That's it," said Roxy.

"These are the cries of London town," Les spit out eagerly. Crickets. "Come on. That's legit! Then how about Theseus and the Minotaur?" he shouted in desperation.

Roxy looked at him crooked and asked, "Do I have to worry about you too now?"

"No. It's cool, it's cool." They can't say he didn't try. Let the record reflect that Les Watts gave it a go.

Roxy set the nachos on the bar in front of Catfish, who got down to business. She also asked the bartender for an ice water and suggested the old man stay hydrated. Roxy and the rest of Dream Demonical had spent the last two months rehearsing once, sometimes twice a week with Catfish who'd come over to Didney World West and go over his songs. He knew most all the greats ranging from Muddy and Little Walter, to Sonny Boy Williamson, Sonny Terry and Big Walter Horton. Twig helped his Pops whittle the list down to twelve solid tunes that most times ran out to about forty-five minutes.

"Next time you see me start heading up on stage," Roxy told the rest of the group. She then dashed up to the front entrance, grabbing two wristbands and also had the doorman put Izzy and Alyssa on the guest list. Deftly crossing the busy room, she exited through the backstage door and made a beeline for the bus, giving it a 'Rap tap tap' on the side window. Movement inside and a click and the door rolled open revealing the boy and girl sitting close on a blanket spread out on the floor of the cab.

"We start Catfish's set in a few minutes. Here are passes to get in if they lock the back door on you. Also, I put both your names on the list up front. You think you all might eventually come inside?" Roxy said.

"For sure we will," Alyssa said and it was the truth.

"How about you there," Roxy to Izzy. "Getting antsy?"

"No way, quite the opposite," he replied.

"Good to hear," Roxy said. She executed a loose rendition of an about face and disappeared back inside the venue.

All alone again, they were. Just can't wait to get deeply held within. Izzy had been running the numbers and if he left Phoenix the next day at 1030 he should be able to make kick-off, which was at 1630. But he thinks west coast time is one hour earlier than Arizona, which means he can leave at 1130 Mountain Time, question mark? Is he trying to figure out daylight savings time right now?

"What are you thinking about?" asked Alyssa.

"Time zones, irony, fate and freewill," said Izzy.

"Because wrinkly clothes?"

"Ugzackly," Izzy smiled. "The ultimate ironing in my life is that, being somewhat musicianish, I cannot whistle. Among the many drawbacks this deficiency poses, I have absolutely nothing to do while I work, and am helplessly unable to convey my sincere appreciation to attractive women as they pass by. As I'm a dog person, this shortfall also affects my ability to gain the attention of stray pups as they might dart towards traffic. I will probably never attain any great standing in the bird-calling community, and my chances of rising to understudy to lead whistler in some world renown acapella group diminishes everyday that I remain without a whistle. Thanks to today's technology, my aspirations to officiate competitive sports are still intact. Though this seems trivial considering the life I could've had."

"Truly a pity," chimed in Alyssa.

"So here I am, six ways of miserable, and my dog is a fleeting memory. Pancake flat on the interstate. In summation, learn to whistle. You will never be bored on the job, women will have a better self-image, and your puppies will be safe and secure.   Who doesn't know how to whistle anyway? Communists and Fidel Castro, and they probably learned long ago, only to abandon the practice because none of the other dictators were doing it."

"When did you have a dog? You didn't tell me you were a musician. And who really wants to be in an acapella group? Even one that's world renown," said Alyssa.

"The dog is just a bad childhood memory. I have a ukulele I mess around with, and yeah, I guess acapella has recently fallen off in popularity."

"Is the ukulele here in the van? Will you play me something?"

"I could try. I can't guarantee you it'll sound good." Right off he began to reconsider. He was not a good singer. He felt he was already losing much of his mystique. He was hesitant, and began to try and weasel out.

"Oh, come on. Are you really gonna tell me no, now?"

Izzy didn't know exactly what he was doing. Everything was so bizarre to the point that this girl was now so very real, and becoming more like someone who would require an end, if they were not to continue on in this mode of deep entrenchment and connection.

"What do I get if I give you a song, one song?"

"So greedy is he. And you already got what you get."

He kissed her. She kissed him. They kissed one another. Kiss. He held her. She held him. They held one another. Hold. Reaching into a closet behind the girl, the boy pulled out a small case not but two feet tall.

"Would you like the rock, the country, or the jazz?"

"I would like a the country, please." She quipped, a little Italian.

The two of them sat there cross-legged as he took out the instrument and strummed one chord, then another. The tuning was close enough. With a slow and deliberate hand, he began to lay down a simple introduction. He cleared his throat away from the girl.

"Dirt road in the twilight, woods so cool and dark. Up ahead pale neon, somewhere a dog barks. Honky Tonk moon, keep shining on my baby and me." On it went and goes continually in some sense. Lazy summer blue smoky haze; easy in my soul melts away. Stars are twinkling bright, the hoot owl calls all right. Honky Tonk moon, shining: baby and me.

Some worlds began. Others were flipped and upended.

Izzy played and sang while Alyssa listened. Hands moved and thighs were put upon. Her soul strings were heartily tugged around. They both felt each other far beyond the basis of fingers and such. Touch, deep down and desirable. Much of what was shared spared no room for scared. Frightening to be so unaware. Reality scarred with heavenly torture barred from ordinary gain or lost despair. Yet frivolity. Surrounded by the hand-stitched idle inclusions. Izzy finished the last chorus and had a hard time meeting her eyes. She still watched him anyway. Made her presence known.

"Who is that by?" Alyssa asked.

"That's that Randy Travis. By way of Dennis O'Rourke."

"Oh, for the years I have not lived, but only dreamed of living,"[7] she said. The two sat with much energy passing through, around and between them.

"Who is *that* by?" he asked.

"That's that Nathaniel Hawthorne. On living."

Soon small talking would not suffice, though they had touched on several massive moments. They were exchanging experience in large quality amounts; aesthetically reorganized trash. Militant intellect negotiates dissent. Burly old dude yoga, Satan's old ugly lemmings or sweet oracle, undying life. Sacred prose in reverent innocent tones: human emotion and reliable timing. Dismantling every considerable option negating syntax towards realizing ultimate comprehension triggering inherent ontological nuance; asymmetrically recurring truth. Idiosyncrasies demonstrating entity's nature through inclined traits yelling as the medium utilizing sound in concert began, and the glorious suffering oozed out door cracks and the aging foundations.

Alyssa felt walls and windows closing in, on, and around her. She wanted badly to obey this thirst for security; know the ledge. It was an act of balance and shifting sands, two structures battling hurricane force whims. Master of the dance falls face down in the dirt. (Zartan's Englewood's Nietzsche. (Because if at first you don't succeed, try Crystal's meth again. Then it's crazy, then shhh.) Play it cold, for what? To be cold,

72

pulls bit.) Lethargic anguish masquerading entirely non-toxic: gregarious. Lowly orphans agonize, trembling hopeless in nefarious gloom. Nervous literal allegory utilizing gaunt heresy to eradicate revolt: from the cheap seats.

Cracks on the snare drum echo random hits, your time has meaning. A repetitious bass line forms a familiar pattern, in between hidden harlequin assists, reflects melodies of notorious youth. Outside evil naysayers, the eternally meddling yucksters lurk. Pocketing hucksters perks.

Most souls seek palpable energy, allowing cosmic elements and enchanting next level imagination, garnering happy times ending never making everyone naturally telepathic. Proletariat empathy amplifies celestial existence, but wherein lies the cancerous onslaught negotiating friendly liberation in cohort's travels?

How made is their philanthropic regime overthrow, gathering readily enabled stable society? Progress obliterated vehement exercising regurgitating total yin: anhedonia and ennui, versus positive reign of substantial periodic elation resulting in true yang.

• • • • • • • •

If only to calm the tempest, she sought colossal oaths made memorable inspiring true meritorious entrance necessitating triumph, needing conquered ornery undercurrent rampaging alongside gargantuan effort, and superhuman talent reaching effervescent natural growth, truly healing to achieve peace over war ending righteously with a king's plate of biscuits. Good real angst, vivacious yummy on the side.

Is it just that principled respect inviting developed ego comes before the fall? But it's not even spring, and what of this ledge I don't know about? The Rhythm Room was bleeding mellow etudes lacking obscure dissonant yelling and at the bottom of it all, Alyssa wished now only to hold a frequent resource in existence, necessary deal. The boy and girl still sat resting their backs against the bench seat's base. She reached down and found his hand and slid hers into a locking grip of solemn solace, with a silent prayer she thanked the night for the moon above.

"Izzy." She said his name.

"Yes, Miss Alyssa?" He said hers.

Now *she* was unable to look *him* in the eyes. She wished she could say something earth shattering, groundbreaking, mad-hattering, or soul shaping.

"Will you play another song?" was all she could muster.

She did not see but felt him smile. He raised the instrument and lightly strummed the strings. He sang her Stardust, "steals across the meadows of my heart." The music of the years gone by: A tear did slide down the Rose's cheek; sweet tones and the fears fell by the way. Why ride by the bayside transport her to a land where she playwright, scenes from a dreamscape as the day's closed blinds. "Beside a garden wall when stars are bright," the song then ceased and they were again in each other's arms, for a wonderfully long time. Alyssa climbed up on Izzy. He sat holding her and they danced as she let escape soft moans. Making time. Getting lost. Being found.

• • • • • • •

Inside the venue everyone had found their feet. Those on the floor swayed fro and to the beat. The musicians fell on solid footing laid back in the groove. Catfish was bringing it home on Sugar Mama, signaling with his right hand while his left held the harp to his mouth as he shook and jove, going high to low pulling hard on hole two. He brought down his right arm and the band dropped a heavy chord and the toms and kick drum fluttered beneath the decay of the stinger. The crowd applauded. Catfish slapped the harp several times on the palm of his hand, clearing out the condensation.

"This next one's called, 'I'll Fight For You'," Catfish spoke into the mic. Twig strolled over near his Pops and turned to face Moe and Les in the back row of the stage. He started a four count just loud enough to be heard by the rhythm section, Roxy and his Pops on each side. Same time he said 'four' he picked three high wailing notes on his guitar as the drums, bass, and keys all hit on the downbeat. They were off, then moments later a harp riff ripped up and dug in on the flat fifth. Twig was still piercing the room with screams released from his amp through his guitar from his fingers through his soul from the mind of Elmore James. By way of Richland, Holmes County, Mississippi, USA.

"Gone off on your lonesome, not a soul by your side. Just weeping and tortured, been treated unkind. But all along, I told you true, I'll fight for you." Elijah sang, back in his mind he was waist high deep in the muddy river water of his ancient youth. Most songs in his set he'd been singing a good bit over half-a-century. Twig was front stage right beside his mic stand hotly mean muggin' the world. Still buggin' about his 'drugged out' Pops, handling heavy on the microphone, easy speak and slack tilt steady preach while Roxy and Moe were pushing thunder strokes, smacked axe reattacked. Roxy was stage left in front with an eye line to the drums, center back. Les was in the back stage right next to Twig's Marshall half stack setup. Dream Demonical's usual arrangement was Roxy, Twig and Les across the front, stage left to right, respectively. Twig was always smack dab in the middle. Les was never much too active so he didn't mind being pushed to the back so as Catfish could have his moment front and center.

Later in the night when Demonical performed, Les would get enough face time, though most of the attention would be on Twig and Roxy. Desean, called Twig, did often shine bright like a diamond in the spotlight. The focus made him do the hocus pocus all but danced and set right ablaze. Roxy made the call to put him center stage so she wouldn't get the drama that comes with the pressure position. It doesn't seem like six feet of stage displacement would do much good deflecting heat, but she did the math and those are the certified results.

"But all along," Catfish belted out, "I told you true," a quick low squiggle on the harp: "I'll fight for you." He bended, bent, his bendings whipped back down to the low fifth drawing in on hole one. "Guitar!" yelled out the old man and Twig braced his feet, found his stance split dimensions with a high sharp shrill piercing knife of a note and he was shaking it all out wildly. Setting loose a loud lightning bolt thunderclaps madly a torrent of raw rapturous reverence to the forbearers of good juju slash bad voodoo, a real bold extension to mention motion the crowd swells roar expulsion the ride of impulsive hoots 'n' hollers by blue-collars, rowdies, and rude reckless foll'ers of the true path. The blue jazz, renewed blast of tempest torn battle worn wood craft, a blood bath of tendon sees pick stabs some rancor some slaps muddy hand core allegiance to band stand the beauty while soothing with the face of an angel divine. Nine and three more's sublime inch subwoofers low throbbing with all the heads nodding then proven in unison lone tear drop sobbing in sullen grave robbing the dead come to life once inspired.

Catfish was comping along underneath his boy, who brought it back all the way around for a variation on the opening verse twice as gone and he cursed, "Hot damn," out of nowhere. "But all along—I told you true—I'd fight for you." He gave a signal and they all brought it back home and out. The crowd was responding well. Catfish and his group were about halfway through the set. The old man was feeling it as they burned through Who Will Be Next by Howlin' Wolf. After that he turned around and shouted, "Peach Tree, Peach Tree." Then he reached down, took a swig of his drink and moved back up to the microphone. "This another one by Sonny Boy Two." He came in quickly with a jut-jigga-jut-jat and all the business kicked back in.

"Looka there, honey, mercy me," and all the like, like "Way over down by the peachie tree."

Then they did 'My Babe' by Little Walter, and 'Baby, Please Don't Go' by everybody else. Slowed it down, sped it up, Messin' with the Kid, Juke, Sonny Terry's Hot Headed Woman. Somewhere in there it did take a Mellow Down Easy, all of them is Too Young to Die and it was just a Mean Old World anyway you slice it.

Down on the floor a saucy lady whooped. Catfish said, "Honey, you sweet times seven," and that was how it ended. Finished. DD-CC al Coda. The stage lights went down and the house music came up. Movements began on and off the platform, as Catfish and his gang unplugged and started to carry off their instruments and gear. Superheromanz stood by making preparations for their set at 2130.

It was 2120. Buck arrest time throne, gamma ray headphone, shorty got backbone slack tooth liars, pass me the hammer and the needle nose pliers, Beatle knows whyers. Stack six logs by your best sled dogs; request rest longs by the heat'll grow fires. Moe's drum kit stayed put as the middle act had permission to use it to keep the setup and turnover time down. Roxy placed her bass in its hard case, slid it behind the stage out of the way. Les stood close by holding a bottle of partially drunk water.

"Les, give me a smoke, man." Roxy said to the keyboard player.

"You told me not to give you one if you ask. Plus I am quitting right now, so I don't have any on me," Les replied.

"Liar. Come on, I haven't asked you in like two weeks," Roxy pushed back.

"Alright fine, but please don't ask me for any more. This is supposed to be my last pack." Les removed the Newport hundreds from his jacket pocket. He slid one out and passed it over to Roxy who smiled gratefully back at Leslie Watts, aka Lo-fi. She pushed open the backstage exit to go grab a lighter from her Jeep. She looked over to where the bus was parked; instead she saw a red ninety-something Ford Mustang with no Alyssa Rose in sight. Roxy knew and also didn't know exactly what had happened. Out loud she said, "Of course they go and disappear. I just hope somebody's still got some sense."

Chapter Thirteen • Minions of Faith, Mustard Seed

The Rhythm Room was on Indian School Road several blocks east of Central Avenue. The boy and girl headed west, deciding to turn south on Seventh Street based on Alyssa's limited knowledge of the valley's layout. "I know if you go south, you run into a mountain," she had said. There were cars out, lights on, and the heat soaked pavement. Flagrant. Just relay come fission. Vagrant display cold fade coalition and the organisms *breathe,* with a heartily stressed *'eathe'.*

"Band-aids strip club," Alyssa pointed out the window.

"Bible Baptist Church," Izzy said. "To the right."

This place had something on somewhere though it was difficult to say just what. They crossed over the interstate and saw the lights of a large plane passing through the sky on its final approach to the airport. Off to the right they saw tall office buildings lit up at the windows, tops, and edges. They drove by a few gas stations and through an older district with quaint designs leftover from decades past. On Izzy's side of the street there was a large stone-fronted structure with seven or eight columns centered on its west facing façade. They continued straight on and up over past the baseball stadium. Alyssa said it was going to open soon, according to what Roxy had heard on the news. As the VW bus crested an overpass, they both saw red lights blinking in the distance, high up in the air, lined vertically and side-by-side.

"Those are the radio towers on the top of South Mountain. You can drive right up there and see the whole city," Alyssa said with great certainty. They went through what seemed to be a warehouse district. This based on the profusion of warehouses. The street sign said Buckeye Road. The area was tolerably okay. "Does it feel like this is what we're born to do?" Alyssa asked, immediately feeling stupid and regretful. What kind of line was that? Izzy's brain wheel was cranking.

"You talking about driving or this business of growing old? Like Go Fish, War, and The Game of Life, on a loop until you

78

die," replied the boy. Their momentum was crushed. They were trying maybe too hard to connect. It was uneasy at times.

Conversational road kill. Aardvark paws fur foal effect. No armadillo no fowl. They drove on feather. Passing another highway the signs said Tucson or Flagstaff, this way or that. Brrr-umping oval railroad tracks, there were regular office buildings, and far ahead the red blinking lines of glowing buzz, a beacon beckons in the night. They were on a bridge and from the look of it there was a wide riverbed below. Safe on the other side, trees began to show in dark shadows. Some were palm, some great and bushy. The detail was limited if not for the scattered light poles which did but hint at shape and form. On Alyssa's side, at ground level read a sign that said 'Tires.' This was the south of Phoenix. Passing a Tastee Freeze they stopped for a red traffic signal at Broadway. Resuming easily on down the road in a mostly residential neighborhood, on several walls there were graffiti, tags, and some more elaborately colorful spray-painted pieces, art.

They went by a Spanish church that said something about "Iglesias." Further down a more traditional chapel, whose message board read, "Connect, Grow, and Serve." After Roeser, more trees, homes and a school, empty lots opposite a corner shop on Seventh Street and Southern Avenue. A large church reflected a touch of culture with its architecture, the tower at its front. The boy and the girl made out its placard to offer some welcoming take on this humble South Mountain community.

"Do you know what's at this mountain besides a mountain?" Izzy asked.

"They have horse stables and some ancient native ruin-type stone habitations."

They were both still in for whatever, basic alley oaths not clever. Along for kicks: the sock it to me of it all.

"You have on decent walking shoes?" said Izzy.

"Yessir," she replied. "You want to know something about me?"

"Yeah, sure. Why? You want to know something about me?" A basic crosscourt forehand return.

"Ask me a question," said she. "I will be as open as my dignity allows."

He was two-thirds pleased that this course had been set upon, for direct and honest communication was tops. Alyssa took the deal to be a freely offered, legitimate shot at the core of truth, a glimpse into the man's being. By pure instinct she suggested to Izzy they turn west, move over to Central Avenue to continue south, because people have inklings and she might've recalled this from a time before. She spied an Arby's and had her standard positive reaction associated with the restaurant for its seasoned curly fries and quality roast beef sandwiches. Alyssa couldn't remember if they'd eaten anything back in Payson. She was kind of hungry, but it wasn't a priority. Also, shouldn't she be thinking of a question for Izzy?

"So, what are we doing once we get to the mountain?" her asked.

"Exploring," Izzy said. There was a vast natural expanse; he had a flashlight and they had limitless terrain inside and out of their collective bodies range. Part of it sounded like bullpuckey, but it did also make sense to Alyssa about the exploration of each other. The both had gotten a bit whacked out. Izzy really only seemed to be about thirty-five percent hippy. More like he just owned a VW bus and read a few books. His van wasn't covered in bumper stickers and window decals. Small feathers hung suspended from the rearview mirror.

"What year were you born?" Alyssa asked.

"Sixty-four," him said.

"Where were you born?"

"Portland, Oregon, Multnomah Country, Pacific Northwest, USA, Earth."

"What were you doing when you were twenty-two?"

"How about I get to ask you something? To be fair."

"Alright, have at it. Ask away. What would you like to know?"

Izzy paused for half a minute. They both leaned forward to see the tower lights high above. They were close. "What is your essence or redeeming quality?"

She digested the words she'd just heard. Thought of their meaning. "Eesh, your question was so much better than mine. I would say that my essence involves umm, believing in the goodness of humanity, second chances or even just first chances. Life is a gift, evil is an aberration, you know. Every-so-often I get burned but I think I live a fuller, richer, more realized life because of my belief in humanity and such."

"Well, your answer was way better than mine so I'd say we're even. But nobody is keeping score, so—" he trailed off.

"Oh, I'm definitely keeping score," she sassed a bit at which Izzy smiled and they both enjoyed the moment.

As they drove, a road sign warned of a hard right turn up ahead. The posted speed limit fell to twenty-five, then to fifteen miles per hour. Protective railings appeared on each side of the road. A massive earth and rock formation was there on the right, which they hugged close by as the van curved around and there was a slight pitch slanting towards the inside of the road at the turn. Now no more houses, just desert bushes and rocks visible within the lit range of the headlights. The bus was traveling west now and Alyssa told Izzy that the ranger station, stables, and the rest of it was just up ahead. There was trust between the two, though really he was pleased just to go for a drive along with Alyssa Rose Twyst. Though he only knew her for the moment as Alyssa Rose. Currently their cloud of intrigue only thickened as it hung about these two love-stricken.

"Whose turn is it to ask a question?" she said.

"That'd be you now."

"What?" she exclaimed, "Are you—interested in?" Oaf! That was plain yogurt.

"I am interested in words. Written, spoke, and sung. Blue notes, blue skies, fresh air and fruit pies," said Izzy.

"Oh yeah, and fruit pies?" Alyssa jabbed.

"Apple, peach, cherry, most any kind of berry. Blue, straw, huckle, boysen, banana cream is in there too."

"Banana cream-berry pie, huh?"

"You know what I mean. I might have an apple or cherry individually wrapped Hostess fruit pie back there in the pantry." Izzy motioned towards the back where a cabinet was set stocked with meager quick snacks. Most of it was boring protein, the savoriest thing being a can of tangy barbecue beans.

"Definitely, maybe if I could have the cherry," Alyssa said.

"It's a done deal orange peel," Izzy said and the girl smiled.

"Look, the old west!" Alyssa said pointing out ahead at the wild western saloon style storefront dimly lit by one or two lamp poles. There was a faint outline of a corral. He thought a sign said, 'Ponderosa.' If they stopped they might see horses stalking or hear their breathy snorts. There were scattered lights at other parts of the property, but the bus pressed on generally unfazed. Izzy's goal for some time now had been to drive all the way up to the red blinking towers, and park near or beneath them, to gaze out at the glorious cityscape. On the same southside of the road as the stables, they both caught a glimpse of several medium-sized single story structures. At first glance, the huts seemed quite empty and barren, comprised entirely of crude stone and brick. Temples. Our pilots two stayed midstream in the current, drifting on in the dark. Izzy slowed down. Up ahead he spotted a ranger station in the middle of the road. Warning blockade arms extended out on both sides barring advance. Reflectors on the arms flickered from the headlights of the approaching camper van. They rolled to a stop, temporarily stuck.

"Closed?" Alyssa said. "Since when do they close mountains?"

"Communists," Israel said. He shifted into reverse, backed up a bit turning over to the right and swung the bus hard left in a U-turn, with his mind set on heading towards the stone ruins. Maybe check them out, seeing as that a trip to the red lights above south Phoenix's mountain would not happen this night. Though in a way, it already had happened and was now an expanding experience.

"What say we explore those stone houses, then we should probably get over to the show, see that we all get where we need to be," said Izzy. Alyssa wondered if that meant anything, but was reassured that they weren't bailing or splitting right off. "Reach into the glove box and fish out the flashlight, please and thank you," he told her. She leaned forward and lifted up the glove box door as Izzy switched on the overhead dome light. There was a purple ostrich feather, a boomerang, three decks of cards, literature, a dozen lighters, a small toy sixty-three T-Bird, and near the equator she did find a flashlight in amongst the bulrushers. Alyssa grabbed the dormant saber, placing it safely on her lap.

"Can I ask you one more question, Izzy?" again she said his name.

"Please do."

Alyssa gathered her thoughts, in a more controlled delivery said, "What is *your* greatest gift?"

"I gave my grandma a beamer, nah." Izzy considered her query as he scanned the roadside for the ruins. Was she asking for the best present he ever received, or the greatest gift he's given? Did she want to know his prime ability, or deeper still some innate spiritual talent bestowed to him by a higher power? Was he overanalyzing too much? Was there a wrong answer? Was there even a right answer?

He saw the ancient adobes, pulled up beside them and off the asphalt onto the dirt shoulder. He kilt the lights and shut off the engine, remembered he was still on the hook for an answer. It was quiet save the seeping silence of the desert.

"My greatest gift is, uh, this night I've given to, no, I don't know. Patience. Patience is my superpower; sincerest apologies if that doesn't do it for you," Izzy said.

But that did do it for her. Game, set, match Mister Dufrene, though she only knew him as Izzy, or Israel.

Alyssa switched on the flashlight and it filled the inside cab of the van. The front doors opened, and the two bodies each hopped down, closing up the vehicle behind them.

"Keep that light on the ground and watch out for cacti," Izzy called out.

There were two main structures separated by fifteen or twenty yards. The first domicile was a simple four-walled cube with open windows and faded lettering on the side facing the road. Izzy and Alyssa moved on towards the next, much larger dwelling. As the girl shined the light the entire length of the building they saw many rooms and passageways in between. There was no roof. The luminous beam cast into, out of, and around all the walls of stone as well as the vacant gaps where windows were made. They stepped onto a smooth walkway, passing an old-fashioned water well with a short double sided roof, but no rope or pale to add another dimension to the scene's sense of realism.

"How old do you figure it all is?" asked Alyssa.

"Looks pretty old. There must be some placard posted telling when it was made or discovered," said Izzy.

He remembered the red lights that they followed here. He turned, glanced up and for a second was reminded of the angle your neck takes when you look up to the tops of the colossal skyscrapers of New York City, Chicago, and other metropolitan hubs. Izzy heard Alyssa say something. He saw her entering the stone hut through an access point on one side. He heard exclamations of fascinations, and shattered expectations, at this skeletal construction's treasures. That it might embolden such a reaction was splendid. His eyes adjusted to the night, the moon offered perspective as he walked up and reached out his hands to steady his entrance and avoid a knock on the noggin.

"This place is dope, right?" said Alyssa.

"Aye Lass, it's gr-r-rand," Izzy said in a Scottish brogue.

"Looks to be seven or eight rooms here, all the way up through the front."

"It's quite a spread. The walls are mostly smooth, a few cracks and rough spots but nothing too—ouch! Sharp." Izzy pulled his hand back from where he was feeling because he'd been surprised by an edge.

They moved slowly along to the front and larger sections with the girl leading, shining the torch onto Izzy's path at tricky passes. She wanted to see every little bit. She would sit down and stand up in different spots, popping her head out the windows to check the view of each room's past occupants. In a few more minutes they came to what seemed to be setup as the main room. The boy and girl wove in and out of the maze of passageways like time. Alyssa suddenly stopped, cut the light, turned and reached out grabbing Izzy by the arm. She stepped in close to him and gave a slight, "Shhh."

"What?" Izzy whispered.

"There's someone laying in the far corner over there."

"Give me the flashlight," Izzy said.

The boy took the torch then scooted around Alyssa, turning the beam on and peaking into the room. He saw a person lying on their side wrapped in a gray baggy coat.

"Hello, you!" Izzy spoke way too loud for Alyssa's liking. She shushed him and slapped his back, pulling aggressively on his shirt.

"Come on, leave him be, we've seen it, now let's go." Alyssa obviously had no interest in bothering this soul any further.

Izzy relented and they made for an exit in the adjoining room. That was about the full extent of exploring they could do in this particular spot. They cautiously crept away from the ancient ruins. Izzy pointed and Alyssa cricked her neck back to gaze up at the towers atop the mountain, some blinking red, others lit in a steady glow.

"Give me the light," Alyssa said, and then walked over to the well, bending over to have a peek. She shined the flashlight down inside, but then came up with a very disappointed, "Nothing." They passed again by the smaller building, gave a quick look in one of the open windows. All that she saw was more of the same nothing.

"Do you think we could go look around at the stables on our way out?" Alyssa said.

"There's a good chance of there also being somebody there who would appreciate our presence even less than that dude we just saw," Izzy said, purely rational.

They got back to the bus and Izzy opened the door for Alyssa, offering his hand he helped her hop up in, closing the door securely after she was seated. Izzy walked around the front, jumping in behind the wheel. The engine fired to life. Alyssa stowed the flashlight in the glove box.

"What's it like driving around in this bus all the time?"

"Hmm," Izzy considered her question. "Maybe it's kind of like traveling around in Santa's sleigh I guess."

"How's that?"

"People get a kick out of it until they see it's just me and not actually Santa or somebody exciting."

"Aww, I think you're exciting," she said in a conciliatory tone.

"Well, thank you kindly," he replied.

They pulled out slowly, rolling the windows down to take in the fresh night air as they headed back towards the city. Soon they saw the downtown buildings brightly lined up in the distance. Back to life, back to reality, back over to and north up Seventh Street. A daring chase waged against your boring everyday monotony. Like a box of those spray cans of whipped cream fell off a truck and landed right in front of your own backyard. We call those ones good days.

Chapter Fourteen • Numbing the Rumblers

Las Vegas, Nevada

Truck felt like true grit grown savage walking down the fallow road with airs of danger lurking from the stench that lingered thick in nearby lots and alleyways. Sonny gave him the spare key for the van, adding, "Don't be stupid, you'll be fine." Truck's plan was to walk over to the Strip, or a remote casino, and spread twenty dollars across one or several slot machines. He figured it was about three or four miles he had to cover. He'd been strolling for nearly an hour already, so he should be very close to the Boulevard. Traffic had picked up in the form of cars on streets and peoples on feets and cabs would drive by, slowing down at times, then speeding off. There were sprinkled establishments of ill repute and some more suited for those sanctified by a certain source of pious ceremony. Maybe somebody goes to church on Sundays, prays at the altar of their Lord and Savior. Then the next body and soul goes to church five times a week and that place is the corner liquor store. A seller of libations, cellar door of consecration's ritualistic metaphor, shut the screen door tete-a-war, per instigated carnivore. Neon green semaphore out front of these premises wore: "Booze whines lottery," in clear and brown glass pottery. All with lines like blown jazz artistry.

It was way past the pleasant folks' bedtime. Drown your head time in the drink, moon, and dead shine of the taunting place your bets line in the sand, which begs for choosing, hit or stay your pickings losing. Loosening patience from your pocket's safety linings. Taste refining golden lockets next for pining pawning rockets soaring high ghetto stock markets bull or bear, buyer beware of love and secretion; either/or leads to neither shore's completion. Have you got the time good man? It's twenty-two oh fifty tan.

As he walked, Truck saw a massive shift in sight chiaroscuro. Civilly disobey each David thoroughly, kicking rocks and breaking empty bottles. Tricks for trade cars heavy on the throttle, some spots were burning fierce, ferocious lit. In crack and crevice the shadows find shade. Last Vegan bowl of lard there for the taking. Past champions' swollen guard bread for the baking. Clime worth raping, dime dirt scraping, and the eagle passes time skilled mind predating. The killer prays his dinners not escaping. The diner's dollar pie price is inflating. The wartime peace keeps are constabulating. The small blind crook cheats limping while debating. His pot of gold is stolen while he's waiting. Around every corner, behind every door, redemption isn't something you do not settle for. It might be the next hand you're dealt is the winner. Aligns the complex plan to score booty thinner. Hot ass was everywhere. Truck wasn't shy about looking. Was a woman what he's after? Cackles from far off spawns the baddest kind of laughter.

Right there first in line was the MGM Grand. Truck weighed in his mind whether he should get a drink or put all of his resources into a go at the slots. One beer would only make him want another, so he might as well increase his chances at winning. Optimism prime, he put forward in his being. Finding his way to the casino floor, Truck drifted about trying to gauge his surroundings in an intimate manner. He located a water fountain and restroom, made a pass once through the blackjack tables, then changed his twenty bucks into quarters. Holding his cup full of eighty coins tight to his chest, he came to the slots trying to get a feel watching which machines were being played, triangulating a spot to initiate his attack. Around him sat old folks and little silver-haired grandmas, serious game cats and slick Warren Beattys. Each gambler was locked in modus operandi, while second-string scramblers were hanging on standby, just in from Van Nuys. Truck had never been strongly superstitious. He knew about feel and rhythm. He believed in the transfer of energy and striking when the iron was spicy hot. He put a lot of stock in proper timing, the effectiveness of repetition and hard work. Combined continual and forever on a loop. He reached a row of slots, counted down nine machines, and sat on the stool in front of the Nth degree of money down the drain.

Quarter in the slot: One, two, breathe, four, five, six, pull and listen. Watch, feel the cup 5.67 grams lighter, low—adrenaline fires. Weight. Release. Let go. Accept.

Quarter in the slot: One, two, breathe, four, five, six, pull and listen. Watch, feel the cup 5.67 grams lighter, low—adrenaline fires. Weight. Release. Let go. Accept. Project move after third pull.

Quarter in the slot: One, two, breathe, four, five, six, pull and listen. Watch, feel the cup 5.67 grams lighter, low—adrenaline fires. Weight. Release. Let go. Accept. Stay on course; I'd rather die than flee.

Nun-convent tunnel wisdom wood holed that cheese booths free self-perseverance. A portable snack vender rolled by announcing special menu items and Truck heard, "Gouda, swiss, or cheddar." It happened in Monterey (jac), a long time ago. I met her in Monterey (jic), in old Mexicoan fiesta (mix) Mack Truck stayed firm on the accelerator. Kept on, pressed on, "Pull and Listening," asking please do come fly with me, on the street of dreams.

"Don't worry 'bout me, angel eyes." He mumbled when a relatively attractive woman did a double walk-by. Who knew what angle she was working as a motivating force.

"You make me feel so young. Where and when?" She was obviously on the prowl, lustily groaning out the proposition in a soft yet coarse sotto voce. Vulture poaching culture and innocent, insensitive being brings the dolce vida, slinking.

"Pinche baboso," Truck said loud enough to convey displeasure of the deeply guttural kind, back to the gutter with yall.

"Fine," and she left. Her ass was okay.

Quarter in the slot: one, two, breathe. Returning to the lectern at hand. The background music was a soothing amusement, proven infused with big plans. Twenty coins in, five bucks spent cast off in a hopeful daze. His cup gaining less weight, second by second, a collection of fruitless plays. Wasn't meant to be, persistence doesn't automatically translate into victory. When his cup was mostly empty he moved machines, forgetting how to count and then his breathing fell off. The first hints of exhaustion tugged lightly on the sleeve of his shirt, the leg of his pants, subtle nuisance.

He was constantly rebelling against zealous yearnings for it, needing it. At the same time not sure if he could handle it, the win. A small win most likely, but there's that chance it's a nice win or a great big halo to the merry mother of good glory holler lu Jah praise. This was the quarter slots remember, so yeah. Sonny just said, 'Don't be stupid,' so I won't be. His mind was racing, but outside he was just a guy in a black shirt, jeans, and ratty sneakers. The type you know probably it's best not to test with. Part of him felt like an extra inside myriad obvious variants, increasing excitement though his arc had hit a bit of a dip. No faith amicably marauds in loving yall close, blood at least. His brothers both now are sleeping just a few miles away. His healthy ornate neck orchestrates regality dressed in a simple chain with a cross and his father's dog tag.

For the raucous constant barrage there somehow rest a sick and eerie steady insignificant lullaby engulfing nothing captured entirely. Truck came from an adeptly understated strict tradition enforcing righteous ecstasy, alien antiquated subtle concept emanating tactical insipid calm and existential science of the enigmatic realized in chaos. Many strangers who knew him not thought he looked the rabid aggressive, greatly enthused caveman, while the secret was his tendencies toward the exaggerated creative charismatic energy never tiring rampant irrevocable complexity.

Truck rattled the remaining coins in his cup, scanning the casino floor. He saw colossal optical light escaping over rainbows spread out across the massive room. Then his focus turned to the crass and cantankerous spectrum of unsettling noises disturbing the soulfulability of this late Saturday night hedonistic vibe; life crushingly real. He had an idea how he could salvage some semblance of a victory, so he decided to stop and save the last four quarters for something to be bought at a later time, perhaps on his trudge back to the van. He thought about folks who take cabs and wished he had a pocket full of bills, plastic holographic seals. He remembered the opening beat from 'Eat the Rich' by Aerosmith, and he hit an invisible snare drum with invisible sticks in a repeating dotted eighth and sixteenth note figure again and again. Perhaps there was a flam. Five coins left: cinco el Presidente Washingtons, Señor Jorge if you please. Picking up the fifth to last twenty-five cent piece he held it flat in the palm of his right hand. Standing up off the stool he concentrated all of his energy into the tiny medallion that may or may not have any actual silver in it.

"Daddy needs a new china cymbal!" He closed his fist on the coin and blew once a mighty wind in between his thumb and forefinger. "Down the hatch, make it a match, big money-money baby luck, come on." Truck dropped in the coin and tugged hard on the pull-arm and then released. The spinning started and spun and stopped and nothing came. No luck, some loss but basically no shame. Just another no name, playing the win or lose game. He wanted a candy bar, so his course of action was set in motion to work a plan to get his hands on a hundred grand; the easy way. Sugar baby, sweets.

January 24, 1998

The Rhythm Room parking situation was tight. It took Izzy some time working several angles before he was finally able to shut off the bus and set the parking brake, leaving it in first gear. The two got inside and began hunting for Catfish. Dream Demonical was on stage in between songs. "Original, for the masses!" Twig shouted in the microphone. Then came four stick clicks and the whole band dropped a singularly hit note, "I ain't no drive-in movie," Roxy sang boldly. Two more bops in unison, she finished the lyric, "Don't project yo shit on me!" From Twig's guitar came a heavy pulsing chug. The pounding of the bass filled the swoon with a kind of jilt. Flitting shimmer on the hat stick worked with skill. Fist pounding on electric keys, thick clogs stomp down ribbit frogs and junk clowning on a hot pot of newt stew. Bad brood witches brew kettle in the black mood, white heat sacrifice the flesh feed fortunately tortured on the porch swang seat.

There were people standing all about the bar. Most of the tables in the showroom were full. The dance floor was occupied by a swarm of shakers. The hypnotized were in trances all across the club. The listeners heard hope and a healing vibe, energized by the dope and the feeling right. They all were moved and good to go. Alyssa said she'd find Catfish. Izzy told her he'd get them drinks and come help look for the bluesman. The two entered tangled in a double handle grip strangle holding firm quick conveyances of closeness. Pressed off and apart, now mixing in through the crowd, Alyssa walked pensively towards the edge of the stage half of the room, scanning for her friend Catfish.

The sound of vehemence and violence coursed through the venue's layered atmosphere. In an instant the band cut off mid-beat and Roxy said in the attitude, "It's not all about platforms and stale ass platitudes." Twig interjected, "What's platitudes?" With whimsy, "Exactly," was her reply and she fingered four notes fast on her bass strings, the song erupted once more and the train came smoking chock full of coal. "It don't—change nothing, relay some junk about truth," Twig spoke-sang the line. "Tracks get tough, mind get rough, both heart and soul—body-body," Roxy answered and the vocalists dueled for the education of the audience and themselves and their children's children. Peace unearthed guitars will towards men. They played out the song, now a good piece into their second set, could say the home stretch. It had been a packed house almost all night, so they may pocket more cash than the originally guaranteed amount.

Roxy began in on a bit she did to introduce the gang. "Hey folks, we are Dream Demonical. Original. For the masses! It's been great and we hope to see you all again. Give it up for Twig there on the guitar and vocals." Applause. "Mister Namaste, AKA Moe Nasty on the drums, hittin' the skins." Applause. "Les Watts, on the keys playin' all he gots." Applause. Twig stepped to his microphone and said, "Roxy on bass." Then tons of woots, whoops, and whistles erupted from the hall.

Les switched his keyboard to an organ setting, he padded out a sustained chord and after a few moments Moe entered with a soft but slowly building roll on the snare drum. Roxy came in on the bass and they played 'Sunday Morning' from No Doubt's Tragic Kingdom (1995), quite apropos as it was now past midnight, in the antemeridian hours of Super Bowl Sunday, January 25, 1998.

The truth blame in with disease. The booze phlegm bended the knees. Salute temps pending the seize. Vermouth tent vending for freeze. Galoot gent sending the bees, (heebee gee type) do keep fending the keys. To the west wild that plot, new thought sounds get the blue rot, flows on the seventh of seas. Spark a root pot, archaic logical dig, in the loot spot. Waller up, give it a kick, bug a boot shot, new bohemian crude, bought a new yacht without any warning, cascade level pouring. Working on the new docks like a longshoreman shorting wages, they keep drain down go snorting, while the cylinder breathes circuitous purporting. Sap apoplectic spittle beads, and drops of sweat'll speck in bleeds, golf reeds. They got a new view and many in the spectral onlookers wanted it badly, and it was this recognized vibration how most of the men longed after the dark-haired tattooed girl onstage singing, not giving a fuck and moving hot as shit, very seldom unaware of the power she yielded and concealed, always wielding without hesitancy. Unfairly brandishing her skin and round tight body draped in black and denim torn glimpses into divinity. In this holy sacristy of the gospel tunes as high up in the belfry swung and clung the sacred chimes calling out the blessed urchins dirge by surgeons skilled incantations. With voiced enchanters pant and surge while solely workin' out the kinks and cluster bombs refute the rest compute aplomb. Composed disclosure love composter blows your floakin' mind hole open. Spoken speak in spankin' beef or bacon raw or ready for the taken saw confetti party makin' celebroke the beat is breakin'.

Alyssa found Catfish sitting up against the wall where they had started out the evening. She took a seat beside him. They shared a brief glance that said hello and nice to see you again. Izzy had taken longer than he thought fetching the drinks. When he finally got to the barkeep he didn't know what Alyssa would want, so he got two bottles of water, then stood in the back of the room scanning for Catfish and the girl. He noticed the pair on the far wall, so he began heading their way, keeping one ear on the music, which sounded familiar all of a sudden. Bap | bap, "We in the goosebump bidness," said Roxy. "Can I get a witness?" A hypnotizing tone started high on the guitar and floated steady on then dropped an octave. The bass entered high then dropped and the progression continued until upon finishing, returned to the upper notes cycling on in that same manner and loop while Twig spoke poetic in calm calculation. Everybody came to just be one with the wind and sea. As Twig kept spitting out truth Roxy laid back off the mic dropping long heavy sustenance, feeding the air. Space rumbling bodies shoe strangs bouncing wall to being to breast, to arm pumping to back of head, floor to the concrete, the booty swang jiggle out a step in the pond. Feet dipping in to do that fluid scoot, cruising with they top down. Druid to it, lute it and shoot it. Screw it, nudist. Prudish sewage's take on the same old damn thang. Foolish ladies on the prowl comma run. Bullish boys comma all's good fun. Rampant egotistically filling a void, crammed Danishes with Crisco oil, a plan to devolve. Two feet couple eyes, hands free supple thighs, can of something to quit; stop. Rein it in; pain is in, real accessible, feel from within a bloody vestibule the hell with all the rest of you. Test a few, testament all inhibition's interstitial intervention super writings on the wall; quiet room old Arizona killer fashion kind of gal. Sitting pretty, finger in the air, tasting the heat and desire of the room, getting them to feel thangs. Root bangs—

Israel Dufrene sidled up next to Alyssa and offered her a water which she took. He thought he'd offer the other bottle to Catfish, so he did and it was accepted. At least that was something.

"I think I've heard this song before," Izzy said.

"Yeah, this morning you and Roxy talked over it when you were stranded on the side of the road," she reminded him.

"You're right," and Izzy sat back listening hard to the music pouring out of the musicians of Dream Demonical.

Peace, the word, the way: wisdom, love, and a gang of Tanqueray. Cool, calm, nukeyalur bomb, rather put a light upon a nukeyalur com. Communication, feed the nation, cause commotion, ride the ocean waves-waves Jesus saves the drinkers thinkers jokers smokers. Something in the drumbeat just doubled and by the looks of Moe's stick work berzerking he'd kicked the hi-hat and stray tom hits into overtime.

Scene, the sun comes up like a red star rise, beat come a bump, bump. You been done got down for a minute get clicked hit a win and get crunk, crunk. Ya hip swang like a chicken wang; got style kill shot like a hit main. Tone dial cold sweat in a heat wave best pump rock in the spot make a big bang.

Izzy remembered it was something interwoven, but he couldn't remember the rest of what Roxy had told him.

"The paths to enlightenment are varied and voluminous," Roxy said.

Twig sang: "You better get up a double shot of somethin' somethins down with the chicken and dumplin' dumplins. | | Less miserable, less problems, Rome set of Sistine columns. Traditional, pure: the vine, the branch, the cure. Love the lovers, love the haters, embrace the barrier's Yorkshire terriers. Lo-fi, forty-five, phonic interwoven—"

"Dream today," shouts Roxy. The bomb drops softly, everyone settles and they all take it in. Cheering erupts from the crowd; they all know the night now nears its end.

"Thanks, we got a couple more. Please tip the bar staff and drive home safe," Twig announced. "This next one's called Mercurian Jazz Cigaretrograde."

Moe started with a prepared four-count fill and the rest of the ensemble came in and the audience again was in a trance and at ease. Demonical had massive range and could tailor their sets depending on what genre show they were playing. They could legitimately fit in at a rock show, reggae, ska, blues, funk, punk, metal, or even a bit of edgy mainstream pop. Labels are for cans of green beans and dog food. It's bad news believing all folks aren't on the same basic level, equal footing, or general commonality.

Izzy asked for and was given a sip of Alyssa's water. Afterwards, he felt a strong inclination to grab hold of the girl's hand and press it into his. He thought of whom he'd have to answer to if he decided to bypass the Super Bowl and stay with this woman. Was this an illogical course of action? Or was he being more rational than ever? After several more minutes of the sickness and salvation flowing forth from Demonical's lips, the gears shifted and a calamitous barrage of hits and notes and Twig and Roxy madly grinding on their axe blades. The axiom of noise seeped through the battling girls and boys. Out of nowhere it seemed that an impromptu pit was forming. Moshed the people mashed disaster fast approaching peak resistance to their souls encroaching on achieved nirvana.

Crack, thunder stack of molten flapper jacks bemoan the jolt as everyone on the mics uttered, "Jazz Cigaretrograde." Back into the fray, scorched persistence. Burning earth the racket grew and off the tops volcanoes blew as death escaped retold as true expatriates thoroughly and through. The echoes view too towering more. Some on the floor spectating began gyrating gladly bouncing out of time no hesitating just a crooked line vibrating and the room was one, now bulging with renewed sensation. Satisfied admittance to recompense an evening's pleasure came and whence.

The stage beholders laid the onus on the artists who came to spawn and enter tamed. Rework engorged by lion's tooth engrained, inflamed like Zion's loot retained. Momentarily obtain estranged gripe on totality of a reality. Relative to one shared second. Absolute retaliation perpetrates on consecration, visualized actualization of a damn good time.

One time. Spend it if you got some. Smoke it if you got, umm. Love it if you got one, Shogun if you shotgun. Secondary image unrelents raw sentient mention of the waning dim percentage buzzed and tinted. Zen and tempted, mints and whimsic swayed the valley ground below. Speakers spake and amps lified. Vast approaches taken, tried. Witness strobe and quaken spied on we the people testified.

Space warz and star trax, heavy on the beeswax, round go the warp drive bevy of a Sleestaks. Fluffy purple ski slacks dry clean only, multiple terrestrial phone call homely. Land of the three foot six armed monster, man all the photons stand by to launch her. Out into the dark grey matters not where, belief is suspended or they really don't care.

Ordinary folks most speak in prose; air quotes the dawn quixotic. Still hyperbolic gestures flow expose those gone neurotic. Les in the front row, across from Moe, was now standing on his stool with one foot up on the keyboard as he was balancing with a slight shake. His arms waved for control, to keep from falling steadily stomping on a cluster of keys. The entirety of Dream Demonical was all—pounding—over-and-over. The loud clatter increasing, most of the universe is into the preach they are sailing a humble made dwelling of pie. Peaches. Alyssa smells like to Izzy. He knows that many things are right in the way that fall the cards, and he's lapped up the proffering gentle and sweet wined the bagels. Oven of lovin' the winter was centered and focus was hopeless he fell justly for her grace. Slides buy the altar, partaking in the custodian's ritual concomitant saturation behind these cool gymnasiums, the second thirst day of ebony monthly. Saving every savory mulch just to restore Romeo-stasis.

"Thank you. Goodnight!" Roxy shouted and the stage went dim. A grimy rock mix pumped in over the house system. Some people clapped wildly, others headed for the door. The remainder made a move towards the bar and restrooms. Alyssa told Izzy she was going to go, "Say hey to Rox," who was currently winding cables, packing things up and also shutting them down. The beautiful Rose glided around the edge of the room, hopping on stage and stopping next to her friend as she was setting her bass into its hard case. Roxy said something and Alyssa began speaking while Izzy watched her mouth move and then stop. He saw Roxy's lips moving and after half-a-minute Alyssa did a little hop of a reaction. More words from the bassist followed by a nod of the Rose's head, and an acknowledgement in the affirmative. The girl scampered off-stage, back around the wall towards where Catfish and Izzy were sitting. She had on a smile.

"Roxy said there's a house party in Tempe, and could you please help transport the gear there and then you're off the hook clean? But you can stay and hang out at the party if you'd like or crash or whatever, it's up to you," said Alyssa.

"Sure homie. If you purr fo' me." Swerve to gourd he said it just like that.

She sat sweetly on his lap. Izzy hadn't had this much of such a kind thing like her in a good long time. The sensation was instantaneous and she felt body heat and awareness. They was a thing. Were a thing that was happening. Catfish couldn't help but chuckle at the youths' exuberance and confessed peculiarity. He wasn't one to discourage connectivity in the grandest sense. Even then a perilous underestimation of the scope a heart can hold. Unfathomable by a friction, sometimes overthinking can be underwhelming.

Superheromanz had cleared out their stacks of equipment, so Roxy and them had plenty of room to put gear near the back exit as they prepared to load. The Cherokee was still close to the backstage door. Izzy brought the bus over as a couple of exiting cars honked and who the hell knew the motivation leading to these noisy excretions. No one said much as they carried out cases, amps, and drums to put back in the vehicles. Didn't appear like too many people were hanging out, though some came by and met or thanked somebody in the band. Catfish had a small crowd around him still inside kind of listening at him, and looking him over trying to get something maybe to rub off or to have a whiff of the real thing.

Once most of the work was done, Roxy went up to the bar and spoke with the manager about getting paid. The gentlemen went back into the kitchen area, and when he returned, produced a wad of bills. Roxy shook his hand and took the money, turned and walked slowly while she counted the cash, then slid it into the back pocket of her jeans. She came up on an older couple talking to Catfish. The lady there was squeezing his fist, saying, "God bless you, wonderful, amazing, thank you so much." To which the old bluesman cricked his head and gave her back a, "You are too kind." The couple left. Roxy stepped in and elbowed Catfish lightly in the ribs.

"You and us all got an extra two hundred bucks seeing as how the night was so good and lots of people came out," said Roxy.

"Yeah, did they like it? Maybe we get a chance to come back out?" Catfish said. The weed he smoked earlier had all but worn off.

"Good possibility of it," she replied. "We're all going over to my friend's place where they're putting on a little something. I could find you a spot to take it easy, or you can go at whichever speed you wish."

"Oh, I feel strong. Got many hours left in me still."

The two walked out the backstage door where the rest of the crew was hanging around the loaded automobiles. Roxy went to Izzy and passed him a twenty-dollar bill, "For the ride." He tried to give it back but she won out in the end, only seeking to stay fair.

"Follow me, fifteen minute drive, we'll unload first thing into the garage," she said also to everyone. Then wiped her hands twice out in front of her signifying they were clean and clear. "Regulators!" Roxy called out.

"Mount up!" answered Les and Moe. Twig didn't play along. It was part of their shtick and the intro of Warren G's hit 'Regulate' featuring Nate Dogg (1994). The engines fired and passengers resumed their positions, as music started leaking out of different rolled down windows.

Cruising east on Indian School Road past 16th Street, they got on 51 South then onto 202 East into Tempe. Exiting at Priest Drive south into the neighborhood just below the dry Salt River bed, they were all talking and relaxing. The Cherokee was holding Roxy, Les, and Twig. In the bus were Izzy, Alyssa, Catfish, and Moe.

"One Nation Under A Groove, man." Catfish said while Funkadellic (1978) played on the Vee double-you's radio.

About having a chance on something, ready or not. Put a good mind to it. Roxy pulled into the driveway of a home with a short stocky palm tree in the front yard. Izzy stopped alongside the curb just past the home's front property line.

Small talk, guys. Big words, nice ideas clever wit transitory effects barley lager than the blooze pourn down the glutinous gullet gambling debt up hops the shark of responsibility. Early mornings common waned tomorrow. Bottle caps away the cobwebs ban the sorrow until they're numb, fad and heppy.

• • • • • • •

As they unloaded the contents of the vehicles into the garage, Izzy noticed a classic station wagon parked in the open cavern. Looked to be from the mid-to-late Fifties. The body was clean with the paint in a progressive stage of patina. On the rear window of the passenger side, a sticker read, "Neoclassical Postmodern Recalcitrance." Could be a Dodge, Pontiac, or Oldsmobile. Didn't seem like a Ford or Chevy. There was a roof rack over the back half of the vehicle's top. It had premium chrome rims. The tires had "BF Goodrich" in bold white lettering, opposite were the words "Radial T/A".

Roxy was making sure their equipment was packed tightly up against the wall so that there was room to move freely in her friend's garage. "This is Louie's place. He's helping us all get home tomorrow. You probably want to go make sure your bus is shut and locked. It ain't the best neighborhood." She said her piece, reached up and started pulling down the garage door manually. Alyssa and some of the others were hanging out front as Izzy walked towards his bus. Roxy closed and latched the door, staying on the inside. She headed in the house for a whistle wetter, while sound selector chose the pressure dropped, the call: Safe at someone's home that counts for one place that's a known spot on the journey's charts.

Tuned up, into obscurity. Out of body, off the grid. Over the wall: on the lam, under the radar, around the bend. Louie lived alone with three dogs and more than a couple rooms full of musical instruments. He's a collector, a vintage protector, and an upright prosector. Bass vase vahs, cadaver's heart, the neck wood-flaked with snakewood baked in brownie bars and deep guitars the doghouse string bass viol. The bottle broke the seal. Again a place was real, the touch and much the feel;

101

of beer can chicken style Creole. The deal; backyard grilling with a keyed low filling, "Oh low rain." She was Louie's girl, Lorraine. Good friends they were all. Got along splendid. It started sprinkling a faint drizzle. They were safe under the covered back porch patio next to the grill. Roxy, Louie, Catfish, and Lorraine in peace and quiet chilled.

Meanwhile out front.

"Oh, it's so nice, the midnight showers," Alyssa said to herself out loud.

It was a mild treat for them to be in a more southerly climate than usual. Izzy walked up to the group in the yard lit only by the front porch's light. It was the girl, Moe, Les, and Twig talking about the show and nothings random when Israel stepped up beside Alyssa.

"Sup, poser?" Twig said abruptly to Izzy.

Izzy let a beat pass then said: "Oh, you one of them supposers?"

"Yeah, so? Suppose I am," Twig responded, making Les chuckle.

"Was that a funny joke?" said Alyssa.

"Yeah, real funny joke. Like your boyfriend's fucking hippy wagon," Twig said.

"It's a 1969 Volkswagen Type 2 Westfalia Camper," Izzy replied.

"Nazi school bus. You a big Hitler fan? Got any good pamphlets?" Twig chided.

"Twig," Moe cut in with a slight plea to knock it off.

"I have no ill will towards you, man," Izzy said.

"Get some," Twig told him.

"Ease off," Moe said. "Go hustle inside and see what's to drink, or what food Louie has on the menu."

"Yeah, let's all go in. The rain is picking up," said Les.

"Yes, Les. Let's." Alyssa added, very impressed with her wordsmanship.

They went in through the front door, into the front room, dim and basic. Twig and Moe kept on through the kitchen and back patio area, while Les disappeared down the hallway like a shifty secret agent. Izzy and Alyssa sat on the sofa, sinking

102

down towards the Earth's core. There was an entertainment center across the room with a television and various sized speakers placed all over. A large window faced the street and had thick draperies out of seventeenth century Scotland. At least two lava lamps could be seen from the pair's perch on the couch. A leafy house tree stood hanging back in a corner. The stereo played Jamaican ska, roots and rocksteady. She Will Never Let Me Down was on the radio. Toots. Johnny Cool Man, noise from a bonnie tube amp, Les was shaking a keyboard jam vamp with his right smoove hand. A quick trill between threed notes, a figure felt like Lusianna trim. Leaking, sifting, trickling down the hallway; rippling, tickling ivory consonants, drifter grifting thr'over continents realigned in fervent nonsense. Scented wafts from back porch loft hits. Izzy and Alyssa in pheromone fits, and unspoken both they wants it. Read Wisconsin at Algonquin.

It wasn't really a house party. More like a friend of Roxy's opened his home with welcoming arms. I forget who it was told me there were three dogs on the premises. Not a canine in sight. No barking was heard at any point between now and their arrival. Conversation and merriment waved, flowing ebb and to fro-manic pace to climax lull and interest fully sustained. Then a space and silent listening: eruptions, laughter and the balance of a calm, secure Saturday night, Sunday morning.

Out back it was a right thin den of thick thieves all besieged in some stout contemplation. Aggregated communal ideation under one thought, glob of gooey chunklit chomp, concentrated sun spot. Tetrahydrocannabinol sick fibromyalgia shot the sheriff when they was a Ladmo Bagginses nostalgia.

All were ingesting something, snacking munching chips or chewing jokes and grunting. Yips and yaps, back slapping happening in subjective lucid slackening port of call for leave and napping just to view truly a grand thing. Understanding on one's level shared upheaval frees the deviled eggs brought out by sweet Low-rain to dull the hunger, feed the pain.

"There's finely chopped celery and onion bits in these," said Lorraine.

103

"Makes 'em twenty-eight times better," Louie assured his guests.

They were placed on the table around which Roxy and Louie sat. Lorraine took the chair next to her man. Twig and Moe sat on a couch against the back wall of the house. Catfish was on a lazy boy, rocking back and forth. Moe hopped up to put chips and four deviled eggs on a plate he got from a stack on the table. Roxy reached forward, took one deviled egg, and leaned back sinking her bite into one half of the treat. Creation shone. Snack spree zone.

"How's them taste, Miss Roxy?" Catfish asked.

"Good, good. Little bit of crunch." And she lifted the container from the table and held it out within the old man's range.

"Thanks," he took one in each hand. "Midnight picnics are always real nice. Eh, specially on an evening like here."

"Pretty much flip-flop weather if you ask me," Louie said.

"Whatever's on that grill smells real good," said Twig.

"Only a few more minutes and we can tear into it. I also have hot dogs if the chicken isn't sufficient," said Louie.

"I told the guy and girl in the front room there was food out here. Same with the dude playing on your keyboards," said Lorraine.

For a while it was a perfect pow-wow.
Braggadocious banter four-horse cow town.
Rustlers back and then they're broken southbound.
Puffed each up then spent consensus kowtow.
Stories mixed with subtle yeeps and clown sounds.
Pisser patter hints approach big shout down.
Towel thrown in admits: "Fine then I bows out."
Low-rain wrapped in holy ancient gown shroud.
Scraps and gristle tossed to vagrant ground hounds.
This and that we got from lost and found pound.
Jesse's there the basset short and round mound.
Jenkins guarding all day now he's wound down.
Georgia Mae is sweet, she wears the lounge crown.
Chilled and drowned the feast released a twelve-ounce.

Cheers. Several drinks were raised. Triumph was praised. Well wishes and side dishes, gold blisses and "Who this is?" Louie asked. Les, Izzy and Alyssa slinked out the patio doors onto the back porch, and in the smick of a grin perspective changed. Collective ranged a shifting in communal density. Most of those became verbose, featuring multiple trains to follow. Explain the hollow course less invasive, slight motive to extract food for their faces. The Rose and Israel grabbed hot dogs, which weren't completely cold. A gripful of chips and a taste of Satan's ovaries. There's celery and onion in those but they're delicious Low-rain told them, to be sure. The thunderstorm and the native lord of the land and maid marinate multi-grain. Then grim and barren and okay, Sue mistress of mayhem and the Les, sir of two evils and even Alyssa were kind of looking at Izzy expecting him to say something.

"What kind's that wagon in the garage?" Izzy asked.

"A Fifty-six Dodge Sierra," Louie said.

"What is Neoclassical Postmodern Recalcitrance?"

"A way of living," said Louie.

"Yeah, man. Thanks for the grub," said Izzy.

"I didn't get your name."

"I'm Izzy."

"Who is he though?" Twig mumbled under his breath.

"Nice to meet you, man. I'm Louie. You can thank Lorraine for the chow."

"Nobody is who," Twig said, losing the war, maybe slightly winning the battle.

"Don't go and vanish all the way," Roxy called out as Izzy and Alyssa headed back indoors. Les got some snacks and sat on the couch between Twig and Moe.

Each consciousness faded differently into the morning, many losing steam seeking sleeping spots for the night. Twig and Les sought to spend one more minute making music. This left the back patio couch all to Moe. He said it felt right tropical for crashing outdoors. Blasting out snores, they now would be forced soon to retreat indoors. Louie and Lorraine grabbed a few things and shut up the barbecue before retiring and leaving Roxy at the helm. She told Catfish he could have

105

the spare bedroom; down the hall, first door on the left. That left Roxanne Rawlins watching, hearing Moses Prallums chopping logs and the dogs entered the house through their special small hole in the wall. Flap-flap, flap-flap, flap-flap. Roxy thought of where she was as well as how she had got there. Where she wanted to be and how far she still had to go. This night had been a small reward. Those feel so much better when deserved. The more entrenched she was in these music digs, the more certain she could be to never get stuck out on an island all alone. She'd be the rock, if she could only put a sock in Moe's craw. It gave her heart a thaw. She burst a quick guffaw.

"There any hot dogs left?" snorted out Moe. All the food had been taken inside to the kitchen already. His eyes closed but his head shifted so Roxy couldn't be sure if he was asleep or wake-talking. "Roscoe P. Coltrane," clear as day. Having some kind of dreams, Oscar Meyers and the Duke Boys.

Roxy'd had enough of Moe's rough snuffling, so she got up carefully and like a ninja went inside closing the sliding temple gate slash patio door behind her. She shuffled across the dining area into the front room where Izzy and Alyssa were tucked into a corner of the sofa.

"Sorry to barge in buds, but I've got no place else to turn," said Roxy.

"No offense, but we'd like to be alone," Alyssa said.

"Oh, major offense you sexy bitch," Roxy said and they both laughed.

"We can go out to the bus, get cozy," Izzy offered as an alternative.

"Cozy tea cozy, Parker C. Posey, Keyser T. Soze," sang Alyssa. She sat up, stood, stretched and twisted slapping Izzy on the knee.

"You all did outstanding tonight, Roxy. I'm glad I got to see you play," Izzy said.

"Thanks, man. Fine ending to a fine day." Roxy sat down as Izzy arose from the anti of grave moods; tidings galore.

The tide meets the shore as the lovers once more climbed aboard the V-four foreign-born shack on wheels. Bench lays back reveals, the bedding attacked, luscious lip smack she steals. Strong embrace, clothes off peels, and inside she squeals as her ear lobe he feels with his tongue lightly suckling. His belt she's unbuckling their skin firmly bodies barenakedly touching, emoting erupting then calm. They hold on.

"Why does it feel like tonight is so important?" she asked him and also herself.

Sigh. Pause.

"I think that it's best if we don't speak of importance, or try to categorize feelings, but just appreciate our shared experience and let it be," Izzy said.

"Thanks a lot, the Beatles." Alyssa wasn't totally pleased with his response but she wouldn't allow it to ruin the moment in time.

They fell asleep intertwined. Her head on his shoulder, his hand in her shirt, their legs wrapped together, center of the universe. Burning magma and hot flames fired off in their cells. Cores. Coerced old souls. So-called coarse fold, off course nearly sold.

January 25, 1998

Late next morning, Izzy lay awake with Alyssa by his side still in slumber. He had been pondering his situation for either ten minutes or two hours. He seemed to have figured one or three things out in his deliberations. Alyssa gave a little wiggle and knocked her elbow on one of the near cabinets with a sold thwack.

"Aww, ambushed," she said, rubbing her arm.

"How'd you sleep?" Izzy asked.

"With my eyes closed, deathly still," she jested. "No, it was good."

"I'm glad to hear it. I spent some time thinking this morning a lot about what is important. Like how you said last night."

"I remember you said basically we should leave it alone. Enjoy the fact that we have it at all. Whatever it is," said Alyssa.

"Yes, well for me, 'it' is this synchronization we've had for the past twenty some hours. I know that that is only a small sample sized slice but, uh—" he paused, the two side by side lying down and he looked at her and she was staring at the ceiling breathing gently. "Would you want to come with me to California?"

Alyssa's face expanded, eyes widened, mouth opened and her jar dropped. She took a quick, audible inhale.

"Really? What about the Super Bowl? You'd take me along?" Alyssa excitedly.

"I just have the one ticket. We'll go to the stadium and sell it. That will cover gas and then some. Ice cream cones and souvenirs, general amusement," said Izzy.

"Oh man, oh man," she chattered.

"So you'll go? Or can you go?" Izzy asked.

"Oh man, oh man. Yes! Of course I can. I will, we will," said Alyssa.

Izzy took a deep breath in and exhaled. "Good, so—"

"But don't I need things? Supplies, resources, clothes," said her.

"We can get all of that as we go," said he.

"Man. Okay. So when do we go?"

"It's about 0930, so pretty much now."

"Well, I have to go tell Roxy," Alyssa said. "I have to tell Roxy that I'm going to California!"

They both scooted up and sat on the edge of the rear bench seat that was still down in bed form. After straightening clothing, hair and what not, Izzy unlocked the sliding door and the two of them climbed out and stood stretching.

"You really want me along on your trip?" Alyssa said in a serious tone.

"I really do. Honest. It's the only thing I want."

She leaped towards him and wrapped her arms tightly around his torso and squeezed. He held her closely. They stood there each trying to hug the other one to death; but to a good death, where you're reborn and live on with the angels. Izzy and Alyssa separated and the girl headed inside to talk with Roxy.

"How am I going to be having adventures stuck in one place?" the Rose said to Roxy.

"I mean, it sounds great. Just, it's so quick."

"Not really, if you take into account everything that has happened since yesterday morning. It feels like a proper build. Now's just the pay off."

There were a couple light knocks on the front door, and Israel Dufrene entered the room where Roxy and Alyssa sat on the couch conversing.

"You looking to run oft with my girl?" Roxy said.

"I'm just a wanderer, roaming around, good deeds and such. I promise," Izzy said.

"Don't misunderstand me. You must take good care of her," Roxy said.

"Swerve on my mama's gravy. You will get her back safe," said Izzy.

The boy and girl ate potato salad and tortilla chips with salsa for brunch, while Roxy listed off things she wanted them to bring her back from the coast. No one else was yet awake. It was Roxy who stood out front and waved as Alyssa rode off in the Volkswagen bus. Izzy steady at the wheel comma righteously determined at the helm.

Roxy was twenty-seven percent sad because even though it wasn't permanent, she felt the loss of a close friend and her only girlfriend. This made a part in her heart hurt, which she then shrugged off because feelings is nothing except weakness and folly.

Izzy gassed up at the corner petrol station on Priest and University. They traveled west, taking 143 South to Interstate Ten West and were on their way to their destination of San Diego. Izzy planned on taking Ten West to Blythe, then California State Route 78 South meeting up with Highway 8 near El Centro, then on west to Qualcomm Stadium.

"The company you keep is sure a thing to behold. I've never met anyone like Roxy, and Catfish is a whole other thing altogether," said Izzy.

"I heard him once take to saying soothes. He swore to us all that there was a darkness coming most fit to ruin lives and send people spinning into deep despair. At least I believe that's how he put it," Alyssa said.

"Has anything come of it?"

"No such deep despair that I've seen, just some sour attitudes."

"That's only life. See that brown case by your left foot. Hunt through it and pick out something to listen to," he told her.

She lifted up the rectangular container, unsnapping one side. She opened it and saw a bunch of cassette cases that she started to sift through. Beastie Boys, War, Dwight Yoakam, Cypress Hill, Sublime, The Pretenders, Pearl Jam, Sonny Rollins, Tom Petty, Joan Jett, Maceo Parker, De La Soul, Fred Wesley, Stevie Wonder and Jimi Hendrix. Skipping around she saw Stone Temple Pilots, Miles Davis, NOFX, Sheryl Crow, R.E.M., A Tribe Called Quest and Dixie Chicks. Some names she knew and others she didn't. Alyssa chose the one that said The Best of Creedence Clearwater Revival, Volume One. After removing the cassette, she handed it over to Izzy. He took it and glanced at the artist's name, smiling as he injected the cartridge into the clip. The mechanization of music, the ribbon fed and turned and read Proud Mary. Good God she was pretty there next to Izzy. On some levels it didn't make sense, but felt rightly natural to enlist this angel as shipmate on his voyage. She had speckles of freckles on her face and long hair that was many shades of dark and light bronze. Now alive and dancing free from the air streams creeping in through the windows cracked.

There were countless miles ahead. Izzy wondered if the girl could drive a four-speed manual transmission. He wondered if there might ever be a need. Hopefully not, though that would be a hot scene. Rose mobbing down the road at top speed or cruising slow, with no particular place to go.

January 25, 1998

Sandy egg oh Padre, wholly roamin' order. Fly across the highway, California border. Bug upon the windshield, orbiting the sun. Mankind knows it ain't the only one. What do you do with somebody in the second hour of a six-hour trip? "We'll probably stop here quickly some time soon." Izzy kept his foot steady on the gas pedal, checking blind spots and mirrors on a rotation. The bus was cruising easy at a hair under sixty-five mph. Felt like sixty-three. Shifty sweet eyes, baby had a simple yet complex guise. Contact high, he caught when she touched him. Brushed right by when she slid back into the center cab. Next she started whistling effortless swinging phrases with some bounces at the end of the line, over and again with slight variations now and then. Izzy heard rummaging sounds as though a raccoon, Procyon lotor, had found a trash bin full of goodies.

"What's going on back there?" Izzy asked over his shoulder.

"Customs. This vehicle matches the description of a group of smugglers known to be seen working these parts," Alyssa answered.

"Smugglers of what?"

"I'm not at liberty to disclose that information."

There was more digging around and a faint whistling continued. Izzy didn't have anything in the bus necessitating secrecy; still it felt odd as this girl continued her search.

"What's that tune you're whistling?" he asked.

"Smokey Joe's Café, that is," she replied.

"Who's that by?"

"The Coasters, that be. Catfish showed 'em to me."

"Charlie Browns?"

"The very same," she said, then more digging and song.

112

"Ah-ha! And how do you explain *this*?" Alyssa climbed back up front holding a small flipbook photo album.

"Knock yourself out," he said.

She cracked open the booklet. More exploring, buses, people's past are all game.

"What's this on the plate next to the French fries?"

"That's an alligator po'boy. Like a hoagie, some would try to tell you."

"Where were you at that alligator's on the menu?"

"New Orleans. Lots of places there have all types of interesting food. Turkey neck, crawfish pie, jambalaya, filé gumbo."

"And the alligator sub was your favorite?"

"Red skin potatoes, boiled. So much goodness stuffed in the pot to brew," Izzy said.

"Who's this with you on the army tank?" Alyssa asked.

"My younger brother. He lives in Colorado Springs."

"There's some of a little dog. Then he got puffed up and hairy with, dreadlocks?"

"His decision not mine. He got back down to slim but passed away over a year ago. Fourteen years plus he lasted," Izzy said.

"What are you all dressed up and posing like Saturday Night Fever for?"

"Halloween. I found the vest and pants at a Goodwill for four dollars."

They drove, each other happy and some squirming toes at what might lay in store for them. They stopped in Blythe, a couple of hours in. Izzy topped off the gas tank. Alyssa went inside the store for snacks and found a rack full of all kinds of music on cassette for sale. She had maybe ninety-three bucks to spread out. The cassettes were two for ten dollars. She picked out Alanis Morrisette's Jagged Little Pill (1995) and CrazySexyCool by TLC (1994). Earlier when the CCR tape finished, Izzy had her swap it out for Red Hot Chili Peppers Blood Sugar Sex Magik (1991). Immediately upon acquisition of her two new tapes, she was thinking ahead to what the appropriate tactic would be to get her tunes playing. She really had no say slash pull apart from what sway the boy gave her. She'd in one way given herself over to his care, though deep down and even at the surface she felt absolute freedom. Whimsy Cal E. Fornia, here we will be headed in your general direction, now come forth. Show yourself. Present arms and faces, charms and places. Hedonistic belief alarms the faithless. Quantum chase-test. Who's the vagabond in great response equator's shapeshift? The question on all our lips.

"Do you believe in Hollywood as being the Whore of Babylon?" Alyssa asked.

"How's that now? I know it ain't exactly the Pope or the Temple Mount, but—"

"You know. How for most of the twentieth century filmmakers have been steadily shifting the nation's morality, blurring the lines, the evolution of propriety," her said.

"And you are against this, yes?"

"The bad guys aren't supposed to be the good guys. Everybody wants to be cool. I'm pretty sure that's not even a quantifiable thing. This van of yours is obviously cool. But is that somehow linked to your own identity? You are not the bus. The bus is not you. It is just a possession, an object. It is 'your' bus. You are its owner."

"Am I on trial here now? I thought we were baggin' on Hollywood."

"The film industrial complex. Eff eye see. Fic. Shun fic, shun. They put these things in movies for cultural street cred. Kevin Costners and James Earl Jones drove one in the baseball cornfield flick," said Alyssa.

"I saw one in Heat with Al Pacinos and Val Kilmers, during part of the big showdown when it all pops off; the bullets, battling, and blood. I would not say by any stretch that the Volkswagen bus is the symbol for cool. Or represents as much."

"Ipso facto life. Drew Barrymore in Mad Love, Lucinda Dickey in Breakin', both had VW Beetles because that showed how they were cool and tastefully edgy. In Pretty in Pink, Molly Ringwald even drove a pink Karmann Ghia."

"But originally you slammed Hollywood, and now Volkswagens are being propagandized as cool?" Izzy was searching for the connection.

"No, cool is okay; but ultimately harmful as it only drives a wedge between that which is cool and that which is uncool. Heaven forbid you be the latter. You shouldn't label people as undesirable or lacking some unnamable essence. There shouldn't be clubs where only the cool are allowed entry or access. It's sections within sections, and judgments upon judgments. That's class war anti-justice elitist bullpuckey if I ever saw it. I do not care for that one bit."

"Hey, to whom are you preaching? I'm with you on this all the way."

"Well, Hollywood might have its toe in your corner, somehow; indirectly." Alyssa said.

"What if we just choose everyone? So there's no side picking and opposing forces. Just progression together in one direction."

"Hmm, no. That's that twenty-percent hippy part of you talking."

"Yoga say, there are many approaches to washing one's clothes; Laundromat, washboard, riverbed, dry cleaners or a bar of soap and a waterfall," he replied.

"Or you could take care and be cautious; keep out of the mud and gutters."

"Who you calling mud, honey?"

"Who you calling honey, bud?"

They both paused and it felt like something was up for grabs. Like the secret to the circle being completed.

"Bugs Bunny, I believe?" said Izzy.

"Works for me. Drug money?" posited Alyssa.

"Yes, mucho."

"Seriously though, if you'll allow me this request; don't call me honey," she said.

It was fun, this thing called the chitting and chatting. Amusing and endearing and you learn things or two. Theirs was felt pleasure in the process and maybe half a teaspoon

115

callous or coy, but only in the nicest way. Alyssa picked up her purse and set it on her lap. She would just ask.

"Can I put on some of my own music?"

"You may do whatever you wish, Miss Alyssa."

"Thank you kindly." She unwrapped the TLC tape, deposited the plastic wrap and empty case in her purse, and popped the cassette into the stereo deck. She had CrazySexyCool on compact disc at Roxy's; it was one of her favorites. She hoped it received a positive reaction from Izzy at the wheel. The album started on an intro with a heavy solid beat, a dude hyping TLC then they whisper, "Crazy- Sexy- Cool-" for a second, then the first song starts which is at a Creep. Ultimate chill and mellow.

"So these girls can be cool and it's no problem?" Izzy pushed.

"TLC ain't Hollywood."

"Got it," he said and they listened to the song. Kept it on the down low. Nobody is supposed to know.

The twenty-fifth of January, snifter from apothecary, warrant to suggestive forms of jest with magic propertarie. Shared their bared there's interlinings working silver tales and pining truth and hopes, soft expose the blues in nature's shining. The sun beat down. Bassline rolls, the hat ticks time, the mood right swoles.

"I seen a rainbow, yesterday. I almost forgot, while we were talking in the woods," Alyssa recollected.

They stuck through to the rivers and the lakes that they knew used to prove useful new residues left the proof of one single sun day. Trace amounts, hallelujah sing praise. Drink it in eyes of blazing landscapes are they moving?

"Is this moving too fast?" Alyssa ast.

"Not at all. I can make upwards of seventy," Izzy toad her.

All the shade fades away. Sped the day in display out the window blade grasses they stayed fast awake. Relayed escapades and adventures they'd made. While betrayed did their winks and their waves body languid point blank and in sight plain behaved the great spirits played straight spatial renegade taste in a base marmalade. Marvel odd. Plausible

116

audible laudable thinks thoughts born release, seize plots torn—begat get got gone, ready-or-the-not fit, fought, fun. Thread to the one come a lot more than the either had done asked for. In store, floored gorgeous on the wood grain dashboard wardrobe. Lion in the wickerman sword phone redial. Speed style anchor all aboard prone to see, while distracting visions of a sapling chord tone grapple.

He was thirty-three, she was twenty-two.

He'd seen many things; she'd seen plenty too.

Free and humored beings, present fluid flings, like a plethora of gleans they were privy to. Introspection station. Who you with? Zulu nation. What's your cargo? Good vibrations. Do you declare an infiltration? I do declare I doves. What's your faces? Fond of aces arms embrace his wander near the hidden places found in space the given stasis loose and lean vamoose shoelaces.

Vaysis vahses, worthy causes basic taste of what's not blasé. Paws they posit laws they lozenge, smooth and silky legs and soft lips. Beg your pardon, loins stray garden forms stay hard and pulses throb, the games a star ten. Shame is lost the flame accosted licked at burning skin. Casualistic Zen: causal naturalistic vixen den. Spy ritualistic healing, spurt she'll cleansing, spurred jewel frenzy newly sensing true ungrinching long indentured wellspring. Shell seed by the seashore sing more for tough years I traveled on the gravel saddled up the strawberry roan and rodeo the rails.

Riding gladly side-by-side the light it did prevail; time sluggish slinking snails. Wind whispers on the sails. After the end of Waterfalls, Izzy reached down and slid the case of cassettes over near his seat. He lifted the cover open and with one hand grabbed the Beastie Boys Ill Communication (1994), removed it from the case and hit eject on the tape deck.

"There's still more songs," Alyssa said.

"We'll put it back in again soon," Izzy reassured her.

They shared a bag of Fritos and some red licorice whips. They kicked it root down, discussing what that might actually mean. They got it together, and in between. Izzy said that as

117

second in command of the vessel, she should be sworn to a sacred oath.

"Say this after me, 'I, Alyssa Rose, vow on this most sacred oath."

"I, Alyssa Rose, vow on these most sacred oats."

"To stay alive and out of hardship and troubles whenever possible."

"To be staying alive, out of hardship and troubles, at all times."

"To treat this hunk of metal with the utmost respect," Izzy said and slapped the dash with his palm.

"To treat this hunk of metal with the utmost care and respect," she also slapped the dash.

"To be kind to everyone, except maybe sorry ass fools."

"To be kind to everyone, except for sorry punk-ass fools."

"Do you have anything you want to add? Oath-wise?"

"Hmm. And I swerve it all on my grandmama's gravy. Forever and ever, Eggmen."

"Eggmen," Izzy repeated. It did now feel more official to them both.

"Your important looks of vitality embody years of understanding. It means a great deal to me," Alyssa said.

"Thanks. Right back atcha, kid."

"Don't call me kid, bro."

"Don't call me bro, sis."

"Don't call me sis, pops."

"Ooo lady, that's cold."

"You can call me Al. Sometimes people do," said Alyssa.

"Thanks. But I don't think I'll be one of those people," said Izzy.

"Who calls you Israel?"

"Mostly the governmental authorities."

The boy and the girl continued south towards Interstate 8. This would take them west to San Diego and then Qualcomm Stadium, and Super Bowl XXXII.

Chapter Nineteen • Bump Goes the Diamond Mine

January 25, 1998

Mumbles: "Never had a better Saturday in Nevada." Shadow magic matter. Proper strata compound data equals prequels compen-sat a Mack Truck propped up at an angle idle with the window and the seatback sidled. Down loose upright battle tangled war to fight the urge to join the day. In the distance a dog spoke, the bark of lounger.

It felt like noon. Boonz in the back and Truck in the front were both eighty-five percent asleep. Sonny had emerged from the Ford Econoline and walked over to an alley to relieve his bladder. They had to be at the gig site at 1300 hours for setup and soundcheck, so there was no need at the present moment to wake his band. Eventually Vincent, folks called him Sonny, would have to sick the proverbial hounds on his friends if they thought they were going to sleep through the day. Walking to the corner convenience store, he bought a cup of coffee and a donut to go along with his Cheetos leftover from last night. Today could turn out to be a good day if Dystopian Squalor Syndicate could get through the show this afternoon. Then they would really be able to get down to the business of hitting up the Vegas attractions.

Sonny wasn't big on gambling or Vegas shows unless it was a comedian, or if perhaps there was some nudity involved. Showgirls and Rita Rudner, that was his bag; the Smothers Brothers and a sideshow gal with three tatas. Was that Las Vegas or the Ukraine? He was no longer moved by normal stimuli. The only music that could reach his soul now was traditional blues like his Pops used to play; where four-four was only an ideal, a sometime thing. When he performed, it was to release tension and pent-up aggression slash frustration. Sonny didn't feel like a musician, but more like a lumberjack or professional wrestler. He used to destroy gear at shows for the noise it made, the rush it gave, but that practice proved to be too expensive. He decided he would go back to the van, listen to Fishbone on his CD Walkman and count the minutes until they needed to make the short drive to the venue. He downed the last bite of his donut, chocolate glazed. Sonny got back to the van, slunkered down in behind the wheel as it was the best seat available. He fished out his disc of Give a Monkey a Brain and He'll Swear He's the Center of the Universe (1993), his headphones and CD player.

Gone for a swim upstream. Remnant options dim unclean. Proudly rambunctious prim, pristine; loudly dissonant blasting class free christening gypsy king. Glistening tank tracks belay the whip cracks. Heavy is a thing left unseen by the herd that bellows beneath trampling footsteps. Scampering crooks theft creak under the weight of the bridge of sloppy tuning, be foreword in your wanton lack of disc repeat and random consequential fuming. Choice beats flown over guitar filled sweeps and non-committal chaos lost in yelled conviction. For a moment, words meant something. Or at least stood for everything altogether in one accordion or some crazy Creole instrument. Mint gum, seen that piece-wood floor. Scary being small food leather sent fun a Dorian jump, lazy citation.

Lemon Meringue is the apple of his mind's pie licking mouth chops orange, a tangy flavor on his lips, and a crunchy tongue in Cheetoed cheek. Smitten smacking double trickle heart attacking hindrance accessing windowed dressing. A rustle and Truck shifted a second, swallowed a snore.

Outside the clear pane glass, midday sheer pain basked in the kind of well and much worse off asphalt walkers you'd expect, in the down time ice of the hurricane sugar stalks the inner sense and lurks the dangers hidden near. What a difference the dark makes. The dank marks the darling masks the dancers be wore. The morning goner last eve's gore is garnered in the gutter store. The off pour of the grievous war amongst the carnivore, flaunts the red caped matador. Daunting keeps the final score while mortals fight the men of lore stab madly at the wounded core, the coil subhuman toil the spoils of yore. Passed by did one loud chopper roar.

"What's all the damn commotion for?" Boonz grumbled.

120

"It's getting near that time when we have to roll over to the jobsite for setup and soundcheck," Sonny said.

"Can we get something to eat first?" asked Boonz.

They hit a drive-thru on the way to the gig, ordering burgers and fries. Boonz and Truck started eating their lunch in the van. The Syndicate soon arrived at the multipurpose club, which was already advertising for their live music and Super Bowl viewing party later in the day. Boonz went inside to locate their contact and find out where to unload. The club's day manager came outside and gave Sonny directions to the back door around the rear side of the facility. Sonny finished his lunch, and then the three men began transporting equipment from the van to the stage.

There were various sizes of TV sets set all around the room. A slightly raised platform was against the wall opposite the main entrance. Pregame programs were already playing on the screens. They cut in highlights of past championship games, as well as footage of the Broncos and Packers from the regular season. People were at the bar getting a jump on the drinking. Groups of patrons were scattered all about eating appetizers and the like, some in yellow and green, others in orange and blue.

The sound technician asked the guys to give him two songs. They played and the familiar flow returned to hands, fingers, and vocal chords. Did and done. They shut their amps off and stored their instruments in their cases. Boonz walked up to one of the bar staff to see if they had any kind of tab or gratuity for the afternoon. They did. Each ordered a beer. They all sat down at the bar, starting in on their two plus hour wait until show time set for 1530. They discussed if they would stick around to watch the game or spend the evening on the Strip. Truck told the others of his walk about town last night and how close he had gotten to a big score.

"You went to one casino and blew twenty bucks. That hardly counts as being out about town," Boonz told Truck.

"Hey man. Least I was out doing something," Truck said.

"Sure Mack. You're a real man of the people," said Boonz.

121

"Damn straight. I walks proudly amongst the living," said Truck.

"Come on now, don't start. There isn't one way that's better than the other. Haven't you all heard of scientific relativity?" Sonny asked them both.

"Haven't you all heard of scientific relativity?" Truck parroted.

"That doesn't sound like a mellow Sunday afternoon conversation," Boonz said.

"Choose your own facts and create a life experience based on the direction of your chosen frame of reference. It's similar to moral relativity, but it deals with truths and not so much the notion of right and wrong. So Truck, you can maintain your worldview; and Boonz, if you choose, can then agree or build your own factual platform or belief system. And never the twain shall meet. Mark my words; there are multiple ways to accomplish the same task. Short cuts and detours, a little clemency goes a long way. Or start your own religion, and worry not of your neighbor's troubled soul. Sammy, can I get another brew?" Sonny said to the bartender.

"Sounds like bullshit to me," said Boonz.

"Or, is it the best way to get along with your fellow man?" said Sonny.

"That would probably involve compassion and empathy. Your thing of holding opposing or alternate viewpoints seems like it would cause obvious rifts in society. More like the antithesis of utopia," said Truck.

"That's a dirty word," Boonz said.

"It's basically the framework behind our national democracy," Sonny said.

"Yes, and usually the differing parties don't get on too well," said Boonz.

"Scientific relativity isn't around to get folks hand holding, singing peace and love like friendly field mice," said Sonny.

"Yeah, that's what drugs and booze is for. Two bruises more!" Truck called out.

Beers in the early afternoon was par for the course of a day in the life of Dystopian Squalor.

"It's like what I been trying to tell you about golf," Sonny started in.

"Oh, how about you don't try and tell me anything about golf," Boonz replied.

"Same as with good cake and swinging clubs, it all comes down to consistency. If you find a way to do something and it works, repeatedly and it's functional like a frame of mind or set of beliefs, do it," Sonny stated. "You don't have to succeed at everything to be successful."

"Ya mutha," Boonz said offhand.

"Successfully made two babies. Graduated college," said Sonny.

"What about the icing," Truck said. "On the good, consistent cake? Big part of cake is the icing; otherwise it's just a loaf of sweetbread. Is that like a part of golf too?"

"Yeah Sonny, great question, he makes a legitimate point. How do we account for the icing in all this business?" Boonz asked.

"I was obviously including icing in with the cake when I said good cake," Sonny replied.

"Wool, I mean, there is a definite separation between the two parts," Boonz said.

"Vanilla cake, chocolate frosting, separation," said Truck.

"Pineapple upside-down cake doesn't even have icing," said Boonz.

"It has pineapple. The pineapple is the icing," Sonny said.

"Okay Seinfeld. And maybe a nice melted butter could be like an icing. So then toast with sprinkled sugar is like crispy cake, right?" asked Truck.

"I think we're getting away from the idea of consistency," said Sonny.

"Is there any link to pie in this equation?" said Truck.

"Hmm, death by saccharization," Sonny sang.

A chance to wave the flag of the fool, the fellas flew and flapped their yaps unruly grew and from the outside it was a truly Yule-type view. Pipe dreams sound sweet, repeats the echoes as they were sang. You can take away the drum but the beat will never change. Ever charge, ever large; women

123

complain the men harangue, the mood was leisure and lazy with an undercurrent of dormant adrenaline. Adrenalang. Adrenal slang. Kerrang bang zang go the volleys. There were more Broncos fans than Packers, more men than women in the space spread out. The vast expanse was slowly growing in peopular density.

Buzzin' buzzin' peach Schnapps fuzzin' cheap sangria Robitussin mixed in. Was or wasn't he with or did she nix him? Stout concoction brought by luscious vixen. Wantress servile sexful thick elixir. Eyes far off inspect then lick their lips with shameful bets their wits against her. My oh how those blissful tits perk. She is the true champ on any given Sunday, Tuesday through, with Mondays off six days a week and sometimes seven. Just alive to make the leaven blessed increased the way she's living rest in peace, prays for giving. Her shirt reads, "Quit work, make biscuits." The first half of the motto stretched nicely across her breasts. Truck had spun 180 degrees on his stool to watch her walk between tables out on the floor.

"Sexy," Truck said maybe a fraction of a decibel too loud.

"Keep it together, man," said Sonny.

She was talking to, and taking orders from a new group that came in and was seated in her section. Truck wondered aloud what her name might be. If she had a nametag they couldn't see it from the barstools. She had short dark hair, seemed spunky and lively. Her height was medium and made her look not to be messed with, taken lightly or treated without some basic level of respect. Still, she was fun and playful with the patrons right up to the unspoken (but very real) line that was not to be crossed, or shit would get lost. Not unknown to have rude ones tossed to the curb. Security was given word to remove trouble for the sake of keeping the overall balance in check and under control.

"June," guessed Truck. "From Jackson, Mississippi."

"Rochelle, from Rutledge, Tennessee," Sonny said without looking.

Boonz looked over at the waitress scribbling on a notepad. "Maybe Caroline from Louisville, Kentucky. Or Mary

124

Katherine with a K, and she goes by 'Kat', from Campbells-ville, also in Kentucky.

"Here she comes," Truck said and spun around, the three musicians all facing the bar, leaning each in their own kind of comfortable.

June Rochelle Mary Katherine entered the bar, walking up front past the Syndicate. Some pleasantries were exchanged. Boonz stared down into his drink.

"You all need anything from the kitchen?" she asked.

Sonny connected with her eyes, politely told her they were fine and thanks for asking. He said she'd be the first to know if they were overtaken by hunger. As she listened to Sonny, Truck focused in on her nametag, which was white with red letters.

"Hey uh, Charlotte. You from here in Nevada?" said Truck.

"No, I'm from Clemson, South Carolina," she replied.

Truck nodded, turning back to his beer, feeling he had successfully maneuvered that interaction. She was beaming radiantly in her natural state, and she had work to do.

"Alright, thanks fellas," Charlotte said, heading off to check on her other customers.

The three boys felt enriched by the encounter. They thought she might be a student at UNLV or some other local school. Working her way through a degree, architecture or dental medicine. Maybe there's a kid, or she's a recovering addict or used to strip and is now going straight. Truck told all that he refused to believe there wasn't something greater at play in this portrait of a young woman.

There was only about an hour left until Dystopian Squalor would exit the ordinary world, and step on stage as the most immediate representatives of the rock and metal lifestyle. This transformation fit organically with the rousing crowds of football fanatics, and the generally rowdy types populating sports bars on such occasions. On a smaller TV set above the bar, there was a news program playing. It was the only screen not set to the pregame festivities. Pope John Paul II had visited Cuba to challenge Fidel Castro to welcome in change; a story

125

played about President Clinton denying sexual allegations with statements and images of Slick Willy and the First Lady; something about a Spice Girls pay-per-view concert. Michael Crawford, AKA the Phantom of the Opera, has filed suit against the MGM Grand claiming they fired him unfairly; breaking news about Oprah, Patrick Swayze, and mad cow disease. Titanic was crushing the Box Office at movie theaters. Seemed like mostly a drag, so Truck turned back to his beer, while he surveyed the room for Charlotte.

Crisscross web of applesauce, best moss on the southside of lost paradise, press posh sped ahead fastest Ford Fairlane in the west Galaxie a mustang stomps across the screen. A live white bronco fighting restraint, a bit in his mouth and nostrils flaring strength rippling through its flexing muscle. Tone blank, maybe some soundtrack low beneath the chuckle's conversation wades. Somewhere cheers enthuse then fade while those abuse their rival's state.

"Cheesehead fat tub-of-lard triple bypass frozen ass dumb-nut deep-fried Twinkie sucking fucks."

"Go hump a tree, hippy snowball banging ski-pole licking log cabin smoking squirrel munchers."

"Muenster and gouda rules. Medium mild cheddar drools," old lady say.

"Mile high my ass." Didn't much come of words. They were all mostly busy drinking or eating, lost in the atmosphere of the heir to the zone of what ultimate victory might feel like. What some of them would describe as a moment. Justice timed to elate, now to inflate the belly boastful confidence of insecurity.

"Can you imagine how much money is moving around on this game?" Sonny said

"Much," said Boonz.

"Maybe lives destroyed or fortunes made. Can't figure out if I want in on it, or if I should keep it away like the plague," said Sonny.

"Stay away, Sonny. Life's best with a view," Truck toad him.

"Man, you gotta put a foot down, put some loot down, skin in the game. It's called action, go go go!" Boonz said.

"Boonz, you're in no kind of spot to make recommendations on how a body should live," said Truck.

"But I've got basically no chance if I don't ever ante up. But also no risk," Sonny said.

"People go all their lives, every week picking numbers and scratchers for what? Maybe a ten dollar winner every other millennia," Truck said.

"Could be like buying a dollars worth of hope to get through the week," Boonz added.

"That's a rosy take on the lottery," said Sonny.

"You know me. Sunshine and smiles," said Boonz.

"I do. More like moonshine denial. You're unkind and wild," Sonny said.

"Did you write up the set list, Sonny? Any changes from the Show Low lineup?"

"Same originals. Switched around some covers."

The club was filling up, and with room for more, looked like it could easily hold three to four hundred. There was a lot of open floor, standing room to be found aplenty. The bar manager talked to Sonny briefly about maybe playing a few songs at halftime, but that didn't seem like it would happen.

Not that they were too interested, but the loyalties among Dystopian Squalor had Truck and Boonz pulling for Green Bay, with Sonny staunchly backing Denver. Boonz had family in Wisconsin, thought the Packers were the be-all and end-all.

The soundman came by the bar and tapped twice on the countertop with his palm.

"Maybe fifteen minutes until you want to think about taking your spots on stage. We're gonna try to have you finish right before the national anthem. I'll give you a signal at ten and then five minutes out."

Neither Truck nor Sonny emptied their second beer. Boonz was still working on his first. This worked well for them, as they could have a couple drinks during their set, not having to worry about inebriation factoring in or causing deterioration of their ability to perform. That type of drunkenness was rarely an issue, but it had bit them once or twice. Truck still felt bad about it, so the lesson had been learned.

"What are we starting off with?" Truck asked.

"Obligation to the Feud. Then No Trades or Tattoos into John 3:57," said Sonny.

"Yeah, that sounds good. Doesn't that sound good, Boonz?" said Truck.

"Yeah man. Hey, I say maybe we pull out Predatory Chronic Psychosis. And Fire for one of the covers," Boonz proposed.

"Fire would work well after 3:57, keep things moving," Sonny said.

"And it's not long so it shouldn't affect time," said Boonz.

"What about One-Note Jam right before it?" said Sonny.

"Uh, probably no One-Note Jam," Boonz said.

"Yeah Sonny, probably no One-Note Jam," echoed Truck.

"Freaking monkeys. You sound like a broken record. I'm just trying to put on a good show," Sonny towed 'em boats.

"One-Note Jam ain't a good show," Boonz replied.

"How you gonna tell me folks don't appreciate comedy?" Sonny asked.

"Is that what that is? Comedy?"

"It's a statement; a commentary on what is music and what's entertainment."

"Who has ever told you One-Note Jam is entertaining?" asked Boonz.

"People," Sonny said flat.

"Well man, people lied."

One-Note Jam was kind of a gag-bit. Sonny would deliver this elaborate setup for a supposedly extraordinarily meaningful song. He'd pump up the crowd real good and build and shout out a hard four count, then Truck gave a big fill over beats three and four then: BOMP!! A single stinger on the downbeat and the people are left hanging. Voilà: One-Note Jam. Sonny thinks it's funny, but sometimes it feels more like a dirty joke. It usually only confuses the flow of a show. Seldom is it ever understood. So One-Note Jam must wait for another day. Vincent "Sonny" Frye was on the short end of a two-to-one vote.

"Hit the head now if you need to," Sonny said to his crew. "Then we meet at the stage in five."

Boonz popped up and disappeared. Truck peeled off and slunk away. Sonny asked the bartender for three bottles of water. He carried them over near the back of the stage behind their line of amplifiers and drums. Everything still looked like a partially packed sports bar. Little attention if any was focused on the medium-sized stage that routinely played host to live music, open mics, comedy, and karaoke depending on the weeknight or time of day.

From the edge of his field of vision, on the periphery Sonny felt eyes upon him. It was a curious presence. No ill will or bad vibrations.

"What kind of music are you going to play?" a woman asked him. She wore an orange jersey with a white number seven. She had a green bottle of beer held tightly to her chest.

"We play rock. Songs you can move to. It's not just screaming," Sonny said.

He saw her nod silently as he slung his guitar over his shoulder, plugging into his tuner. He started in on his low E-string. The woman was watching, nodding.

"Are you like Guns N Roses?" she asked.

"I, personally, like those guys. But we, as a band, are not like those guys," Sonny said.

"Mm-hmm, I dig." Hers was an amusing attitude, as he tuned the A and D-string.

"So like, Metallica then?" Crazy lady. Guess she was okay, nice lips.

"No," Sonny said. He wouldn't expend any energy. Prep. The G-string.

"Then it's like Green Day? Or like Pearl Jam or something?" lady say. She really did want to know, but didn't know how to ask what she was wondering. Barely bending the B-string. Starting in on E.

"You know Fishbone, Bad Brains, Black Flag?"

She cocked her head sideways, spinning gears: "No. You know Bikini Kill?"

"Yeah. You heard anything about Dystopian Squalor Syndicate?" said Sonny. Nothing was registering but she sure liked watching. "Miss, you wait three minutes and you will know exactly what we sound like." This made her smile and even out.

"Can you play Bon Jovi?" she took one last go at it.

"No ma'am. Get on now," Sonny said causing the lady to wander off back into the maze work of tables and gaming machines strategically placed throughout the room.

Truck snuck up. "What'd that lady want?"

"To know what we sound like," Sonny said.

"Oh yeah? What'd you tell her?" asked Truck.

"Lenny Kravitz on crack."

"Yeah, that probably would be something," said Truck.

"Something that would be," Sonny said.

"What would?" Boonz stepped in.

"Nothing, nevermind."

"What would be something?" Boonz asked again.

"Leonard Albert Kravitz on crack rock," Sonny sang it like a song lyric.

Are you gonna go my way? Sure. One ticket please. New York City. Get a rope. Red please. The ricochet whips.

They took to the stage. Each set to work hitting switches, checking connections, adjusting bolts and nuts to get the tensions just right. There were rigged spots and floodlights but none were on. The sound tech dipped in and said some lights would come on, which basically means they've got the green light to begin. Sonny told him thanks and could he raise his guitar in the monitor mix. The room had a humming mixture of speech and atonal noises. A tunnel of echoed murmurs that melted off and Sonny listened as the multiple sources of music all cut out. Glasses and bottles clinking, arcade clatter, a rack of billiards cracked then was gone just on cue. Truck sat at his set doing doubles and triples on the kick drum and toms. Waggling arms in a kind of stretch, Boonz stood in front of his amplifier, back to the room, sound down low going over lines.

Sonny was ready and walked over to Truck, propping his right forearm on a crash cymbal stand.

"Obligation, No Trades, 3:57 and Fire," said Sonny.

"What's after that?" Truck asked. Sonny didn't say as several spots lit up the stage and he flicked up his guitar's volume and chunked two round open D chords, strummed and landing on a loose twangy pinch harmonic that bent and rolled out into a clean vibrato as he hung onto that note until it turned into feedback, which he corralled, collecting some pressure in the space between him and the amp he was facing. Sonny walked to the microphone and said, "This is the Dystopian Squalor." Then he started picking a percussive pattern on his guitar.

Truck started soft eighth-note flams on the snare and it got loud quick, then sixteenths beating vicious. Boonz set it off high up an octave on the D-string; two loud hits on a G. Groove entry, intrigue and a bottle of get down.

There were a good number of patrons present for it being an hour until kick-off. It's always fun to play for a large crowd. Though this wasn't currently one such homogeny. Most folks were still at the bar or around their tables, but there was a nice swarm mobbing over towards the source of the music. The Syndicate's style of performance wasn't flash. No leather studded accoutrement, wild colors or tight pants. Nobody's shirt came off unless it was a hot outdoor festival. On the whole they were mostly minimalist, though Boonz played a custom five string with the low B. Sonny had a Gibson SG Classic, an old Fender Strat for busted strings or emergency backup. Truck's kit was a rat rod of piecemeal drum manufacturers. Vintage rims with the rear skirts but an amalgam of quarter panels, hood scoops and mismatched doors. But the body was clean. Get a listen and let it purr, give it more, feel it roar. Brutal tight, with half-a-millimeter of room to let it rumble, fuel and fire. Eight cinder blocks fall from a second story droptop turbocharged double particle accelerator pedal's pushing fast and furious.

On the floor, one body put a shoulder to the chest of another and the noise boiled blood, hooked in sharp talons to

131

inflict instigation. Commotion propagated thicker crowds. Thin skin looking out for offense in the loud battleground threat abound steady shouting up for more. Pound on the floor from below with a broomstick, down keep it else I call the cops weren't around. Bricks verbally thrown, the hand was shown and the seed of a target sewn.

A woman nearby said something cautionary to her friends. There was a definite pit forming, violence swelling in its wake. Sonny gave a glance across to Boonz. They both shared a look of satisfaction that they'd near on incited a riot right out the gate. This could be a real good day in the hood. Sonny stepped off the microphone. The bass and lead guitarists played a line in unison, swaying slightly with a head nod every quarter note. Rapid fill a Mack Truck crashed heavy on the four and then it settled into a solo for Vincent Frye.

The rabble still they roused, elbows fist and mean, while soldiers bounced. Sonny looked out and saw a silver flash of shine rise in the air from down in front, the heart of chaos. It was a second before it registered. Then he saw a man grab the object, pushing at it then the flourish disappeared. From the mosh a massive blast flashed a flame and Sonny thought he got hit in the chest with the business end of something sharp. His pick hand went limp and it was hard to stand. He heard screams and panic, then Boonz was leaning over him and there were just cymbals ringing. Sonny couldn't see much but bright light from somewhere up above. He didn't know why he would be lying on the stage floor. Boonz was shouting.

"Sonny! Fuck. Sonny! Fuck, man. Truck, man, call an ambulance! No, go tell the bartender to call an ambulance. Sonny," he kept saying, "Sonny!"

Feedback. No input, no output.[8] Boonz knelt there talking to Sonny who was no longer listening. Not even a minute and Boonz knew what death looked like. Standing up painfully slow he began to remove his instrument. Drawing in a deep breath, he released an ominous growl. With a guttural yell he spun around to heave his bass hard and hurtfully against the world crushing dreams, hope, and spirit. One son. Done living, sans justice for any and all.

Chapter Twenty • Freetrade & Appetizers

January 25, 1998

Izzy's plan to move the ticket was that they'd park off the stadium premises and walk around the parking lots, entry gates, and side streets to locate an interested party or fan trying to get into the game. He had done business before buying and selling odd items in random ways. A part of him thought he might be able to turn his one lower level ticket into perhaps two upper deck seats. This seemed a lot less likely, so Izzy was already resigned to taking the first good cash offer he heard. He and Alyssa had decided that after they got paid they'd drive over near Mission Bay, find somewhere out of the way and watch the game on TV. Preferably at a bar, café, restaurant, or any general place of pleasant vibage and atmosphere that offered snacks. Izzy wasn't sure if he'd get pinched if the wrong people saw him trying to sell the ticket. Alyssa offered to hang back in the bus, but when they arrived there were people selling clear out in plain sight. Still they would not be flagrant.

"I think we should rehearse a little backstory," said Alyssa.

"Backstory for what?"

"You know, for if anyone starts asking questions."

"I got the ticket from my uncle. What else could someone ask that we'd need to rehearse for? It has all the seating info here listed on the front," Izzy said.

"Well, what if like you said we get pinched, and our stories don't match up, hold water, drama, miscommunication and shit goes down?"

"No shit is going down."

"Aww shit. It's going down. You want I should hold onto the goods? Stash it in my bag?" Alyssa was playfully accentuating.

"Just keep an eye out for cops and authority in general."

"Bad boys, bad boys. Whatcha gonna do, when they come for you?" Alyssa sang and did a rudegirl dance, kind of swung

133

her arms in a freeing motion with some twirl to it. "Police nah give ya no break."

"Take it down a notch, Peter Tosh," Izzy said.

"Just having fun, Don drum on," she replied.

"Alright, but let's stay focused and on task."

There was a steady creep of vehicular traffic, legged globs of hype milling about all over. It was easy to blend, almost easier to get lost or lightly accosted. Juice and enthusiasm were oozing through the air, buzz flowing from the stadium feeding contagions to the viral beast of footballed up energy blowing dandelion's lightning bolts on a deep post route up into the clouds. 'Go long' called out, blue angry-tude eighty-nine contraband marching brass mob slash concubine ultra slam Ickey Woods touchdown shuffle. Others Lambeau leaped on friend's backs or in rampant pantomime street side renditions. Interpretive modern glance daggers stare down with ice glares the championship crown bears the sound growling beware on fair ground. Premonitions of the pound: commentary mostly crass and out-of-bounds. Cutly fresh and grassly mown, with orange blue and yellow groan. Mean scene, beanie chic, triangular cheddar hats peek above the undertow in lands of giant's eagle's wings. Foam number one fingers, zing the zingers, fine women and they skintight leopard lookers lag just behind the righteous ass.

"Okay. We're newlyweds from up north. Jim and Sally Nesbitt. These tickets were our wedding gift from a relative. We got here but have to fly home to Idaho for—your dog has the bird flu. We sold one already. Deathbed. Despair. Eh?" Alyssa said.

"Hold on," Izzy motioned for her to wait up.

"Tickets," a guy said quietly, stopping nearby.

"One for sale," said Izzy.

"How much?" asked the guy.

"Four hundred."

"What level?"

"Plaza, section seven," Izzy said.

"Two-hundred," said the guy.

"Nah. Trade down for two together?"

"Don't have two same section. Two-fifty?"

"Nah. Thanks anyway," Izzy answered and the scalper disappeared. The boy and girl moved a little further down their current path.

"You don't want two-hundred and fifty?" asked Alyssa.

"We can do better. It's a good seat. Thirty-five yard line."

"Hmm. You want I should upgrade our back-story? Maybe your dad has leukemia and we need the cash for a bone marrow transplant."

"It'll sell itself," said him.

"So cloak and dagger, isn't this? Aren't we?" said her.

A blimp was flying overhead, for a second it cast a shadow on the ground where they were walking. Several other buyers slash sellers came and went. Some approached Izzy. To others Izzy did the approaching. There was plenty of time for dealing as the pregame festivities were still underway. He'd heard the Beach boys were going to perform, as well as Lee Greenwood, and the songstress Jewel would sing the national anthem. Izzy had the last scalper up to three hundred, but still didn't pull the trigger. He told Alyssa that if he could get three-fifty he would take it. Israel Dufrene spotted his next mark on the sidewalk ahead looking far across the lot at the stadium, glorious and grand, cramming full his field of sight.

"Take my arm," Izzy said, and Alyssa attached onto his left side.

"You need a ticket?" he asked the man in a pleasant tone.

"If it's a good seat, I do," the man answered.

"I got one visitor's side, forty yard-line, Plaza level," Izzy said.

"Oh yeah, for how much?"

"Four-fifty," clean and cut, matter-of-fact.

The man put his hand to his jaw and kind of felt for his beard, which wasn't there. "What's the row and seat?" he asked Izzy.

"Row thirteen, seat nine."

"I'll give you three," said the man.

Izzy paused in thought, and then countered with, "Three-fifty."

The man again tried to find his beard. Said, "Show it to me."

Izzy rotated his cupped hand, letting the man see the ticket to check its authenticity.

"Alright." The man turned his back to the road, then came back to face Izzy with an outstretched hand holding folded bills. They exchanged ticket for money. By the time Izzy flipped through the two hundreds and three fifty-dollar bills, and before he could say thanks, the man was already gone and headed for the nearest gate. Beyond that, his entry into the most venerable and pro, the supremest of all bowls. Spiked punch included.

· · · · · · ·

Izzy and Alyssa Rose both felt a rush of adrenal flush flitter as they started briskly speed walking, by Olympic standards, back towards the bus and further freedom. Then the girl leaped, failing to contain her excitement, a nice victory it was.

"Hey, no running," he warned.

"I'm skipping," she replied.

"Well, definitely none of that either."

Izzy felt young, he saw her smile and it looked amazing and real. Upraising spear rites unlimits revealed. In a second split they were both in a sprint, burning legs warm body works left right left stride dodging around certain demise. To run was the prize. No one could stop them but their own surrender to fly. Strange looks they'd sunk their hooks, relayed shakes loosed forlorn webs cover. Crooks gangway, straight booked, straight back to the bus roundabout the oracle course. They made post haste; laid waste, roll tank pocket bank and a handful of change their ways. Órale, got gain.

Alyssa tagged the side of the bus first though Izzy's effort might not've been one hundred percent present. Enjoying the view. In another minute they were back on the move. Twenty-one minutes went by, and the Volkswagen bus pulled into a parking lot within an easy walk from the streets with shops and restaurants, places for people to inhabit for some stretch of

136

time.   Izzy secured his anti-theft club-lock on the steering wheel, and they headed towards a welcoming clump of commerce and huttage.

"That looks so nice," Alyssa said of a large establishment.

Izzy could see inside the windows, multiple televisions where Jewel was visible inaudibly singing the anthem.   It seemed sufficient, Izzy said, and so they agreed they'd go inside. Upon entry they met a hostess.

"Table for two," Izzy told the young woman.

"Sure. That will be just one minute. What is the last name?"

"Dufrene."

"Thanks. It won't be long," said the hostess.

They sat down on a solid wooden bench.   Now in the background they could hear Jewel singing, "O'er the land of the free, and the home of the brave."

Izzy thought how if things were different he could've been in the stadium right now. It didn't really bother him and he kindly grabbed hold of Alyssa's hand, playfully intertwining his fingers with hers. The restaurant felt a bit more like a dinner joint. There was a modest sized crowd, as they could see into the dining area, it seemed an older populace. Some gray hairs and wheelchairs.

Out of nowhere: "I'm just not sure how much credit you can take for that bus. I mean it's not like you built that," Alyssa said.

"Hey now, I have heaved and hoisted and pulled out and dropped in that engine with two floor jacks and pure ingenuity. I've maintained and cared for, fixed up, sweat and bled over and into that machine," was Izzy's position.

"Okay. Points for that."

"Miss Rose, I am not really feeling this spot here. How would you take to going elsewhere?" Izzy asked.

"Fine by me. I'm along for the ride."

Izzy stood, followed by the girl, and they slipped quickly out the door. As they left, Alyssa heard the hostess call out, "Dufrene, party of two," trailing off in confusion. She said nothing to Izzy, only kept continuing down their current path, floating on high the waters cresting this vein of service and industry. What happened to the Dufrenes? Who can eat at a time like this?[9]

The two docked in another port further down, tying off at an outdoor café where they sat beneath a large umbrella. They ordered chips, salsa, and some specialty-seasoned home fries, curly to their close acquaintances. Comfortable and composed, the fresh oceanic afternoon air rivaled the football game in thrilling liveliness. It was a good time. They had drinks, and in their minds no doubt or darkness lingered. There was plant life (probably fake), tall stalks of green leafy camo adding shade to their spot. The Packers scored on the opening drive, a twenty-two yard pass to Antonio Freeman from Green Bay quarterback Brett Favre. The Broncos answered right back with a fifty-eight yard drive and a Terrell Davis one-yard touchdown run.

Izzy's hand was messing with Alyssa's foot; the ankle of her leg sat propped up resting on his thigh. And they both did lounge. What a blessing passed right over Sunday's best address announcer, interception Tyrone Baxter. First and ten, Denver is on the move again.

Onward Broncos soldier marching down the corridor, the field of play hits and velocity makes havoc on a body's constitution. With pro-size execution, of buttonhook pistol grip deep routed electrocution. Buzzed by each advancement toward the plane marked six-point contribution. Fusion. Elway runs a one-yard goal line intrusion. The lead sled of Cadillacs, Davis monster smack attack the fundamental function of a killer running back. Tyrannical domination, total destruction of your defensive line's *face* may mask their *fear* they run in place can't touch; get near. Itty-bitty blitz left tackle fits of rage and sighs resign. Their powers blind, even combined.

Izzy and Alyssa shared the screen, true blue evergreen efficacious entities, Norma Jean Aloysius Beverleen. Green Bay had the ball and was driving. Favre's safety was at the mercy of a rushing Atwater swiping caused number four to let loose the ball handle and the Denver defense recovered

138

possession, increased momentum by number twenty-seven. This time only resulting in a field goal of two score and eleven yards, making it seventeen to seven, in favor of Denver. The teams then traded three-and-outs. With less than eight minutes left in the first half, the Packers started back on their own five-yard line. They began a deliberate and methodical forced march down the field. It was impressive and punishing progress. After sixteen plays the Pack stood six-yards from the goal line, close to getting back within one score of the lead.

All the chips were falling in Izzy's favor. The salsa was chunky with an appropriate amount of zest. Green Bay's quarterback connected with his tight end for the touchdown, and the half finished with the Broncos ahead by three.

At the same old time as the game, simultaneously the lovers caught up in a fifth of passionate rage, raised a slice of lime on the lip, a light hand upon her hip check level one two for the halftime extravagancies. Barfly relevants and skillet fried elegance, portrayals of sides, dishes and haute and spicy pigskin cuisine. Dip it in, dip it in, rack of ribs, salute a cent'anni. Good health, keep your chin down kid.

There was a blue-collar pro-Packer proletariat single feller seemed down like a lariat had him wrestled around by the neck. World was on shaky ground, this ancient in a daze near on seventy-eight years. And is this what it led to? His gaze fell to Izzy who was sunk down hunkered and comfortable.

"You all pulling for Denver?" asked the old man.

"Yessir," said Izzy.

"Christ, if back-to-back titles ain't the last temptation since the Packers won Super Bowls One and Two in the late-sixties. Broncos been in control, seems I got problems if Green Bay don't step it up," said the old man.

"Umm, crack heads got problems. You have a slight situation with mild discomfort," said Alyssa.

"I guess you're right, young lady. Crack heads do got crack though," old man say.

"If they're good at it they do. Still, you did win last year. You do have that," Izzy said.

"I just feel afflicted, and I'm a light sleeper so who knows the effects it could have if this keeps up," said the old-timer.

"Well, don't give up yet. You have a whole other half," Alyssa said.

"That is the truth. But who knows if I even make it that far."

"What do you do?" Alyssa asked.

"Oh, I used to do things. Not so much anymore."

His mood was dark, onyx. Slam rocks well. They asked what his name was. Marlin Brandon he told them. Susan Sarandon flashed in Alyssa's mind. Scrolled across the inner side of her forehead. Off she goes coasting, then thinking and then blank. Doing the Paul Schrader, raging bulls, seeking pay dirt.

"Think positive thoughts. Goodness will come," she said, his spaced invader.

"That sounds like rules. Don't care much for them. You a ruler?" Marlin asked.

That's one third of a yardstick. Boys will be boys, men men, and cranky old fellas just about whatever they want. God bless you please Missus Robinson. Tide comes in, tide goes out. Pinch of Skoal, seabound gulls, purple shells, and people skills. Jesus Moses, Mary Jane and Buddha's Judas wafting through the air. Alyssa looked sideways at Marlin.

"What's your problem?" she asked kind of true and sincere.

"Alyssa. Sorry, sir. Let's be civil," Izzy said apologetically.

Sanctimonious territory, sacred monkey ass ceremony, sanctum onerous cerebral viscosity, he was thick skulled and numb-noggined from time to time. She was straight rude and felt justified if her heart was aware and connected, as well as something else about being in the right now. Nice and necessary or muck the fans up confusing what is proper yet edgy as marshmallow. The solution to the egg old question, "Can't a body just get along? Down the road, with ease."

"You must be one of them truth fairies," Marlin unleashed a spring of demonic laughter, adding. "You a witch?"

"Way to go Miss Rose, *now* you riled him," Izzy said.

"The only *real* magic is in timing and the fire of the sun," said the girl.

"Exactly what a witch would say," the old man was a good bit inebriated.

A foursome minus one they made. Aphorisms on display, appropriate weight yet to be sayed, the will to war had honed its hate. Scion timid, relate I've id free, the gang within the game. Words convey, thoughts betray, berate, irate arose with tempers flared.

Fee fi foe fum, sugar pie honey bunch, smokey was a tempting song of a grin, short while 'til the month of May, but today was about the My Girl high city. Marlin Brandon stood, nearly knocking his head on the large shade umbrella over his table. He stretched or had a spasm that shook his limbs, and for an almost octogenarian, he got around okay.

Izzy wanted to ask Alyssa about her family. Or were her parents around, or did she have siblings, or where was home if you don't count Roxy's place? But he was resolved to patiently continue communication, allowing information to present itself naturally. Like how you might expect things to go down.

In an ordinary flow—

January 25, 1998

Three hundred and sixty-three miles east and up a little, Roxy was loading what she could into her Cherokee, while preparing to drive back home. Catfish had already said he too had lost interest in the game, or might've just been gone too long from his own place. Roxy said either Moe or Les had to come along with her, otherwise Louie wouldn't have enough room in his station wagon to transport the rest of the gear and people back to Payson after the game was finished. Moe said more than the game he wanted the ride in the wagon, so he pulled rank and Les was marked as the third and final crewmember to make the trek up north with the first group.

Louie's girl Lorraine hadn't seen the forest or the trees in a while. She had the next day off, so Roxy told them they could stay at her cabin for the evening as a thank you for their hospitality the previous night. Louie's main concern was bears.

"No worries man. I've got a bear guy. Sprays the whole encampment on the regular. Zombie squirrels are the *big* issue, if you want to worry about something." Roxy was trying to soothe, distract, and also jab at Louie to stay on his good side.

"Bullcrap, you do not have a bear guy," Louie shouted at Roxy out the open door. He kind of wanted her bear guy to be a real thing.

"His name is Bart. Les tell him," Roxy told Les who was in the open garage door holding his keyboard stand.

"His name is Bart," Les told Louie, who was standing in the kitchen. Catfish was already seated shotgun patiently waiting while Roxy checked and double-checked things.

"Les come on. Everything else goes with Louie!" Roxy hollered.

"What'd she say?" Lou asked loudly at Les.

"That's everything she says. See you all up there," Les translated, walked out to the Jeep and slid his keyboard stand into the rear cargo area.

The engine fired and Les wedged in the back seat with the equipment. As they pulled off, Catfish took in a deep slow breath, held it for a few seconds, and methodically exhaled blowing steadily the air out of his mouth. The whole process was audible if you were paying attention. Roxy was.

"Everything alright over there?" Roxy asked.

"Oh yes, fine. Just having a moment of my meditations. Last bit of trip left. Only gettin' settled," Catfish told her.

"Don't worry about Twig. He's recently been kind of sour," said Roxy.

"Oh yes, he'll be fine. Has to learn some about adversity. My other boy is taking on some big challenges. Don't want him in over his head. He's strong, but you know me being his Pop I have concerns. Who knows, maybe I'm bothering myself for nothing. So I do my meditations. That's the best I can do, sometimes toss in a little prayer," Catfish said.

"Breathing, praying, talking through it. Those are all good approaches. You know I saw him Friday in Show Low. They were sounding real good," Roxy said.

"Twig might've mentioned that." Again a deep breath and you could see his chest expand, shoulders raised up then he exhaled medium-slow. It would've made quite a noise if all that wind went instead through one of his harmonicas.

"Sure nuff he's a rollin' stone," said Roxy.

"Back down the road I'm goin'," said Catfish.

"Rox, you gonna put some music on?" Les asked abruptly.

"Wait 'til we get out on the highway," she replied, then directly switched on the radio and some noise came out low in the speakers.

"I got *all* the secrets to the highway," Catfish sang. Built on the backs of those destined to make the journey. They took off out of that place in a hurry, sauntering's just too slow.

"Who sang that one?" Les asked.

"Big Bill Broonzy, Charlie Segar, and then Little Walter Jacobs in the late-Fifties," he told Les.

143

"I think Clapton's done a version," added Roxy.

They were returning to the edges, places that were more easily understood. They hadn't done anything, but chased away a good lonesome roam.

The trio took turns improvising mournful and forlorn verses of fleeting and solitary abandon, together. Elijah took in another breath, and a more forceful focused stream of air exited through his mouth.

"How's it I never saw you meditate before?" Roxy asked.

"That last one was also a prayer. You praise Him on the inhale, and ask for your blessings on the exhale. My Ma, she did that and taught it to me."

"Does that make it work better?" asked Roxy.

"I can't speak to the results, but you feel fine and more tranquil like," said Elijah.

Roxy merged onto the freeway, which would take them east to connect with the Eighty-Seven, or the Beeline Highway as it was often known.

• • • • • • •

Back at Louie's, Lorraine was offering Twig and Moe some sandwiches that were mainly bread, but also there was some meat and cheese, though thin on vegetables, and lacking little chocolate mints, but hey. They all told her thank you so much and wasn't she sweet. She asked did they notice it weren't so much bread but rather a dinner roll sliced? All were in one accord that it was even better than they had originally let on. Twig gave Moe eyeballs that wasn't Low-rain the most pleasant kind of bother?

Lorraine said the way she knew the rolls were classy was they had a light spat of flour and the bag they came in was "fancifully sleek." She told Twig and Moe she knew some things about "grooming and such," because of summers she had spent in Missouri, though she said it like "Mizura." Louie was familiar with this bit of history. He was having fun watching his guests chew and nod while the second half of the game got going.

144

No one was overly invested in a declared patronage to one specific side. The woman was encouraging in a general sense, since she returned from the grocery store talking about Americana, and how taking part was a sacred piece of our national heritage. Said there was an amazing Tostitos chips and salsa display that moved her, "in a grand style." A profound realization of roles reversed with universal snack dispersal. Walker Herschel had a commercial, artificial flower flare when the chips and salsa dried up middle of the third quarter. It is the law of man to ingest finite amounts and wash it down to come back later for fourths and fifths; an infinitesimal gesture at worst. At best you feel love and warmth.

"Do yall think I look like Christy Turlington?" she asked.

"Gosh, Low-rain," Louie said. "Leave them fellas be and let 'em eat."

Doing the Little Bobby Darin's World, how we kneel son man de la soul. Where somewhere you be yonder see, find a seat and park it. She tells them very well she is a rational radical. So they'd taken off in the '69 bus. They was singin' in the eighty-sixed '86 Jeep Cherokee, no Desmond Dekker was playing yet. Rudegirl Rainey was a mini-flirt plainly and felt far ahead of any curve. Nerve she had in bulk, and when told could easily hold her words. Birds. There was a tick in her mind, some reminder of the kinder kind of unloving homes. At the same time she realized her overreaction, and adjusted accordingly. Her roots were dark and substantial, boots, Docs, conversed and damn chill. Is anything else consequential? Of course, elephant gents, sporting dived funster wallets.

Chapter Twenty-Two • Absolute Crap

January 25, 1998

Three hundred miles northwest the pandemic bites our toe. Yo toe, yo toe. Feefty are too. The paramedic said maybe there's hope and chance in amongst all that blood, but they took Sonny off the oxygen. Now law enforcement is taking statements, having a good old time at the wake again. Finishing watching replays on the big screen of Denver quarterback John Elway flipping horizontal like chopper blades after busting out eight yards and taking the Broncos to the one-yard line. A moment later, tarantula dexterous tramples down the defensive front line, touchdown. Extra point and the score is Denver 24, Green Bay 17.

Boonz had already told four different cops that he only saw Sonny fall back. That the crowd didn't register. Or he could've been asked four times by the same officer. Or maybe this was a dream, but that was a lie, and fairy tales are for children at bedtime.

Sonny's just asleep. Sonny now sleeps forever.

"He's on his way to begin again." Truck was already mentioning reincarnation.

"Fine." Boonz couldn't listen. Kind of guy makes a dime out of fifteen cents. Then Truck said something about killing the Buddha on the side of the road. Boonz wanted space and kept going out the back door to breathe, but then another cop would bring him inside and ask more of the same questions. He couldn't get away from his dead friend, and his friend's death weighed down heavily on his everything. Weary was every cotton-picking minute's scream inside. He could only think about driving quickly away from this hell trap. Or he could maybe get lost in a strip club, or fuck multiple prostitutes or start and not stop drinking. Score meth or try that heroang for the first time, or find the guy who shot Sonny and ask for the next round in the chamber for his own crooked sorry face.

Kill Buddha, fucking kill *me* flashed through his consciousness. This feeling is not good: a pang of horror and the scourge of Dystopian Squalor's existence was floored. Regurgitations per minute increased. Fly heaving pain. High anxiety. Vera Wang. "Breathe," he heard Truck say and felt a hand on his shoulder. "It's easier if you don't put up such a fight with things."

"Just let me freak out, man," said Boonz.

"Yeah man, right. But that battle's not worth a wage," Truck said.

"I'm putting together my own little rebellion."

"Come sit down in the van," Truck led him shuffling, bent over and off axis.

Mack Campbell slid open the van's side door, guiding Boonz to a seat on the floor. Then he (Boonz) scuttled backwards to lean his weight against the inside of the van, and the blue beanbag chair. Truck sat at the edge of the door and heard mumbling.

"What's a rebel? Mercenary recompense. The price paid, Herculean request. What the fuck has got into people?" Cuneiform babble on; tsunami foams rabid Machiavellian justice. Illogical vacuum, lleno de mierda de toro.

Great white stark knuckle tension in his fist Truck pounds out aggression on the wall of the Seventy-five Ford. Hard time breathing, thinking he needs a bigger throat, more air. Steeled reserve to overcome and take the lead. Doing the Roy Scheider. Squints through salty tears, not a dry face richer for the wear. Grits his jaw and feels the war with the beast of sorrow and loss. Flourish of energy ripples through his spine, a slap to the ego of the rock star trap. How much more pointless could this tragedy be? Desperations feel maxed out plus one. Memories distorted, managing to fall apart. Doing the Rob Reiner, dreamt of escape in a Maude diner. Felt like a scrape and a mauve shiner, as if he'd taken a beating a long timer. Shook his body a hairliner fractured his current will to go on.

"Go on, man," said Boonz. "You don't have to keep it together on my account. This whole business is a fucking wreck."

147

Everybody knew everybody too well to put up a front or façade. They would need to find some means to recover. They lost a brother, a branch of their triumvirate. Part of Boonz in particular was dealing with the shock. He had a faint notion about the ramifications and fallout from Sonny's murder. Murmurs, "It wasn't real." He could drive the van off the Hoover Dam. Pills, raid a pharmacy. Maybe if he took this all out on somebody's jawbone or eye socket. Chop down a tree: power tools, a chainsaw. It seemed he had so many options and directions to go in, but it was the pits. For whatever it was worth, Truck was somewhat available. Their bond had suddenly grown tenfold and that was real and now. He was almost certain Sonny was dead. Truck was real because he was sitting right there. Blood was real and dried on his (Boonz's) hands and in spots on his clothes. He could see the sun above the horizon. Belief in all else was shattered. This city felt so strange. Love was nothing, meaningless, and alien. How he yearned to stop worrying and just swing on the spare floor tom that sat beside him. What is music? Why are we playing here? Are we playing? Is this serious? Is this fun? This is not fun. What end am I serving? What about Sonny's Pops and brother? Who's going to make *that* call? Nothing but questions and confusion, grasping at straws, man. Illogical cause, the one and only reason to pause. Stuck. Do something random in this pandemonium.

A plain-clothes police officer came up to the open van door and stood before Truck and Boonz. He asked if they were the two who were on stage at the time of the shooting. Truck nodded in the affirmative. The detective told them they'd be able to get their equipment soon. The coroner would be moving the body in the next few minutes, and would they be staying in the city tonight? Boonz told him no, that they would go back to Arizona the minute their gear was loaded. The lawman double-checked their names and asked if they had a next-of-kin contact number for the deceased.

"His Pops lives in Payson, Arizona. That's as much as I know," said Truck.

"Thanks. Sorry for your loss," said the officer, to which they both sort of mumbled in acknowledgment.

The bar manager gave them an envelope and apologized that it wasn't more. He looked crazy. So soon come the reparations. It seemed odd, and the cash got stuffed in the glove box. Deep down where the shadows maintain peace.

Time passed, things were quiet for the first time in a long while. Truck sighed, "You can't tell me I never tried." It sat a moment.

"What are you talking about? Like we successfully failed and that's bookends?"

"You know we won't find another one like Sonny. Who *knows* how long it would take to even get back up and operational on even the smallest level," Truck said.

"Yeah I know, but just don't straight up and walk away."

Afraid and flailing, stuck out in the wailing wind; punished for crimes of commitment, sacrificed for some bit of humanity. To this end: To remain being and not simply cease to exist because here comes the monkey wrench and there goes the works. You ever hear a paperclip spat out of a pipe organ? Like mushroom soup clouding up a nice rabbit stew, trace elements of radish and radiation; a pinch of paprika for pep.

Depress.

January 25, 1998

In a relatively calm space off the coast in Mission Bay, Izzy and Alyssa watched as Green Bay tied up the score at twenty-four a piece. The Broncos punted and the Packers kicked it right back. Now, Denver had possession of the ball with three minutes and twenty-seven seconds left on the game clock.

"This is it," Izzy said. "Elway has a chance to take the ball down the field and put us ahead."

Alyssa had never really before cared about the outcome of a sporting event, but because it meant so much to Izzy, she was feeling emotionally invested in this game of the pigskin. America. The Green Bay fan that had been laying into them at halftime was now in his own zone of terror and anxiety. Everyone on the patio would either yip in the positive, or yap vocal negatives with the customary bodily flinches depending on which team made a play and who it benefited. The Broncos ran a sweep to the left. There was a fifteen-yard facemask penalty that took Denver close to the Packers thirty-yard line. Terrell Davis busted out a couple yards to the right side. Then Elway rolled out to the left, completing a pass to number twenty-nine for a big gain. They were set up first and goal-to-go at the eight-yard line. A holding penalty moved Denver back ten yards. Davis took the hand off again, breaking through the line all the way down to the one. That run gave him 156 yards rushing for the game. One minute forty-seven left in regulation. Second and goal, Elway hands off to Total Domination, who crossed the goal line through a hole the size of a small vehicle, six points. That was Davis' third rushing touchdown. They flashed up on the bottom of the screen that it was a Super Bowl record. The extra point made it 31-24, Denver.

Now, with a minute forty-five left, the Packers needed a touchdown to tie. After the kickoff return, they were set up at their own twenty-nine yard line. Next play was a hand off to number twenty-five, resulting in twenty plus yards, bringing the Pack out across the fifty and into Denver territory. Clock is ticking down under a minute twenty. A short pass for no gain, and Green Bay calls for a timeout at one minute eleven seconds remaining. When play resumes, a quick pass from Favre to Dorsey Levens gave the Packers first and ten at the opponent's thirty-five. This was followed by another pass to Levens on the right side for four yards. It's second and six, with less than forty-five seconds left to play. There was an incomplete pass across the middle. Antonio Freeman had his hands on it, the clock stopped at thirty-six seconds. Third down and six at the Denver thirty-two, Favre took a shot down field, but Steve Atwater and the Denver secondary cleanly laid out the intended receiver. With thirty-two seconds remaining the Packers faced fourth down. The players were still getting up from the previous play's collisions. Heartbeats were raised. The ball was snapped. Favre dropped back, stepped up into the pocket and threw across the middle where Broncos linebacker John Mobley broke up the play. The celebration began on the Denver sideline, in the stands, and in Colorado while twenty-eight seconds were all that was left. One more snap, just to take a knee, and the victory was sealed as John Elway was mobbed, lifted, and carried on his teammates shoulders as the game clock hit triple zero. The new world champions were crowned. Final score: Denver 31, Green Bay 24.

Izzy took a huge breath, looked over at Alyssa Rose who shone and glimmered.

"Wow," she said.

"Wow is right," said Izzy. "Now if I could only just have this feeling on a continual loop, coursing uninterrupted through my veins."

"That might seem nice, not sure if it's sustainable. Sounds more like a manic episode, or some extended adrenal binge."

"Yeah, the good stuff," Izzy said.

"Now to the beach?"

"That be the mission at hand." With that, Izzy paid their bill and the two left the establishment's perimeter. They stepped back onto the shop-lined path, going in the direction of the VW bus. Their chariot sat awaiting their return.

Israel hadn't put much thought into a plan for postgame. The beaches weren't far off, and that could cover most the rest of the day. Toes in the sand, they could watch the sunset on the vast oceanic horizon. Besides, an itinerary is basically rules, and therefore a sort of hindrance against liberation. These things like curfews, operating hours, and daylight savings time are the constraints and tools used to limit individuality, which at its core is a priceless asset. They are simple mechanisms that man and womankind have set in place, in an attempt to "maximize efficiency." Some kind of vinderfall, good fortunes blown in on an easterly breeze.

Inquisitions of definitions of relation played quietly in the minds of the boy and girl. Words hardly matter when looks like these they share, sideways glances and soul smashing smiles. How sick and twisted the two must have appeared to even the slightly cynical witness. Losers lost hatred recusers toss caustic through the window, out the back hatch, over the left shoulder, away from harm and into some whole other realm. Enter dimensional warp drive train robbery. Errant daydreams lit by evening sunbeams creeping soft heat in cracks and crevasse. Inflected spoken bravas. Told her how good she looked. She made him feel so. So what, so why, so willing to try on wings they glide emotional rampage overt surrender, good real amble vibe incandescent trailers yall.

Yowzah. Ya dig. Ya know?

Holding hands, ankle pitcher shows. Touch. She felt so good to caress in the van yesterday, when she wasn't even fully naked. How she must look stripped down bare. These thoughts made Izzy experience a small degree of lust and desire. He wondered what kind of reaction she'd give if he

152

told her: Positive or negative, good or bad, sweet or naughty? He was sick, his mind in high fever on different levels he was in realization of this girl here. Bliss swirled near. Blustery.

She looked at him and said, "Hey lonesome."

"Hey," Izzy replied, which visibly pleased her. Her bent lips emanating joy.

"Are we thinking about walking or driving to the beach?" Alyssa said.

"I say we drive. Find a good spot. Easy access."

They dipped into a couple shops to browse the local wares. Alyssa rummaged through assorted shells and beach themed trinkets. He would sneak up on her, and then she'd tag him good on the arm. They stayed light and playful. In the moment on cloud nine, triple seven straight jackpot of pleasure with a dollop of delight.

Making it back to their vehicle, Alyssa had only purchased a postcard for to write a note to Roxy and tell her, "Hi and all's well." On the picture side there was a glowing sunset with a sliver of the shoreline sand showing and "San Diego" printed on one side of the border. Izzy walked around to unlock Alyssa's door. There, sitting cross-legged on the asphalt in the shade of the bus were two smiling faces looking up at him, a man and a woman. The woman raised a hand and waved by wiggling the tips of her fingers. Like lost puppies their eyes begged for the world not to just stomp them out cold. Please hammer don't hurt 'em, they were froze as ice pickles, pop rocks, and goose hair.

"The truth, Sara," said the man.

"Nice kids they look like, a guy and a girl. Oh, and she has freckles, ask them," said the unknown woman who might be named Sara.

The seated man sat up, lifted his right arm and placed his palm against the van's sliding door.

"Hey, hi, hello I'm Dirk. Benchwobble's the name and this lady here be my one and only lady fair, Daphne Sarasota DeMariantnet. We have adopted this vehicle as our Mecca. At this very moment, we offer prayers wishing blessings on its owner and occupants. Is that you?" The man held his hand out in greeting. Izzy noticed that the man wasn't exactly making eye contact, but no doubt it was to him that he was reaching.

"Go on already," Daphne said. "He'd like to make your acquaintance."

"Yeah uh, my name is Izzy and this is Alyssa Rose." The two men shook hands.

"Buddha be praised. Lift high the Lion of Judah. I do apologize friend, we'd stand but there are people after us and we fear being spotted. Hauled off, incarcerated." At that, a frightened look came across Daphne's countenance.

Izzy didn't want to get too involved in this man's tale weaving, but the couple seemed about the epitome of harmless and docile. Most of all they didn't appear a massive liability.

"I'm afraid we'll be pulling out soon," said Izzy.

"Do you suppose we could slink in down low inside of your bus and discuss things over an offering of the herbal kind?" The Dirk held up a fat joint, rolling it between his fingers. Izzy was hesitant, but in the end succumbed to temptation and his fellow man's charms. He unlocked the door and slid it open. The new couple did slink in and sat on the bench seat. Alyssa entered the cab, sitting on the box seat behind the driver. Izzy surveyed the area and saw no one who appeared to be searching for anybody. He stepped up, slid the door closed, and took a seat on the floor next to Alyssa's spot.

The curtains were adjusted in a clandestine fashion. Izzy pulled a cloth divider across the front width of the bus, cutting off the outside view through the front windshield. The fuzz is always watching. All took a few seconds to regain a sense of balance, as half had been on the pavement's hard surface. Izzy wanted to get at least one suspicion straightened out.

"Sorry to be blunt, but can you see alright?" Izzy asked the frail old fellow.

"Yes, I'm only mostly blind. Mind you I can handle my own in a fracas. I probably couldn't tell you the number of fingers you're holding up, nine out of ten dimes. Zen crimes, pluckety hen chimes. Only machinery I'm qualified to operate is a toaster, and even then I might get a singe. I kid. But it does hurt. Who would like to do me the favor of sparking this?" said the Dirk of Benchwobble.

The mood was light and Daphne gently grabbed his hand, sliding deftly down to his fingers where she gripped the joint and took it as the Dirk let go. Miss DeMariantnet exuded great civility and grace for her relative youth. Though there was a feeling that she could bite and snap if necessary, in defense of her companion. She lit up with a fire from out of nowhere, drawing in a quick sip then handed it out across to Alyssa.

"Thank you," the circle hit a time warp. "Is Benchwobble your real name?" Alyssa misted mind sport.

"Many an actual being knows me by it, family included. It has been handed down among many of my past peoples. If that holds any weight," the Dirk said.

Daphne nodded slightly and Izzy inhaled deeply the dank. Big money, big money, spin spun he went, saccharin a rally round the planet's den honey.

Big ebola five alarm chili, thrilling. Swig handful of jive and yarn willing, weaving. Shady woving bouncing off the ceiling. Wheeling in a most wild way. Laughs of belly grabs and swelling. Telling fibonacci kamikaze bold-faced libels. Then some seismic numbers game and nine sided die rolls, though only once theta do be alive.

"What are you all up to here in the bay?" Izzy asked them.

"Well, I is basically a royal print-sesh, journeying the global circuits," said Daphne in an odd accent.

"We don't usually get into details. Often strangers can't help but judge and criticize; it's in their nature. We understand, even the kindest soul, so no offense or anything. We are a self-sufficient traveling troupe. Out to join the milieu," said Dirk.

"Don't act like we're a couple angels, Dirk is usually 'drug adjacent' with his nose in the honey pot. It is part of our process," Daphne half said to Dirk, half to Izzy and Alyssa.

"Look, I didn't go to college just like you," Dirk said to Daphne. Then he looked in the direction of the others across the cab. "We all didn't go to college. Nobody here went to college."

155

"I went, just didn't finish," Izzy conceded.

"Of course, no one here finished college, incompletes all around."

"Pinkies down and nobody gets hurt," Alyssa tossed out, trying to add levity.

The Dirk chuckled and raised his hands both to the sky, playfully pleading, "Occifer please."

They all carried on and burned down the house.

"We're over from Arizona for the Super Bowl," said Alyssa.

"Fantastic! The Super Bowl, yes. And when is that?" the Dirk asked.

"That was just this afternoon," Izzy replied.

"Yes, of course. Stunning game, a spectacular display," said Dirk.

"Come off it, man. You didn't see it?" asked Alyssa.

"No, I suppose not dear. I was here with Daphne in this parking lot," Dirk said.

"How long were you waiting out there for us?" Izzy asked.

"Oh, not long in the grand scheme of things. Would either of you care for some mescaline?" the Dirk put forth.

Israel looked at Alyssa who had on a strange face. "Thanks, but no."

"Just polite, that is. Good business. The lines are generally clear and defined. Most folks know when they've crossed over to the other side," Daphne said.

"I'm sure we're fine on this side for now," Alyssa said.

Pause, pause, space and thaws.

"Daphne knows a right squared away fella got a proper shack just up the coast. Short walk from the beach, all the amenities, shower, toilet, a real normal-type setup. I reckon we might could go in like double trouble team toil and struggle o'er the fire's burning coals and the cauldron's bubbles. What say ye brother Israel?" said the Dirk.

"I'd say you haven't shown but only about six red flags, and my cut-off is at seven. You two need a ride up the coast, that's fine. Not sure how much more I can really do for you," said Izzy.

"That's all I was asking, man. Daphne can give you directions there no problem. Maybe thirty minutes, right?" he said to the lady.

"Right," she replied.

Alyssa told Miss DeMariantnet that she reminded her of a young avid lavishing gardener, and had she ever seen The Killers. What about Killer's Kiss or The Killing from Fifty-six? Daphne told her sorry, no, but did she sometimes feel like a Bonnie and Clyde, or maybe Juliette Lewis with Woody Harrelson or Brad Pitt, driving around always up to no good. Alyssa said not so much, but that she hadn't been at this traveling thing for too long yet. Daphne said Izzy and her looked like 'spitting images' of Sailor and Lula from Wild at Heart. Only Alyssa's hair was a lot less blonde, and Izzy didn't look nearly half as rough as Nicolas Cage, in a good way. Alyssa Rose said thank you, how Daphne was just a sweetheart, and if the boys get lost they could turn this into something more like a Thelma and Louise. She asked if Daphne knew how to drive a stick shift, adding that she could but it weren't a pretty thing or point of pride. Daphne said she had never attempted a manual transmission, but she was willing to give it a go.

The Dirk was pleasantly being. Izzy said if there were no objections, they should just head out on their way. Benchwobble said something about the best use of a half-hour. This made Daphne laugh in the most satisfied manner and sing out, "Dark wing Dirk! When there's trouble you call BW."

Izzy opened the shades. Crawling up front he fired the ignition as the sky was changing. In the light blue, now crept violet ribbons. The horizon turned purple with reds and crimson at the edges. The engine warmed. Alyssa in the back said something about world domination, which was answered by the Dirk of Benchwobble with some gibberish including the likes of 'zoinks' and a hard 'gnarf.' There is after all a limit to the number of references one human can accumulate and access, spanning decades of cultural crazes, fads and frenzies. In Izzy's mind flashed faintly scenes of G.I. Joe, Voltron, and

157

Thundercats. There was something in there, he was certain. How far away he felt from the place he thought his home.

What is home and how is the family? Who is blood and why's this man so freely unencumbered, yet so cambered. Smooth low riding too pumped and bat reset up third eye motion dew scoop dropt ops hood roots and a brand new handbag. You know we like to drive stuff around here.

"You whot?" said the eyes of Mademoiselle DeMariantnet.

Quite obfuscatorily sew. Make it buttons. Rear view peer through pure blue retinals; jet set vestigials of the haze flown high.

Space-time warp smash cut to: The Reckoning...

Roxy pulled her Jeep Cherokee into Catfish's driveway in Payson. He invited her and Les in for a drink and general relaxation. Just being back where the tall trees were was satisfying, the ones they pined for. There wasn't much unloading of gear, as all Catfish had brought was an attaché case of harmonicas and his small tube amp. The rest of the equipment was drum hardware and instrument cases, which would eventually end up at Roxy's place. All three musicians seemed pleased about extending the weekend a bit further. Catfish said he'd get out the good mugs. Roxy said she'd prefer the ugly mugs and that got an easy laugh. Everyone was already sat down in the living room and settled on couch and chair. There weren't any noises save the steady breath and heavy peace that descends upon you after returning home from a long stretch on the road. Roxy could sense the feeling and blood funneling back into her gas pedal foot.

They all agreed it was good that they had made the trip for the show, though felt better now for having completed the sojourn and docked base in their port of origin. Catfish looked for a moment like he was gathering up for a long draw on an old recollection, a deep pull out the sofa bed and get comfy. Then he fell back, leaned out, stretched and shook his shoulders collapsing fully into his recliner. "Mercy," said he.

"Your set last night was real solid. Was it how you expected?" Les asked Catfish.

"Singin' songs ain't science, man, it's more like magic. A lot more feel than formula," said the old man.

"Lightning struck a match and fried a fret fool," said Roxy.

"Most times, I try to be offstage, out of sight. It's less stress on your constitution. I'll get up now, once and again, but man I ain't made up for it full-time no more. Your all's bodies can survive that abuse, but my bones just won't have any of it. I used to be built to run on like this for weeks and months at a time. Now one day has probably put me out good," Catfish reflected.

"Aww, come on. Let's have a go at it again tonight. Re-party!" Les prodded.

"I told you, it's purnounct 'Rep-ar-tay'," Roxy told Les.

"Ooo, piano man. What I gave you, and look what I got back," said Catfish.

"WAH-wah. Fats Waller in the pit of hell," zanged Roxy.

"Thanks. I will take *that*, as a compliment," said Les.

"Ugh man, that breaks it all up. You're breaking it all up. In true repartee, or general smack talking, you can't just drop one bomb and walk away. Follow it up with something. It goes back and forth, as part of the game. Otherwise, it's just plain incivility, Hiroshima and goodbye. Does any of that make sense?" asked Roxy.

"Re-party! Rooksy Collins, Paul McCartney and buffalo wings," Les replied.

"Ooph, no. No re-party. Party is over," said Roxy.

"We've only just begun," sang Les.

"No bueno Karen Carpenter."

"Hey sues kreesto redempto, stand back here comes Charlie Musselwhite's Southside band. Nineteen sixty-seven, or sixty-six," said Catfish.

"How do you figure that?" Les asked.

"Our Beloved and Sovereign was a woodworking man," Catfish said.

The three unwound further and let loose talking about who'd fetch all the drinks. They waxed poetic on foods they craved and wished they had there on a platter. Les finally relented then pitched forward off the couch. He made his way drudgingly across the room and into the kitchen. There were always beer cans in the fridge. The strong liquor was kept in the freezer. Les saw a mostly gone bottle of vodka, and a near full fifth of Southern Comfort. He removed the chilled, frosty bottle of brown spirits. The label identified it as one hundred proof. He took three mugs from the cupboard, setting them on the counter. Two ice cubes dinked in each cup and Les poured about three fingers all around, unsure if these were the good, the bad, or the ugly mugs. After stowing the bottle, he grabbed one cup in each hand, pressing those two against the third, clamped and carried everything back to the living room. On the wall beside the kitchen door, Les saw a blinking red light indicating a new telephone message. He would tell Catfish.

Les entered the room focused primarily on not spilling any alcohol. He heard Roxy say, "But that's not on me."

"Now I don't mean to cast dispersions—" Catfish said.

"Do it, cast 'em, disperse away," Roxy told him.

"It's just that, at some point, you have to get rid of all the excuses. Face things head on," said Catfish.

"Recuse before you abuse," Les said, trying to ever be the monkey wrench as he set the mugs down on the coffee table amidst his friends.

"Try not to be unreasonable. Play your piece and be passionate. Excuses are shaky terrain," said Catfish.

In a loud faux-operatic tenor profundo scream Les bellowed, "Everyday it's one more thing, smacks me up so bold. Now I've gone off by myself, no excuses left to blow."

"Alright, everybody simmer down. Hand them drinks out before you make a mess," said Roxy.

"And why is everyone preaching at me all of a sudden? Prop 101, yoga say, Propaganda is propaganda is good or bad is a shady biz," said Les.

"Don't start on with the yoga man," Roxy warned.

The three retreated each to their icy mug of strong tasting stench. Enlivened hooch it hits your nose and warms the inside brush back, high and tight. Retaliatory torch the neck chin music fast fried cheese stickball and the first stoop step is home plate.

"It's rare you be conscious and totally happily blissful. Mostly it'll happen in the middle of a dream when you start flying or find some heavenly rapturous treat. There ain't enough hours in the day to do absolute nothin'," Catfish said.

"How you mean?" Roxy asked while all imbibed.

"There really aren't that many truly bad people. Most folks just have a rotten idea of what's funny and fair game," said Catfish, as he took a big breath and continued pontificating.

"An oh-mauzh to a montage, cinema floss and camouflarge; camels slog the channels barge the panel's

161

sergeant-at-arms marches darn the pararde root. Berry eye scream float by, the marshal second lining rolling flambeaux and preservation hail two jabs bands brass funneroles lay a body dim to rest. Rebirth in Algiers Point of the lost resort on Lake Pontchartrain's shore when the waters don't reside out NOLa's way. Crawdads crowded in the pot with the road's kill it potatoes party dons pretty down to clown up Tchoupitoulas and over to Saint Charles, North Rampart and Dauphine, plus near on all of what's in between. Shoot out ninth teen ought sixth ward inner Metarie-physical state of not minding the muther-uffn swamp air. Take a sip." Catfish finished his verbal mist saying something about sinners maybe pray more than the pious, excluding the Pope and upper management. At least if they have any sense they do, pray more.

"We're all sinners," said Roxy.

"Yes Miss Roxy, and how much sick can most men take before they just fall face down prostrate at the altar of something? Supplicate," said Catfish.

"Okay, so what are you trying to say?" asked Roxy.

"Thankful's all that I am," Catfish said.

"Good. Me too. Les, you alright?" Roxy said.

There was no music or television or radio noise and this encouraged peace, freedom of thought, and the basis for a lively comma slow-paced discourse, bona fide sampling.

"Ah, people," said Catfish. "I don't get it." Editorializing. "They're missing a great deal of what's at hand. Fingertips."

"You're buzzing, buzzed, you drunken cuz," said Rox.

"Amicably," Catfish poked, stoking the fire.

"Tell me what don't people understand?" asked Les.

Catfish told them something about breaking stereotypes and roads in Minnesota. Gave a miner a soda at a mini-seder and the dark invader bade him a vote of good confidence, man. Others are just bereft of belief, concept in conceived. A bass clef up one's sleeve, an arid zone of sweet tea, another brisk sip and relief. Release of deep seeded reeling dis ease.

"Honestly, if I can be that with you now," said the bass player for Dream Demonical.

162

Roxy was weighing whether she should risk an open heart. Narcissistic bearings spunly needing greasy gets the- uh, tension. The will starts the doubting second-guessing apprehensive window dressing, pick your chin up shoulders back; she took another swig and squinted slightly in her viren mind's condition, people's home was low the lighting sitch. Natch reack shin wanton satisfaction, movement jury's prudent ego's Judas sprite or Brutus. Ceasar sin or Jewess bluish blush and fluid rouge a flush, flew through and touched her wrist not much but such that nights is worth a strutch. Mince comet's cure her come to lean left on a chronic crutch: upon whuch witches clang. She clings to also spruce and pine-fruit apple acorn nuts, and what's she doin' now, a tradgic klutz in matters over minding sores on souls ka'latter. Batter up, duggin' in, bare the teeth get Hopi, link them sync and dine the meaty buried marrow truth and treasure there.

Everything was quiet. Condone the bone reliant sired shared. Fowling up her mind and clearing out her heart. And she wonders if they knows. Outside the cold air blows, winduhs rattle.

"Old man, was Alyssa looking like she knew what she was doing with that Izzy, or did she ever seem gone or without her head straight on?" Roxy said.

"I can tell you the only thing might benefit from some prayer is that machine they is traveling in," said Catfish.

He tipped up his cup, draining its last drops. Holding the mug in one hand around the top rim, he rumbled the tumbler, wiggled and clinked his mostly melted ice cubes around quickly for a second or two. Three fine it must've been. Half a set, go again. There are tries and regrets, wins, losings and bets. Bluff solid big streak blind stab bless it river.

Roxy envisioned an ideal scenario where Les and Catfish asked all the right questions. She'd be able to clear her conscience and unload her woes without risking injury to her fragile heart's carcass. She hated to cry or even tear up, as it had been drilled into her that this was weakness showing and is usually a marked sign of failure or cowardly retreat. She angered herself, inside criticizing her sniveling desire to

163

surrender, let go, release, and overflow. She breathed in deep and let out a heavy sigh. If she could only allow herself to tell Catfish that maybe she was a machine that could also benefit from prayer as well. Her left brain or right brain, whichever had the capacity to feel sympathy slash empathy, reminded her that Les would hang out if she even hinted his presence might be appreciated. She very well may be alone soon, faced with a lack of company. Louie and Lorraine would at least be up later, possibly to stay the night. So she could if she wanted to, put off fretting and find something instead to be happy about. It'd all no doubt be lies. She felt as though things were not so right. Is there no pride, solace, or comfort taken from the accomplishment of a task completed? Yes'm.

Breathing simple, she noticed Les fidgeting his hands' fingers. He was practicing rhythmic and melodic figures on invisible piano keys. Dumb calm Les. He caught Roxy's glare, froze as he sensed some pointless disapproval, and had no wish to complicate or coerce any further negative reaction. Smart kid he was, for his considerable youth; his relations told him and he took it as truth. Catfish said he'd really like some nice vermouth. No ways uncouth, Sundays vamoose: Duluth in nineteen sixty-two. Unstayed reboot, check-raise held suit what stakes, what's goot— the black jack booth. Roland eye in bad Cali's lined strewn with waist pieces hip shot from the dark passenger window. Shades drawn, Roxy slipped her sunglasses on. Slumped down as far as the couch cushion would allow. None of 'em felt like going nowhere anytime soon. Catfish started a quiet and low down croon. In the sweet by and by, sang a song about meat on a beautiful shore. Picnics and cakewalks saddled with altruistic rage. Self-defeating. Roxy wanted to sleep and Les thought she looked it. All were hanged over and pitched sideways under cast shadows overhead. They'd need to switch on a lamp, or else in a short time be left in pitch blackness. Surrounding no sound. Neither Puget nor any other, minus the pin drop ball peen spin stop needle pop vinyl waxen capture. Still shot, zero activity on the radar. Motion stature invisible wave of solemnity whooshed through the room's occupants. Cloud surfing shit kicker bootstraps loose and a skin quipper.

The beau ideal: to converse with profound intensity, sharing thoughts and feeling, achieving intimate rapport.

"Guys, I feel like dookie. Turd brained, ashamed and just plain phooey," said Roxy.

"Aww lady, come on. What's going on?" said Catfish. Then he raised his feet, and dropped them heaving forward adroitly, standing up good and tall.

"I don't know, it just doesn't feel right and steady," Roxy said.

"The work is done, relax. Bring it down," Catfish told her as he walked over to a wall, flicked a switch which activated an orangeish yellow glow, providing at least basic outlines and light for safe maneuvers. He entered the kitchen, hitting them lights too, hollering back out if does anyone want anything to eat? They mumbled no as Catfish opened the freezer, grabbing the bottle of Southern Comfort and elbowed the door closed.

"You have a message on your machine," Les shouted.

"That I do," he said to himself, walking over to the wall-mounted phone and pressed the button under the blinking red light.

"Hello, this is a message for Mister Elijah Frye, regarding your son, Vincent. Please call us at—" and the male voice listed a number with a seven zero two area code. Catfish zipped the tape in reverse to copy down the rest of the digits on a notepad with a pencil there for just such a purpose.

"702 is Vegas," Roxy called from the living room.

"Yeah, he was out that way for a big show's what he told me before we left yesterday. Oh, I hope they didn't get themselves into trouble," said Catfish.

"You gonna call them back?" Roxy asked.

"I'll have Twig ring 'em up when he gets here. He does better with all the yessir and no sir business. Plus, they didn't sound too urgent and who knows if they're even open this time of night on a Sunday," Catfish said.

"Alright, whatchu doin' with that bottle?" Roxy called, and he could see her head peeking up from the couch.

"Gonna drink it. So's we all don't feel like dookie," said Catfish.

"Hey-oh!" Les scrummed. "Have you a minute—To witness my discontent—Of darkness and the heavens bound together?" Followed by Roxy on a quick air drum fill ending with a stick on the hi-hat. They both kept on, "Eyes are two of them, neuron blasting pools. Mellow on the throne flown loud over the crowded." Les and Roxy had successfully musicked. Catfish stood perplexed at these childrens.

"At certain times in existence you two do present me with the heebees," Catfish said. This only broke Les and Roxy up more. A reference to the Bee Gees was made. Shadow Dancing Nineteen-hundred and Seventy-Eight.

"Any given moment his brain gets blown," Les said.

Everything kept multiplying, the laughs and joviality. Sat he, that Catfish in a void. They's all jus' sssssss tone.

Duh.

Chapter Twenty-Five • They Are All Our Martyrs

Truck and Boonz left Las Vegas numbly comatose. Exhausted from the scope of desolation, sour-brained and sore from loading, struggling to carry this weight of death that they shouldered. Boonz took the wheel and Truck right away told him they could switch whenever, so just say the word. Since then nobody had spoken.

The first hour was wretched. Stunned they sat in silence. It was difficult not to give into the anger brewing beneath the surface. Finally as the darkness outside set in, Truck decided to turn to the community CD case in search of comfort. The only thing that made any kind of sense right now was Green Day. He slid the disc into the deck, it turned for a few minutes and then Longview came around. They were reminded that music does offer some good, for all the crap that making it a living brought along. Green Day was basically a three-piece like the Syndicate was. Or had been when Sonny was around. Sonny ain't around no more. Tupac was also shot in Vegas a little over a year ago. Le Parish, as the sane would say, the bloody Crooks. Shoot, just this past March they did the Notorious Biggie Smalls with a drive-by in Los Angeles. Neither of them really had any say in the matter. Robert Johnson, Brian Jones, Selena, Doug Hopkins, and Mia Zapata were taken early. Miles Davis, Willie Dixon, and Richard Pryor passed on from heart failure. Freddie Mercury and Eazy-E lost out to the AIDS. Little Walter died premature from all types of shady practices. Some folks just don't get choices in this business. Cancer took Bob Marley and Bill Hicks. Others voluntarily feed the poison to themselves. Quiet deliberation. Infernal contemplation. Suicidal ideation, for some it's a hobby, a good way to pass a Tuesday afternoon. Cobain pulled his own trigger. Sonny had nothing. Not a damn chance. It was hard not to hate the whole of existence. Tre Cool came in after a silence, singing an acoustic song all by himself. With the distorted guitar, bass and drums gone in the mix, Truck could hear Boonz putting it to the Ford Econoline's engine. He peeked across at the speedometer, easily up over eighty-five.

"Let's not us go run into more cops," and Truck felt miserable for saying it. On the other hand it was a rational fear. That must count for something. Bradley from Sublime did his own dirty deed. That shit, heroang and addiction links you into Hendrix, Janis Joplin, Jim Morrison, Andrew Patrick Wood, Michael Hutchence, Shannon Hoon, Steve Clark, Kristen Pfaff, Bob Stinson, Stefanie Sargent, Jason Thirsk, GG Allin, Bon Scott, Keith Moon and John Bonham. John Belushi, River Phoenix, Chris Farley and Elvis also put in the work. Stevie Ray Vaughn, gone in a copter crash. Frank Zappa, prostate cancer. Jeff Buckley drowned in the Mississippi River. Plane crashes ended the lives of Patsy Cline, Ritchie Valens, Buddy Holly, The Big Bopper and most of Lynyrd Skynyrd. At that moment, Truck couldn't help but wonder if any part of Boonz's mind was aware of the precipice off to the right of the road. A typical short railing ran alongside the highway, a sad deterrent from the massive dark pit that could offer an answer to the pain that ails the fallen soul. To destroy and crush, like the insane urge to slug old ladies, or turn your car into oncoming traffic.

Truck switched out the CD in the stereo for more Green Day. Chronologically, Insomniac (1995) was the next album after Dookie (1994). He skipped it though, putting on Nimrod (1997), which just came out at the end of last year. The music started quickly with a barrage of eighth note snare hits as the guitars ripped in on the first track, Nice Guys Finish Last. Fuckin' ay. Sonny was like the nicest hardcore shredder he'd ever known. He should've been a contender. In his bones he was just good people. The best. He was a monstrously creative force, whether it was writing music or cooking a casserole. Dammit but the rage would not subside. Fucking Nevada cowboys.

"Man, this whole thing's like a right large Chinaman in my armor, you know?" Truck said, realizing he and Boonz were best off working together. They must remain on some basic kind of good speaking terms. Their target destination was the band's small cottage in Flagstaff. It functioned as a rehearsal space slash stash house where they all had a bed. Maybe they each had an extra shirt, of course a communal tube of toothpaste. They filled the gas tank before leaving Las Vegas, so that should get them all the way home. The two remaining members of Dystopian Squalor passed through Kingman and were now facing a buck-fifty straight east on Interstate Forty.

From his periphery, Truck could see Boonz staring out the windshield. He was gripping the steering wheel, stiff and intransigent. It was some sort of dance, rebellion against reality, refusal to come to terms. He had at least two solid hours to hang in this limbo provided by the freeway. Untethered from actualization. Fettered in consternation. Squared in bleak Czar station. Deceives reincarnation with a savory sweet libation. Boonz lifted a bottle from the floor beside his seat. The lights of the dash panel illuminated his brow and the bridge of his nose. He took a long pull off the forty-ounce. The dirty sour sloshes, it swashes and swished around in bliss. Incontinent, indulgent endocrine blend with insipid O'Doul's-esque odour. Subordinate ordinance with which to get bombed. Tanked. Sherman and Peabody cleanse. The pilot barreling down the empty interstate, mortar fires the pistons in flight, spark away the time flees, shells littering left and right. There's no turning back, on into the frontline this weary battle occupied territory, a couple warn bucket seats rolled across the rock they rode.

Why we kindly thank almighty heaven do abide.

"Boonz man, you got a mean, mean way about your ways and means. You like a pitbull fightin' in a tight pair of baggy jeans," Truck took a stab in the dark.

"What is it you want? Just let me drive," Boonz said.

"The Green Day is good though, right?" asked Truck.

"The Green Day is good," said Boonz. Truck considered this to be something in the vein of progress.

Now he (Truck) was antsy, so he rummaged around the cab for something to gnaw on. On the stereo came one of his favorite lyrics. The vilest conglomeration of four letter words ever uttered. Death, love and libel. It made his crusty insides crack a smile. His hand came up with a thin plastic pouch. It was Sonny's jerky, with some scraps still left in the sealed bag.

Truck fetched out about a three-inch piece of meat, tore it in half with the right side of his bite. It tasted saucy, no doubt the label boasted of authentic barbecue flavor, some legit brand like Bull's Eye or KC Masterpiece. Sonny was generous with his time and attention. He shared his energy, mostly led people down the righteous path, and all that utha mutha jazz. Truck had his first questioning thought about what is closure and how could he get his hands on some.

Shut the blinds on my left pinky toe, into the darkness drove. Vicissitudinal wind speed sign waves flash mileage and the splash of reflection from markers lain out in the black lined white steady spine, flyin'.

The sanctuary that the night supplied was of little comfort to the fractured beings burrowing the tunnel straight on through the natural expanse. Fucking get home already, though they weren't stopping for shit. The music caught Truck's ear as a trumpet and trombone were messing around over an upbeat circus feel. Old time party jam sped thoughts up. Felt odd. Nothing is in the right place. A wish there might be such thing as a take back. Do over. Rewind. Billie Joe spoke of a morning princess, scantily clad. Misdirected energy. The song ended, Truck was relieved. A thick and deliberate acoustic guitar plucked a lick. Pause, and a solid picking pattern yielded a steady driving pulse. The lyrics came in, simple and sincere. Some bit of emoting bubbled down deep. He couldn't, wouldn't explore or entertain even the idea of getting in touch, digging in. Truck knew he'd start talking to Boonz if he went down this road, asking questions that would only turn him away more. It was too risky right now. Truck had to let go a little tension.

"You want me to take over?" Truck asked.

"Ask again in an hour," said Boonz, after a slight hesitation. "You know this means we're off the tour."

The beautiful unknown: ultimately golden. Truck thought he understood what poignant meant. No idea how to spell it though. Antidisestablishmentarianism keeps Rome the fuck out of Provo, and Jesus all up in the Constitution of the United States. Amurcan engine nudity keeps the competition stiff;

170

stifled, automatic rifle on the range with red tracers all the while light filled the night field. Torched photons shoot halogen missiles graze the hair razor triggers the road red rad burnin' barren calls in bogeys up ahead. Down on the front edge, in Boonz's mind every vehicle on the approach was a deadly game of chicken up against him. Drive me a Murkeree, flat out at a cliff above the sleeping pits of hell. Dead man's tales don't tell you no. How much say do you give a damaged psyche if a dark demented stranger do you wrong, side your swipe, suicide fake over. Even the thought and change in wind pressure makes him at the wheel close with death. Again. Just like Sonny was erased. What was his middle name? Vincent 'Something' Frye. Things you thought you knew or didn't ever stop to learn.

What's the play in times like these? How long, how often, and how do we do in remembrance of he? Say words at a gravesite, life etched in quartzite. Nothing's gonna feel right, what can bring me down? A pack of flocking pet vultures, circles round the sepulcher, the candle lit in honor of the souls. A rising temple flourish hearts alive, with flutter freshly bled and fried in butter breaking bread we line the gutters holding signs that beg, uttering: 'Will wake for feed.' Willing to wait for freedom. Got a right to mind bend, bug pick and eat 'em.

"What are you mumbling over there?" Boonz said.

"We're all being plant food and fertilizer," Truck said.

"Thanks, sunshine. Get more music, something faster."

Truck snatched the CD case off the center console, leafed through the pages using the small traces of reflected light to make out which albums he was looking at. Illmatic by Nas, Sonny played that often en route to shows. Ten and Vs. from Pearl Jam; Core by Stone Temple Pilots. Faster, something faster, BAM! Punk in Drublic, NOFX (1994), he slid it out of the sleeve, retrieving Nimrod from the player. The loading mechanism took hold and the circle began spinning, reading rhythm rocket rampant distorted twitching guitar spit thick, heavy, loud, and fast out the speakers in the front door mounts, echoed by the empty walls back in the rear. Floored. Enter four bars of eighth note snare, building doubled by pulsing bass

171

fed into the system with rapidly smacking kick drum over and over driven forward under fierce scratching visceral rhythmic cranking smashed Boonz in the back of the head. Gave it to him something good.

'Talk to me like you know I got a shotgun,' his dad would say. 'Fuck you,' sixteen year-old Boonz would tell his old man. 'That's a start,' he'd tell his boy like it was a game. Like this was good and normal behavior in the ways of father-son communication. Get your kid so scared and mad. Then after the shit goes down you feel like you were definitely one of the more competent parents. So yeah, Boonz had plans on talking to his own kid, if he ever has one. He had something like a steady girl in Flagstaff. She had a solid job and loved to wonder and what if about future things like kids, locations to live, plus crazy goal-oriented suppositions. She always secretaried and administratively assisted really well no matter where she was put. Boonz had done his own what ifs about Esther playing some role as manager, but what does that count for now with no guitarist or singer. What if he (Boonz) played guitar instead of bass? He acknowledged that with his current chops he could maybe play punk, but he was a long way off from fronting a metal band. He could stay on bass and takeover vocals and find someone to plug in at guitar. He was seeing that he had options ahead, decisions that could be made. In a sense he was rightful heir, next in line. He just wanted Dystopian Squalor Syndicate to live on. Felt it was bigger than just Sonny. Even though it was his idea and vision originally, Sonny's that is. Boonz was older than everybody. Was that good? Is Truck the asset here? Will he want to go off somewhere, or just hang it up?

Now along with this rotten mood, Boonz wondered if he could trust his mind with such an inquisitory onslaught. Maybe he shouldn't make any judgments, or instead go find some acid in Flag and checkout.

It was he in the road with his fiddle tucked directly under his jaw, jammin' with a smile, shouting nonsense. Longing to detach for a length of laborious trail, lift off into the night. Forget. Be forgotten, flail without bondage or binding.

"You okay to take the wheel?" Boonz said.

"Yeah man, of course," Truck replied.

Boonz pulled over to the roadside, shifted to park and slid off the seat into the back of the van. "Thanks," he told Truck, who popped into the driver's seat. After buckling his seatbelt, he put the van in gear and drove off. He felt something knock against his foot. It was Boonz's empty bottle. Truck kicked it away from his seat and grabbed another chunk of jerky. He could sure go for some real food, a substantial meal instead of bits and pieces. He thought about Chinese takeout, Oreo cookie blizzards from Dairy Queen. Stuffed crust pizza. Sleep. What might tomorrow be like? Truck never knew any dead people, let alone saw them die. Battle cries, fight back lies like it'll all be fine. His hands were supine on the bottom curve of the steering wheel, gently guiding the old brown van, flying pure as the straightened arrow. Crooked feather on the wind, guarding rail slight refractive bends the pitching shadow's shallow current over the night's trails. Bats and a slat moon on the rise, sliver size.

A silent Boonz was in the back making Truck feel half abandoned, but not really. It was just a feeling and everybody knows those don't count. What does count? What is important and what's fodder? What's something he oughta not let loose, the canon's juice with natural enzymes, intravenous divination sum blind traveling bandwidth. Interstate north forty backwoods chop the top off the Grand Canyon, slackwards rolling down the rock faced jiggered, scarred and mortal haggard nostril flared they flagged her cross the way. Chew tobacca spit klong, unincorrigible diphthong; brutal rush with a neutral touch to the hidden oracle in his left temporal lobe. Was that the future or a suture come apart, the cruise controlled the lonely fart; if a finger's pulled alone in there would anyone cheer it? Three toots for flat you lends their ears four cheers. Lift a cheek in honor of the fall and soldiers spring up soils the wintergreen smelling tree shaped air freshener on the rearview.

Pee you stink tooth, geek proof me roars into the soul. The ayes have it and the bleat goats on. Baaaaad juju, voodoo mama said she saw a body on the river float, bye.

Chapter Twenty-Six • Surfboards Up Mofos

January 25, 1998

Izzy followed Daphne's directions. They never strayed far from the smell of ocean air. After making good time on Interstate Five, they exited the San Diego Freeway at the Mission Avenue loop in Oceanside. Continuing west they came to Rotary Park and Benchwobble said there was a pier and good sand. Izzy and Alyssa agreed to drop in at the beach before going anywhere near the house that the Dirk and Daphne'd been talking up since coming aboard. The wheels on the bus went round and rolled slowly coming to a street running horizontal to the shoreline called the Strand. It was said there were limitless such roads across the globe. Miss DeMariantnet told how this particular one stretched all up and down the coast, the pier divided it in two. Revise and conquer. Six of one, Hoffa doesn't the otter. See of wise guise in the ocean. Made mend, weed hemp leaves trace amounts to nothing much along the lines of foot traffic, flipper rovers unseen in and around the structural supports beneath the pier.

There were youths out and drunken adults crab walking the sideways, even on past where it ends. Izzy found parking in a lot just south of the main concourse and kilt the bus engine, the crank pulley spinning to a rumbly halt.

"We could still make Haight while the sun don't shine," said the Dirk offhand.

"What's that?" Alyssa asked.

"A reference to the Bay and a midnight run's my guess," Izzy said.

"The breakers break her off once nicer by the boardwalk," said Daphne.

They'd all contributed. The bus was secured. Izzy and Alyssa headed towards the fishing pier. Daphne DeMariantnet gave her arm to the Dirk of Benchwobble who undertook a leisurely waddle. The walk was calm and covered lightly with only a small whip of wind from off the water. Some grit grated on the sand on which they strode.

"Mmm, tasty like a raindrop," Daphne held her hands out offering an open palm to the sky in supplication. A hint of gentle mist was about the place. With the blind man anchored to her right elbow crook, it was fantastic the freedom of motion she enjoyed without flinging or jostling His Grace. In fact she was dancing, forward at about two miles per hour. Not that Izzy or Alyssa were watching, but the Dirk had a great smile upon his face. Real close to her breath, Daphne sang a rhythmic melody, full of about twenty-eight nahs. Then said, "say it Dirk. Please, for me."

"Huh. She's got the look," Benchwobble said very reserved. They both chuckled, which caught Alyssa's attention, though the couples were a solid twenty paces apart.

"They're singing. I think they really care for each other," said Alyssa.

"They're partnered up. That's a way to do it," said Izzy.

"Don't they make such an interesting pair? Yeah, they are rough around the edges but it's sweet," Alyssa said.

"What in the world can make a brown eyed girl turn blue? When everything I'll ever do I'll do for you," Daphne sang to Dirk, "And you go—"

"La la la la la, she's got the look."

Up ahead, Alyssa spun around and walked slash strode backwards holding Izzy's right hand with her right. They'd merged onto the walkway that led to the pier's entrance. While Izzy looked out on the ocean, Alyssa watched the Dirk and Daphne cross a road and make their way onto the path. The two girls caught one another's gaze. Daphne gave a finger wiggle wave that was immediately reciprocated with a smile and wave from Alyssa who then twirled back to face forward.

The lamps were lit that lighted the pier, both sides like a jungle trail lined with torches leading to some shrine at the base of an ancient temple. There were palm trees faintly glowing in the night. They could see a wide ramp leading up to the raised boardwalk.

"Loving is the ocean, kissing is the wet sand," and Daphne dipped her head towards the Dirk and she squeezed his hand coercing one more, "She's got the look."

This was one of many games they shared. Not all were song based, but this one seemed quite apropos for the current setting. Izzy was stopped and Alyssa had removed her sneakers, now burrowing her feet ankle deep into the sand. The Dirk could see only a faint fading light source and so kept his eyelids shut, taking in the scene with his other senses. Daphne had been to the beach earlier today, though this area in specific she considered a sacred region. She was moved and in extraordinarily high spirits.

"They have a restaurant out there at the end of the pier," she said proudly as her and Dirk arrived on the sidewalk beside Izzy.

"You are sure working your toes down in there," said Izzy to Alyssa.

"Some days don't require socks."

"And some days shoes won't suffice. Boots."

"Oh yeah? Aren't those generally reserved for cowboys and cowgirls?" Alyssa asked.

"Shitkickers. Military too. The working man's—but I guess they also extend into everyday fashions," Izzy said.

"Ohs ma toes fills sews goooood," and she threw a shoe and stuck Izzy in the left thigh.

"Thanks Miss Alyssa, may I have another?" Izzy said, turning the proverbial cheek.

"My feet, AKA the proof. The sand is AKA the pudding. I.e. carry the C, the pudding is infinite, washed by the proof of a hundred thousand years," said Alyssa.

After a pause, Alyssa stood waiting for some reaction. It was like the sound of a Wild West pistol cocked back, but silent. Just the space hung, the timing had elapsed. Izzy looked up and past the girl at the distant dark waters. He was kind of hoping to swallow the moment and let its tension dissipate. Alyssa Rose looked at him and the Dirk and Daphne who smiled patiently.

"Is this you trying to not call me on my bullshit in front of company?" Alyssa asked.

Still Izzy stared out at the ocean, not tense but strangely. He nodded and told the girl yes, he did not wish to call her out,

176

very terse and plain. The Dirk sensed some slight element of discomfort and felt moved to help.

"Oh, well don't do anything different on our account. We're happy to just hang about, and stay out of the way," said the blind man.

"Yeah man, and we appreciate it," Izzy told him.

The dispossessed tertiaries were out, some predators, some pray for deliverance safely through to the next morning unscathed. There were two towers a ways down the pier, one on each side, connected by a catwalk with a sign on the shoreside. Izzy bent down, picked up the projectile sneaker, flipped it up in the air and caught the thing after several rotations like it was what people do. Alyssa hopped over beside him, plucking the shoe from his grasp.

"Don't you want to put those on, to walk the pier?" asked Izzy.

"I was planning on hitting that shit raw!" Alyssa got a laugh from the Dirk and Daphne. Izzy told the Rose it was a good one.

"Birds be crappin' though, look out," Izzy warned.

The Dirk let go a deep chuckle, sort of a mixture between Santa's ho-ho-hos and Jaba's moany dirge of deep pleasure.

"Crappin' indeed," said Dirk. "Look out!" With bells on the two couples crept on and through a small car lot, onto a ramp, which once scaled set them at the beginning of a raised pier extending forth into the swushing tide.

They started; soon Alyssa went careening starboard and out onto an extension, peering over the rail to the shoreline below. She saw the breaking waves in the reflected lamplight of the promenade that she hung off of. When the waters receded she could make out the sand, and a shell or two rippling the film of sea settling still, before once more the waters broke forth and filled the floor with cresting current.

It was your standard oceanic view. See a scene set a walk a long pier, illest tree us strucks her. Whisked her window unto three dimension'll last time traveled this close to ad infinitum. Even sum level near wents the green meadowed forest. Natch aural bay noir sounds clear and flowing. Derivative. Done.

177

Folk being folk. Lies from the pit of hell and all damnation. After the storm derides, post-humorously when the laughter passes. The novelty of earth took her fancy for a turn.

"Man, the beach. Just like tropical islands," said Alyssa.

"It's the coast. Where the land turns to sand, and meets with the deep blue," Izzy replied.

They continued further down with Alyssa hugging the edge, slipping her sneakers on because she had in fact noticed more than one spot of bird droppings. Closer now the tower's sign read, "Ruby's." Daphne said that was the diner way down at the end of the walkway. Alyssa felt almost otherworldly as if she were approaching a portal, where the winds and mist and sounds and smells were the ancillary effects of interplanetary time warps; smash cut to the other Rose on the other side on her own alternate journey, like a pleasant ride at the amusement park. She abandoned this absurd dual-reality for the chance she might climb up in the towers before her. Daphne said if she remembered right, you usually couldn't get in unless there is somebody with a key. Or you got a ladder and scaled up there, which she knew happened only on rare occasions. Izzy told her the Broncos were newly crowned World Champions, and how that easily ranked as worthy of a trip up the towers. Daphne agreed it was, though maybe not so much here in Oceanside. Besides, there weren't any ladders handy. That was good enough for everyone, then Alyssa asked Izzy if she could get up on his shoulders. He said to just leave it, but she said no and it was only to give the Ruby's sign one good smack. After a bit of climbing, supporting, holding and balancing they'd gotten stable. She stood her feet on his shoulders, inched out and over and SMACK. She whacked the bottom of the 's' in Ruby's, yelled 'ouch' and immediately had Izzy bring her down. She slid slowly and landed in Izzy's arms. It was a thing meant to happen all the way through. In her mind she was trying to distinguish between this being a vacation, or had she made a more permanent change to her lifestyle? She wondered if this was temporary, and if so when would it end? That can't be the way to approach things, only worrying about their ending. She tried to insert her consciousness back into the moment, realizing she was now being carried down the pier. The present was so much nicer than her angsty paranoia, so she rested her head on Izzy's shoulder, listening for his heartbeat. She felt his embrace, his strength and arm around her back, the other firmly clutched her upper thigh.

The two couples made quite the contrast. The Dirk helplessly dragged half a step behind Daphne, while Izzy cradled Alyssa effortlessly in an easy squeeze. Upon first glance, both sights were sweet and a mind could weave stories endless. Our heroes two looked like America, beautiful and bold. The blind man and his keeper struck a much more European look, some eastern block pairing of necessity where gender and status mattered less, with functionality at the forefront. Either way the foursome strolled on unaffected deeper out over the shallow waters. Alyssa Rose opened her eyes, seeing lights out in the distance. Ships or gypsy skiffs adrift, spelunkin' for sunken treasure trunks and rambunction, with passion in the fashion of sinking song, plinking stones skipped gently whipped with hoots hollered echoing eerie.

"Do you think there's people surfing?" Alyssa asked, raising her head slightly feeling it'd be too much to have Izzy carry her over to the ledge to look. She did not want to misuse any sway or diminish her place in his good graces. Just then she was set down bum first on the boardwalk's ledge, a bit off balance she clung to Izzy's shoulders as he slid between her legs. Alyssa's back was to the waves, she held his face to her chest while he wrapped his arms around her body, they were linked and nearly as one. He closed his eyes, and she saw the future. He breathed in her warmth. She felt his exhale buzzing. His "Mmmm," spread into a low growl that shook them both and she writhed, squeezing him harder with everything in her power.

The Dirk and Daphne continued slowly, surely down the pier, entrenched in their own machinations. Would they encourage Izzy and Alyssa to join on at the community, maybe travel further up the coast? Daphne asked if they might be well off traveling east, and what's realistic with their limited funds?

She wasn't above tricks and had put in work as recent as a week ago. The Dirk considered her a saint for the sacrifices she made on their behalf. It wasn't unusual for him to wait outside motel rooms or within earshot of parked cars while she would do the deed. The Dirk and Daphne's connection went far deeper than simple sexual orgasms. They were each other's guardian angels in a committed symbiosis. She was unafraid and courageous, born in Montreal, raised in Baltimore. He, Benchwobble, had the lexicon of Kentucky, the lilt of Looziana, by way of Mississippi, where that Jackson is.

"No Daph, I tell you that's much more than posturing. That's oblivion. They are oblivious," Dirk said.

"You want to see if I can pick you up like that?" said Daphne.

The two laughed at the thought, but in Daphne sparked an urge to test her strength. The Dirk was a meager five foot eight, maybe one-forty after a big meal. Daphne might've had an inch on him, but she was sturdy, fit and durable. And challenges, she lived for those, a chance to dare fate and prove her worth.

"Let me lift you up," Daphne said.

"Oh, let's not," replied the Dirk.

"I feel so strong, all through my body," said Miss DeMariantnet.

"Please, let's just stay calm," Benchwobble's voice wavered.

"Trust me. I will not let you down—" She turned towards him, chose a basic fireman's carry, bent over putting her shoulder to his stomach, bracing at her knees and pressed up raising the Dirk, holding securely the back of his legs. She stood tall, gaining balance by widening her stance.

"Hooo-ey, don't drop me woman!" yelled the Dirk who didn't quite know what to do with his arms. So he flailed and clenched at Daphne's shirt, back, and butt region.

"Hold on Your Grace," Daphne warned and began a slow spin at a very conservative pace.

"Oh no," said the Dirk as he realized his orbital rotation. "This is no good, please. Daphne, please."

180

"I'll just take it easy. But try and not wiggle too much."
She arrived at some mild pre-established tempo gently walking
with her feet baby stepping to the beat-ch. Then way down
low from his belly grew a groan deep and steady toned mellow,
"Ooohhh." The fellow flew around though floundered fisht in
the misht did abound, finally got a hand on that round
backside, having a whale of a time. The long droning 'Oh'
was bumped up into a woo-woo-woo as Daphne put in a slight
up and down element, that gave the Dirk a rhythmic pressure
against his abdomen. She slowed the spin down with the Dirk
still woo-wooing as Daphne placed him feet on the ground,
holding him steady to recover.

Izzy and Alyssa remained intertwined with muscles taut
and bodies burrowed up against the railing. The Dirk and
Daphne both took seats on the ground, leaning up against a
small kiosk on the side of the pier. There's worlds and then
there's this their world, inside and apart from what is without.
Baby d'you take me to be your webbid whispers on the
amphibolous winds or sterling tributaries longings listed,
ambiguous mystery trimmings? As them lemmings rubbing
ambidextrous tender all-in Rose's nipples prim unsober anti-
ambivalent in the very least. More overheated gland secreted
beg repeat and clinch the freedom of release. Izzy thought to
mount a full on assault to love and cherish, til death and perish
won't they part, for nothing now not ever or in this instant.

"You know, I want to *be* something," said Alyssa.

"I do. You know, I want to *do* somebody," Izzy squeezed
her tight.

"Gross," she told him. "We at the beach, man. Eye aino
beach sand." Alyssa was crazed, not making any kind of sense.
No kin to any lack of chival-rinse; lost iniquity and inner
scents. Feral moan. Fever moon on a Sunday night living.

Subtle subterfuge and shrapnel lining winter's brood with
parts colliding. Danger springs and snared entrapment on the
limbs of them they're dining. Hungry. Satiate. Satisfied. The
two played through all the way down the pier. Took time.
Shared space. At the end of their trek was Ruby's Diner just as
promised. You can even see the restaurant from way back at

the start of the boardwalk, its entire length being lit. The diner had at least two stories. The building was wide and pale blue from the night. Shadows and light played from off the yellow bulbs. There was room to move and walk a full three hundred sixty degrees around the building, with a clear view off into the deepest blue sea and beyond. The splash of waves hitting the pier's legs down below dominated the soundscape. The boy and girl would talk and then sit in silence. Minds raced and eyebrows raised. Eyes glazed, caught contact out of the periphery or dead on stern 'em down. It was pleasant enough.

On their way back in, Izzy and Alyssa picked up with the Dirk and Daphne who had had sufficient rest and recovery from their big to do. They all made their way to the shore, taking time to remove all footwears to tip a toe in the sand and surf. Izzy asked Daphne how far off the house was from where they stood. She said it was not even a mile south, that they could take The Strand down the coast, then Wisconsin Avenue east to Tait Street. Hook a right and over a block to Hayes Street, there it was on the corner of Tait and Hayes.

For sure there would at least be somewhere safe to park. Access to a kitchen and bathroom and the inside space itself. Izzy said thanks and he was sure when it came to it, the arrangements would do fine. And then for no good reason Izzy questioned his commitment and motivation. Was Alyssa purely debauch and indulgent escape? He had options and little to no overhead if he found a desirable place to stay put. He also had a job offer in Denver with his uncle. His brother told him there was always a couch at his apartment in Colorado Springs. That was less alluring. Is staying on the road realistic? Maybe yes if there was a destination at the end of it all. Or no, is that the whole idea, to go, go and go even further? Disappear, live the junkie life, Bramboles and a Canterbury wife.

"What do I need to know that you haven't let on about yet?" Alyssa asked Izzy as they stood in the chilly surf and made big thoughts. He did not answer. The Rose took note of how leverage was an actual thing. She did not worry. She embraced mystery and grabbed Izzy's palm in hers.

"Sometimes I think I should just go somewhere and, wait—Have I told you this before?" Izzy asked.

"About writing? Yes, but go on, give it to me again."

After a beat, and with some enthusiasm, Izzy said: "A some wrongs!" But if it were to be spelled as he delivered, it'd be 'A SUM WRAWNGZ.' It wasn't a joke, and it wasn't a funny. It was kind of a line, and some part truth. Said the butcher to the cow. The girl thought there was indeed something to it.

Izzy and Alyssa told Daphne, 'fine let's see this crash pad.' They got back to and loaded in the bus. Windows down, system up, that's the way we like to crup. Creep, crawl by the cobweb wode the ways eyed to the next episode.

Miss DeMariantnet gave them specific ground rules for the house. These came down to don't make sudden movements, and warnings of at least one bird who lived on the premises, clipped wings so it often walked on the floor. There would either be an empty ghost town vibe, or a party brewing with lights and sounds, bottles passing the rounds; the tribe tripping. Upon arrival, there was a dim crystal glowing without any protectorate beside the white front door. Tall indoor artificial foliage lined the outside front wall.

"Around here we call it the Tait," said the Dirk.

"Who calls it that?" asked Alyssa.

"Us, them, people," the Dirk replied.

"No they don't, nobody does. He jokes," said Daphne.

Miss DeMariantnet went straight to the doorknob and tried it then shook her head. She looked under the doormat, around the upper frame for a key.

"You don't think you could just knock or ring the bell?" Izzy said.

"It's best if we slip in. Make no fuss," Daphne said, lifting up some of the plants. She reached into what should be soil and on the second try came out with a key, which then unlocked the door. Alyssa wanted to make use of the facilities. Daphne told her she'd point out the restroom once she set the Dirk up in the parlor. Izzy took a seat, put his feet up, and started to get a feel for the place. It was a ghost town. Daphne switched on a lamp. There was an empty birdcage on a table near a cutout of a wall that looked into the kitchen. The ladies went down a hall. The Dirk told Izzy that this bird they got here could speak some.

"Can it fly at all, with clipped wings?" asked Izzy.

"Daphne tells me it hops real well, can do short bursts of flight. Not sure if I have met this one. But you know," said the Dirk, sitting up on the edge of a recliner.

From the dark corners came a clicking sound, and a beastly pterodactyl-esque scrawk that echoed, and then vanished just as quickly.

"I can't even tell where that came from," said Izzy.

"Should be in the next room over here behind me." The Dirk motioned towards the birdcage adjacent room, which also had access to the hall and the rest of the abode. Izzy asked if Dirk had been here before and was told that he could not say for certain. The shadows were still thick, as the small desk lamp illuminated little.

"Surfboards up mofos," followed by several chirpish clicks and flutter.

More listening and the Dirk said, "Yes?"

There was a small clatter. "One eight seven," sang the voice from somewhere.

"Equals sixteen," said Dirk. "Pair of eights, double infinity. Quad fours."

Izzy was hearing, watching, waiting. Looking for connectivity and logic in this random nonsense.

"Murder death kill, RAWK!" Menacingly.

The Dirk had it all come flooding back over him. "Of course. Many birds I've met. This bloak can and will dish it out good," the old man was speaking up and projecting.

"Stanislas my boy, how have you been?" shouted Benchwobble.

"Murder death kill!" from the bird with renewed vigor.

"Yes, kill indeed. And how is Suzanne?" the Dirk retorted, snickering.

Izzy had no idea what was going on. It was either very funny, or unnervingly terrifying comma disturbing.

"So you two know each other?" Izzy asked.

"As I have said, this is the Tait. That cad in the kitchen is Lord Stanley. He says he's got nothing but good intentions," said the Dirk.

Izzy felt like he was in a battle of wits with the drunken town philosopher. Good fun. Dumb. Daphne came back out with Alyssa in tow. She (Daphne) told the Dirk to leave the bird alone so as he wouldn't get riled. To Izzy she said they were more than welcome to lie out on the couches. He said thanks, but they would be fine out in the bus. Either way, Daphne said, you saw where the key was. To Alyssa she said that she hoped to see them tomorrow, and that if she needed any necessaries, her and the Dirk would be in the first room on the right side of the hallway.

"Murder death kill!" again, loudly from the bird.

Alyssa said nothing but gave Izzy a frightening cringe, and mouthed, 'Let's go.' They headed back out to the transporter, as Daphne called 'Good night,' behind them. The evening felt early and so the two set out to walk to the beach. Seems about right for a couple such as them. There was always love and laughter. It was natural and noticeable. Izzy felt it his duty to watch for obstacles. Maybe the slightly ominous dread he had was just good old red-blooded North American vigilance and concern. Just like Washington on the Potomac, Lincoln on the penny, or Cassius Clay on the verge of Islam and immortality.

Chapter Twenty-Seven • Here Enters a Realization

Louie and Lorraine sat side by side on the front bench seat of the old Dodge station wagon as it barreled north towards Payson. Twig and Moe were tucked in the back with stacks of drums and bags of cables and cases of instruments. The large gear, kick drum, speaker cabinet and amplifier heads were in the far back cargo space. Louie had his right arm stretched out on the seatback behind his girl. The windows were cracked and the air in circulation was cold and crisp with the scent of pine and mountain.

"Yeah man, I saw your brother play back when they had to sneak him into gigs because he was like only nineteen." Louie was talking to Twig about one of Sonny's earlier groups, where he was one of two guitars and hadn't yet started singing.

"That was Underdog Overlord, right?" Moe put in.

"They were more punk, aggro-maniacal but still tight. Good drummer. Twig you were probably in junior high or something," said Louie.

"I was playing. Act like I don't know what's what," Twig wouldn't take any shit.

"Hey, if you have half of what Sonny's working with, there you go. Roxy already told me you can hang. She just can't tell you that or that nasty ego biz might start up," Louie said.

"Yeah, I heard enough stories about the woes of talent." Twig had, from his Pop and others.

It was getting on near 2100 hours. They would drop Twig and some gear at his house in town, and then Moe would guide them out to Roxy's. His bike was there and he was ultimately responsible for the remaining equipment. It'd been a good Sunday with the Super Bowl and the feeding they all got from Lorraine. She was excited for this trip, small though it may be. In a way it was her reward for the time she put in being a gracious hostess. Benevolence come full circle.

"Homeruns is rare kid, ain't everybody can hit 'em. And grand slams? Forget about it," said Louie.

"What man? That makes like zero kind of sense," Twig challenged.

186

This train of logic was indicative of the trip so far.

"And sometimes you know who though? Randy Travis," said Moe.

"Ooo, he's nice. What do you think of Dwight Yoakam? You know he was in that movie last year," said Lorraine.

"Yeah, he's alright. You know Randy Travis shows up on Matlock every now and then," said Moe.

"Isn't Matlock for old people?" Lorraine asked.

"No baby," cut in Lou. "Matlock is for everybody."

Them Bones by Alice in Chains was at a light blare on the stereo. Twig only wanted to get home and static. He could've spent this whole weekend working on his truck. Now he would be back exactly as he was before. Stuck. With a list of tedious diagnostic checks he'd have to run to figure out why the Chevy Tahoe had quit on him. He was coming away with sixty bucks, which was his cut from the Rhythm Room gig. That money could possibly cover the repair costs for his truck as long as it didn't need some pricey component. Could just be a loose connection in the ignition circuit. He wasn't sure he wanted to get into the steering column. He could test the starter. Up until now he'd just given it a good shake and jiggle. Once he gets the Tahoe going he won't have to be dependent on hippy vans and know-it-all bass players. Roxy ain't all that bad, but still. Plus his Pops has appointments and errands he needs rides for. Twig still had some resentment towards Sonny, because of he's hardly ever around and kind of bailed on the family, but who cares. Twig would probably do the same if he had the chance.

They hit Payson and Twig directed Louie through a few turns, then pointed out Roxy's Jeep, telling him to pull into the driveway of the house it was parked out front of. The wagon's passengers emptied and stretched, while Twig walked around the vehicle to grab his gear and be done. Moe stood by Louie and Low-rain, who were both saying how much nicer it felt here. Moe nodded. Twig carried his four-by-ten cabinet to the front door and set it down, returning to the Dodge. He grabbed his guitar case and amplifier head, heading back across the front yard.

"That's everything Lou. The rest goes out to Roxy's. She is probably inside if you all want to come in," Twig said setting the amp head on the cabinet, turning the doorknob, pushing it open.

Louie was shutting the back of his Sierra wagon when he heard voices from inside the house and music playing somewhere in the background.

"Hey now, what's this come washed up along the riverbank?" Roxy called out upon exiting through the front door. She gripped one hand each side of Twig's cabinet, dragged it easily across the home's threshold, and then popped back out.

"Rox," said Moe as she slid-skipped-skid over near the wagon's nose, kicking tires on her way.

"How was the drive?" she asked Lou. The night was very dark.

"Easy and nice," answered Louie.

"Don't the cold air make you feel alive, like breathing it in is more real and substantial?" Low-rain said aloud tucked up next to Louie. She had on a denim jacket with her extremities tucked inside the front pockets.

"It's underniable," said Moe.

"Do you mean undeniable?" asked Low-rain.

"No. Under-niable. Less than deny able, can't do it. Not worth trying," Moe told the group.

"What are you talking about, Moe?" said Roxy.

"He was doing it most of the trip up," Louie told her.

"Make sense, hey. Be normal," Roxy said as Twig emerged from the house.

"Yeah Moe," said Twig. "Let Rox preach on normal at you; crazy tattooed woman all slappin' that bass for a living. Tell us about normal."

"I got my shit together. We did the show," said Roxy.

"Glory, glory tell it on the mountain," sang Twig.

"Everybody here's got their shit together, Rox. We all stand victorious, yada yada, we yabba dabba did it," Moe said injecting his energy into the air.

"Yeah, did your Pop tell you about Sonny's message?" Roxy said to Twig.

"Didn't mention any message to me," Twig replied and then went back inside.

"Do yall have to leave or what's going on?" Roxy asked Lou.

"Yeah, no I don't work Monday, so we got tonight and pretty much all of tomorrow."

"We should also go out and do something, maybe the Natural Bridge," said Roxy.

"Oh, I've heard of that. Let's definitely do," said Lorraine.

"Whatever, yeah. Let's nature it up," said Louie.

"Psshhaw," from Roxy, and Low-rain let out a laugh.

"Nobody says that, babe," Lorraine said.

"Alright, why don't you get back on Moe's case?" Louie totem.

Inside the house Twig was in the kitchen listening to the message on the machine. He lifted the phone off the wall, got a dial tone, and punched in the number wrote out on the note. Written. It rang. He looked at his father in the next room, sitting back in his recliner. It rang. Let's see what mess Sonny got himself into. It stopped on the third rung.

"Detective Reese," said the neutral voice.

"Yes uh, my name is Desean Frye. My brother is Vincent Frye. Calling back on behalf of our father Elijah who someone is trying to reach," Twig said.

"Yes, thank you. Is your father there with you?"

"He is, just prefers me to talk to you is all."

"Well, I'm sorry to have to tell you this Mr. Frye. Your brother was shot this afternoon here in Las Vegas County. We were unable to save him. We have his remains and will help coordinate transport once everything is processed," the detective finished.

Twig's head rang, heart hung and mind spun. He forgot to breathe and time stopped. Smash cut to: the Reckoning dead.

"His remains," Twig repeated dazedly.

"Yes, I'm sorry. His body. Would you like me to put you in touch with—"

189

"No. Who did it?" Twig cut him short.

"We do not currently have any suspects. We will remain in contact," Reese said.

"Remain," Twig echoed in a trance.

"Sorry." Click. He'd placed the phone back on its hook and did not let go, thinking maybe this would keep reality at bay. Nope. A wave overcame him. That cop just told him Sonny got shot and died. He felt weak, leaning into the wall for support. Dead. Death means life's over. His brother was no more. This is bad. This is not good. Desean wondered when the sadness would start. Pop didn't know. Looks like he is feeling something pleasant, happy, drunk. Is this information that should be kept quiet? The only noise was Jimi Hendrix's Blues album playing at a medium volume. Bleeding Heart by Elmore James, 1965, first released posthumously as a B-side to It Hurts Me Too, recorded 1962-63. It Hurts Me Too originally recorded and released in 1957. That song is based on a Tampa Red number from the early-Thirties. First recorded by said Red in 1940. A mid-tempo eight bar blues, Junior Wells had a version in the Sixties. Then Wells and Buddy Guy had another take on it in Seventy-nine. Clapton released his interpretation on the 1994 album, From the Cradle. Powerful. You know what it means to be left alone.

Was this a joke? No, this is real. Now it's just him and his Pop. Shit. Before it kind of felt like it was. But now it is. He thought about his mom. He didn't want to start thinking about that. He'd prefer to stop thinking altogether. Go numb. Maybe if he shared this burden it would lessen the intensity. Twig walked to the freezer, opened it and removed the Southern Comfort. Twisted off the cap, took a mighty swig and the ice cold liquor burned his esophagus. Warmth lined his gullet. He considered the ecstasy of breaking windows up with rocks in high school. The time Sonny brought him along to slit some tires on a rival's truck. Cheers to the catharsis of demolition and destruction.

He drank once more. From the looks of it, Roxy, Les and his Pop had dipped into the bottle some since their arrival. If he could get a blunt together, wouldn't that be more conducive to mourning? He realized there might be an appropriate response to this situation. He was concerned he was doing it all wrong. Twig knew in his gut he couldn't escape this. It was his place to step up, walk in to his Pop and tell it straight.

His feet began to move. He was ambling towards the front room; bottle in hand, the freezer door left open. He was taking action, although he did not feel ready or sure. Coming up beside his Pop, Twig stood staring at the floor, on through to the earth's molten core.

"You gave them a call? Don't tell me Sonny got locked up or somethin'," Catfish said.

"No," said Twig. He hadn't thought about what to say.

"You ain't heard of glasses?" Catfish motioned to the bottle in his boy's grip.

"Yeah, oh." Twig realized he had hold of the SoCo so he set it down, capped on the coffee table.

"So what's with Sonny then?" asked Catfish.

Twig took a few good breaths, then got down on one knee to be level with his father.

"Pop. Sonny got shot and died." It was out.

Hendrix's right hand hammered on and off in that psychedelic trill. 'About this time, we'd like to present you to the Electric Church.' The organ droned underneath and in the spaces in between.

"They told you that?" Catfish said with a temper.

"The detective told me, from the number on the message. Las Vegas County, where Sonny was. Somebody killed him. They didn't say how it happened." Twig put a hand on his Pop's arm.

"Aawww." Catfish said, angry and bothered. "Tsssss," he hissed in frustration.

"I know, Pop," Twig said. Catfish looked him in his eyes. They didn't get the chance to even tell him their goodbyes.

The word spread. Sonny got shot and was dead. A cloud of dark sorrow befell their circle. The reaper, that square. Bastard ass mofo dared not spare one soul. Ergo despair flows through Rox and rivers silt delivers shocks, shivers death's toll.

El gazpacho Gestapo gestalt bravacho.

They all were sent out to deal. Conjugate. Was alive is gone, are alive am here. Try to cling to the animated. People you could hug, talk to, and who answer back. "Think only of the past, as its remembrance gives you pleasure,"[10] Lou told Roxy that night. Said it was from a smart cat from another century. Everyone ached for Catfish and Twig. Time went so slow because you couldn't escape the sluggish chore, chugging forth, acknowledging every second you aren't unconscious or under the influence. Even then the nightmares peak; wreak havoc on them beings. Repulsed, full of disgust.

Sad and mournful—

Chapter Twenty-Eight • Devil Got His Dune Buggy

Up and over in Flagstaff, zombified forms, Truck and Boonz lugged in gear like ants in a processional bringing gargantuan bits to their queen, being the band house. They were unloading. Loathing. Lament. Unhinged, untethered and floating. No stomach for further goading. Spent. Bloating gut wrench, gun toting and limp, noting the dim state in which they sat once the van was secured. Their sadly accessible, empty fridge stained rug space had a large hole in its heart's center.

Sonny's bag of barbecue beef jerky was down to its last few pieces. Truck fetched out a small strip, two remained. He pressed closed the seal on the pouch, for freshness, to preserve. They both wanted to pass out, shut down. Think about; deal with tomorrow when it was only necessary, like a week from this Tuesday. Maybe never if that's an option. Felt like the end of something, minus the resolution. Like the early part of a large task, fantasies of escape, and a wish to bail, bypass. You think about what it means to quit. In moments like these, rehab's for everybody. To die: your birth but guarantees. The cleric makes the cross sign before his solemn prayers chime in the heaven's decrees. Angel got its due; devil got his wings.

Sacred vice of sentient breather sucking wind to see. Dawn's early light, wished he'd never saw. Patience's last legs, good luck making it to the head to piss. Fuck your damn alarm and the day job. Truck thought he might tire his brain out, run his mind ragged to the point he'd crash. Boonz balanced battling anger and depression until he was drained and unconscious. Some clip that turned out to be. Anti-tripped a fiend blocker, tears on your pillow. Liturgic acid, lethargic sackin, le dirt nappin'.

193

Back on the blessed west coast, amuckst all the gory Love and Laughter, sat a couple of nits wits ass down in the sandy shore. Dinah in the distance, someone's in the kitchen, aye no. Pass the time away, hear the whistle blowing, early in the morn slash late night swarm. Blast calm palm trees shadowing Shenandoah.

Alyssa was humming, 'Fee fie fiddly eye oh.' Kinda imagined herself sorta riding on the rails. Wondered what it takes to be a full on bum. She figured it was mostly commitment. Based on what this guy once told her, that was one of the tenants of the Marine Corps; the other two being honor and courage. To totally commit to freedom or lack of bindings; sure sounded like fun.

Or, to be fair, had she been slowly and thoroughly corrupted, manipulated into a believer in the wacky idea of feeling happy, well and good as the ultimate existence.

"San Juan's in a chicken spit shynah," sang Alyssa.

Izzy wanted to keep on a good face. Odd. It was impossible to not smile around her, so he'd already given up on triangulating how to be debonair, whatever that was. Stupid cool. Are cool, is cool. Is acting, am act cool? How is look cool? Cool is real. Real is cool. Real is real, cool is basically unnecessary and only serves to cloud and divide. Sometimes everything and everybody's always all versus. Doesn't make much sense unless you get off on that whole trip. Us-them, they-we. You, me, her, she was easy to watch and fun to listen to.

"Where's your family from?" Izzy asked.

"Aww," after a pause. "Well there's probably tons of ways to answer that. Seems folks with identifiable origins put more stock in where other people come from. While those who mostly hail from nowhere in particular don't usually pay that business no mind."

"You sure talk like you're from somewhere," said Izzy.

"So what if I do?" she added in mild indifference.

"Okay. So you and yours rather just came into being from the general ether?"

"So what if we did?" and she slugged him hard in his left bicep.

They made out, and then lay out on the beach, with nature's noises and each other's breath breathing heavily in their ears. The two had come some many miles, feeling very far away from that one spot there on the roadside where they first caught eyes. Now swept up in an adventure neither knew where it would lead. They were oblivious to most everything else, each one massive in the other's mind. Yes and yes and yes they wished that this "them" remained ongoing and continuous. A pleasant stroll back to the bus, they fell down on the bed and shared past experiences and future designs.

Alyssa softly sang of the sand, man.

Acapella.

Chapter Thirty • Almond 7770, Their So-Called Life

The argument could be made that Earth is just an immense archipelagic mix of water and land. Rock and the rinse washed up against. Probably some scientific numbers guy could give you the ratio of actual surface areas, but guarantee you most all humans be in the dirt terrariums, houses and society. The ocean is one odd-shaped aquarium. You do however get some kooky overlap right where these two divergents meet. It is this gray area shore enough. Folks on boards riding waves, ships and seagoing vessels, some wind-harnessed craft gliding effortlessly over the silken choppy drink.

This morning like most, Lalo sat out in the surf on the only board he ever owned in all his life. Of course he'd borrowed others before, even at that he felt blessed in utilizing such craftsmanship. Born at a young age to immigrant farmers, who had died at a ripe stage with considerable karma. He let another wave go by. Luck had left him caretaker of the house at Tait and Hayes. The address never changed, but the occupancy was up and down all of the time. It had been just him most of this past weekend, though he had noticed today that the Daphne girl was back with her blind man.

Doesn't matter now. Lalo saw his swell coming and only waited a few beats before laying flat on his stomach and digging into the current. Pushing with his arms and cupped hands to maximize speed, gravity flinging him downhill as the approaching inflow raised him up. He slightly changed his angle and popped right up onto his feet. He dropped into the breaker gaining balance as he rode. The adrenaline surged in his body and he pumped down several times to increase acceleration. Lalo tucked low momentarily, banking hard left and was headed up the wave for a split-second, then spun his torso and arms quickly to the right which whipped his board back around. More pumping and he stood up to watch the crashing foam finally catch up to his feet. It didn't get too much better than that. He was fully satisfied if he were to die today; the kind of wave that'll put you at peace with the world.

He paddled into the shoals, and then turned over, stretching out on his board to look up into space. He was searching for the early morning moon. To achieve ego death on Dagobah; home planet in the system shares its name. Telekinetic cruiser rays are two units in the background. Sluis sector swami land, vector dark force side of hash and nectar exile light stood undetectored flit about his flat so fleet of foot. Yoga say, Dalai Lama do. Tarot Chi go maybe so: squish like crepes. Who's wet? Brahma beware, venerable Vishnu bids the Buddha adieu. Ra, Jah, Zen Gunga Din. Gawd awmighty, Baba Looey Abba hymn. Maharishi mountain grass, man with megaphone blocks the pass of lost resistance Haile Selass, he brings the revolution. Jehovah, Dionysus. Adonai, Nanak and Isis. Sihk the truth, and yes-sweet Jesus don't forget Our Blessed Mother Mary.

Lalo crossed his chest and reached upwards towards the sky, holding high the heavens. That was his daily prayer, slight return. He rolled off his board and into the wakening universe. Standing up he tucked his board beneath his arm, strode onto the beach and straight on through, retrieving nothing because it was all that he had.

For the first time out front of his home, he noticed the old Volkswagen camper, curtains drawn. Its color was like a faded light almond. There was a spare tire mounted on the very front, with a black cover smoothing out the edges. Looked like some kind of roof rack on top in the back. Like it might hold a couple boards if you strap 'em down good. Approaching the van he recognized it was a decent spray can job. Hardly a speck of gloss, but okay if you take a few steps back. Had an outlet jack right there behind the driver's seat to run electricity. Shiny moon hubcaps with the VW logo embossed in the center. The window curtains were a light blue, having some beige pattern printed of something but he couldn't tell just what. Then the fabric moved and Lalo thought that he spotted eyes watching him. His intention really wasn't to snoop, so he headed inside, content with the reconnaissance he had put in.

"Swerve to goblins, he had shorts and a surfboard, that was it. Sort of an ethnic look," Alyssa said.

"What does that mean?" Izzy asked.

"You know like he had flavor. Maybe a rich hickory smokehouse zesty barbecue spiced out tanginess. A little 'hmph'." She made a motion with her hands indicating the amount of 'hmph', which was actually quite a bit.

It fascinated Izzy how she often made no sense, but at the same time represented some profound reticence he was drawn to. He explained to her that surfers were probably all over the place, this being the beach and all.

"Yeah yeah, I got that. But this guy was really giving us the eyes," Alyssa said, then got back to more 'splorin' like she called it. She popped the cushion top off the box seat behind the driver. Made some noises, moved some bits.

"Oh—my—gourd. What, is this?"

"That's a book I picked up in Denver."

"It is so frigging huge! How many pages are in there?"

"Wool, it ain't hardly proper form to speak of page numbers, but pretty near on a thousand."

"Holycrapathousand? What's it about?" Alyssa asked.

"Tennis. Film. Rehab."

"Wow, that's crazy. How far in are you?"

"Oh, I am *very* in. It is happening."

"Yeah, like what page though?"

"Wool, I technically haven't exactly got officially started on that one yet."

"Right. And what'd that hunk of timber set you back, fiscally speaking?"

"Jacket says $19.99, Canadian."

That soaked in a minute. Alyssa thought about Dudley Do-Right, Alanis Morisette, maple syrup, and ice hockey.

"Oh, I'll stare at the title page, feel its composite weight. Peruse excerpts; consider lines, names, and places. Let it all simmer," Izzy said.

"Yeah, alright. Sweet. Anything else you want to declare? Literarily?"

"The Naked and the Dead, Norman Mailer. Written in Paris in like fifteen weeks."

"Oh yeah, is that one very thick?"

"Around seven hundo."

"Pfff, and that's it?"

"Hemingway. Tolstoy. Pynchon. Cervantes."

"Well fine, but I say it don't seem that impressive unless I don't know, maybe you actually got to flipping some pages. Crack them sons-a-bitches open." Two beats. "In*dulge*," as she drew out the second syllable.

Izzy tried to save face by adding that he was re-reading the Tolstoy and Mailer.

Alyssa said that she wanted to make use of the shower. She asked Izzy if he'd come in and hang out while she was inside. He said he would. Izzy slid open the van door and they entered the day, wearing yesterday's clothes, he in shoes and socks, while she was only in sockless sneakers. He knocked respectfully upon the door.

The man with flavor opened up, still shirtless, and cleared his long black hair from off his brow. The man spoke first, "You Daphne's friends?"

"I'm Alyssa, that's Izzy. She mentioned that we could use the bathroom."

"Right on. Yeah, whatever you need," said Lalo.

They entered and the surfer plopped down on the couch. Alyssa went down the hall. Izzy closed the door slowly and began to hover, formulating a plan. Instantly Lalo realized these were the inhabitants of the VDub bus out front. He was wondering whether or not he could finagle a ride, or get a peek inside at the interior.

"Whatchu call that paint job?" Lalo asked.

"Oh, that's Almond 7770, aerosol," Izzy told him.

Lalo just nodded, inside gave himself his kudos due for calling it. This man with the van had some uneasiness about him. It wasn't negative energy, but slightly restless and hard to put completely out of mind. The television was on, volume low. MTV was playing the video for Santa Monica by Everclear. Izzy heard the shower come on, took a few steps further in and slunk down into a recliner that rocked a little back and forth because of his momentum; object in motion, the chair being the outside force. Israel had heard this song before

199

but didn't know its name, so when the artist and track info came on in the lower left portion of the screen he kind of automatically said, "Santa Monica," out loud so the thought would take hold in his memory.

"Yep. Good shit," Lalo replied.

"Where's that at about, in relation to where we're at now?" Izzy asked.

"The city itself is at the end of Interstate Ten West. Right up next to L.A."

"What's that as the crow flies?"

"Maybe an hour and a half. Just I-5 North to 73 North to the 405 North and bam, Ten West and there she is," Lalo said. "You heading that way?"

"Don't know yet. Just learning about the area."

There was a flutter and flapping, then a scroungy white bird sat up atop the couch. Izzy observed the foul thing. Its head twisted, shook, and swiveled like some fit of rage had possessed its vertebrae slash entire being.

"Murder death kill! Rawk," he sqwookt.

"Chill out homie," said Lalo.

"Chill out homie!" echoed Lord Stanley.

"He knows you're watching him," Lalo said to Izzy. "It's best not to pay him any attention."

Focus was back on the TV. A black and white shot of a shack flashed, then a dirt road, a face with tears, and the words showed Tennessee, Arrested Development (1992, Chrysalis).

"They always got good variety on early mornings. Less commercials," said Lalo.

"Who's aware?" said the bird.

"Now he's jealous," Lalo told Izzy sotto voce. Speech was telling his story of a magic kingdom.

"Who's aware? Who's aware? Big bad wolf!" blared Stanley.

"Chill out homie," Lalo said in a warning tone.

"Rawk," and the bird clicked and clucked in displeasure.

"Doesn't that get at your nerves?" Izzy asked.

"He's not usually this boisterous. Totally disappears if there's more than a couple people around," said Lalo.

"Another place, another land," Izzy sang along in his brain.

"So what're you all up to?" Lalo tried to sound harmless and interested.

"Trips and journeys mostly." Was all that Izzy gave up.

"Right," Lalo said while nodding.

Alyssa appeared from the hall running a brush through her hair and saw the bird on the sofa back. She watched Lord Stanley preening, hopping around, finally he looked right at her for a moment.

"Hey bird," said Alyssa.

"Chill out homie," said Stan in polite response.

Alyssa kept brushing not wanting to excite this wraith. She saw the TV just in time to shout out: "A game of horseshoes!"

"Surfboards up mofos," was Lord Stanley's heinous harangue.

The Rose paced easily over next to Izzy, sitting on the armrest of his chair. He looked up. They smiled at one another.

"You wanna get outta here?" Izzy asked.

"Sure. That's a thing I guess. Getting the fug out of dodge. Where would we go?"

"Away."

"Never to return?" Alyssa asked.

"Probably not to here. We go on to the next place. Arrive anew," said Izzy.

"What about the Dirk and Daphne?"

"We've already done right by those two."

They said their goodbyes to Stanislas and all the rest. The Dirk put up a futile effort about him and Daphne coming along but Izzy shut that down. Lalo was watching Kurt Loder break in with news of a shooting last night at a concert in Las Vegas, as the vagabond pair climbed aboard the VW bus. Izzy and Alyssa shoved back off into the mighty estuary that funneled all the lesser runnel riders and adjoining tributary travelers into the major flow. Barged in on the highway, nestled down and sifted through the scenery as it passed them by.

201

They talked about what's a Lead Belly. She was unfamiliar, but when he sang a little Aww Black Betty, bambalam, Alyssa said that it definitely sounded familiar. She asked if he'd seen My So-Called Life, which was a TV show about this girl Angela, played by Claire Danes, who'd just been Juliet to Leonardo Dicaprio's Romeo in the most recent movie version of Shakespeare's tragic love story. Izzy learned about Rickie and Rayanne. There was a dorky neighbor Brian and a great deal of time was spent on Angela's crush, Jordan Catalano. Alyssa said her and Roxy would watch My So-Called Life almost every time it came on MTV. She figured they'd seen every episode maybe four or five times over.

Izzy tried to relate by telling the girl about his longstanding relationship with The A-Team. She said her younger brother had the black van with the red stripe, and a giant Mr. T action figure with a string on his back, that when you pulled it he'd say one of his catchphrases. She then launched into several of said phrases.

"Study hard in school," Alyssa said in a deep growl. "Always listen to your parents." It was not a good likeness. "Murdoch you're crazy!" This got a good laugh from Izzy, and so they both started doing their best Mr. T impersonations.

The boy asked her if she could drive a manual transmission. Alyssa said she was very limited. That she had once drove a tractor on her friend's farm and its surrounding roads and fields. Also she spent some time behind the wheel of her grandfather's 3-speed Ford truck. Izzy thought about the benefit of a second driver if they did any massive long hauls like he was considering. Maybe they would find a place to get her some time at the wheel of the bus. Plus highway driving was simple, basically once you got into fourth gear it was just a matter of cruising, keeping in between the lines. In general she seemed like the kind who wouldn't balk at a challenge. He took the tractor story as truth. The fact she knew the truck was a 3-speed was also testimony of the girl's capability. If they took it slow, what's the worst, she'd stall some. The clutch plate was relatively new. How much damage could she do in small amounts? Seed planted, shone soon.

He set his sights on showing this saintly dove something oven extraordinary scale. Izzy considered the temporal side of Alyssa's left earlobe, how he longed to taste it, and hear her vocal moans. For a second he madly wanted to four-letter word. The concept hit him so heavy and real. This current manifestation would expire as all else.

"Stick save and a butte," she called out.

"What's that now?"

"Hockey speak. My dad is from Minnesota."

They had the itinerary of itinerants, the migratory habits of wayward transients. Unsettled to say the least. Perambulatory twice parked perambulance chasers. Free range beau hue rodemance in a twister tale. They were on the move and in a mood.

Music played. Advances and chances were made. Voices and choices, stances and glances were given. In assurance and warmth they were bathed. You don't have to acknowledge truth, it just is. Love is not a word told, it is a feeling shared. It is though quite absurd, bold and rewarding if you dare. It's people willing, motivated to say yes.

As phony as the speed of light is attainable in a foot race: When are we gonna sit down and grab a grip 'a' boot lace? They'd drive on, stop in or cruise past places; see nothing really, sample wares, watch faces. Nowheres particular, their rectangle vehicular was rolling sweet and cycular, seventy horses strong. Four words, marching on.

Chapter Thirty-One • Expression Continues, Aunt Sally

January 28, 1998

Three nights had gone by and the taste of things was sour still. Today was the funeral service; they would put Sonny in the ground. Emotions were much less likely to stay buried. The only coping was on the coffin covering, satin white. Twig had picked it out, pure and holy.

There was no justice. The scales weighed heavily towards despair. Little could console but how the wailing sorrow bared. Pain is life's exhaust. Inglorious wretch and rancor unaccost assuage the snake birnt Pentecost. Refrain less say curd then you might suppose those Christian folks be haviorn in a shack that's decorated with the cross.

"All is lost," Catfish had already declared more than once, wanting peace.

The people around only thought of how they might help offer relief. Met with passive resistance. Blessed assurances, things will be fine. There'd been old ladies from the church on rotation out front singing hymns. It was a sure real venomous dreamscape.

Part of Twig wanted to hate and be spiteful, foul and rude. But every chance he was presented he deferred to compassionate concern. There were so many posers. Early on, Catfish had asked Roxy to sing a song at the service. This gave her a purpose and distraction all in one; respite from the storm. From the suggestions given she'd gotten the list whittled down to Day By Day, or The Sweet By and By. She was ready to do it unaccompanied, though she still wanted to try and see if Twig would back her on acoustic guitar. More lucid by far, the music imparts, entomb supple car. Are, rollin' in my six-fahr. With all the candles burnin', swingin' down sweet chariot, let free life.

Those with their ears on, eyes pealed noticed for the last couple days strange figures lurking, looming about town. The back alleys and front steps were littered with scrawngy loiter squads, scattered and hid in shadows. The squalor had arrived.

The story of Sonny's death was in the papers and on some local news capers for the first few days. People lost interest because they never apprehended any suspects back in Las Vegas. Another free man shot down for no good reason. There were fans and friends who felt obliged to make the pilgrimage to see the body put to rest. They sojourned and stood vigilant, sleeping in their cars or packed in transitory lodgings. All had respects they wished to pay the family. Nobody thought there'd be any kind of unwelcome sentiment between the rabble and the residency. The clash was unobserved for the most part. For a certain sect, this small town was now regarded as a sight of sanctuary. An element of extra creatures, rodents stealing scraps. Pass the time in silent daytime naps.

Truck and Boonz were making plans to come down together in the van the morning of. The mourning started early and truthfully had never ceased over the past three days. A girl traveled with the remaining members of Dystopian Squalor Syndicate. She was in a relationship with Boonz. She had motives of her own, machinations as to what she could get out of this tragic drama. To sell her concern, this Esther was prone to paroxysms of woe and unrest. She was unafraid to emote at random. She sat in the back of the brown Ford van speeding south down Interstate Seventeen. Boonz drove, Truck would take the wheel on the way home.

Moe had been telling everyone that he was available for whatever, and to please just call if they needed anything. He didn't really know Sonny that well, but considered Twig and Catfish to be family. Them and Roxy were also visibly, audibly, and understandably shaken. Their bodies seemed beaten, voices wavered and weak. People got affected in different ways. Individual responses varied. Timelines did not necessarily match concurrently.

"Who is it never has been knocked down?" Moe said to Catfish, trying to relate to his loss. He was at Twig's house on standby if a ride was required, or an errand or to shoo away the boo birds. Offer, soothe words.

"I ain't your dentist. Don't tell *me* 'bout your fillings," Moe said, attempting humor. Feeling it out.

"Graham cracker pie crust!" Twig in a moment of clarity. "Tell one of them church ladies that's what we could use."

Food in large and small Tupperware was piling up in the fridge and freezer. You could put on twenty pounds easy if you weren't cautious. Careful, though indulging felt good. Quell, console with a casserole. Something like 1400 they'd all get together for the last goodbyes. Graveyard send off, bookends, pin drop death-rottle. There would be a preacher to officiate the service. Catfish said it weren't out of the ordinary for spirits to rise or remain present after the life passes on.

Les had been staying out at Roxy's since Louie and Lowrain left town Monday night. They all mostly did nothing, then tried to engage in activities to get their minds off the misery, only to revert back to idle suffering when overcome with reality; this was the cycle. Empty painful hurt felt in between fleeting alleviation from distress.

Roxy told Twig her and Les would come over around noon for lunch and support. Twig and Sonny's aunt came down from near Chicago. It was their Mom's younger sister. Her only daughter was escorting her. This was the only family blood to show for the ceremony. The two of them had flown into Phoenix the night before and drove up to Payson early this morning. Aunt Sally spent some time talking to Catfish about the boys' mother. Twig was slightly intrigued that these visitors might have some insight into his Moms. The rental they had was a 1992 Chevrolet Caprice Classic station wagon, huge, because you can never have too much room; spatial, palatial. The weather was amazing, relative to Chicago, so they rode everywhere with the windows rolled down. The air circulation was intense and a thin coat served as the ideal equalizer. Sally's daughter Maya drove. The vehicle's heat was engaged and entered this temperate vortex down by their feet in front. The wagon was five years old, though to Maya it felt like it came off the lot just yesterday. She had no car back home and was always feeling trapped. Not any more. Maybe in her dreams there were rides such as these. This was the kind of car you'd see some gangster slap hydraulics on. Hopping down the road riding slow. Massive thumping bass barely contained, seeping all out of the trunk where woofers blared. For now, it was fuzzy smooth jazz coming through the stereo speakers on a weak signal hardly cutting through in the wooded elevation. This was good smooth jazz, real smooth jazz, and old smooth jazz. From back when you might not even call it jazz but standards, pop charts. Music. Yeah, you still take a hit before going on stage, but it's the good kind of buzz what allows you to create, produce, and enhance the minds and ear holes that you enter. Expand; engage in vibration creation.

Sally's thoughts drifted off into the late Fifties and Sixties, Thelonious Monk, Max Roach, and Charles Mingus. The tune on the radio ended in a flourish of bop and flurry on the sax, bass and percussion.

"That was the New Oscar Pettiford Sextet with Pendulum at Falcon's Lair, 1959," a too-cool disc jockey said with quiet gruff. "Next up, Sonny Rollins. On the Sunny, Side of the Street." A tenor sax and trumpet hit and held out a long warm note, fresh and lively. Steady then swelled up, fell in as the melody dropped, bit and kicked; took you for a light stroll with soul. Hope, thinking that the levee might hold. Bold, powerful stride as it goes. But yeah, put all of that nastiness aside. The things; all of it'll be alright. At least for the moment or it gives the now a meaning, the ability to progress without deterioration. The nuisance and nuance of a bad trip or fucked up situation. It is senseless loss and pointless desecration, hapless destruction from witless protection.

No, Sally told herself, she would keep it together. She would not be counted as one of those wailing uncontrollably. Which isn't to say that surface sorrow is shameful, she only wanted to be strong. A rock to lean on, Maya wished that she might find her own role in this small patchwork family trial. That she would lend contribution. She'd eventually feel guilty if all she did was drive her Mom to and fro. You're old enough to rent a car, you're old enough to be supportive and offer words, deeds, or a timely hug. Her cousin and his dad, Catfish, both looked like they had a few stories for sure. Maya had some memories of Twig's Mom from her youth (Maya's youth); when for a while Twig and Sonny lived with their

Mom, in the same house in Chicago as Maya and her Mom. It was the sisters, Sally and Laura, her and the boys, but back then they were called Vincent and Desean.

Her Aunt Laura died after some time, from illness, though it didn't seem to surprise anyone that much. The boys went off to live with their Dad down in New Orleans. Here they were, almost fifteen years later, death at the doorstep once again. In the house and getting comfortable. Grim reaper put his feet up on the coffee table. Just flipping through last month's National Geographic. That's real places and worldly information that they'd had a subscription to for decades.

Aunt Sally and Maya had finished with their errands, and now headed back to attend the lunch that Catfish asked they come by for. They were bringing disposable plates, cups, and utensils; options other than tap water or alcohol for drinks. Usually there was tea at the house but things were lagging, tasks undone. Sally told Maya they would be doing some cleaning before leaving for good. This was to prepare her for the necessary headspace needed to tackle scrubbing dirt, grease, and grime. They pulled in out front of the house with their sun tea, apple juice, picnic items and cleaning supplies. Maya parked the Caprice wagon behind a dusty yellow Jeep Cherokee. She noticed a mean army green motorcycle with sidecar in the front yard gravel.

Inside the house, Catfish was showing Moe a Bible passage he wanted to read at the service. It was something about entertaining angels. This whole business was giving Moe flashbacks of his hometown and all the Bible folk he grew up around. Seems everybody gets God near the grave. Gaudily say a prayer when the sickness falls, cancer comes. Drop to your knees and bang the drums. Worship the Lion of Judah, Lamb of God, let mercy rain down upon us; the innocent ones. The wicked lightning strikes, destroys as chance deems fitting.

Sally buzzed the doorbell. Moe let them in with a smile and a, "Welcome back." Maya had hands full of beverages, which Moe took right away. They left the liquid detergents, spray bottles, and sponges in their vehicle. Catfish was there in the front room. Aunt Sally sat down across from him. Moe carried the drinks into the kitchen where Roxy was figuring out which of the Tupperwared food items they'd need to warm up in the oven or microwave. The deviled eggs and ambrosia salad had already been steadily disappearing.

Les brought his keyboard over and was back in Twig's room, both now jamming. They started slow in A blues. The organ setting played against a clean electric guitar, one of Sonny's old Gibsons. Time stopped when the four-four time began. The beat hadn't quit since. At the twenty-one minute mark Twig stomped on his Boss DS-1 Distortion pedal. Les comped lightly and kept a strong and steady left hand bassline, tossing in some scattered stride. He would go into double-time near the end of phrases, then back to a slow four as Twig was pulling, bending notes and blending over many kinds of rhythms. Harmonic melodies made of dissenting dueling vibrations of strings and sounds. As of a natural course Les got around to pounding on the middle-low register of the keyboard, finally giving the practice amp he was plugged into some decent kind of workout. Twig started swinging on chunky round chords with a lot of fret noise and muted upstrokes; maybe it was metal with a gun to my head. He transitioned into pentatonic goat head bleating death stricken trilled out hammer-ons, with a low crying gut wrenching wish to not stop until his fingers bled. He engaged his Dunlop Crybaby Wah and found a tempo to pulse, while he played against Les who now kept slapping up high then wiggling octaves between the thumb and pinky of his right hand. Les loved to hold these waggles and hit the middle fifth or flat third to keep up movement and the momentum. He was getting good at using his index and middle finger to improvise melodies, or pound rhythms as the octave trill was maintained or walked up or down. It was soulful. It was mindless. It was time traveling, space shattering freedom. The door to the fourteen by twelve-foot room containing the music making was shut, closed, not open, unwelcoming. This was Catfish and Twig's day. This was Sonny's day. And it was a sunny day, though it felt heavily overcast. The shadows did abound.

Cloudy mind can't see the sun or hear the laughter, have the fun. Cloudy mind can't feel the rain; stave off hereafter savor pain. In veins, the blood remains the same. The heart it strains and pangs. Twig stopped, wrapping his left hand around the neck and strangs to silence them. He reached down and picked up a beer bottle from the floor next to his chair. He took a swig. Les quit playing and sat up straight to stretch his spine.

"I don't know, man," said Les. Before the jam, Twig said something about expectations. Les was staring at a Soundgarden poster pinned up on the wall, the album art for Superunknown (1994).

"I guess expect the sun to rise," Les expanded. "Trust the stars will shine. The tides will continue to break upon the shore. Believe that good indeed exists and will always prevail over the aberration of evil."

Twig took another pull off the bottle. He nodded his head slow, set his beer back down and started to play the bassline riff from Born Under a Bad Sign (Booker T, 1967), clean tone tapping to the beat on the Wah. Over and over the smooth lick he played, with the low stinger at the end of the phrase.

Out in the front room, Maya sat on the couch next to her mother. They both were exchanging chitchat tête-à-tête with Catfish as he leaned back in his recliner. In the kitchen, Moe and Roxy continued prepping for lunch. Rolls were warming in the oven. There had amassed on the dining room table myriad trays and displays of food. It almost looked like Thanksgiving. Except this was a Wednesday in late-January. They had gathered together to celebrate a life and acknowledge its passing. Moe already had a plate full. The microwave beeped, indicating the green bean casserole was sufficiently heated. Roxy could hear Catfish reminiscing. The whole house listened to Twig telling stories, and generally rebelling against peaceful surrender.

"That is just his way," Catfish explained his boy's music to Sally.

"He's very expressive," said Sally politely.

Oozing down and out the hallway was a darkly aggressive groove, with overtones of relentless, restless angst and fury. Catfish looked over and stared out of the sliver of window uncovered by the curtains, and he talked to the world and the room as one.

"Musicians just loiter until the beat drops," said Catfish. "Only then they become players. Makers of noise, bangers of toys; any old kind of vagabond voice peace fighter."

The two ladies gave him a chance to continue. He did not.

"I really like that. What you said," Maya told him.

"That's how it is. Twig will get his fill at some point. Then he'll stop playing and remember. I like hearing him though. Helps me not forget," Catfish said.

Roxy hollered in that they could all come and help themselves to the spread whenever they wanted to start eating. Catfish commented that he thought he could go for some food. Sally and Maya answered in the affirmative as well. The three stood and made their way into the kitchen. Twig and Les played on. Roxy being sympathetic brought them a container of deviled eggs, some biscuits, and bottles of water as a subtle hint to discourage the vice of alcohol as an escape. The deterrent of despair, she slid in unannounced as an assassin but her target was to unload nourishment, letting her presence be felt for the good. Everybody did what needed to be done. All ate, gathering strength and courage for the event that lay before them. The mood was somber and sedate. The meal they shared was at a minimum pleasant. Yet it represented a wealth of accumulated well wishes, and a benevolent gesture from the community. Plus also a good bit 'a' gravy.

The boy and the girl in the bus on the road made San Jose by Monday evening. They stopped for a time first in Santa Monica, and then in Salinas, where Alyssa worked on shifting between first and second gear. She practiced launching the bus from a dead stop on a section of streets with very light traffic. She only stalled twice and had a resolute, steadfast, and positive attitude. Izzy cut her virgin voyage short to end on a high note. Tuesday morning they drove into San Francisco, where they mostly sight saw, but did park and walk to get lunch from vendors down by the wharf. After a bit more of a driving tour, the true blue bohemian crew, a brood of just two, set off further north now on the 101. The switch from Interstate Five would take a bit longer, but provide a magnificent experience, traveling right along the Pacific Coast.

Tuesday night they stopped in Grant's Pass, where the 199 connected back to the Five in Southern Oregon. It was quiet there, and easy. However slight, there had been a marked change in tempo since leaving that thing called California. The longitude shift brought with it different senses. It was late as they hit town. Izzy was busy hunting for a spot to drop anchor. Alyssa saw a giant caveman. She tried to show Izzy but he was caught up in scanning the surrounding streets, lots, and neighborhoods.

It's the Rogue Valley, US Route 199. It's the Zone 7 historic climate, Reinhart Volunteer Park. Once they found a safe spot to put in, it's the locale where Izzy and Alyssa made love again. In fact, they had not since outside of Roxy's show Saturday night in Phoenix. It's the feeling of security when you hold onto another body. It's the warmth. It's the beating heart you hear when you place your ear to the chest of someone. It's the moment after you've both finished and she squeezes you tightly, asking with immaculate timing: "What's your stance on mating?"

Izzy laughed out loud. Then he became silent, taking a moment to consider her inquiry. Maybe she was being dead serious. He tried to gather himself further.

"Sweet Rose, I am absolutely pro-mating. I've not ever really done it this freely. But I want you always. Under the covers and neked. Plus for babies and copulation."

"Hmm," she took in this information. Then milking the extreme attention that was focused on her, said: "My stance? I like to be on top."

They were both very amused, and made more time lying down on the bed of the van. They shared a strawberry Pop Tart. Izzy locked the van and they both drifted off into sleep.

The next morning they were rested, and had scrambled eggs at a diner near the Rogue River at Riverside Park. Izzy got to see the caveman. Alyssa did several laps driving the bus in an empty parking lot. She took to the street and got it up into third gear, cruising at about thirty-six miles per hour. The Rose signaled right, rolled to a stop, feeling like a champion. Izzy took over, hit up a gas station for fuel, and they connected to Interstate Five again heading further north through Oregon.

They passed by Green, Roseburg, and Sutherlin, making Eugene in a couple of hours. They stopped in Salem for some gas, hot chocolate, and a big bag of large marshmallows, because it was the right thing to do. Continuing on they arrived in Southwest Portland some time on the other side of noon. Izzy merged onto the 405 north, following the signs toward Washington Park. He was aiming for the north entrance to the park. First stop, the Portland Japanese Gardens. All of his knowledge about the city was from an in-depth magazine piece he'd clipped about Portland; it was decided they'd begin from the outside in. They passed beside downtown, exiting near Southwest Alder Street, then worked their way west to enter the park by the Number Three Reservoir. The last legs of this portion of the journey were taken slowly and savored fully by the transient couple.

It had so much green, so lush. With so much life, such rush, enlivened and invigorating. In among the West Hills, the Tualatin Mountains lay on the western border of Multnomah County. The edge of the basin, within a cannon's shot of the state of Washington. You say ketchup-mustard, I say Portland-Vancouver. Tomato is to potato, gizzard strips and Portland

Harbor. But still love is all around. Columbia River slash the Mediterranean Sound. Maybe with a monster three-man water balloon launchster, you could lob a volley across the barges in the Washington state shipyards. Twenty-twos and Forty-fives, aim high, Portland Meadows. But I degross, in a civil society we get past divisions and surface incisions. It's the anecdote of the antidote since antiquity and the antebellum. The anti-venom for the anti-derivative antics of Auntie Em's anticipatory ante-up and throw it down attitude. The antelope play, the buffalo roam, and the anti-dis and anti-dat grift is all stacked. The anti-virus is the anti-coagulant nurturing cure for all the early days. Seldom is heard such discouraging words, snack on anti-depressants and raw roots and verve. Anti-biotech ain't gonna getcha nowheres. Now here's Cyborg Joe, so plug in or disengage your weapons systems, Vonda.

• • • • • • •

In nearby Goose Hollow, on SouthWest Prospect Drive, there did appear a glowing blue point of light in a closed off backyard; six feet above a healthy lawn, hidden by thick trees and brush. The light then extended straight down, making a vertical beam of neon fluzz, with the sound of a million warm tube amps bluzzing as the light stick expanded out on both sides to form a large rectangle, in the shape of what you might call a door. A portal. A passageway to another dimension of a Portland at the polar opposite of the good, kind and humble place we know it to be; somewhere else along the spectrum.

A sound like joy, glee and voices free began faintly then increased and 'plop' out popped these squirrels three. Just furry as could be, each landed one, two and fleed the open space took cover deep in bush and tree. The blue light beam, in a suck of air and vacuum, rushed back up to one pure dot then vanished, puff, no traces be. Like when you switch off the old television sets, minus all the lingering pitch and squeal.

These squirrels looked like your basic plain tree bark brown, with lighter flurries under their carriages and bushy tails. They did however, each wear on their noggins, leather flight masks with goggled lenses to protect against the intense pressures of interdimensional space travel. They hunkered close to discuss the execution of their mission.

"Big Daryl, you go north, Little Daryl head south. I will go west. Everyone keep your sensors on. Blue homing beacon if the target is located, red beacon for distress. We will search, and then meet back here at midnight to report our findings. If unsuccessful we will all head east. Let's make this better than San Diego, guys. And if we come across the Danger, escape to the hills."

"Yes, escape to the hills," said Big Daryl.

"Yes, the hills, got it," added Little Daryl.

"Chameleon mode for day flight," said the lead squirrel.

"Yes boss. Got it boss," from the two Daryls.

"Go, go!" and the three broke off. Both Daryls immediately took to the air spreading out their patagia, increasing the tautness of the kite-like membrane, connected from ankle to wrist. They accessed their amplified abilities, as powers bestowed upon all Guardians of the Envoy to the Council of the Living. Also maintaining happy thoughts, as is the most key element in flying sans a strong updraft. They each triggered a switch on the side of their multifunctional facemasks. Cloaking engaged they took on a light gray hue as did match the overcast cloud cover above the city.

Larry the Ancient watched his two squad members vanish into the sky. He retreated under cover of the brush. His superiors back home had given precise instructions as to where Larry would most likely meet their mark. A powerful tree was said to be near Goose Hollow. That unbeknownst, it even now drew him and them, and maybe others to its treasured trunk, the shelter of its branches. The Ancient had only to stop, listen, and feel as it began to pull him in its general direction.

Larry hopped a fence and scurried across a road into a thickly wooded area. Even now, his sensors were hot which flushed his system with adrenaline, extra clean mojo. He sped around the ground beneath the covering canopy, and came to another road that he cleared in three strong bounds. Across a dirt field, he hugged closely the edge of a pond, scrambling back in among the powerful bristling pines. His heart beat heavily and he was incredibly alert. This mission he was on could mean a place for him in the pantheon of Greats of the Seven Dimensions. He would be able on his final day to rest well knowing he'd made his contribution to the universal well-being. With respect paid from the Council of the Living itself.

But the squirrel was determined that he must focus. This reminded him of when he played tennis and would be serving for the match. Thoughts of victory would creep in and distract from the fact that there was still work to do. Work to be done. Larry came out into the open, leaped up and spread his limbs wide. He thought of how he *did* win the tennis tourney, which made him rise and float. Higher he flew and with a tap to his temple activated his stealth mode. He glided over massive fields of flowers and flourishing colors. Passing over more trees, and of all things below him laid a strip of several tennis courts. Fate seemed to be smiling down on him as he alighted on a tree branch, turning leafy green. He looked around, sniffing and listening for sounds. Larry the Ancient could taste his own anticipation for what he hoped would soon transpire.

· · · · · · ·

Izzy and Alyssa, rolling at a crawl down Rose Park Road, passed by an amphitheater and gardens on the cityside. At one point a view opened up towards the east. A snowcapped mountain stood off in the distant day. They were now in Washington Park. Izzy came around a large bend and pulled the bus over among some other vehicles in a small lot off the asphalt track. They disembarked from their craft. Izzy filled a water bottle from a gallon jug of drinking water, the expedition would continue now on foot.

Izzy began down a path into the middle of the Japanese Gardens. Alyssa taking longer to look about fell back for a moment, then quick-stepped up to the boy, grabbing his left hand with her right. She felt him squeeze and then relax into a careful clasp.

216

It was reminiscent of northern Arizona, but more humid and a tougher chill. She was wrapped up real good in a sweatshirt with hood that Izzy had given her. It read Colorado across the front. There was a rock garden with raked sand, and the flow of Karesansui. A flat garden alternated white sand and brilliant green patches of grass and moss. This setting had more natural magic than any place she'd ever experienced.

The two crossed a handmade bridge, marveling at all of the wild plant life brimming up everywhere they turned. It was pleasant even in the winter months, though the colors weren't as vibrant, and the foliage not as fierce and luminous as in the spring, summer, or fall. Their walk brought them to a pond, and they crossed another ornate bridge over still waters, venturing deeper in on a path lined with short bamboo stalks driven into the earth.

"Look," Alyssa said, pointing over to an elevated mound upon which stood a giant glorious specimen of an old life form.

Securely anchored by a broad trunk, with arms raised up and out. Over its limbs extended fingers, toes, elbowed and reached away to touch the heavens soft. There was very little pigmentation. Leaves were light in general. Still an iridescent glow shone off the moss and epidermal husk of the hallowed colossus.

Alyssa Rose stepped over the short bamboo barrier. With small slow paces she moved beneath the furthest reach of the maple's tentacles hanging down. Izzy followed suit and saw a pond just beyond the lowest boughs of this good soul. Merry old troll indeed.

The interdimensional agent Larry the Ancient deactivated his cloaking device. From atop his perch he descended, watching the man and woman below on a measured approach. Larry the Ancient Wonder Squirrel, LtAWS, hit the ground and observed the human duo becoming aware of his presence.

They watched him watching them, the squirrel stoic as the stone gargoyles guarding the Gothic cathedrals in the darkest medieval ages. Izzy and Alyssa were close now, within ten to fifteen feet. Larry only sat patiently waiting intently.

"Speak friend, our ears are open," said Izzy.

217

The squirrel sat up, quickly glancing left and right. He replied, "Right on."

There was a pause and drops of jaws. His voice wasn't loud. There was weight and authenticity in his delivery. It wasn't like Alvin, Simon, Theodore or the Rescue Rangers as the average human might expect. Nobody quite knew what was which and where was why and who? Though Larry stared squarely at the boy and girl, an eyeball for each of 'em.

"You heard that?" Alyssa said to Izzy.

"Yeah," Izzy said back.

"He has a little hat on," said Alyssa.

"Yeah, you try and say something to him," said Izzy.

"That sure is a nice tree you got," Alyssa told the squirrel.

"Acer palmatum, Japanese maple," Larry answered in Latin and plain English.

Brains were spinning, minds churning, pulses leapt and questions burning. Larry too was battling crippling exhilaration, but this was what he'd been trained for. His actions from this point forward could hold the fate of multiple realities in their balance. In Izzy's head was the Chipmunks vinyl LP he listened to as a young kid. Witch Doctor, Swanee River, Home on the Range, and other American classics.

"Sacajawea," Alyssa said in amazement.

"Jean-Baptiste," Izzy answered.

"These are both great explorers," said LtAWS.

"Are you real, man?" Alyssa asked.

"Yes, I am flesh just as you. I come from the Seventh Dimension," Larry said.

Larry the Ancient tapped a three-digit code into the number pad on his flight mask. This set off the blue homing beacon, which would signal the Daryls and provide them the coordinates for his location. They would need to reconvene. Plus, he could use his crew to reinforce a good rapport with the humans.

"So, the Seventh Dimension. Out of how many dimensions total?" asked Izzy.

"Seven," said Larry.

"Right. Do they all have names, are you able to tell us?"

218

"Of course. There is the Good, the Bad, the Ugly, the Smart, the Dumb, the Pretty, and the Weird. My realm, the youngest of the dimensions, is the Weird," he said.

"That's how come you speak our language?" said Alyssa.

"Those are some sweet spectacles you're sporting," Izzy said.

"Thank you. The design is atavistic of those worn by your fighter pilots in the First World War. And yes, that's how come I speak your language," answered the Ancient.

"Well, I am Izzy, and this is Alyssa," Izzy motioned to the girl.

"My name is Larry. It is nice to meet you both. I should warn you, I have two friends that will be arriving soon. They are squirrels as I am. We only require a brief audience with you," said LtAWS.

"There's certainly no harm in just having a visit with somebody. Unless you all mean to eat us or be generally rude," Alyssa said half-teasing.

"This is humor, yes?" said Larry. "No, Miss Alyssa, I only ingest nuts and berries. Maybe a milkshake or part of a cheese spread on special occasions."

With that the two Daryls landed high up in the same giant maple. They saw their squad leader in discourse with the humans. They disengaged their cloaking and scuttled down the branches. Little Daryl fell in behind Larry the Ancient. Big Daryl hopped onto a large boulder nearby, settling into the scene.

"Now that your gang is all here, do we get to know what's going on?" Izzy said.

"Tell them," said Little Daryl.

"You must tell them," added Big Daryl from his rock.

"Yes. Well, we believe that you may be the one we have been searching for. Perhaps you have some role to play in the ultimate salvation of all existence across the seven dimensions. It has long been told of the man who drives a castle. He would say to us, 'Speak friend, our ears are open.' To him we reply, 'Right on.' Tell me good sir, do you drive a castle?" said the Ancient.

"He totally does! Go and try to deny it, right?" said Alyssa.

"I guess in a stretch I could say yes. But what do you consider a castle?" said Izzy.

"A fortress or enclosure, walls and a gate, shelter from the elements, most likely a bedchamber, and a throne from which to command," said Larry.

"Maybe a cow or a goat for fresh milk," Little Daryl added.

"Well, no cow or goat, but the rest checks out under that criteria," Izzy said.

"Nice, we drivin' castles! But either way, we're glad to meet you all," Alyssa reaffirmed.

"You are kind to welcome our presence," said Little Daryl.

"Acceptance is contagious," said the girl.

"Indeed, Your Grace," said Big Daryl.

Alyssa gave a little start, looking inquisitively at the squirrel on the massive stone.

"Do not be alarmed, it is just a saying we are familiar with. Acceptance is contagious. This is very true," said the Ancient Wonder Squirrel.

"But what does all that mean? If we are somehow to be singled out for some mysterious reason?" Izzy said.

"I only request that you allow me to be of service to you. All that I have and can offer will be available to you when the time comes for action. Do you consent?" Larry asked.

"I mean, if you want to tag along or hang out, that's okay with us. Are your friends coming too?" said Izzy.

"No. The Daryls will return home and await further instruction. I will mostly operate in a clandestine fashion. In general, I will only speak when spoken to. I will be ever vigilant and on guard for situations that may arise," said Larry.

"He's like our own caped crusader, Iz," said Alyssa.

"And what if no situations ever arise?" Izzy asked.

"Better safe than sorry," said Big Daryl.

Alyssa and Little Daryl both agreed and said they were familiar with that saying as well.

The Daryls wished blessings on everyone, and headed back to the yard in Goose Hollow on SouthWest Prospect Drive. They would radio back to have the portal reopened, and then return home with the news. Izzy and Alyssa spent more time in the Japanese Gardens with LtAWS. On the way back to visit other parts of the park, they showed Larry their castle. He graciously thanked them, hopped on top of the bus, and turned himself a faded off-white to blend in with the camper top. He would wait here as the boy and girl got their fill of the fauna and flowers, large greening towers in abundance on all sides and sightlines for miles. Alyssa Rose and Izzy, free in the wild sub rosa fields relief by his side, con esposa the two in sublime paradise where they spoasta. Be. Learned a two or thing about devotion. Speak in contrapuntal screams of emotion. Blush heavy quotients, retrograde inversions exceedingly potent. Imbibing heart waves with a fresh brazen potion. And now apparently, they *might* be the chosen.

January 28, 1998

Riff, interaction conversation improvisatio inspiratio golden numbers mystic pizza topping combinations. Cheese the crust bro, grease the nuts Joe, fleece the klutz broke down on the cusp of the six-oh-nine and oneteen-eleventy East. Inner and outer wheel bearings, fluids flushed and naval staring, tell him parts will take two weeks unless he'll pay the founders fees.

A tired service station mechanic eyed a motorist pulled off on the side of the highway. The shop he worked at was right on the edge of the city limits and could always use customers. Could be a belt, could be a hose. Might need a full tune radiator blows. Gasket leaks, the battery's weak, maybe just a fortnight left 'fore she goes. Like working some putz at the county fair. Got three shots win a giant bear. Rigged though. While tractor-trailers float by, going chig-chugga chig-chugga chig-yo.

Boonz, Truck, and Esther zipped by a poor sucker stuck pluck on the banks of the riverrun as they rode past. Truck drove, Boon sat shotgun, and Esther was in the back of the van, the only other one fully in Boonz's camp. All were in low spirits, but still wanted to put a strong façade forward for the funeral. There was doubt and uncertainty in a broad sense. Across the dashboard, spent wrappers and empty bottles.

Tense. Shun. Abhorrent. Torrent. Spun. Drunk.

"Whatever one thing you are worried about, life is so much more than that," said Boonz.

"You trying to mastermind a plan or what?" Truck replied.

"It's sketchy. They story ain't rote yet," said Boonz.

"Man, why not just let things happen?" said Truck.

"You. You got to consider your options. Decide where your loyalties lie," Boonz said.

"Pap said there's never only one right way to do a thing, unless you're talking about eternal salvation through our old broken and spilled out," Truck replied.

"Pap said, pap said, nobody cares, pap's dead," Boonz said tauntingly.

"Deride and conjure divide. This I cannot abide. You act like you know things and maybe you got plans, but nothing's guaranteed and you ain't shit without a good crew," said Truck.

"I know this. But can I count on your allegiance as a given in our quest to continue and expand Dystopian Squalor?" said Boonz.

"I tend to vote third party write-in. My allegiance is to the rebellion," Truck said.

"—And of course to the Syndicate," Boonz added.

"Sure man, but Sonny is dead. Don't forget that's why we're here. Today isn't about music," Truck toad 'em.

"Yeah, alright. I know. I was just saying," Boonz assured him.

Boonz kept navigating. They would stay on the main drag, then take Main Street west to Country Club Drive and on to the cemetery at the outskirts of town. It was coming right up against two p.m. slash 1400 hours, when the service was scheduled to begin. There was a small procession underway, led by the hearse from the funeral home. It was a vintage Buick from the Seventies, all black but with chrome bumpers and trim. Next in line was Aunt Sally's Chevy Caprice Classic wagon driven by Maya, Twig set in the front there beside her. Sally and Catfish were in the backseat sharing space. Roxy was bringing along Les in the Jeep. Moe trailed the caravan on his war colored motorbike.

Lights were on, signaling the occasion. Some vehicles filed in after that. Others had come to see Sonny put to rest. They were the mangy dirge and well-meaning scourge. You would find people holding onto a heavy influence, which had a hold on their own inner beings. Some hurt badly, some recovering, some only just barely alive. Twig couldn't make sense of the reactions he underwent. He was angry but had no wish to aim it at those around him. It was good that some family had showed up. He appreciated his cousin and aunt being there. Everyone was being gracious and sensitive to his Pop's and his needs, or whatever. Still the thorns stuck him and constantly there remained, an unsettling annoyance. Perhaps this is just what it feels like when your brother dies.

"My Dad back home, they have him on oxygen. People say he hasn't got too much time left," Maya said.

"Sorry," Twig replied. It wasn't nothing.

"Were you and Sonny real close?" asked Maya.

"Yeah," was all Twig could get out.

Suddenly a memory of waves overcame him. They were kid memories, brother memories, and family recollections. Random things that happened in the past. Maybe you didn't always remind each other how much stuff meant, but that doesn't change the fact that it did. Mean something. Mean a lot. Important junk. Sometimes mean everything; because that was all there was. Is. For this or that reason. For every reason Twig was fighting succumbing to emotion. Cursing the damn weakness, a slight glimpse of the bleakness ahead. Sans Sonny, AKA the darkness somber desolate squalid pain and misery. So fucking depressing, to parse the depths of loss, sour-actualization.

Silence is holding. Sigh, let's be bold and release the soul of the golden.

"I once told Sonny how crap things were for me. Said I wanted to take it out on someone, or do something crooked to get level. He promised he'd figure it out if I would just stay cool. Next day we drove out into the forest. He brought along a grip of wooden baseball bats, a thirty-pound sledge, and a TV set he got for three dollars at a rummage sale. We both beat the hell outta some trees, fallen logs, and the TV set before I was all spent. We cracked three of the bats in half and had another two in splinters," Twig said.

"How old were you?" said Maya.

"I don't know. Twelve or thirteen," said Twig.

"Do you remember what it was that was so crap?"

"Just like wanting a good childhood, but getting more bummed. Plus people being all lame and sinister, like bad guys everywhere you would look."

"Then you didn't want to hurt anyone?" Maya asked him.

"No. I guess not," Twig said.

Maya nodded, putting on her right turn signal, as had the hearse that she was following. Pleased with her exchange with Twig, she would not push any further.

The procession all snaked north and was soon split up. Each vehicle found parking close by on the cemetery grounds. Moe put his motorcycle right near where the hearse had pulled in. He was on standby to help organize and enlist pallbearers. It was to be Twig, Les, Roxy and himself. Then he recognized Truck and Boonz coming towards him from an avenue of headstones. It was those two and a short brunette.

They exchanged 'Heys' all around.

"This is Esther," said Boonz.

"Hi. You two want to help carry the casket?" said Moe.

Truck and Boonz said they would. The rest of Sonny's family and the funeral attendees made their way to the area done up with white folding chairs, a white canopy overhead. Moe gathered his crew. As they took hold of Sonny's burial vessel, Truck added a, "Let's keep it slow and easy."

They traversed the solemn earth. There were only some quick exchanges between Dream Demonical and Dystopian Squalor Syndicate on this death march. They noticed the reticent unknown standing far off and nearby, all watching the goings-ons. The tame rabble spy rituals brought off and about most proper. Just rites. Drawn. Enthralled. The six, the men and woman set the casket gently on the frame mount that would lower the body down into the dirt. People filtered in and took seats. Catfish and Twig were in the front row along with Aunt Sally and Maya. There was a pastor present from a local church that they'd asked to lead the service. He welcomed all, encouraging those scattered in the distance to gather in.

"Today, we have come to lay to rest, Vincent Edward Frye. Known as Sonny by his family and friends. Born in the summer of Nineteen-Seventy, to father Elijah, and mother

225

Laura in New Orleans, Louisiana. I have been told that Sonny was an accomplished musician. It is clear that he has touched a good many souls with his talents and passion for life. Many of you here are a testament to his willingness to share his gifts with others."

This settled, and thoughts were thunk. Feels and funk.

The minister continued: "Now, Mister Mack Campbell has requested to read a prepared piece."

Truck walked up and eyed the casket, acknowledging Catfish and Twig. He unfolded a paper and straightened out a couple creases.

"It's hard not to think about what if, you know? What if they hadn't took Sonny and all that. So this is for him. What if? What if the eagle refuses to soar? What if the lion refuses to roar? What if the harlot refuses to whore? Opens her heart, closes her door. What if the whimsical cut out the whim? What if the spinster just chose not to spin? What if the poet refuses to pen? Line upon line, again and again. What if? What if the slacker began to produce? What if the hangman did slacken his noose? What if the shut-in began to uncluse? What if the bass fisher turned 'em all loose? What if? What if the carnivore went vegetarian? What if the Sheriff was chill with Maid Marian? What if there weren't no more shushing librarians? Speak your minds people. Don't let them hush you like they have done to Sonny. There are always changes. Sometimes you think you know if it's for the good or bad. Sonny was good. It's bad that we lost him. Other than that—I don't know. Maybe together we can make it back to okay. Thanks," Truck finished and walked away at a somber pace.

"Thank you, Mr. Campbell," the pastor had stepped back in. "Now Sonny's father wishes to say a few words."

Catfish stood, as did Twig, who walked beside his Pop to a position graveside. The old man began to speak.

"Be not forgetful to entertain strangers—" A slow and deliberate rhythm, emphatic. "For thereby, some have entertained angels unawares. I heard a man say that in a movie. I searched it out in the Bible, there in Hebrews chapter thirteen and verse two.

"Be not forgetful; to entertain strangers. Thereby. Some have entertained angels. Unawares." He stopped to collect himself. With great finality, "We must always entertain stranger's angels. God Bless Sonny, bless you all, and peace be on everyone."

Twig and Catfish returned to their seats. The pastor announced there would at present be a song sung. There was movement in the wings, then Roxy posted up next to some flowers installed on a stand near the front edge of the canopy. Les moved up next to her, wearing an acoustic guitar slung over his left shoulder. Silence. An intense saturation and concentration of energy comma goodwill lingered in the still hollow air. With looks and a small signal Les began to gently coax out a rhythm and played a tag, leading Roxy into the opening stanza, her chords vocalizing.

"There's a land that is fairer than day—And by faith we can see it afar—For the Father waits over the way—To prepare us a dwelling place there.

"In the sweet—By and By—We shall meet on that beautiful shore—In the sweet—By and By—We shall meet on that beautiful shore.

"To our bountiful Father above—We will offer our tribute of praise—For the glorious gift of His Love—And the blessings that hallow our days."

Roxy continued on the second chorus. You could hear Catfish echoing her on the 'In the sweet' and the 'By and By' parts. Then as the call and response came around again, Aunt Sally, Maya, and a few others joined in with the singing. Roxy started back on the chorus a third time, while Les dropped out so it was sung acapella— "In the sweet, in the sweet, By and By, By and By—we shall meet on that beautiful shore, By and By." More voices came in until at last there was a choir in full voice—"In the sweet, in the sweet, By and By, By and By— We shall meet on that beautiful shore."

There was a special moment shared then all fell silent, hung the air with rapt emotion. Maybe the wind spoke, but nobody else. Catfish stood, started clapping up tempo bobbing in

227

between the hits after eight counts opened up and sang right out—

"Soon and very soon, we are going to see the King. Soon and very soon, we are going to see the King. Soon and very soon, we are going to see the King. Hallelujah, hallelujah, we're going to see the King."

Les found the key and laid light moving chords with a little bit of rhythm echoed Catfish clapping, something then was happening. Twig sat shook slumped sideways surrounded by forces, tangible proof that love is a real thing. Makes a body stir. Lit soulful truth, by the vein, the raw, and the crude.

"No more dying there, we are going to see the King. No more dying there, we are going to see the King—" Twig let go. As had the rest in peace they left their release to seek slight reprieve. "Hallelujah, hallelujah, we're going to see the King."

Overall it was a mighty fine customary observance. People gathered in again to watch the casket lowered down in the negative space of the dug out earth, the realization of a life's journey complete.

Twig rose and walked off towards a lane of settled graves; trying not to step on any heads, toes, or chiseled marble stones.

"Jesus," he prayed they spoke each other's language. Pausable friction, God's a disciple jockey, scratching against the record, back and forth. Steady time to the drum beat. (1984's irreparable coalescence.) Yes-yes yall and a bag of them spiceys. Moves on the dance floor. Sonny boy, Sonny boy tell 'em a tale. Give 'em a line to come in off— the ragged waves, from across the bow.

"Hey man, you wanna hit this?" Twig turning saw Boonz offering him a joint.

"Yeah, man. Thanks," said Twig, taking a drag, holding in the smoke for a time.

"All that singing was some shit, huh?" said Boonz.

"Yeah," Twig exhaled then quickly drew in again on the reefer, the sadness.

"You like backing up Betty Boop?" said Boonz, small and easy.

"It ain't so bad," Twig handing back the joint.

Boonz took a couple three puffs. Then he asked, "She let you touch them titties?"

This got a little chuckle from Twig. It was madness how amazed he felt as he recognized it might not be hell from here on out, always and forever. Things weren't over. It just seemed that way at the moment.

"Fuck, man I'm sorry. I wish I could've done something for Sonny. It all happened so fast," Boonz said.

"It's done. Doesn't matter anymore. I might just want to start a rage— Against the machine cover band." The punctuation caught Boonz a bit off guard.

"That would be fun," said Boonz, passing the joint back again. Twig took another toke; the ganja lined his throat and entered his bloodstream's bodily system.

"You ever think about taking over Dystopian Squalor? Not that I mean to take you away from all of what you've got here," Boonz said.

"Tsss, what I got," Twig, dismissively. "That's exactly what you mean to do. I don't blame you. And yeah, I thought about it. I'd be dumb not to look at my alternatives, bullshit like that."

"Seems to make a lot of sense, but no rush, man. You do what you need to do."

"No shit boondoggle. Thanks for the permission," said Twig.

"Alright. Just know that Truck and me are down, and we been there is all. You know?"

"Yeah. Thanks." Twig handed the roach over to Boonz. The two shook hands in some basic form of acknowledgement slash saying goodbye for now.

Twig went back to roaming around the graves. Boonz turned, making his way towards the burial site. Roxy gave him a look as he strolled by.

"Hi," Boonz told her.

"Fucking headhunter," she said.

"Hey, I'm not big on logic and reason, but it's obvious. There's no secret lady."

"Yeah, maybe in *your* skewed view," Roxy told him.

"I'm doing what's right for my band," Boonz replied.

"My my, aren't you important? Owning bands and what not."

"And what about you, Mama Goose? When you gonna let them baby birds free to fly out on their own?" Boonz snapped back.

"Sleaze." Check and mate for now. Boonz could tell so, so he walked away at least appearing civil from a distance.

There were mostly live bodies milling about the site of the service. The lines between stranger and acquaintance were blurred. Fondly recalled stories were shared, bonds inferred. Arms extended, hands shook, hugs happened when appropriate. Catfish sat down talking to Aunt Sally about Twig and Sonny's mother.

"Aww, Laura she was so nice. She raised them boys, you know?" said Catfish.

"Yes, I know." Sally had been there and seen it happen.

"I coulda never done so well as she did. Oh, I was a selfish man," he said.

"We all have that one time or another."

"But *some*times though, not all the time. There does a reckoning come."

"No. No, this isn't that. This is just—it's a damn tragedy. There is never any reasoning with those," Sally tried to console him.

"Yes. That is sure a load to fathom."

Catfish looked off and rested his eyes on a dark mound of soil. There was a long shovel laid across its side. This would be the dirt door shut on his poor boy, Vincent "Sonny" Frye. Got stole. Ripped from off this Earth. Rebirth of the negative essence. Reversal of molecular space. Seed, fodder, nutrients. Feed the fueled men race. Been unfomented. Transported through and entered into an elemental trace. Ashes, dust, and biowaste. Smoke it shoot it freedom base. Dushty asses, drunken lasses, muster passes grace. Blustery fascist face. Most already forgotten, the first begotten, rancid rotten and chaste.

Hate no stranger, straight no taster. Entertaining mangled angels major strafe in dangers pasted rate a crazed witch blaze. Anyways comma anyandalloftheways. Nature's phrase; praised, glazed and sprinkled. The gory daze of a glory haze. An altogether boring pace. Fuck the story-Ay. All but ever thrown a catch and sank. Cut the stank, check the grab, bill the foot to light the kill and stomp the grip, script the flip and dance. Grive, joove, gab and mood: Mick and Stoove, starve and markle mapled spit the hot shook a tot. Knocked some sense into the lot. The word pulled loose and off the bone it fell—

The juices mixed with rocks and gravel fillings.

Crustaceous lava tilling. The granite larval spilling, some final marvel thrilling goosebumps drifted off on the same breeze that brought them in. At who knows whim?

One circle: fin. Fade out, pace in.

It began to shprinkle as Izzy and Alyssa grazed nirvana somewhere in the Rose Test Garden. Then via the long route, they crawled all over the amphitheater and got a good soak going, before eventually retreating back towards the vicinity of the bus. The rain in Portlaned fell mainly unwaned on the strange weather vanes of the quiet quaint hamlet. The desert it ain't, but a fertile peaceful plain. An unwavering dang wet harangue. Quite the flip of a brief burst or pang on the heavenly range, the prim and the downy of Multnomah County. As Izzy approached the side sliding door, he noticed the fringe of a furry tail from underneath the right front wheel well.

"You want to come inside out of the showers?" Izzy asked, bent down by the tire.

After a moment of hesitation, a skittering noise came from the recessed shadows as Larry the Ancient hopped down onto the ground. He surveyed the immediate area.

"Yes, thank you. Have you plans to put out from this mooring?" Larry asked.

The side door slid open. Alyssa stepped up in. Izzy from the outside reached into a slender closet space between the bench seat and the rear passenger window. His whole right arm had been swallowed. Finally, he pulled out one of his several stashes throughout the vehicle.

"Yes. Please," Izzy motioned and he and the squirrel both also leapt into the van.

He shoved the door mostly closed, leaving it a couple inches ajar so as to not make things too stuffy. All settled and the scene was most fine under the petulant sky. Izzy sat next to the girl on the bench seat, setting a small carved wooden receptacle on his lap. Trust her tranquil treasures beat roving the betrothed.

"When do we depart?" LtAWS asked.

"Oh, not too long," said Izzy.

"Would you like some ganja, Mr. Larry?" said Alyssa.

"Oh, I can always easily scavenge up some nuts, bugs, or tree bark; any of which will be sufficient nutrition for my mission's duration," said LtAWS.

"But ganja isn't food. It's a magic herb," Izzy totem.

"Yes, of course. I am very aware of man's propensity to ingest various mind-altering substances."

"But you don't trust us?" Alyssa asked.

"It is not a matter of trust. It has been told of the soldier who submits to potions of pleasure, losing sight of his duty and obligation," said the Ancient.

"Who was it told you that?" said Izzy.

"The commanders of the Guardians of the Envoy to the Council of the Living."

"So then it's forbidden?"

"No, only highly discouraged," said the squirrel.

"And so what if instead, we highly en*couraged* you?" said Alyssa.

"I believe that is what you are doing now," answered Larry.

Izzy had a joint out, and was rolling it between his fingers, loosening the dry leaf inside. Larry the Ancient watched him handling the small white stick. He felt no ominous apprehension. Alyssa asked if their encouragement had been at all effective. Larry answered that it had and that he would perhaps try a small amount as a measure of good faith.

"Hey now, we don't want to force anything on you. Just being inclusive is all."

"No, no. I insist," said LtAWS. "By all means, light it up."

In Izzy's mind, Alvin had just told him to spark one. Your team wins the Super Bowl. You travel about freely and without hindrance. A girl walks into your life, still the blessings that be in her eyes abound. Now a sentient fur ball from a fabled dimension sits here clear as day, and how far away is Cortez? What is Denver? Why is Colorado? When will any of it make sense? You'd think at the pace he was going there'd be some gigantic magnetized payoff at the end of the track they were shooting down. Twas a zippy and yet involved, arduous slog. Soon to re-enter into a head full of fog: a better daze—a howdy clause.

233

"So Larry, these Guardians of the Envoy to the Council, right? You work for them?" Izzy asked.

"No, I work *with* them," LtAWS replied.

"But they give you rules and restrictions?" Izzy said.

"Yeah, screw them guys!" shouted Alyssa.

"No, do not screw them. All is done for the greater good. Now let us consume your ganja. And will this be the kind laced with the PCP or formaldehyde?" said Larry.

"No man. What? It is only the purest kind," said Izzy.

Larry the Ancient Wonder Squirrel sat up on the box seat across from the boy and girl. Izzy lit and hit, passing to the left. Alyssa inhaled easily and leaned forward handing the herb over to the Ancient. The southern flying squirrel held the joint with both forepaws working around his front teeth to form a seal as he puffed several times to maximize the flow of burning grass. It tasted like a fresh campfire. The smell was reminiscent of his youth in the woods around Pine Bluff, Arkansas, USA, Seventh Dimension of Earth, (AKA Weirdsville). Larry felt a rush and thrill at the idea of a new experience exposed to his own being.

The doobie made its wade around the mystic triangle thrice and then some change. Izzy and Alyssa were silently transfixed, watching the little space traveler getting used to the buzz, his weedfaring tee aitch sea legs. Outside the rain picked up in a constant caress that pattered on the roof and windows. A verisimilitude of verve in a cornucopia of rhythmic harm honeyed, resplendent and celestial. Peek out to see the ground drowning. Noah-Noah whatchu know about characters arc de triumph and tribble-ations? Then the flood doesn't destroy. The planets continue their revolutions—

Around Pandora's Double Xerox helix box—

Bridgetown Brigadoon imbued this bountiful city of Alyssa Rose's awakening; that why *not* make things ever only always amazing? Stumptown bud saloon door flapping, boots' spurs jangling, blown in with the tumbleweeds at dusk. Bumblebees that buzzk. Ill tip static automatic trip emphatic spell of musk. Liquor in a hidden flusk, opened coat out, "Whatchu need? Rolux." Flagrant noble tricks, aged obelisk. Local bubble ups on the cusp a couple yups. Yip the coyote calls, shrieks in coyote drawls. Long and open vowels, strong and vocal howls; sigh lends gruff in growls. Hierarchy barking fouls with slim and ribsy sharking scowls; teeth. Hungry beast, starving artist motivated by the kill, stalk and slaughter, graver still the ravenous raw, veinous meal.

"Can I do some more driving today?" Alyssa asked.

"So, you also are fluent in the operation of this machine?" said Larry the Ancient.

"Semi-fluent, mildly able. Barely competent," answered Alyssa.

"Oh, she's better than all that," Izzy said.

Alyssa straightened up all proud like. The squirrel smiled and resumed looking all about the van's insides, its intricacies. There were words and language, small colorful labels placed in generally random spots. The curtains over the windows were a gentle blue with tan squiggles. Several small hatches held who knows what. Larry turned and peered into the front control area. He saw two single seats, and the helm, which was a great round wheel. It was all very crude relative to the massive cargo ships and personnel transports back on his home planet. A highly reflective panel was attached inside the top of the massive front window. From this hung a peculiar thick twine weighted down by two birds of a feather, flying together. Intertwined, interwoven. Izzy told Alyssa that she could drive for a bit once they crossed over the Willamette. First they would stop at the waterfront to see if the rain would let up some. This would allow them a walk along the riverside's park and pathways.

"How many gears?" Izzy's quiz popped off.

"One two three four-banger," said Alyssa.

"That's cylinders. But okay. When do you shift?"

"Second at ten, third at twenty-five, fourth at forty. Ten twenty-five forty, then on and on as fast as the fates allow," Rose rambled.

"Where's reverse at?" the exam continued.

"Push down, left, and back," said her.

"I will say that your confident tone leads me to believe you would make a gifted pilot," Larry said to the girl.

"Yeah, she's got the knowledge down. Still must put it to good use, be consistent and improve. And at our core, what are we?" Izzy asked. "For extra credit."

Alyssa gave this serious thought. Because what're you gonna do, not think a thing over? Maybe breathe before you let forth with your speculations. Crazy idea. That's if you're interested in words and language. Written, spoken, or sung. Blue notes, gray skies, fresh air and fruit pies. Root beer and soot wise. Rutty roads to roam down in a moose-size goose guise, laying golden eggs buys the true prize. Freedom. Time to calculate a sentence. Guarantees repentance, as the truth lies.

"We are, (dramatic paws sub claws out draws) a high volume hunk of inert metal. The locale motoring freight train, rectaganol doghouse on wheels." Alyssa dropped this and sat back to watch the reflexive ripples extend out into the brains of Izzy and the squirrel.

"So the legend goes," Israel said with glows.

"Allegedly," said her.

"Oh?" perked LtAWS' ears. "Is there a mythical narrative of travels in such a vessel as this in which we sit?"

"Ah yes, there is an alleged legend," Izzy said.

A gleeful expectance bubbled in the squirrel and certain parts of Alyssa did also tingle.

"Good Israel, would you share it with me now?" said Larry.

"Say, let's move out. I'll tell you something about what's a VW bus. Like on the road; rolling," said Izzy.

The roach was field stripped for disposal and recycling. The wooden box stowed back out of sight in the closet beside him. Izzy then climbed up in between the front bucket seats, sitting behind the wheel. He had the key turned, and hit the ignition's push button to fire, get the valves pumping, crank pulley spinning. In his mind he started the clock counting down from three minutes, which he'd give the engine to warm before putting it to work in the cold, damp climate. Izzy put a Beach Boys CD in the stereo and I Get Around came on. He

236

was once again pleased at converting the front to disc brakes. Drum brakes would be mostly for crap in this tempestuous drizzle. He used to have a 1965 Pontiac Bonneville that was an absolute mess in any bit of moisture.

There was a Waterfront Park, Governor Tom McCall, on the west bank of the Willamette River. Alyssa slipped into the passenger seat humming a tune, then immediately broke into the lyrics of I Get Around. Only instead of singing 'girls,' she replaced it each time with 'squirrels.' Her annunciation was clean and elicited a, "Huh ha," from Larry.

Nobody was going steady, because it just wouldn't be proper to abandon your best *squirrel* on any given Saturday evening. From Larry's perch in the back, he heard the girl's version above the song coming from out of the front speakers.

"Huh ha! No it does not say that, truthfully. Tell me are these the real words?" LtAWS was confounded.

The music continued unaccompanied—Moving around, getting down, getting back up again. Two solid minutes of surf, cars, and girls comma squirrels; just enough bounce in the get-tar that you might call it good old Rock N Roll.

Larry watched the Rose sit blooming turned a smile beaming joy and pure amusement multidirectionally.

"No sir, that's me having fun. Beach Boys don't sing about *squirrels*," Alyssa said.

"Might've had some more fans if they did," Izzy said.

"Huff, I did for a moment there believe you," said Larry just a bit let down.

Little Deuce Coupe started playing as Izzy shifted into reverse, backing out, glancing left and right, not very unlike Larry had done upon their all's meeting. Be on guard.[11] The road was wide, barren, and surrounded on all sides by massive pine and the dark green-canopied forest. They meandered cautiously still stuck with a curious tourist mentality. Passing again by the diverse gardens. A last look towards the amphitheater, they caught a glimpse through the timber lining the lane. Izzy collected his thoughts. It was all so seductive.

"In or about the middle of the twentieth century we had this thing called the Sixties. A lot of what was going on then leaked over into the Seventies and far beyond. Spawned by a shared tide and revolution in places like basically everywhere, folks ignited, lit hearts and minds, which fused action and fed the general unrest."

Larry the Ancient listened closely as Izzy spoke. He climbed up to sit on the back of the captain's chair. Looking out the front window the three witnessed the city appear as they left the cover of the park.

"The Summer of Love in sixty-seven. Woodstock in sixty-nine. La Onda at Avandaro in Mexico. New Zealand house-truckers. 'Peace convoys' in the United Kingdom at Stonehenge, and the Isle of Wight Festival in 1970. Piedra Roja in Chile. People gathered. Bodies mingled minds and moved about. Others followed around the Grateful Dead, lost and hungry wanderings of all kinds made use of Volkswagen campers and all sorts of Type 2 transporter vans. Show me a better way to do it. You can't," Izzy finished his oratory.

LtAWS considered this, decided it could be nice in another life. "They tell us stories so that we know their character. We accept them and embrace the novelty," quoth the Ancient.

"And Monterey Pop, flower children, and all of the music too," said Alyssa.

"Yes, many epic unifying moments and passionate individuals that informed the larger consciousness of humanity," quoth the boy.

After rounding a wide bend, Izzy pointed out they were on Columbia, which should take them right to the River. Alyssa gave him a sideways glance, putting to question his navigating prowess.

"Rand McNally," was his only reply.

Sailing in a southwesterly course (according to the dash-mounted compass and street signs) they crossed over a highway. The pace of traffic was careful and calculated due to the vertical misting.

"Wwwaaaah tis thah tone un yur yoozingk inard?" Larry blathered.

Laughter erupted from the girl and boy. Alyssa told Larry could he try that again.

"Yes, uh—Yes and who was it dipping your dope joints in embalming fluid?" Larry asked. "I am certain I have heard of this practice."

"Maybe some degenerate tried that once, but this stuff you're on is one hundred percent natural," Izzy totem.

"Vur evil bod ids who zey. Fibe?" Larry felt the earth tilt, unable to follow at least half of what was going on. He'd get wobbly then work to focus. Was he already letting down the Council of the Living, or is this just pleasure and the feel of existential growth? From the buildings, they passed into a swath of green and lush thickets. Ahead in the distance, a great structure breeched the horizon shooting up and nearly out of Larry's sight from his spot beside Izzy. There were other less impressive nests of flesh in zest concession. Blocks apparently necessary, some form of GDP.

"Therse hubs ub comerts ur resurdances?" said Larry.

"Probably offices. I would doubt if anybody lives in them," Izzy answered.

They all watched, looked, and rolled through these articles of architecture, finally turning south on Naito Parkway. Izzy pulled in off the road, gliding to a stop next to a shuttle bus temporarily parked crooked over two spaces. The rain was light. Izzy fetched an umbrella for the walk. The passenger window was left cracked so that Larry could move in and out. He said he would most likely stay put, run some diagnostics to judge whether this smoke had left him permanently impaired.

"Alright, man," said Izzy.

"Furnub takoy, Sam," said the Ancient.

Izzy chuckled, then set off with Alyssa. They walked up through Governor Tom McCall Waterfront Park as far as the Morrison Bridge. The two stayed snug under the open umbrella. Grass fields, cement trails, dusty avenues watered down and slick in spots. A few boats were out on the river, though most stayed safely docked in the harbor.

Larry the Ancient dozed off after determining he was probably damaged beyond mending. Undoubtedly to be stuck forever in a haze, calling people Sam.

. . . .

When Larry was a young lad he acquired some land. He set up a small farm on a meager plot in the Arkansas Timberlands west of Pine Bluff. He was out on the plow in the field preparing his soil for planting. The crop came in light last season, so he extended the perimeter of the area to be tilled on the northernmost side. This meant more work but also the possibility of greater yield when harvest arrived.

A neighbor might argue that he had exceeded his legal property line, but Larry knew his deed well and the additional space he was cultivating was definitely a part of his land. He wanted to get the seeds in the ground soon. He would still need to put in the better part of an afternoon scouting the forest. He would collect fallen acorns from the nearby red oaks. He must also find suitable thatch for the repairs required on his den.

Larry's wife was at home now nursing their only child, who wasn't but ten weeks old. They were coming out of their first full winter together. Hopes were high for the coming spring and summer. Without warning and from not far off, a scream shattered the morning calm. Terror froze him for an instant, and then recognition flooded into his system. It was Rebecca. She was being attacked and her cries were of dire despair.

He bounded forward twice then flew the length of his field in a second split. As he hit the compact sod, he transferred all of his momentum to thrust fully again. Larry sprung up but kept his projection angle low to maximize the terrain he could cover, while staying under the branch and limbs that hung above the pathway. He heard nothing but Rebecca's shrieks. He realized she was now fighting back against whatever creature was encroaching upon her. Another bound off the dirt as he flew higher and could finally see his nest.

It was a damn hawk! Blast that two-bit vulture with its beak slashing all through where Rebecca stood, no doubt in between the wretched beast and their child. Larry's current flight pattern would take him right into that bloody creature's spine. Hopefully it wouldn't be too late. He came down with his hind legs extended forward, so that his front paws would be free to go after the buzzard's face.

POW! Larry stuck it right below the neck. A near dead hit on the upper vertebrae, if the dirty chicken hadn't turned slightly at the last moment. A deathly piercing squawk echoed out through the woods. The stunned bird attempted to jump up and fly away, but its first few flaps were weak and it only landed again close by. The hawk-eye realized it was only another rodent that had done the clobbering. Larry saw it contemplating an immediate counter assault. It screeched, spread its wings and popped up flashing its talons in a show of aggression and murderous intent.

In a fury, Larry ran at the brute and quickly pounced up aiming his full force at the body. He saw the bird raise a claw. The squirrel opened his patagium to draft upwards as he smacked the side of the gnashing beak away and bashed the lousy magpie right in the face with a brutal follow through. This sent it flipping feet over head and backwards into a pile of brush, dust, and feathers. It scrambled madly. Jumping away it finally flew off, injured and dazed in a crooked line, dodging trees while trying to steady itself in retreat.

Plain old Larry turned and scurried back to the scene he had just broken up. Then he was suddenly around a campfire recounting the event.

"'My baby. It ate my baby,' was the last thing she said to me. I sat there on the ground with her. As my dear Rebecca breathed her last. Then and there I decided I wouldn't ever be caught sitting idly by, waiting for the next evil to come and destroy my world. I sought out how I might fight for good. I dedicated myself to always stand on the side of truth, justice, and other such lofty business."

A voice across the fire hollered out, "Tell 'em the one about Clyde the Glide, Larry. Don't nobody wanna hear about all this heartache." A crash of thunder shook the earth, left the scene saturated with chaos.

"Whatchu all know about Clyde the Glide?!" Larry the Ancient shouted as he was roughly woke up by the bus door sliding open.

Alyssa jumped in and set down keenly behind the wheel. Izzy was backing in as he shook raindrops off the closing umbrella.

"Get ready Larry, I'm taking charge," said the Rose.

"Hey, what do *you* know about Clyde the Glide?" Izzy asked Larry.

"What? Nothing. He is a folk hero from my dimension. Is this true that Miss Alyssa will now perform maneuvers in your vehicle?" Larry asked still half groggy.

"Yep. Now's your chance to escape if you know what's good for you," said Izzy.

"Pssh, me drive 'um doghouse Ay numba one big time G.I.—keys, please," said Alyssa, major league sweet.

"Alright, talk me through each step," he said, handing over the key ring.

"Mirrors." She adjusted the rearview, looking left and right to scan the sides.

"Shifter in neutral, key in ignition, turn right one click. Oil and alternator lights. Second click, start engine." She pressed the push button and the starter spun. The motor fired up and the girl gave it a little gas. Izzy told her to let it warm. Seat belts, check the wipers, you'll need lights and are you sure the side mirrors are good? The weather was mild enough so that no ice had yet formed on the roads. It was okay driving conditions.

"Hey, take it easy, for the kids. We will get through this," Alyssa feigned grim sincerity. "What about you pick out a nice album for the ride?"

"I say we listen to the road and surrounding sounds. Focus on managing the rain and this machine," Izzy was not leaving anything to chance.

"Lame," said Alyssa.

"It is very wise to eliminate distractions when operating any transport in less than ideal conditions," said Larry.

"Yeah, yeah. Safety first. You all make a good point," she submitted. "Next time though, music."

"Why don't you try going in and out of reverse a couple times?" said Izzy.

"Clutch in," she said, Izzy nodded.

Alyssa pressed down on the shifter knob, felt the stick drop and she moved it left, back, and set it. She gave it some gas, releasing the clutch enough for the bus to move slightly backwards. She pushed the clutch back in, moving the shifter to neutral. She switched on the headlights, and put the wipers on intermittent.

"Just feeling it." She pumped the accelerator pedal a couple times and felt the engine vibrations pulsing through her foot. It was alive. They were connected.

"How's it look on that side?" asked the Rose of Izzy Dufrene.

"All clear," was the reply from her navigator.

The girl shoved it back in reverse, rolling out into the open lot. She found first gear and then started with a jolting hiccup. Once in gear she crept easily forward, and then to a stop before entering traffic. Izzy told her to stay in the far right lane as she pulled out smoothly northbound onto the parkway passing by the Portland Marriott. Alyssa soon spotted the entrance lane for the Hawthorne Bridge. After coming to a complete stop at a red octagon, she carefully drove onto the green-beamed relic; only partially aware she was now over the river's flow. She accelerated, stomped on the clutch, found second and let it back out. After a slow acceleration she got into third gear a little early, but was focused on the road and so everything was steady. She heard no complaints.

"It's a truss bridge, built 1910. Maybe the oldest vertical-lift still operating in the US," Izzy said of the marvel they rode across, paraphrasing his nearly memorized Portland pamphlet.

A cyclist traveled along beside them, but Alyssa remained focused on the road both near and far. She rolled along in low third gear doing a little less than thirty mph. Fairly confident in her shifting, mentally going over what she'd learned, now trying to make every action natural and smooth. Ahead, the camper commander saw a group of stilted concrete freeways, which she'd soon be traveling beneath. She noticed the top tip of her left wiper blade was loose and waggling. She'd tell Izzy about it later.

"That's the Five," Izzy said, indicating the freeway traffic up ahead.

They came out onto a raised roadway that stayed above ground level, until a few blocks down where they met the asphalt in between a small park and a fast food restaurant. She guided the bus to an easy halt at a red traffic signal.

"This is Grand here. Let's keep going, and make a left on Seventh Avenue," Izzy said.

They continued and made the turn north.

"Sweet. Just relax and stay like this. We'll run right into Sandy Boulevard," said the navigator.

With every stop and go Alyssa was feeling more comfortable, accelerating faster and making a sport of it. More than once Izzy said something like, "It's not a race," or "Where's the fire, lady?" To the latter Alyssa snapped back, "*I'm* the Firelady!"

LtAWS was quite verbose. He was commenting on how in every city and every population, in every dimension, we're all basically the same, "Ants in a molehill." The boy asked what that meant, and was told it had to do with the difficulty of the individual to understand life in a larger context; existence in relation to the collective. To this Izzy nodded in some degree of comprehension. Without warning, from the girl arose an even livelier, "I *AM* the Firelady!" She was just having way too much of a good time.

"Me smoke'um Ladyfire!" Alyssa yelled with a rambunctious warrior spirit.

Larry let out a gleeful squeal of squirrel appeal to match the girl's erupting enthusiasm. "Faster, faster!" the Ancient implored.

"Whoa whoa whoa! You all calm down. Alyssa, don't listen to that squirrel. I'll put some music on. But let's not get carried away," Izzy pleaded.

This was agreeable to all parties. Izzy weighed the risks of putting in Ten or some other Pearl Jam. That might overload the karmic balance though. He settled on a Toots and the

Maytals bootleg compilation. It started with a cover of Take Me Home, Country Roads (originally recorded by John Denver, 1971). The disc started spinning. A piano walked up into a steady pulsing hold, padded underneath by the bass and drums. A soulful singular voice began humming warm colors, storytelling in a soothing way without any actual words. Then the instruments cut out and somebody sang, "Yeah—Listen!" Near flawless allocution: in the Western tradition. Truest fountains—floating down the riviera.

"Do you even know where we're going?" asked Alyssa.

"Forward. Ahead. The next spot," said Izzy.

"Uh, could you please be a little more vague? Where am I?" said her in revolt.

"Rip City, Little Beirut," Izzy replied.

Alyssa Rose was not amused. She didn't like not knowing where the end was. It made her think of bigger things. Mountains. Molehills. Whatever real life was, and how could she keep that far away? Izzy sensed her frustration but couldn't help it, her being so amazing and on her game.

"Hey, you're the one driving—" Izzy paused.

"Don't say it," she warned.

"Miss Daisy?" said he as a question and in a horridly offensive Southern accent, the Carolinas.

Boooooo! HiSSSsssss.

Then Izzy 'Ooo-ed' and cringed all up. It was a crass and tasteless joke. Hardly humor at all, fathoms beyond proper. Speak your nasty, talking absolute xenophobia. Larry took a double take.

"Ladyfire daisy phase!" LtAWS babbled on.

The girl did impress with the guile of a good goosebump. Tingled the flesh to watch her work that apparatus. Touch made manifest in the subtle wake of rippled road and conquered intersecting sign waves reading, "NE Sandy." A bit of magic she thought of beaches and dogs from Annie; AKA the Little Orphan.

Up upon the rooftop side to side, water spilt off the edge could abide the tide. Somehow fitting, storm cloud spitting. Toots sang a ditty 'bout Pomps and Pride. Trumpet and

245

trombone built up under a 'Do re mi fa so la ti' don't stop, for this life is a blissful sight. And this day could be forever night.

"This song goes nice with your suspension," said Alyssa.

"Yeeee-uh, sometimes it really syncs up just perfect." Izzy saw she was really getting it.

He gained a closer understanding of her. This woman he'd developed an attachment to. It was strong and she was powerful. He wanted Alyssa, desired to feel her body. But he would not stop the time she was having, just to satisfy his carnal appetite. Is it better to want than have? Better to desire than possess, more thrilling to covet in your heart than hold in your arms? There is something to be said about anticipation; delayed gratification. Grass is greener, weeds is shorter, dandelions is more dandy.

There were places and things the girl tried to take in, but it was all devoured in the now on which she rode. Realized, relaxed, and inspired. Izzy reached over near the wheel and turned on the heater to defrost the front window.

"I must've been going to do that," said the Rose.

Contentedness. Quiet supplication.

Peaceful acceptance of a passive petition, and then she slapped Izzy *SMACK* on the top of his left thigh. He reached over and squeezed her right thigh, right back. Larry the Ancient was moved by their playful affection. So much so that he punched Alyssa in the ear.

"Hey! What was that for?" she said, rubbing the spot where he'd socked her.

"I apologize. I thought it was a game of tag. I got caught up." Larry had to check himself. He was reminded that his mission was not to have fun or be on vacation.

After turning east on Glisan Street, they were headed through Kerns towards the center of Laurelhurst. Cruising the drag, over the speakers a chorus singing: "She will never let me down." Layered full with counter melodies and voices calling chants in echoed harmony.

"How am I doing?" Alyssa put to Izzy.

"Ay numba one big time," he said.

"Any idea what's next?"

246

"We'll grow old together. Go Fish and Texas Hold 'Em. Commiserate."

"That's gotta be a line," said her.

"Sometimes regular talk can be lines too," said him.

Izzy pointed down the road. Said the Coe Circle roundabout was coming up. He told her they wanted to go north, so she would first need to turn right and follow around basically three quarters of the way and then exit. Alyssa said she had it. They started in alright, but she missed the exit so Izzy said to stay on the circle to catch it next time around. After one full rotation they were all quite optimistic about the next shot. After the second rotation, Larry was fearful as Izzy's energy introduced an element of doubt. After three whole rotations full of a hyper-as-shit Ancient Wonder Squirrel, and a strung out Rose, Izzy nearly had his hands on the steering wheel, as once the one thousand and eighty degrees were through, they flew out of the loop northbound on East Chavez Boulevard.

"Broadway and the Hollywood Theatre dead ahead. We'll find you a nice place to put in," Izzy said.

Everyone was still getting over the adrenaline from the wobbly navigation of the roundabout. The objects in motion had nervously awaited the action of an outside force. Thankfully it never came. Finally, in the form of the parking brake, and the ceasing of motion, the safety of being still did eventually arrive.

January 28, 1998

"What're the fowl sayings? How duck they go?"

Doth tree men woods tanned are own contraption. Introspection.

"Pigeon-toed, dovetail—Crow's feet, eagle eye," Boonz rattled off.

"Chicken wang," added Truck.

"Chicken wang, turkey nerk, bird brawn," said Boonz.

"Pelican briefs, hawk a loogie."

"Nay. No loogie hawks."

"Hawk eyes, Buzzard butt. Parrothead!" Truck nailed it with that last one.

"I think that's all of them."

"Pterodactyl tongue, vulturrrre—" Truck stuck in brick thought concentration, penetrating rock sensation.

"Fine man, you win," Boonz conceded.

"Vul-turrrrre—vulture voiced?" Truck unsure.

"No," Boonz again in the negatory.

"Vulture culture. Peckings and chewings," said Truck assuredly.

"Jesus!" said Boonz, furiously near losing it.

"Where?" Truck looked around, acting like he was searching for his Loft and Savagery, then shouted, "One more time, kid."

Twig turned the key and the starter spun, nothing ignited, just cranked and cranked. Failing to fire, somewhere faulty.

"Alright, man," called Truck. Twig switched off the key and slid out of the slightly lifted Chevy Tahoe. "Looks like your alternators got shit flying out of it. That noise ain't good either; that's friction. New one is maybe ninety bucks, maybe less. The install is easy. Whenever the part store opens up tomorrow, you'll be back in business less than an hour after. Easy." Truck finished talking.

"Wish I could of figured that out sooner," Twig said.

"Nah. It's tough without a spotter," said Truck.

The three guys stood around the open hood, underneath the covered driveway with a glowing bulb buzzing yellow overhead. It was dark out, calm and serene. Inside, Catfish sat talking to Aunt Sally. Maya was on the sofa next to her mother. In the kitchen, Boonz's girl Esther picked at a tray of raw vegetables. Seated at the table's edge, she was propped up on one elbow so as to have the ranch dip in reach. She heard muted speech patterns seeping through the cracks around the kitchen door. Boonz and Truck were talking to Sonny's brother. The old folks in the front room were decades back on some trip about memories and meaningful happenings.

Broccoli, green and clean. Good even without dressing. Tends to get stuck in your teeth. Guess that's the way with most food. No kind of reason not to eat something. Plus, she'd been so focused on keeping her caloric intake low due to this piece of cake she'd been eyeing since mid-afternoon. It was the only corner left. All white icing, yellow cake. With none of the colored frosting staining its purity. Red, blue, and yellow frosting is almost never sweet, or in the league of, "Hook me up an I.V. of that, direct injection." You don't need to be decorating funeral cake anyway. 'Keep it classy,' thought Esther. Keep them pinkies out on a cherry tomato. Pop. Pull the pin. Brace yourself. Be sure to keep your lips sealed. As they say, loose lips makes cherry tomato's juices spray all over. The place. Seemed like they'd all made it through the day. Can't say unharmed. People lost bits of themselves; had holes, vacuous empties littered hearts on the mend, lined spirits healing waters wept in sorrow. There'll always be a bitter tomorrow; borrowed against the chance to make even odds.

Collect what's due. Wet dew on the pastures.

"Here's what let's do—" Catfish off again.

Esther had to time the whole thing right. Don't commit too soon; get too far in. Not supposed to eat within two hours of bedtime. It was such a big piece, though. Doesn't make sense somebody making it so substantial. But there it was. Should she save it for tomorrow? Have some, half the other. Would that be not okay? If it sat out, the exposed cake part would dry. But also the icing was improving its consistency with every hour it congealed; got crispy almost, if you're familiar. It's similar to cold pizza in the morning, but a much more subtle transformation. Not to take anything away from cold pizza. There's no mistaking the potency of pizza plus time equals an experience. Full circle to Esther telling herself that celery scooped in the cake's rich frosting would be totally acceptable, totally fine. That's crazy talk. Dunked the short stalk in the ranch and shook it, dripped then quickly transferred it up to be chomped, torn in two. Celery has that same tendency to lodge in one's teeth. It was a clean break and a noisy chew. Makes you feel like you're really making a difference. Eating raw vegetation from the Earth, that's the noble work. It's coexisting and not surviving off the death of another being. The carnivore is a necessary thing. Not trying to say what's what by any stretch. There isn't any good or bad. Besides, everything is chaos, snowballs, avalanches, downward motions, spirals, and uplifting inclinations. *She* was gonna be a part of something big.

Boonz had told her, many times. Laid it on heavy about the attainment of certain levels of success. The storm they needed to create to infiltrate the machine that was the music scene comma industry, if that's even still a thing. Esther would act as a mouthpiece, and representative for Dystopian Squalor. Publicist. She could see the possibilities, bits of glamour, phone calls, and meetings. Deals; networking with producers and promoters. She always had the band's best interest in mind. She could do it. She could do the shit out of it.

This weren't some hostess gig, or a bullshit clerical office position. She knew Boonz had promise. The whole situation could easily (or with some well focused effort) turn into a rocket ship to the moon and beyond.

Boonz was walking a line trying to get in good with Twig. She knew he (Boonz) could talk. Knew it real well because she had some kind of mouth of her own. She usually always had a feeling which way to play it with folks. Also, she had the realization that having those feelings probably meant she was a bad person. It's better to know than to be a fool, plus etcetera and so whatever. She never cared because what—are you just gonna change? Who does that? You take what you get; hand you been dealt. Chips fall where they may. Authory BS that still might contain some elements of truth, forsooth.

From outside, Truck came into the kitchen, pushed the door closed, and walked over to the table. In a few seconds he had a pile of deli meat and cheese in between a sliced roll. He took a bite and scanned the desserts. Cherry pie, fruit salad, angel food and the remains of a more traditional cake with white frosting. Swallow. Another bite of his sandwich. He didn't see any more deviled eggs. Casseroles, rice dishes with queso, lasagna. Rolled tamales, pulled pork and sloppy joes. The dinner hour had officially passed. This was overtime, taking care of business.

Boonz was left in the carport with Twig who was putting tools away. Roxy had already left with Les and Moe in tow. This was mainly to give Twig, Catfish and them the chance to let the day come to some kind of quiet conclusion. Deep sighs outside accompanied by visible puffs of winter breath.

Twig was unsure what today really did accomplish. He did not experience any release of pressure, or alleviation from his emotional distress. It was crap. He didn't think it had anything to do with shedding tears. Everybody is different he kept reminding himself. Ain't only ever one way to do anything, except extra magically delicious through the lard and savory hot sauce churro.

Boonz followed Twig into the kitchen where Esther and Truck were sorting things out. They put lids on containers and placed much of it back in the fridge. Boonz grabbed some black olives out of a bowl. Intentions unannounced, Desean Frye walked into the front room towards the hallway and the back of the home.

"Twig, your Aunt Sally would like to say a family prayer. If you'd sit down here with us for a minute," said Catfish.

"No, thank you," Twig attempted a courteous dismissal. He'd had enough of the rites and ceremony, the pompous circumstantial shit. All of a sudden he is supposed to beg for mercy and ask God for a good night's sleep?

"You should join us. For your father," Sally said.

"You don't get to tell me what I'm supposed to do, or how you think I should act, or what to feel or care about," Twig stated coldly, quick to incite all up in a riot.

"Son, why can't we just settle and get a foothold? Against the rapid waves and rushing current," said Catfish.

"Don't call me that. I ain't no Son, he's gone. Fuckin' everybody just get out!" Twig shouted.

"We'll be going. It's okay," said Sally and she stood.

"You all ladies don't need to leave," said Catfish.

"No Elijah, we'll be fine at the travelodge," Sally said in retreat.

Truck and them heard the fracas from the kitchen and slid out the carport door to their van. Esther was cradling a large hunk of funeral cake on a plastic plate, licking frosting off her fingers. They would crash in their Ford Econoline, and check back in the morning. Aunt Sally stopped briefly beside Catfish, laid a hand on his shoulder, closed her eyes as she mouthed a few words of invocation. Then she followed Maya out the front door as calmly as her emotive framework would allow. Twig and Catfish were left alone in the house. Tempers were at a medium-high simmer.

"Man, if he'd told me anything like you might wanna know, or gave you some words, I would've said that already. Right off I would've told you," said Catfish.

"I didn't say goodbye," said Twig.

"Why? What would you've told him?"

"I would've said hey, and take care."

"Well, we have to make peace with the way things are. I ain't expecting you to be happy much. Please, just don't— You'd be wise not to feed that fury that's burning all inside you now. You know I've said about how the danger lurks. You give it a nest, and it will turn you bad," Catfish totem.

Desean Twigglesworth Frye knew a little bit about garbage people. Dark-hearted and vile, the fiendish filth. Diabolically depraved, degenerate souls. They wore their damage and

252

vitriol on the outside. The dirt-smeared rags and sharpened Gwar noir. A switchblade and hulking spiked shoulderpads make impressions cloud and leer. Crooked stares from the normals. Those of the dryer sheets and fabric softener. You know, real jerks. A, B, *and* C-holes.

Twig just wanted sleep. Catfish too would not turn away rest. For the wicked know when a body is weak and vulnerable. The mind gets temperamental; the fighting tired gain an edge.

Outside in the Syndicate's van, Esther was forced into sharing her colossal corner of cake. This was probably for the best. Otherwise she'd've risked an OD on saccharin sugar. They unwrapped sleeping bags and heavy blankets, sprawled out in the back on the floor.

Fade to white, as the light snowfall fell.

The rain had stopped. It was a chilly nigh perfect evening. Izzy assumed the helm after he and the girl had finished scouting their latest port of call. They set out on a broad westerly way, then a northly upward course, arriving soon after at a park offering asylum and the sacred triple shade. That be unmitigated obscurity beneath the umbrage of a tree, below an overcast sky, and under cover of the most post of meridians. Twas late. Twere hidden. Twilight long gone be smitten. It was safe and soundless.

Alyssa told Larry of the movie they watched back at the theatre of the Woods of Holly. The squirrel had once again remained dutifully close to the camper. The Ancient listened as he was regaled with characters, sights, excitements and other bits of the tale of her and Izzy milling about getting cultured.

"You don't say—'How do you like *them* apples?' Brilliant. Your dimension's variation on Boston sounds intriguing," Larry said. [12]

"Wool, it's just a movie," said Alyssa.

"No doubt founded in truth and experience. And this wizard of the mind, you say he began his career as an alien, and generally eccentric jester?" said the Ancient.

"He was a comic. Funnyman actor. Genius performer. A mind a thousand miles a minute," Izzy added.

"Back home we too have our own extraordinarily profound thinkers. They do nothing but consider solutions to the problems that have yet to befall the Living. To hear them spew the Logic would frazzle most common creature's craniums," Larry said.

"What's a—What's one of the problems yet to befall—you know, like an example?" Izzy asked.

"Oh, I don't know. The eradication of maple syrup would be troublesome. If all the cows went out to roost, and never came back, either of these would mean a great deal of tumult. What if Jimi Hendrix dies, or takes up needlework in lieu of the get-tar. Huff! It is best not to ruminate on circumstances so dire and grim," said LtAWS, chupping twice in dissatisfaction. Then he continued: "Left alone to sit and think and wonder life away we ponder vast expanding territories just beyond our limits. Storied Admiral Nimitz. Glory's not a gimmick. Implore; adore the finish. Let not our hearts diminish. Explore the storm, replenish. The source before it's tuckered poor and blemish. Flush and flourish, rush and nourish sick with boorish grimace. So beware the sly and twisted smile, beguile at every minute."

"What's all that, a poem?" Alyssa asked.

"A cautionary rhyme. It is taught to our young and the newly converted," LtAWS said.

"Converted to what?" asked Izzy.

"To the cause of the Council of the Living."

"Alright. But so just to get this right—you have an alive and kicking Jimi Hendrix?"

"Oh dear…" the Ancient listened to the tale of tragedy of the Original Earth's iconic Sixties shaman. Izzy realized that this opened up a plethora of alternate scenarios in the reality of interdimensional navigation. There was a squirrel here. Was there an Nth dimensional Alyssa or himself? Or is it pointless to guess at unquantifiable unknowns? What if there is a higher power at work? Could Larry have a sinister agenda? Or do you just ride the wave as far as she'll go?

"President Roseanne recently renewed his post as Ambassador Hendrix. It is legitimate though, because the United States doesn't do knighthoods. Plain old PhD didn't quite do it. He is our Official U.S. Ambassador to the Enlightened," said LtAWS.

"Is that Roseanne Barr that is the President?" said Alyssa.

"The one and only. Landslide victory following her sudden rise after nailing the Star Spangled Banner at that historic Padres-Reds game at the Murph," Larry said.

"Holy crud Alyssa, that's the same stadium we we're just at," said Izzy.

"Small world, right?" Alyssa said.

"No. *Huge* world," said Larry. "Are you really unaware of how massive the totality of existence is?"

They agreed that stuff was big, and coincidences common.

The park also granted them room to play. Sod too, sit on it—Ay FonZEE! Solace from the squall, which *big reveal*—wasn't there. But maybe might could be found hunkering down around the corner so beware, be warned, and be cautious whenever does that stinger goan bite.

Next up, pinecone kicking at the tennis courts. After which they moseyed along the path, coming upon empty basketball courts in the Hollyrood. Larry amused the boy and girl by sprinting madly across the court, then sailing up to land on one of the rims. Or he'd deflect off the backboard and down through the hoop. Or he would grab the net and swing around like it was his calling in life.

The best part was the noises and the squirrel net zippers. Zing—nothing but the bottom of the night. Covered all the basics unloaded it was fun, and "He shoots, he scores!" Awarded with that scene being hooked on a feeling. High on weed or at least the lingering affects echoing back.

Alyssa told Izzy that tomorrow for sure they would have to go get another postcard to send off to Roxy. For soothing, and providing an exuberant hello. And this, and this, and everything else she wants her to know. Praying, hoping to see you real soon. You doll, you angel. Being is a boon.

Time warp smash cut to: some twelve hundred miles down and to the right, AKA Southeast. Knights had fallen, a chance to get down, and get back up again.

256

Chapter Thirty-Six • Folks, Alternators is Easy

January 29, 1998

Roxy pulled up to Twig's house and saw Catfish sitting solo out on the front porch stoop. She had the motor off and the wheels were still rolling as she set the hand brake, sliding out the Jeep, landing in an easy stride. She was just a few degrees of separation from old Beau and Luke. Like Roscoe P. Coltrane—snowfall in the moonshine on Mayberry Lane.

"How's the family?" Roxy called out as she drew closer to the old man.

"Near on all cleared out," said Catfish.

"Is Twig inside there?"

"No. He's down at the auto shop with them fellas knew Sonny. Getting set to run off and leave no doubt. Tock is clicking," Catfish said from his tin can lawn chair.

"Naw man. You know I'll be here. There'll always be folks around. Twig'll do right," Roxy said.

"I can't stop him. But it's good that he go. Be selfish of me to try and hold him back. It's music. It's living."

Roxy nodded silently and leaned over sideways with a shoulder on the house, propping it up. Some time passed.

"That was a day yesterday," said Roxy.

"Mm-hmm," said Catfish with a weak nod.

Roxy says: "I see the stars, I hear the rolling thunder. Thy pow'r throughout, the universe displayed. Then sings my soul, my Savior God to Thee. How great Thou—"

"Art is a lie that makes people seethe truth. Comedy is BS and make-believe. It's almost all mostly just shining lights. Stories are shining lights, just on the past. You put your own light on somebody. Maybe you feel them putting it back on you. Songs, movies, books, jokes, everything's shining lights. And if it ain't that or tall tales, it's events happening, sources of light increasing. Meanings of things: parallels. Falsehoods are

257

stories that never did occur, often told as actuality, as some evidence or proof—and rambling tarantula's gardens. But ain't no reason to keep a light on me," Catfish told her.

Roxy absorbed this.   Only a slight chance it was all a deception. Very good chance there was a bit of weed mixed in with some dire lonesome dread and despair. A brown van pulled in right behind Roxy's Cherokee. It was Boonz and them. Twig was up front by Truck who had the wheel. At least the engine mumbling out from the exhaust sounded healthy and strong. Sordid fits. The side door popped out and slid open. Boonz exited the back with that Esther girl. Psshaw—like the speed of sounds attainable in a foot race. Truck kilt the engine, him and Twig each executed a dismount.

Sure was some kind of quartet raggedly mobbing towards the old guard posted up at the entryway of the house. Frye Estate. Skillet country grown. Billet potatoes and some eggs rill greazey. Twig walked up and asked could he talk to her (Roxy) inside. Everyone else hung out in the front. Roxy decided she would defer, listen, and try not to be unreasonable. Be an add alt. Don't try to control all, concede goodwill. If only—

"Can you check in on my Pops if I go away?" Twig came right out with it.

"Why would I do that? Man, come on. Just give him a couple weeks. If you end up leaving, fine. But don't you want to do it the right way? Everybody's still here."

Twig let that slide. Sonny wasn't here. She didn't get it, stupid dumb girl. Nobody's ever as great as they seem. Time though does tell us what they nose. Read red.

"What's your angle, Roxy?"

"I care about both of you. I care."

"You care about something alright. What that is who knows? You probably wonder yourself sometimes. Nothing means anything. Everything is whatever," Twig said.

Anyway, he hadn't made up his mind yet. He was just asking. She could stick around, but now they were going to see if they'd be able to get the Tahoe up and running. Roxy felt a small victory, as there had really been no definitive

258

announcement. It had been close. She was already ready to be there for Catfish, although she wished it wouldn't be without Desean. Twig, Aloysius, the Last Frye guy, Twigglington went to get on even rattier clothes, for if their mechaniking required ground crawling, or reaching in the cruddier crevices, oily nooks and crannies. Even though it was 'Just an alternator,' as Truck repeatedly kept saying.

Back outside, awry alright, a fine array of rascals. Catfish, Boonz, Truck, and Esther tackled the early mourning chitters with their chatters pressing mitts with the matters at hand. Amenable; with a ditto here, or a 'ya know it' right there; that which is worthy and amen-able. Holler loot yes, gory-gory. Beseech prista—ever buddy get down. Can't a soul get on at bargaining? The old man was no fool.

"Flagstaff sure would be a step up for Twig now," Catfish said. Nobody'd really told Catfish anything, but like I said— no fool. You take old folk for granted until they start making sensei, sharing wisdom and manipulating perception for the better.

"Yeah, it's real nice and pretty much a full-on city. So many amenities, and a good assortment of churches," said Esther.

"Only an easy two-hour drive," said Truck.

"Yes, yes, you don't need to tell me where stuff is. I used to could quote how far it was to the Strait of Gibraltar," said Catfish.

"But you don't remember anymore?" asked Esther.

"No, I still know." Catfish said. "Exactly it's too far. By my own humble calculations."

Twig came out the front door in a dingy long john camo top. Layered filth encrusted, stained with myriad glorious achievements.

"I don't have a breaker bar," said Twig.

"Between what you got and the tool box from the van it should be no problem," Truck told him.

Catfish went indoors to hunt down Roxy. He knew she'd just had some words with Twig. Part of it still had the rancor of freshly unsettled earth on the grave of his boy. Couldn't even take an off day to recover. Already he was in the trenches fighting for his last child. On top of that was the guilt of why not let the wild roam free? Oats and barley, hops and Marley trots the rebel Rastafari plea—Let my people go; my lifeblood flow, my recollection grow. Patient testing, floating through the ocean wove. It is a rough but somehow pleasant row. Bolt the beams down the hatches batten. Rampant waves tossed back against the windfall clasping thunder strikes, beat to but mostly fro. Goodwill the ghostly sew. Thus as the story goes: abortive and adore we those—

Really though we must repose; séance and curtain close.

"Sorry bros—" Esther made a swashling hand figure absolving her from all of the mechanicality which was now on the ensue. Twig, Boonz, and Truck had moved the operation into the carport. Esther, she hovered about, in and out of the loop and lull of the tempo of the rising sun. Raising fun.

"Cheap comma Ginsu. Kid you need some good old chrome-vanadium Stanley steel. Where'd you get these?" Truck said digging through an open case of tools.

"It's a collection. A set like *that* you gotta build; takes time. Some of them is pre-WWII," Twig said proudly.

"Yeah, ultimately a wrench is a wrench," said Truck.

Twig set the new alternator on the workbench adjacent to the house. Truck was quickly under the hood, pointing out to Twig the bolts they'd need to loosen.

"I have a Torx bit set, and we can get at the fan belt with a ratchet. We might need a half-inch drive adapter," Truck said.

They got to it and soon had the defective alternator out, which was handed to Boonz as if it was the Holy Grail.

"What do I do with this?" Boonz asked.

"Slap some strings on it Bootsy Collins," said Truck, getting a laugh.

They cleared the contact points and Twig pulled the new alternator out of its box. Truck let him do the install. Not much that could go wrong. The battery was disconnected the night before. The new part in, Truck ran the fan belt back around. They hooked the power up, tightened all the bolts, and Twig got the sign to go give it a start. Up and into the front cab, he put the key in the ignition. Turn. A couple weak cranks and then the horses all powered, cylinders fired and it was growling like a Chevy beast is supposed to. Twig sat watching gauges, and for if any engine warning lights lit up. Truck was still observing and listening at the new part for any issue or cautionary squeals. None were to be found. It seemed to come off successful. The engine was revved and then Twig got out, leaving the motor on, allowing it to run for a while.

"Maybe bring your rig up to Flag this weekend, jam a bit. It'll be good," said Truck.

"We have a Saint Patty's gig you could be up for easily with a few solid sessions," Boonz totem.

"Yeah, if nothing else goes bad on this thing I can shoot up there maybe Saturday," Twig said, kicking the Tahoe's fender.

"Do what you need to do man. We all get it. Either way it'd be dope to throwdown on some tasty grooves, right?" Boonz said, the ever-conniving politician with a benign expression across his face.

Twig cared little for anything now that he had his wheels back. The burden lifted of having to depart Payson in a cloud. Reality lessened its streak of bad breaks. For a second he felt something like a good spirit, an agreeable current, and a fresh wind.

Truck shut the hood. "What'd I tell you? Easy," he said to Twig.

Everybody exchanged goodbyes all around, maybe shook hands in a more familiar way. It marked a memorable display of shared trust. Esther did some halfway up high five to Twig that also carried a positive, playful, and weighty significance. Also other business had gone in a forward progression. There weren't so much as words spoken, but grunts and nodding. They exchanged general intent, and partial promises. Twig got made. Boonz didn't get told no. Truck did the Tahoe a solid. Esther was still coming down off the sugar plateau she'd been riding since last night's cake escapade.

"Lucy, you got some esploding to do." Says the Iraqi Unabomber who's making it a family affair; barrel full of belly blasts.

The Syndicate departed, as unassuming as when they drabbled into town. Dealings done handled; body burial down deep. Next soul on the hook, line and sinker. Tooth and nailed to the wall of the link between the I, we and dem. Suture irie kyahn mend. Fyootcha why we goan bend right around the curve, blurred from when? Venn die a grim, fending meekly.

Twig walked in the kitchen door, through the house and passed Roxy and Catfish. Casually, someplace along in the carpeted hall he dropped an, "I ain't goin' anywhere." They heard his door shut at not-a-full slam. Minor victory, a major battle still to wage. Bitter unrest, caustic trial, the battery acid trains the rage. After again they spin the dials. Once more pray burn the sage. Can you hear the sizzle?

"You know, nobody ever even told me how you all even got on started with calling him Twig," Roxy said.

"Because you don't want to be around when he snaps!" Catfish laughed. "Bend but don't break, baby." Sinful snake in a zenful state; whatchu all gettin' on about anyhow?

• • • • • • •

On the highway, Esther snapped up the hand mic of the CB Radio, stretched the coiled cord back and barked, "Faux foe seven eight niner, Penelope Hopscotch over and out." The thing wasn't even on. This *whole* time.

Truck sat shotgun unwrapping a sandwich, piled high with meats, a single slice of sharp cheddar.

"Ahh, salami lake. Yum," said Boonz.

"Dripping natural juices and enzymes. This whole wheat bread."

This whole existence. A tunnel through time with points along the way, the calamitous fray. What es issence? Word instances. Flipmode as in squad.

Prescient coalesce spent—dammit these fucking birds. Why must they insist upon mirrors and smoke? The river rhymes with its own kinds. On and on just give it up and tell us all about the dust mites on the fireplace poker, how Roxy looked like a warrior with a princess smile. Pretty in pink,

262

Bettie Page in a torn black T-shirt. Her jeans were taut around her ass and thighs. Don't take away a man's imagination. Her skin was fair and looked so soft and pure where there wasn't ink in abundant adornment. Her body lay across the couch so relaxed and inviting. Did that do it for you?

Ominous: ominous-ominous.

You trust that brain of yours?

Is morality universal? If you say no then that opens up the door for gay aliens. And I don't mean merry. Equality, or it's some kind of burn on net neutrality. Turnip tickler. You whot? Honey child. Bye-bye black sheep have you any soul? One gram, two grams, twenty-one full. Murder is most often bloody, even if it's only on the inside. A parasite on a pair of dice will bleed you five ways to Friday. His girl.

Warp smash cut time off blade to fact: That's Tee comma Mister, a massive resistor. Maybe you can hire, the stay clean.

January 29, 1998

There's one in every bunch. Leaf or dye? Hippies; hippy who know how to act like well meaning swine. Well mean and ornery spined. Some kind of nerve. Bum kind of verve. Rooted in 'yeah mans' and glory divine; signs stay covert. For my dime convert, be absurd and woken spurred. It was the morning shine, sun peeking through curtains and vine. A light of line stretched o'er the boy and girl half uncovered and still horizontal, in the state of awaking minds. Thursday's the twenty-nines.

The Ancient was asleep up front tucked into a ball by the right wheel well below the passenger seat. Doin' alright as it were. Alyssa lay beside her Mister Dufrene. Watching. His eyes were shut, though she was certain he'd been awake for at least five minutes. His breathing was deep and slow, subtly meditative, measured and calmly manipulated. She wanted to jam two fingers into his jugular and see if she could get the bpms. Count along as his heart beat time. Bitchin' pulse mango. Bananas per Muppet. Beaks pounding marimba. Benjamin pre-mullet. Beatles post Mecca. All of it.

"Hey Elbows—"

He didn't respond.

"You knows; your nose is kind of big."

Izzy didn't care for her calling him Elbows, but the dig at his schnozz was totally reprehensible and scarring. His closed eyelids twitched.

"Well so is kind of your mouth," he phuffed back in playful aggravation. But he gave her no smile and no glance. His eyes remained shut.

She was unsatisfied. His nose was at least medium large, judging it kindly. It was surely nothing a mirror hadn't already revealed to him. He resumed his metered breathing. Alyssa

264

Rose was calling him Elbows because maybe twice he kind of gave it to her while they slept, when he shifted or made a sudden requisition of a reposition. She took it once in the shoulder, and once in the skull. Though it could've been three in the shoulder, two in the head. It was a variety of glancing blows. Who really knows what violent aggression truly did take place? Naught eye said the tonguetwisting trapezoid.

Blind bare knuckle brawls. Good ole rubbin' ups and fertile pelvic frictions. It was the virile crescent their bodies made to fit on the camper's bed, the shared space where they laid down together. His and her legs were still in a partial tangle. Mainly facing one another, though Izzy was mostly on his back. There really wasn't much room for comfort. Alyssa was a solid five four, and if it weren't for her substantial hair, a strong wind might do her damage. Fortunately, for her and also us, she'd supple skin, firm upper legs and byootie. You know, tasteful. Classy. Saucy. Real. Thick. American hips: soft swole tits. She wanted badly to tell Izzy her nipples were hard. Rigid. He did it for her, basically all the time. Is it a sin to say? There were things she still did not yet understand. Now she was even more aroused. Dare she grab and abuse him?

"You said we could get a postcard for Roxy today," Alyssa said softly.

"That's priority number one, the alpha and omega on today's agenda. Forget about it. Or transfix you evil succubus. Are we slaves to the whim of madness?"

Izzy still hadn't accessed his visual faculties. He listened to her proximity through her voice and breath. There was a shift. A rustle. She wiggled his legs with hers.

"Hey Izzy," she said directly. "Look!"

He raised his head, opened his eyes to see Alyssa with a mouthful of curtains and she yelled at him, "I sucka-you-bus!" Although it came out more like, 'Ah thuck ub youb uhhbzs." This was on account of her mouthful of shades.

Their days had been long in the best way. It was near on a week since they'd met. Sounded like such a long time. Eternal. Infinite and immortal sublimity. She never really thought about the future; was the type to tell others to live for today. Planning was only good for making babies. Even then it's not some major necessity. Make due. Push through. Now she wanted much more. That's crazy, more than babies? Give it more than a week out of one whole lifetime. More than whatever less than is equal to. But all that's math, numbers, and calculations. Him and her make some next other level where nothing else matters. Alyssa wanted to engage Israel.

"What were you thinking about?" she asked.

"How dusty that curtain is you were gnawing at," said Izzy.

"Before that," said Alyssa.

"Why don't you throw a sneaker up there at Larry and see if he's just stalking us or what."

The southern flying squirrel (Glaucomys volans), Larry the Ancient Wonder was still konked out soundly. Alyssa had purchased some flip-flops in San Diego, which was what she preferred whenever it was possible. Don't judge. She chucked her left flip-flop over the front seats. It came to rest against the furball's tail. At his excessive age he took a bit longer to wake up. His hearing was first alerted, and then he came around to unfurl, stretch out, and roll about on the rubber floor covering. With a big full body shake he hopped onto all fours, then pounced to the seat cushion, and up to the seatback top. He perched for a second preening, then glanced quickly towards the back of the bus to see the boy and girl alert, propped up and watching him with great interest.

"Good morning to you both," Larry said and resumed putting himself together.

"Mornin'," said Izzy.

"We are postcard hunting today!" Alyssa said it like as if the picture cards should be worried. Take all prisoners. Leave no souvenirs.

"I say we track down some donuts, good chance there'd be a rack of postcards, maybe more," Izzy said.

"What is the more there may be?" asked Alyssa.

"Perhaps a charming street carnival, or some other such enchanted domain?" LtAWS added.

266

"Ya never know," said Iz. "I say we get back on Broadway, take that towards the river. We're bound to hit a hub of commerce." Though that was just a fancy way to say 'store'.

They got around to whatever getting ready was. Then did descend south down 33rd Avenue and west onto the way that was broad. Izzy drove. The squirrel was in the extreme back of the bus, peeking out the rear window at the views. There was that snow capped mountain. Far out. In the distance—

They passed up one grocery store for the promise of greater fare. There was a minuscule break in their dead west cruising when the bus stopped at an intersection sitting below a non-threatening community church. The traffic was appropriate. Alyssa was skipping around on a cassette of Rancid's …And Out Come the Wolves (1995), again for the first time. The neighborhoods displayed nice houses and smaller-sized business-type structures. This was a solid main drag, though not the maineyest. Mainee-ist: that is the other Portland, that is. Caught the light once more at 21st Ave. Green means go, Alyssa pushed play and it was a good beat with the upstrokes on the rhythm guitar. So call it ska if you want, or punk or what you've got when the rock meets the roll. Biscuits. Only thing missing was the horns. You've got to draw the line somewhere. Alyssa was humming, and then she finally busted out on the chorus.

The girl sang about an old friend, stopping by for a visit once more. "Good morning Elbows," Alyssa inserted her nickname for the boy into the song lyrics. Four score cents and change in her pockets, poor and timeless. You'll never break that spirit; alive in the town they were traveling through. Her voice wasn't so bad. It was just the ridiculousness of it all. How monkeys might better mind their manners under similar circumstances. Izzy moped and shook his head; both hands gripping high on the steering wheel. He would not look at her, but did eventually smile and she gave him a good right hook, connecting with his bicep from across the front cab.

Paws up against the back glass, Larry thought about if when it was all over, could he find a pleasant squirrel from this dimension to settle down with and start living again? Would

267

things be different here on Good Earth? If he were able to successfully follow this mission through to completion, he'd very likely get to choose his next living station. He listened to the boy and girl playing. The Ancient wanted true friendship. The mating of the souls, as he'd heard it one way told. Speculative happiness and britches behold, the miracle of procreation. Otherwise, the whole cycle hardly made any sense. Izzy pulled into a Safeway parking lot, dropping anchor away from the store near the Broadway side.

"Donuts," said Izzy.

"Postcards," said Alyssa.

Larry bounded up front, keeping his profile low.

"Do you suppose you might, if it isn't too much hassle, see if they stock packets of ahh, nuts? It's not a big deal. Not a necessity, but you know—" Larry trailed off.

"I *do* know." Izzy knew. "What kind do you want?"

"Oh dear, the kind, yes." LtAWS was fraught with high anxiety, tapping the outside of his brain casing, chirping randomly in deep thought.

"There's probably peanuts, cashews, almonds, pecans—"

"Oh yes, yes! Do you think they would? Oh a pecan—sweet Jesus, gentle Buddha be praised!" the Ancient's burden lifted with the Harley gassed power.

"We'll do our best to find you something nice," Alyssa assured him.

As was customary, Larry stayed in the bus. Izzy showed him how to work the pivot window on the driver's side, next to the bench seat, midway back. It was difficult for the squirrel to handle the manual roll-down windows up front. Larry left the vent window open, and settled beneath it to listen to the city quiet outside. There were cars whizzing by, but only at a relatively gentle whirr. Heck of a lot more peaceful than interdimensional space travel. He'd only ever read books and heard stories about this present universal incarnation in which he found himself. His home on Weird Earth was the most newly minted dimension, the youngest. The Council of the Living had been researching the idea of expanding to an eighth dimension. This would be home to Infinite Earth, and should complete the prophecies of perfect existence. Larry's mission to come and aid Good Earth, the original creation, was testing his whole interpretation of, or even awareness about, the multidimensional realm of blended reality, and the interconnectedness of it all.

· · · · · · ·

Izzy and Alyssa walked hand in hand, her skipping every thirteenth step. The boy held the girl's right hand in his left. Giving slack, take and pull, she his moon satellite, now shielded by a row of parked automobiles. Out of spite she kicked some bumpers like an orange squeals. Not here, not off in the distance, did their even vehicles have a honk in them. The total lack of venom: it's ramshackle denim and tabernacle rhythm.

Skip.

It was the fourth of its kind since departing the bus. They had halted to let a minivan pass in front of their path. Eleven more paces and Alyssa was in the store; program canceled. Resume traditional ambulatory pattern of left right left minus the hop at every baker's dozen. She grabbed a shopping cart, as Izzy said they would pick up a few other supplies. They stopped at the restrooms, putting them to use. The boy splashed water on his face. Back at the cart, they aimed towards where the donuts or pecans might be hanging out. Rolling through produce and the deli, the bakery was spotted. Soon after they stood before the donut display. Izzy solemn in humbled admiration. Nothing fancy, but everything beautiful. Alyssa procured a plastic bag to hold their doughy prize.

"Two of the chocolate covered cream-filled. Two powdered jelly-filled. One apple fritter, one cherry fritter—" Izzy called out as Alyssa bagged the order like a backstreet butcher.

"Maybe we could get some of those with the chopped nuts on top, for Larry," Alyssa said.

Izzy agreed with her. "Yes, two of the chocolate frosted with nuts."

269

A couple maple bars were added, and one more jelly-filled and now Alyssa's bag of donuts was too full. Izzy grabbed one of the boxes that could hold a dozen. He presented the open container to his girl, who immediately dumped her bag, flop-plop and spluttered them things out. She got at arranging them like a puzzle.

"There's eleven," said her.

"So then get one for yourself too. Even twelve," said him.

"Real funny, master gunny." Alyssa got a chocolate cake, glazed.

"That's a dozen, second cousin," Izzy shot back.

"Gross," Alyssa said dropping the donut box flat into the bottom of their cart.

They found the cake aisle and spent two minutes and fourteen seconds squeezing a big bag of large marshmallows. Finally they moved on. Brownie mix, cake mix, frosting, chocolate chips, white chocolate chips, fudge. Then here were the nuts. Izzy snagged a large sixteen-ounce bag of whole pecans. This meant that they were unchopped halves, but obviously split once they'd been unshelled. Like I know anything about the packaging process.

Now the two drifted up and down the aisles with a meandering gander; a lazy peruse. They took on a couple gallons of drinking water. Baby wipes, shaving cream, and disposable razors, because Alyssa asked nicely. In the freezer section, they had dreams of a conventional oven. Pizza, TV dinners, Texas Toast, batter dipped fish and some choice looking mozzarella sticks. Alas, it was not to be. They intentionally skipped the candy and cookie section to not let the needless torture go any further.

There it was. The magazines, greeting cards, and a whole done-up display of postcards featuring Oregon, the Northwest, and most anything you would ever want to have claimed to see. Alyssa saw lots of roses, and luscious scenes of green. Bridges. Cute kittens and puppies saying in speech bubbles how nice things were. Or printed out sweetly well-wished quotes of greetings and goodwill. Also blasphemous images as well, sex and cleavage and as much suggested nudity as big brothel would allow. Then there was a great shot of Crater Lake. She saw a printing of the Oregon flag, simple and bold. It had 1859 written under a yellow crest on a blue background. There were some with the state motto, "She Flies With Her Own Wings," and the Latin: "Alis volat propriis." She loosely linked volat to the volans part of Larry's genus and species she'd overheard him mention. Also represented on the picture cards were a good stock of beavers, western meadowlark, Oregon Grape, and Douglas Fir. On the rack were several references to the capital city Salem, just an abundance of options.

"Roxy, Roxy, Roxy—" Alyssa muttered as she browsed.

She took her time to find the right one, or at least one of the right ones. In the end she decided on the right three. There were the Rose Gardens blooming lovely. A cartoonish beaver that had on a great big-toothed smile. And an amazing aerial view of Crater Lake, framed by treetops, rolling clouds reflected on the water's surface, and the mirrored effect of the mountain peaks echoing against the edge of the massive lagoon.

She had already decided to send Roxy the roses first. She would start brainstorming right away, and write it up in the bus once she had some good material. No postage necessary if mailed in the United States. Nice. Don't need no stinking stamps. They hit the checkout, figuratively. Nobody got hurt. Manners were utilized.

"These are good ones," the cashier told Alyssa about her postcard picks.

Back out at the camper, in her mind she'd already begun composing what she wanted to say. Izzy supplied a pen and raised the pop-up table so that the girl could sit and study on her writing. The boy began in on the donuts. First, he ate one of the Boston creams. Devoured. Then next on to pick apart part of the apple fritter.

Several minutes had passed when Larry, from under cover, asked about the status of his nuts. But not that it was a big fuss. Izzy dug in a bag and pulled out the pecan sack and 'SMACK' he dropped it down over next to LtAWS like a big bag of gold coins.

"Wow!" It was shock and awe, as he caressed the parcel with his paws.

"And here. Alyssa got you one of these." Izzy, from his seat on the floor in the open sliding door, plucked out a chocolaty nut covered donut and set it on a napkin in between the two front bucket seats.

"It looks so good," said Larry, beginning to pick individual chopped nuts off the frosted donut top. Four reels. Eye swurve.

"Finished. Could you hand me that chocolate cake one, please and kindly?" Alyssa set down the pen, blew lightly on the freshly writ ink, wrote small, right large.

Izzy handed over her breakfast. The champion.

"You ever have the fantasy of being a famous Hollywood movie actor?" Izzy asked.

"Actors, is actors, is actors. It's the changing stage that's causing all the drama. Them lights get too hot. Once you let that in—probably never goes away. I'd rather bang a drum on a street corner for nine dollars a day. Get a good tan," said Alyssa.

"Please, could you be a bit more arcane? I think I might understand mostly all of what you just said," said Izzy.

"I am Cyber Ghost. And I'm on some primitive recon."

This continued. They kept on. Going. Where the moment, um, took 'em. Know buddy, no. Sub trouble, ice in the engine vroom. Bail bail the bilgewater's frail trail. Maybe Alyssa got to take a few laps in the bus around Broadway down 15th Avenue, across Multnomah between the mall and Holladay Park. Then back up Ninth Avenue, to start the square-ular cycle circuit again.

Rancid shouted sweet everythings over the stereo sounding, slow and nicely. Maybe much else went down. Or came up to do and did happen. Otherwise, this was just the day of a dozen donuts and driving. Roxy's postcard was on the noon train out of dodge. Forging ahead in that old bus, which carried them onward. Their wagon of the people, which runs around blocks, for free. Lighter than air, on a wing and a prayer. Watch out for that tree! Unmoored in the jungle. Be.

What do we want? Neoclassical postmodern recalcitrance. When do we want it? Soon will do but please, you take care of the childrens if you'd all be so very kind. I couldn't so much as honestly tell you if that whole dozen donuts did ever get ate up. Yes, those ones. Driven the lemurs you fools, of course knots can't and won't be tide over the boardside lip slide. Inverted. Goofy. All he air walked, green haired with an independent streak sticker. Stranger than fractions of a whole, is the singular of an it, or a we beyond the magnificently blissed out mist. Tortured twisted wrist, and blunt force drama jabbed and impaled into the endless essence of nothing.

Perception. Spirit et sanctu itus. Of chaos mass fortuitous hand 'em rappenings. Tappenings hasty chaste they raced down rapids. In a drift most easy, peachly paced. Teasing taste and the wiggleding waist. Waste, just temporarily misplaced. But due not to want. Do. Where, when, and how with our own fairy god squirrel? He hunkered down in the—well, good morning Auntie. Yes, I know you prefer we say it like Awnty.

"Au chante, madamoiselle."

"Who you cat callin' at all Shauntay madam Adele?"

Who then? Who? Hoodoo we stands for us? Voodoo-ey dance amongst the forest backdrop brush'll jump and shuffles once, please do be so divine, as to rustle up some brunch. Such a rough and tumble bunch. Grunt's grind. Part of me will hustle unto—Pardon me the shovel one two, diggin' ditches in the mud. Boots. Working. In estuaries of our minds. Hover o'er mine's harbor's damage. Ravage the savage passageways of dumb blind luck. React and down the cabbage pluck of trampled phrase.

"Word to the world, untrodden and unafraid."

273

The rope persuades to hold its weight and still it gave once the pressure grew so great that none remained able not to holler, "TIMBERRRRrrr." Tump and faller, tip and wallor off amuck or chill and saunter. Either way. All ways. Anyways. Every way, but the loose witch will watch your soul with hungry eyes and subtle tempers flared. Heat red angers spared the rod in favor of the real freight fare. Wee bear (sic) on the prowl; sea fair on the high and freely severed bleed.

It was dark.

The inhabitants of the blackness whispered sinister swishes burly and audible. If you stared somewhere you might could make out an outline. Moonlight reflecting in eyes, gleaning the worth of all mankind. Shaking it off as one might a light dusting of rain. Good to know, yet ultimately just more unimportant factualities.

A casual breeze was at play on the worn rubber seal around the front passenger window. Probably it was the original, the rarest Nazi gold.

The squirrel was a little dazed. Bemused. His flight mask's operating system was turned off, and all he wanted to know was what day of the week it was. He could go back to sleep and rest well if he knew where in time he was; and this would be tomorrow.

"Ruzzle fruzzle buzzle wuzzle," Larry made out from the boy and girl's talk and tussle. Moan and muscle you could hear the bodily friction. Were they mating again, or only burrowing? The noises were more reminiscent of heavy construction: sans jackhammer and wrecking ball, with urgent surge and assertive sprawl. Then the tension all seemed to fall away into a quiet and deafening silence; a fluttering of movement.

"Scuzzle duzzle yuzzle puzzle?" asked Alyssa.

"Yes," affirmed the boy.

For a moment it was as leaves being raked. The van shook. Knight takes rook. King takes queen. Don't be absurd. Don't be obscene. There was a definitive struggle. But is this Friday or Saturday, early morning or midnight? He should need to really stop smoking the marijuana. His tolerance was much

274

less than that of the humans. The experience of it taught him much, while simultaneously hindering his focus and basic task management. His recollection was mostly a blended mix of strange inspiration, and the certainty that the mission he was on was of the utmost singular importance, man.

That's right buddy, I'm talking to you.

LtAWS dozed back off. Then he dozed back on. Then madly blinked like a strobe light, spasms be damned. Hook me up and hit the switch. Waves of memories smashed upon the sandy shores of Larry's psyche. Overactive imagination's juices swirled in the eddies; blurred and heady. It's the anxiety of being sucked under, though the current still drags you on towards home. The Ancient fuzzy fella drifted off, thinking of his own planet. The Valentine's holiday was approaching, and him once again without a significant other. Even in his present significant otherworldly adventure, there would be no ball or festive enchantment for Larry.

He was suddenly next to Marlene, posing for their portrait at the Academy Ball the year of his graduation. It was held annually for the Guardians' new recruits and those veterans posted on base. All guests had gathered in tribute to the Council of the Living and their Envoy. There was cheap wine in plastic flutes, etched with the Council's crest and motto: Sanctus Circus Victus. Their training facility in Virginia, near Norfolk, was a hotbed for big time names and faces to drop in at the Academy Ball, as well as other celebratory events. A message to the troops was scheduled to play soon, but Larry could see the giant projection screen and it was blank.

Marlene jabbed his side and told him to smile. He thought about how uncouth it was to smile. Supposably. The nerve. The photographer told me you already ruined three snapshots, she was saying. You promised that you'd smile for the portraits if I came here with you. What good is a picture with you all scowling? My mother will think there's nothing here but misery and ugly mugs. And if this photo is the only thing I come away with, and you aren't even on a half-decent grin.

"Smile!" and she pinched him hard. Larry smiled through the pain. He did at least make an attempt to curl his lips up at the edges, but no teeth. Marlene, from Mississippi, asked the photographer if Larry was smiling on that one. Yes, he told her. But his eyes were partially closed. "We'll take it!" She exclaimed and filled out the order card with information on where to send the pictures to.

On the large screen, Larry watched an American flag come on, waving so mightily you could almost hear the violent flapping, the hardware clanging on its unseen towering metal pole. A snare drum began tapping out a marching rhythm, crisp and heavy on the first and third beats. Larry thought back on the early mornings of training, when his platoon was out on the parade deck, drilling and working on formations. All you heard was the heel-toe of their combat boots. The drill sergeant shouting, 'Left' and 'left right left' and 'forward march' and 'column left' and 'right oblique' and 'platoon halt.'

Now Marlene pulled him towards the crowd forming around the projector screen. A fife-type piccolo joined in with the steady snare. Larry wanted food. This was probably the last thing on his date's mind. Or maybe it was at the forefront of her thoughts, but as a woman in a fancy gown, you just don't want to be caught hanging around the snacks.

They stopped to talk to one of Marlene's friends who was attached to the arm of a salty Guardian of the Envoy. He'd obviously been in the service a while, judging from the impressive rack of medals pinned on the jacket of his dress uniform. Larry got pinched again. He wasn't sure if he was suppose to smile, speak, or if Marlene was just saying, 'Look at this guy. Now *that* is a true soldier. I bet he smiles for photographs without even being pinched.' But Larry knew this man was the type who only smiles at the jokes of his superiors. Or if a nice old lady were to share a story of her late husband, who had held some high government office.

An electric guitar now joined the snare and fife while the stars and stripes faded away, replaced by an epic still shot of Ambassador Hendrix. He was in a fantastic military dress coat. With his arms up, he held his guitar behind his head playing blindly. It was a familiar and beloved sight.

"You know, he enlisted in the Army in the early Sixties," and variations on the same statement were heard murmured all around.

Larry was trying to do the math, without losing hold of the dream. It must be 1984, or thereabouts. Beautiful feedback, fret noise, and harmonics pumped out through the speakers. Who knows how long until the actual music would begin. Though the Ambassador's ethereal musings could hold an audience's attention for a good long time before even the most cynical attendee might begin to consider a lighthearted heckle. Hammer-ons, hammer-offs, and a pocket full of back flips, fat licks, raff riffs, the all-natural hat trick. Echo and the Wah-Wah, Mama voodoo Papa, solid googoo gaga, make 'em say whoa.

Might be Eighty-five because Larry knew it wasn't an election year. The end of Jimmy Carter's second term was when they first appointed Mister Hendrix to be Ambassador to the Enlightened. President Roseanne was only the most recent to renew his post after she was sworn in. President Carter first dispatched him to China to broker meetings with His Holiness the Dalai Lama. This would ultimately lead to the establishment of Weird Tibet as a sovereign nation. All because of hammer-ons and harmony. The lights in the ballroom went to black. The music continued soothing, with a slight return.

Izzy had a portable mini boom box. It was currently playing a worn cassette copy of Electric Ladyland (Hendrix, 1968). He and Alyssa lay down side by side wrapped in the warmth of a blanket and their own body temperatures. It was dark in the neighborhood they were parked in tonight. The music was low, the tape player now being wedged in a corner of the back of the camper. The boy and girl were already sleeping a little. But one would wake, and then the other somehow soon followed.

"Izzy—" said Alyssa.

"Alyssa—" said Izzy right back.

"Do you have any tattoos?"

"Yes."

"Let me see. Can we turn on the dome light for you to show me?"

"No. I'd have to get out my keys to switch on the accessories." That was a lie.

"Get a flashlight, MacGyver. What's in that cabinet?"

"That's food. No flashlight. In the morning I will show you." That was truth.

"Can you tell me about them? Is there more than one?" she asked.

"I have three. Why are you so interested in tattoos now?"

"I think I want to get one. A rose."

"This would be the place for that. Where at?"

"Maybe like on my ankle. Pshh, maybe on my arm though, I just don't know yet. It will be a beautiful red blossoming rose, or one with a stem, leaves and thorns. What three do you have?"

"A small VW emblem inside my left arm. My uncle did that one with an electric needle-gun we made. 'Teufel hunden' near my right shoulder, in an old German Gothic script. Then there's some kanji characters on my back, but I forget what it says."

"Yeah right, what does it say?" said she.

"It's a recipe for peanut brittle," juked he.

"Liar. Is it the name of the Japanese girl you knocked up in WW-Two?"

"That's funny. You're hilarious—ly racist. And your nipples are toyt."

"Probably because you're playing with them."

"Yes. You're so warm. It's wonderful. Everything about you is ay numba one. Can we go again?"

"No. My blossom must now close. And I think maybe not again until I get a chance to shave my lergs, if ya get ma drift. Doesn't their prickliness bother you?"

"Nothing about you bothers me." He thought about how true those words actually were.

She was the perfect amount of crooked. Not too prim. Fully understanding the ecstasy she was giving her man, allowing him access beneath her shirt. She got off on it. Felt good. Pressed her body deeper against his massaging hands. The fingers feeling tip to tip and they danced. Fast and slow, light and heavy, easy and hard, soft and sweet. Alyssa reached down and grabbed him with both her hands. He also was fully aroused. She pulling and rubbing and holding and tugging. Then she was going down, loving him passionately, trying to destroy his world. She wanted to give and give and take and keep.

In the background, devil music played. I arise beside a mountain—stomp it out, underneath 'a' my foot.

"Thank you," she told him. "For whatever we're in the middle of right now. It's like a real thing, isn't it? Aren't we?"

"Thank me? Thank you. And you're very welcome," he told her.

They did much love to each other. Izzy asked what her last name was. Twyst, she said. But instead they wiggled. And the squirrel slept soundly on his sixteen-ounce bag of pecans.

Izzy, Alyssa, and Larry made many tracks around Portland's varied territories. A wondrous web of roadways and trails mixed with stony paths. Days faded into daze, and then bade the dawn of the next, after a run on the late hours of the last night. Which was not *the* last, only the previous and most recent. A decent way to pass the present hours—

There was no finality. No end of time on the journey's continuum aside from nuke yeller hollow coast and double you double you four, leaving clouds of mushroomy death. Worldwide wrestling with itchy trigger fingers and trembling launch key-chained codes in grave doubt. Buried alive, cherry tomato bomb lit fused and ran. Fled evacuating tear ducts and small and large intestines. Target locked and Hail Marys mumbled making the cross across the chest. Whose heaven will emerge on high? Out on the town, radiation sweeping the nation. The Hazmat suit society. It's the all-new hip crazy raging psychotic 'it' drug. Alyssa got her tattoo. It was a red rose, with a black and gray stem curving around her left leg above the ankle. Its line was natural and clean.

279

"You'll tell your grandkids about this," says the last man on Earth to the corpse of his festering best friend slash dog comma homie. Cry havoc. Say uncle. Speak not of what you suspect, but act only on instinct if you wish to survive; make it to tomorrow. Move forward. Pass Go; collect two hundred and fourteen dollars. But I die guessing—

January 31, 1998

Twig made plans to travel up from Payson to Flagstaff Saturday afternoon. Then it would be baptism by fire, sink or swim. Extinguish or ignite. A test and audition which was really more about did *he* want them, Truck and Boonz, because they obviously wanted him to come directly on board. Twig wasn't unreasonable, not just offer only. Though power and leverage were as always in play.

Twig left after lunch with his Pop, which was Kentucky Fried and gravy. You tire of eating warmed up casserole. Creations from out the lifted lid of the Tupperware. The act of lunching was okay. Catfish was told it was just a jam, maybe an overnight. You know Roxy and Moe are around if anything comes up. The old man had his pride and did not speak against any of it.

Next thing, Twig and the Chevy Tahoe were gone. There was only one soul left at home. Where's my sinkhole? Pizza spring roll, equal people share the weasel way. Hunt and ride for the quick and temporary glide the prairie sized up, grab and cash while the young go shine and vain. Before the storm and trials fall the rain. Thick and cold the Lidocaine. Explained as only rationally insane. Wanting to get and gather, live and gain: bulled lee.

Time warp smash cut to twenty-one minutes passed by.

Knocks came from the front door. Catfish braced to rise from his lazy boy sankhole. Standing stationary, regaining balance, more knocking thudded back and shook the scene so rudely.

"Yep, I hear ya," he said and in a slow trudge the bluesman made his way towards the pestilence. He grabbed the knob and turned and swung it open. The cold air rushed in, changing the room pressure. At least a bit of fresh can't be all that bad.

"Good day sir," said the unfamiliar.

"This ain't visiting hours, man. Who you looking for?"

"I was hoping I could speak with someone about Vincent Frye, known as Sonny. Are you his family? Hi, my name is Flynn. I'm a nationally syndicated journalist. Might I please have a minute of your time?"

"You just did. Plus, it's already over. And if you're coming for the other one you just missed him. He's gone now too."

"Can you tell me about Sonny's music?"

"He knew how to get a room goin'. Didn't care about notoriety or no national syndication. What's your deal again?"

"I want to tell his story."

"Then you better get on listening to his songs. He done serious sessions too. I ain't the one to know about all that. Them boys he played with have all that somewhere."

"From Dystopian Squalor?"

"That's them. First it was Something Overlord, then the Barney Rebels. How it got so calamitous I couldn't say. So heavy it takes everything over."

"Do you know how to reach the rest of the band?"

"Phone book."

"Would you be able to give their names?"

"Look, one's called Boonz, and Mack Campbell. Flagstaff. That's it. Wish I could help more. Don't write no bad stuff, man. They just played what they felt. For people who felt the same way."

"Okay. Thank you, thanks."

Catfish closed the door and locked the deadbolt. He'd have no more of that today. Outside, the unfamiliar Flynn wrote in his notepad: Boonz, Mack Campbell, Flagstaff, "played what they felt, for people who felt the same way." He underlined "felt the same way" twice with his short yellow number two pencil, which was one of a handful he stole from a public golf course in Las Vegas. Looked like he was going back to Flagstaff. He liked the old man, and hoped he hadn't pissed him off too much. Maybe he could get more from him if he played it right. Not in a dastardly way, but like a good bluegrass fiddle. The devil went down to Georgia. The angels spread their wings out into a canopy covering the clockwork counting time.

Twig is driving to Flag, axe and half stack in the back. Engulfed by the tones of Bad Brains Quickness (1989). The sole craft on his voyage to infinity: to tangle the messengers with the quickness. Do not bother me about the totality. Do not blow bubbles on the Queen of Sheba. Youth tasting juice with pursuit and surrender under no conditions: silent tears in the prophet's eyes.

Was it of the end trouble, or the futures of triumphs remained? He was a man in a truck. Going somewhere to try something out. His mind moved, did Enter the Wu Tang's Thirty-Six Chambers (1993). Twig was all about to bring the ruckus to Dystopian Squalor. The Syndicate never put no shame on a nickel. The game is in the backroom, clan up in the front. Big Cliff reloads the seventh chamber in a six shot revolver. Can it be all so simple? The mystery of C----------; true pain man ain't nothing to fuck with. You rang? He merged onto the interstate, Seventeen North, just past Camp Verde city limits.

If it were to be the cream, there would need to be a strong method. Mankind must your necks protect. If he had the chance to speak and herd, be listened to would all but fall in line? What was it Sonny gave? Does there need be a message, or only one emboldened brave? What is music any ornery way? Again the tears welled, sorrow good emotion swept released in flood and wave.

The time passages away. Mile markers go by. The landscapes changing slowly from desert to wooded forest. Brown to green. Swurve to gourd the seldom cacti spined and bristled. Stuck from out the ground unswarmed but chiseled. Housing the critters, shades the bird and lizard—Liz'll frizzle Frye slow whistle. Work.

283

Disc change needle dropped on Nas Illmatic (1994). The genesis seeking any state of mind where it ain't so much life's a bitch; but more like the world is yours half the time, and memory lane slash sitting in the park for the rest of it. One love, one time for your mind, represent—if you look close it ain't hard to tell.

It's all been done before. But it's a nice ride so you try it once more. Twig let up off the accelerator some when he got close to Flagstaff. He would rather avoid any clandestine highway patrol. He had been tagged a couple times before on prior trips north. It was never fun. Plus he had almost a half-ounce of ganja in his guitar case. You best not fought the law, even worse off if you run. Cannonball Adderley county preacher on the radio as Twig switched over to the FM tuner. Hummin' along it felt like it just might supposed to be: This way, that way and then the next—in quick succession.

We'll just count the days backwards until weird debt.

Sonny really didn't get that far. Maybe didn't even ever get started. That's the dream. Completely unaware is the ultimate enlightenment. I was once like that. Then people got to looking at me differently. On account of how I looked different then they remembered me. Everybody calm down, Twig told his self. Thinking if he does this right, he comes out of it all with a band: his own band, basically. He was young and Boonz and Truck would probably offer him gas money if he asked. Though he also just wanted to play. Music. Heavy, mean, and angry. See what these cats can get up to. You watch their eyes, hands, and faces in Texas Hold 'Em. Them sons 'a' bitches won't just show their cards. As long as they leave me the fuck be when it's required, when I say, it's all good exercise for tomorrow.

"Eleven forty seven fallin' off 'a' the globe, could you fly me outta town on a midday float I gotta groove." What the hell kind of radio station was this?

Good one comma A.

• • • • • • •

The Ninety-two Chevy Tahoe was aiming for just above where the Forty meets the One-Eighty. Birch Avenue east of Aztec. It was Esther's place. She had a small two-bedroom house sharing a fence with a larger property. The common area was full of drums, amps, furniture and PA system speakers. Kitchen fridge full of beer and chilling liquor in the freezer. Maybe also the makings of a bologna sandwich, maybe. Hope you like mustards. They got three kinds. There was a back porch, and a yard with barely enough space to do a sit-up; let alone lawn darts.

Twig parked next to the band's brown van.

They were drinking when he pushed the doorbell button. Once greetings were made, they all drank some more and smoked half a blunt, then setup and plugged in. Boonz said there was a microphone there that he could use. Twig snapped his fingers twice up next to the microphone checking the levels. He stepped in close and his breathing was amplified back out through the monitors on the floor.

"This one's called Blang Blang, AKA Dusty SouthWest, AKA fuck ya muthaz Edmond Dantès Caruthaz."

"What key is it in?" asked Boonz.

"X—"

"What's the tempo?" asked Truck.

"Faster—"

Truck clicked them in with a big smirk across his face, inside laughing heartily at Boonz. Dumb Boonz. Thumb spoons, sunny moons, listen as the money swoons. Funny loons, going gaga over Robin Tunney's legumes, bada bings and bada booms. Vroom vroom, the gloom and doom looms o'er the born protracted room. Soar'n.

Soaking in the fumes of the hell bound tunes. What and how's and whoms got the wherewithal to quench the violence soon? On wars the venomous grooves entombed by the raw and saccharin womb. It was a mixture of the falconer's twigs and Foster's brew. The system finds its chosen sacred goon. To take it further flies the witch's groom. To swoop, dive, poke and pick at eyes that sorrow once did knew.

285

The gong it sounds, billows and balloons. Flecked with just a speck of Satan. You could almost hear his get-tar telling a story. The time he got ran up on by a bear cub in the woods. Hoe—Lee—Schlitz malted milk balls and how far away was Milwaukee as the flow crew? Further than the Rockies precious streams and shallows bathed in bluish hues. The reverb echoed slowly out of view. As a song twas crude but soothing and askew.

"Dudes. That was a righteous setting of a mood," said Twig.

"Fuckin' ay—" Truck added, muting his crash and ride cymbals.

"Some of that slap sounded more like Seinfeld or Night Court hey. As opposed to Korn or Les Claypool," Twig said.

"We ain't Korn," sniped Boonz.

"I wouldn't mind being Korn," said Truck.

They played for several hours, stopping indiscriminately for beer, smoke or piss breaks. Esther went from her bedroom to the kitchen, and then to the computer at the desk in the rehearsal room. After a few minutes she went back to the kitchen, and then back into the bedroom where she had started out. Noise was happening. Holy Henry David: thoroughly and aggressive. On donner on blitzen on Walden Pond tripping with Help Me Rhonda and Barbara Ann now spinning in Esther's CD Walkman. Pumped into her eardrums, The Beach Boys battling Boonz and them. Nothing against nobody. She was flipping through a BMX magazine, wondering if Help Me Esther, or Esther Ann had any kind of ring to it. Her name was mostly best befitting a grandma, or else a super-classy high-powered big city businesswoman. Twenty-seven but accomplished. She who just doesn't give a fuck, and it's a family name so go screw.

So it began. So it continues. Opens up boxes of worms and drop menus.

"They'll be selling out arenas and filling up venues," she thought.

Esther wanted to be part of making it materialize; help the ideal be realized, actually. Green lights and golden fields of fierce spots—exploding wheels—flying off and spiraling until in the end the dirt comes down on top of you. That's the dream, right? A glorious death in battle: moriendo modulor.

Nobody gets that infinite wave and fully sustains from the waters offering. Waterworld—Kevin Costner. Although that is a movie and a pure work of fiction. It never occurred. We too do not exist. Pinch me; I feel nothing. Tear out your hair and kick yourself in the mind. Only heartache, love, and laughter are our currency of choice and legal tender. Crack a bottle, gone a bender. What is blind and willing never to surrender? This, the sign of pure contender; thine may enter. Exit comma no. Do not return to sender, source on vintner. Sucka damn and snaps them black and tan suspenders. Twig did shred and then spit shined his oldest Fender's hip line.

"What should we call you?" asked Boonz.

"You call me Twig. That's what I go by."

"Don't you think it makes you sound like small, or weak and puny?" Boonz said.

"No. Do *you* think it makes me sound small, weak and puny?" Twig replied.

"Get 'em Sue!" Truck shouted.

"No way man, it's a good name," Boonz scrambling.

"So whatchu want I should call *you*?" said Twig.

"Just Boonz is all."

"What even is a Boonz?" Twig said.

"Yeah, what's a boonz, Boonz?" Truck also inquired.

"It's a me is all," he told them.

But what in the hell really was a Boonz, anyway?

Chapter Forty • Burnside, Maria OC, & One Last Go

January 31, 1998

The boy, girl, and squirrel aimed to sort of venture down in and through some places in a round-of-bout way. Eventually they found themselves back near the river, cruising up side streets and what not. There was tons of junk to look at. Alyssa pointed over at a bridge where underneath there sat a concrete skatepark. She asked if they could go and watch. Izzy parked on the next street over behind a semi-truck, diesel rig, attached to an empty flatbed trailer. There were chains and the shackles of future cargo—shorts were seldom seen, but everywhere and in great abundance were vigor and spit. The sounds of traffic echoed. Below the bridge was a coarse but resonant chamber. Airwalk, Vans, Converse, DC, and Dickies: all worn and time stamped, well scuffed. A lone curse flies when someone falls and comes the clackety bangings of board and wheels on cement. The deck is solid, unforgiving. Smooth though. Like how you might imagine a bowling alley lane to feel without laying a hand on one; slick.

A boom box was pumping out music with a heavy backbeat. When the shit goes down, you lick a shot. Three lil' putos, look up here and somebody sent out a loud hoot, made a full run or stuck a trick. A kid rolled in and kicked hard twice off the ground for speed, crouched and hit a launch ramp and it wasn't about nothing but the blood rush, that airborne moment. Whilst in flight and moving, the skater missed a grab, punched away his board with legs and arms flailing as them all tumbled hard to the deck. Little awkward flops and then slid to a stop. What go around come around. Then one time you land it clean, ride away, and *that* moment is the payoff. But usually you peel yourself off the concrete, collect your board and go try it again. Ideally you apply some lesson learned on the next run.

A tractor-trailer rolled under the bridge on one side of the skatepark. Izzy and Alyssa walked up near the blasting stereo. A skater girl was tweaking the EQ, cutting out and cutting in the highs and/or lows in a lo-fi tape jockey fashion. At her feet, a shoebox full of cassettes that had "4 SALE" written on the side in blocky black magic marker. Izzy and Alyssa stopped to browse the wares.

"Any of these tapes stolen?" Izzy asked.

"Who you tryin' to get with crazy essay?"

"Cuz, we prefer stolen merchandise, is all," Alyssa said.

"Just don't want no law coming down on us," said Izzy.

"The only hot ones are from my brothers, so—"

"Alright. How much for the Beastie Boys and that Goldfinger?"

"Fifteen," said the skater girl.

"What?" Izzy said in mock capitalist outrage.

"That Goldfinger is like fucking brand new!" the girl responded.

"What do they call you?" asked Alyssa.

"Maria OC."

"What's the OC stand for?" Alyssa earnestly.

"Oregano Crisper—" Maria straight faced.

"Bullpuckey," said Alyssa.

"Octogenarian Cripple—" delivered deadpan.

"Robb & Stucky," quality furnishings.

"Ostensibly Crucified—" eff 'em all right?

"Nay child, give us thy name," Alyssa with a terrible Shakespearean affectation.

"The Original Coaster is what I am. Do you want the tapes or not?" said Maria.

"You got change for a twenty?" Izzy asked the skater.

"Maybe you just want five worth of something else," Maria said hustling.

"Like what?" Izzy bit.

"Fucking like some crack rock yo. Good clean, make that body fiend," she said with a big smile.

"The tapes are good thanks. What about that Beck?" said Izzy.

"Which one?" said Maria.

"The Odelay," Izzy said.

"Yeah sure, that's five."

Izzy picked up the three cassette tapes and handed over an Andrew Jackson.

"You should not be selling crack Maria. How old are you?" Alyssa said concerned.

"Legal age for crack," said the OC.

"What?!" Alyssa Rose was baffled.

Izzy pulled his worried woman away and they waded deeper down in among the remnants and rowdies. So this was the Saturday dusk crowd. A longhaired youth close by eyed Izzy's handful of music then motioned at the tapes. "Beastie Boys is evolution."

Alyssa smiled, nodding in agreement with the idea that the trio was a pivotal cog, and an embodiment of progression itself. Soul warming. The boy and girl stood, sat, leaned and walked around gaining different perspectives on the scene. The steady sounding of spinning wheels in constant contact with the gray concrete. Almost like the rolling of waves, splashing repeatedly upon the varied features of the shore. It was a community vibe of amateur anarchists and nihilist practitioners whose tools were adrenaline, aerosol, and imagination.

God bless the freaks. For they shall inherit whatever mess is left over after the uprising. Apart from the occasional swear or grunt from a hard fall, it was peaceful and calming. The smell of the river was in the air, seeping sweetly through the small sect, slice of life. Those tempting fate with three-sixty kick flips on the flat bottom. The thrill got 'em hooked. Like old people and golf.

Izzy and Alyssa made their way back to the bus and shared a can of Vienna sausages, legs dangling out the side of the open sliding door.

A little daylight was left as they drove off, up over and across the Burnside Bridge. They were pulled north on the 405 then onto US 30(B) northwesterly alongside the Willamette. Beastie Boys Check Your Head (1992) played as Larry tried to understand why crack was so bad with a barrage of questions at the boy and girl. LtAWS said he still might maybe have just a bit if he ever got the chance, but that he would not actively seek it out.

Sailing along with the current, there was massive forestation directly opposite the river. Buildings and habitation trailed off. Soon Izzy took the exit to cross at the St. John's Bridge. Below on the water several barges were docked, mostly vacant. A tugboat traveled around slowly. Riding on the Gothic suspension bridge, Alyssa saw a park down on the east bank beneath them. She asked could they go. They went. They spent time and sopped up the setting sun.

They sat and walked around Cathedral Park. It was powerful and moving.

Back on the road, Izzy hugged the river drifting south on Edgewater desiring to nestle up against the waterway. Now out of the neighborhoods, the pavement dried up and Izzy switched on his high beams as the streetlights had vanished. They crossed a bumpy pass, navigating a dirt road that ran beside railroad tracks. Driving under a bridge the camper merged back onto a lane that appeared less abandoned and bare. After passing through a bluff they exited out near a baseball field. The street sign said Portsmouth Avenue.

The bus snaked in and out, wandering all about then Izzy spotted a glowing up ahead. They parked facing towards nature, behind them a lit facility was wrapped around by a high wall. As soon as the engine shut off you could hear a distinctive sound. Echoing out was the popping of racquet against ball, and ball against court. Then to racquet and court again, until the cycle would be interrupted by a winner or an error. A match or brutal practice session was in progress inside the complex, just the other side of the divide. Heavy footsteps signified a sprint as someone charged the net, mixed with the squeak of rubber sneakers on the hard court surface.

A sign that said Waud Bluff was posted beside a nearby trail.

Someone called, "Five-Love," then a brief silence, audible physical exertion and a 'Pop' but nothing more. "Second." Less intense audible exertion and a felty muted 'hwhip'

291

followed by a 'Pock' from the other end, steps and a 'pop' back, squeaky shoes and another 'hwhip!' A longer pause— waiting— "Where do you want it?" Then came a violent 'POCK' and quick futile steps from the opponent. The lob failed. The overhead smash was easy money. "Thirty-Love."

Alyssa had moved to the back. She was now munching on pecans with Larry the Ancient. They smoked a joint and listened to the tennis. After a brief rest, the three did some minor reconnaissance, down in the trees and shrubberies by the river. Aided only by a single flashlight, exploring further and far enough to skip a couple stones across the water's surface.

The squirrel took off on a joyride of aerial rambunction. The boy and girl stood embracing in the nightfall. Enjoy peace, love and an updraft, full of soaking air. A mist. Kicks the tips of waves, zips up to the treetops and alighted on a long branch. Here LtAWS would wait, standing watch. Posted chief sitting baron of the bully black skies.

Mount up, move out, wrangles the pulsing vein again.

Back on the 30 Bypass near Columbia Park, undercover of dark they connected with Interstate Five headed downtown. Something was happening at the Rose Garden. A major event throbbed with life and buzz. They parked off of Grand Avenue, said goodbye to The Ancient, and walked down Multnomah towards the arena grounds. Right off they discovered it was the Rolling Stones. Talk about ancient, Keith bloody Richards and Mick frickin' Jagger. From somewhere a radio blared Sleater-Kinney's Dig Me Out on a pirate radio broadcast hosted by Eddie Vedder of Pearl Jam.

"You want to try and get in?" Izzy said.

"Mmm, not really," said Alyssa.

"What do you *want* to do?" said Izzy.

"What do *you* want to do?" Alyssa asked.

"I want to keep moving. I want to fly like Larry. I want to just push off and go."

"Me too. Should we leave? Get on out?"

"I think so. We can take the interstate along the Columbia River towards Idaho."

"Let's take it!" she said.

They went on a victory lap over the Steel Bridge and through Old Town where they stopped for fuel and supplies. After driving by the waterfront, the VW bus crossed the Willamette on the Morrison Bridge, riding north to join up with I-84. The lights of Portland fled in the rearview mirror—saw things, all the much more clearer. The realities appear and gone is fear. The animals conquered another day.

"Larry, tell us more about your dimension's Jimi Hendrix," said Izzy.

"As I said, he is not dead. He just didn't ever die," LtAWS replied.

"Yeah, but like, was he saved? How? Or by whom?"

"Yes. He is safe now, alive and picking. Get it? You know, it feels as though my capacity for humor has been greatly increased. Have I seemed more amusing than I was when we first met?" Larry said.

"Swerve to gourd, man. You are the funniest squirrel I've ever met," said Alyssa.

Izzy said 'ditto' and pressed his Goldfinger cassette into the tape deck, Hang-Ups (1997). In the cool of the night, off they sped. More floating scraps adrift in the current's even flow. On course for timely battle with their chosen heathen foe. Teamed with lonely seething bro. All this is part of just another grizzled steaming trope. Tired. Warn. The self the other casualty, profusely bleeding hope. Or gaining, dependent upon perspective.

February 1, 1998

Roxy invited Catfish over for lunch Sunday afternoon. She would pick him up at 1300 hours or thereabouts. Moe was supposedly coming over too. Les had been crashing on the couch, so he had only to sit tight. He was now hunched over the old upright piano—"Thinkering," as he called it.

"What's the name of that song?" said Roxy.

"It's a mash-up of The Liberty Bell and El Capitan."

"Sounds immensely cacophonous, are you supposed to bang like that with two fists?"

"Yes well, I have a slight military music industrial complex. I can only listen to John Phillip Sousa if it's heavily infused with synthesizers and/or pounding drums slash a solid backbeat," Les said.

"How'd that come about?" Roxy asked.

"Overexposure to the fife and snare. Hey, how come you never asked *me* to take over guitar duties—if Twig runs off?"

"We need you on keys man. Plus, this ain't a high school garage band. You hardly have the chops," said Roxy.

"I could help out on vocals."

"Definitely you could. But I wouldn't count Twig out just yet. Everyone's in such a rush still, and like no time has really passed."

She left him to his own de-evolution of vices and went into the kitchen to check on her meatloaf. There were garlic red skin potatoes simmering in a sauce. She had a vegetable medley on standby to steam. Also, Pillsbury crescent rolls in sleeves in the fridge door. Moe would probably bring some beers. The only thing missing was an option for dessert. Les might have some candy or chocolates. He was the type to have a stash hidden. Roxy had gum, Tic-Tacs, and somewhere a box of candy canes from this past Christmas. Sometimes though, she thought she smelled that Theobroma cacao: Three Musketeers, Milky Way, or perhaps something dark. Loco fiends—Cocoa beans, lubricates the vocal scene's hobo sheen. Shining like a diamond when the Popo screens. Lines up a fine line-up of rebellious local teens.

"That one, it was him. I swear I'll never forget the look on his face when—"

"That's a woman, the individual you're pointing at."

"Yes, she did it. Not a doubt in my mind!"

"Very good, and how would you like that cooked?"

"Very well please, medium raw. Rarely do I ask, but could I also get extra whooped cream, and the watermelon pulp, seedless—with the cashew spread, and a nice ladel of grazy ezenly cozering the third lazer of guazamole?"

Of course syrup, stirrups and the surreptitious turnip overturned on the family's last resort. Now back to the dungeon level for the lot of you. Roxy headed out to fetch Catfish. Moe showed up while she was gone. He had brought a bottle of wine because, "I can be just as classy as you all."

Roxy, Alyssa, and Les would always wax poetic about how classy they were or stuff was. They spoke of the slobs, and of the proper way to act and be. And of the things which others should not concern themselves with. The Coasters, Little Walter, and Big Walter Shakey Horton. And was there somewhere a Medium Walter? Or even a Super Deluxe version? Would that not be something? Like chicken served with dumpling. A Super Deluxe Walter Jones with smudge and scruff and scrumpling. That would be the pinnacle of classy—the tops.

Moe sat down at the drum set, rippling rigid rhythms on the snare, stomping time on the hi-hat pedal right along with Les going thunk-plunk plizzle-bap all over the eighty-eight keys. One by one or a chunk all at once, it was melody and anarchy in unison. Jam jelly pudding put in spring rolls flam wooden stick flick hidden hood in melancholy trance. Was wordless and full of expressive connection. Crankin' out a flagrant sound released from all oppression. Voilà vent aggression. Violent digression—adrenaline set free. Let be—it and any

295

other vagrant at the chamber door. Side of face meets quite directly with the floor. Stopping after a while, they entered into a discussion of minimalism. Les laid it out good and Moe cracked his knuckles, spinning his drumsticks around. It was mostly just a break from playing. You can't just play all the time. There must be another outlet slash functionality.

"You know what they say, at the end of the day, less is more," said Les.

"For the most part—more or less, yes I know that. But sometimes more just must be more—and less has to be less, by definition," said Moe.

· · · · · · ·

Roxy returned from fetching the old bluesman, busted in and both guys told her, "Hey."

"What're you all talking about?" she asked her rhythm section.

"Hey Rox, is it less is more always? Or isn't more more also too sometimes?" said Moe.

"I'd say it's entirely dependent upon context," said Roxy.

Catfish strolled in and everybody again said, "Hey."

"How is ever'one?" he asked generally.

"They're having some kind of identity crisis. Les now thinks he's Moe," Roxy said.

"Les is Moe? Alright. I will take that into account," Catfish said, setting his briefcase of harmonicas down on the sofa.

Roxy asked Les if he had any candy in the house. He asked "Why?" and she said, "For snacks. For later."

Catfish took a spot standing next to the piano on the side near the drums. He watched Moe spinning his Vic Firth SD4 Combos. The old bluesman tapped out part of a walking bass line in the lower register on the Wurlitzer, a lot older than it appeared. Roxy got it from her aunt. The instrument had been in the family since being purchased new by some forward thinking relative in the 1940s or 50s; a good investment.

Roxy went to start the oven for the biscuits and put the vegetables on the stovetop to steam. Everything else was warming or being chilled. The girl, she was only domesticated in the sense that she knew smiling was good. This meal was just an interpretation of what Roxy imagined a proper Sunday lunch ought to be like. The meatloaf recipe was straight out of an old red and white Better Homes and Gardens cookbook. She was careful not to go too heavy with the onions. The guys would've probably been just as pleased with turkey sandwiches. Sloppy, sloppy joes.

She heard Moe pick up a beat, and then Les came in light and up high on the piano. Minutes went by. They kept simple and steady time. Roxy arranged the rolls on a baking sheet. A tortured wailing overcame the easy groove. Catfish drew in on the Hohner blues harp, bending reed, scooping up he wagged his right hand to shape and throw the sound, or to mute and get real low. He chunked twice off beat and then let things settle. In the subtle spots you could hear him searching for space, filling in gaps. Then when the feel picked up he held out longer notes, working them over in all kinds of various ways. Like words of tone and recollection, the story was told. Young aged, unold, and newborn foal, shift into bucking bronco bold. The lightning hopping soul-to-soul points on a circuit popping: full on ahead no stopping.

Roxy put the rolls in the oven and set the timer for seventeen minutes as directed. She walked over to her bass rig, flipped a couple switches, lifted a red Fender P-Bass up and slid under the shoulder strap. After finding the key of the jam, she padded along softly underneath what Catfish and the boys were working on. Nobody spoke. The instruments meandered about in tonal conversation, an exchange of ideas. Clever mumblings. Maybe it was music, or just coordinated noise.

Swaying and toe tapping, wiggling jiggling nodding to the dancing squiggling moving around. Under the influence of a feel and forward motion whilst laying back, the lint in their pockets vibrating good. Catfish would drop out or Les would take a pseudo-solo. Moe kept it basic. Roxy walked up and down or hung out on the one; the root. It was mainly twelve bar blues. Sometimes Roxy would switch to a sixteen bar pattern and hit the fourth halfway through like the bridge in funk. Take it to the verge of a respectable composition. Les took cues from everybody. And if there were such a thing as sense to be made, Moe'd make it. Bare naked and sacred, raw sepulcher where good is flawed. Flawed is good and missed notes are generally spot on.

When they came to some kind of consensus ending, Catfish tagged it with a lick and Moe wasn't overly clever on his cymbals. Les didn't really ever stop, but transitioned into some upbeat saloon jive which maybe had a hint of Rodgers and Hart. He smothered a yawn with his left fist, continued playing the melody with his right—banging over and again in maximum catharsis. It now resembled a crude hot cross buns. This behavior wasn't new to Rox and Moe who stood by patiently. Catfish began comping along with full chonky chords. Jamming. Because that is what he felt like doing. That is all he had. If the music would only last, let it go on. The feeling.

Catfish had a riff going from a draw two up to a draw four, junk in between and you hit the draw five and it cries; the blue notes. Babies and spilt milk. Woman's lost her child. You think this chaos might be more than a crazy trip in space. There may be a heavy at the tunnel's end. Powerful, real and satisfying like cool water for the dying. Roxy almost felt like crying. The scene was strangely emotional. Moe came back in with a quick shuffle. He only picked up where the piano and harmonica were. Les started a firm and simple bassline with his left hand. He'd throw in precise offbeat accents to give the partial feel of double-time; a Dixieland trick. Roxy knew they were still in G because she saw that Catfish never changed harps. She liked G blues because it was close to B flat major. She liked B flat because she played tuba up until her junior year of high school. She marched sousaphone. She did not generally fuck around when it came to the bass and Low End Theory. But for now they were just mostly messing around. You try something out, or you bring something back. Les dealt much in the clave. He dealt much in everything. And he had a ton of candy but he wasn't so sure that he wanted to share. One part of him told the opposing part of him that he owed Roxy a lot. He often wanted to believe he was doing her a favor hanging out. Truth was, he didn't really have any place else to go. Boo fucking hoo. We all got problems. Life is problems. Crack addicts—they got problems. This was again only mild discomfort over a slight inconvenience.

Finally they quit. Les started in on St. James Infirmary, humming the melody of the lyrics.

"Has Twig come back yet?" Moe asked.

"He called. Said he be home Monday," Catfish totem.

The timer in the kitchen ringed quickly thrice; high digital beeps. Then it rang again; and again a third group of threes.

"The biscuits," said Roxy. "Let's go eat."

They fed on the nourishment. They finished it all. They left nothing. Who is this 'They?' Don't start. What'd I tell you about that? What's this 'That?' It is nothing but pure trouble and bother. Roxy cleared the table. Them folks set around talking. Les excused himself and disappeared over into the bedroomed side of the cabin. When he came back into the dining nook, he dropped a large bag of Hershey's Kisses down in front of Roxy. It was the right thing to do.

Les Watts walked over to the piano, defeated, getting right into his thinkering. He could not be happy for the gift he gave. That bag was supposed to last him the whole week. Now he'd have to get out his Starburst early. It'll throw his whole candy consumption routine all out of whack. Oh, to be a crack head, truly understanding priorities.

February 1, 1998

In Flagstaff: The Syndicate, AKA Twig, Truck and Boonz plus Esther stayed ensconced in their dystopian enclave. The woman was the only one to leave on errands, except for when Truck took the van out to deliver the Pennysaver. Somebody might go out back for fresh air, or a look at all of the nature.

During a break from their Sunday afternoon session, Twig endeavored down the street. He found a park with two pairs of tennis courts, some grass, and a play area for children. A light snow was on the ground. Past the park was a tree line, the beginnings of wooded hills. He did not know, but the Lowell Observatory was not far off, just directly west of his location. Twig would greatly appreciate a view like that, perspective.

You simply must make a choice at times. Not everything is black and white. The lead singer of the Jackson Five had a song about that. But Twig wasn't sure if it was Black *and* White, or Black *or* White. Did that make a difference? If it's And or Or. And infers dual possession. Or signifies taking sides. Could he have everything? But if he chose one path, did he have to walk away from all else?

An oddly smiley dreadlocked gentleman came near and asked Twig if he had a lighter. He told him no. Then the strange man asked him if he needed anything. It was probably drugs he meant. Desean "Twig" Frye shook him off and walked away. In his mind, he considered if going by the name Twig would ultimately hurt his image. He'd never thought of it like that, in the business sense of things. But what, would he just go by Desean? Ain't no kind of fun in that. Moe called him Diesel sometimes. What about Dizzle or just D? He would talk to Truck about it. Was it too much long haul tractor-trailer speak for one group? He knew for whatever reason Boonz was uncertain about the name Twig. Desean didn't really care either way. Twig Frye—burning branches. Diesel Frye—D, Despot. Sean was too much like Sonny. Fuck. He fought off a sudden swelling of emotion. He fled into the cover of the pines. He kicked pinecones. He threw pinecones. He picked up sticks and snapped them. He buried his hands in his pockets to regain warmth.

"Dystopian Squalor Syndicate," he said. "Diesel, Truck, and Boonz," he tried out the sound. Tried to think what it was Sonny said. "The Syndicate, The Squalor. From the Dystopian Halls of Valhalla. Original!" he pronounced forcefully. "For the masses—for the massive." Demonical had borrowed that.

He stopped and felt the corrugated bark of a tree, broke off a loose bit and crumbled it in his hand. Twigs break easy. Diesels could take out a brick wall. Tough. Formidable. Strong. Was a change like this good or bad, or good *and* bad, or neutral and meaningless? It seemed like the time to find one's direction. The time to make bold decisions, to discover the truth of what he was, and how hard he could drive himself. He tried to visualize the destinations that might now be within his reach. No limit, like the soldiers out on Tchoupitoulas. Bathed in the muddy waters, baptized in the river. Destined to achieve some degree of rock stardom. Or was he a Judas? A lamb in wolfen mittens. Pardon the fallen chains on a young man's inhibitions. Release Lake Pontchartrain into the streets drowned with ambitions.

You take your shots, or you shake your tots; pole dance your way through college. Knowledge. Two-year, four-year, whore-queer: Lost Angels or bust. Good luck with the relocation. Found bums easy, got a light-smoke-dollar please, for a loaf of whiskey? Eat dirt, mud pie shepherds on the lectern with the stink eye. Wink, sigh, think, try; Neptune's just a blip upon the night sky. Fruit fly or bumblebee, buzzing about 'What if' it's like a jungle flea? Diesel just kept wondering while he wandered. He hit a noble fir, openhanded and playful. But only enough to rouse it that it might entertain him with answers to his questions.

"What is my name, Tree?"

From up above a small branch fell, striking him on the shoulder. It bounced onto his shoe and came to rest beside him on the ground.

"Very well tree, you have spoken. Cool mountain air, who do you say that I am?"

In the distance, a Peterbilt 379 semi let out two long horn blasts into the ether.

"Very well cool mountain air, you've had you're say."

Desean looked around for someone else to ask. There was only him to be found in all directions. He could not see the sun. The gray-clouded sky looked uninviting. He thought of a useful inquiry to make of his own self.

In sincerity: What do I want to be, above all else? Dead. Then second most, and related to a name. Remembered. Yes, and who will remain in their hearts and minds, and on their lips? What will they call you? That man—that bad man—the fire, the fury. You're being difficult. Stop being such a punk. The dread. The rabble. The filth. The scuzz. Buckets of seething rancid blood, the warrior clashing unrelenting dropping foes at will. Oh yeah, who's these foes? We could just be anonymous and not give a fuck like we don't do already. The nameless face, the faceless race, those who give and run the chase. Scour the hillside on the trail, the fiery heathen dragon. Slack on—

"Daggon Bilbo Baggins be gone," the plan well she is back on. Sought out, brought out. Found the one spot on the beast to blow its heart out. Whispers to the marksman where the shot should then be taken. Soaring earth be shaken. Castle walls be quakin' makin' seven hundred seventy-seven degrees of separation. The heat, the scorching burn implores the songs of pure temptation. Decrees throughout the nations; slick clandestine infiltrations. Statements. Incandescent saturations. Violet flows of viberations. Entrenched in vibrant throws of concentration. He hit a wall; shook his brain. Groans— because heavy thoughts can hurt, the wicked pain of contemplation.

"Denzel would know what to do."

Yes, my precious; the pathway beyond discretions. Crew well my man, my dear and dying sinking sand. Freed we stand on solid land to breathe as libertines of no oppression. Walk-walk journey-journey stop drop roll, fuzzy dice it'd be nice to take the Chevy off-road, spinning tires through the sludge somewhere. Four wheels drives a cat crazy conquering boulders and terrain: a dirt nap victory lap. Try not to end up on your ass, or tumped over in a ditch all kinds of sideways.

Roam Rome travel gnome, frequent flyer over hills and gravel roads. Hunting after deer meets and doormats, boar's head and bear's feet. Beer seek must feed, just need drug and alcohols tweak the drama that my head speak. Dumb sheet. Always making tougher many more things. Some sleet, as he drifted back into his mooring. Front porch floor creaks, open screen door spring eeks. Back in Esther's crib, a strange home; the lair of Dystopian Squalor.

"What's up, Twig?" said Truck from the couch.

"Yeah Twig, what was up?" he thought inside. Snake eyes, for the sake of a guise, you roll the muthafuckin' roulette wheel. Realize some other kind of level.

"No man. From now on—call me Denzel."

And so it was.

Denzel, Truck, and Boonz ran through some ideas and a few songs from the Syndicate's current catalog. Then Pantera, Rage Against the Machine, Soundgarden, Linoleum and The Brews by NOFX, as well as part of Kill All the White Man. They could probably improvise for forty minutes and most crowds would be down. It was brutal slayings of metal preying on the palm mutes and pinch harmonics. The sound of death's inner sanctum was running rampant in their den of creativity and destruction. Rough. Loud. Murder and the cops stopped by later that night because of multiple noise complaints.

It was your typical atypical B-movie subplot: Kid gets break, turns back on old life, changes name to Denzel, rocks shit out of planet. Just like Annie but with distorted guitars, and no Rooster or Miss Hannigan. But there *is* an Alice in Chains, so there might could be a rooster after all. You know he isn't goan pass away.

At one point Esther asked about how Catfish was doing. "My Pops got a pension and the house is paid off. There're folks around. All them from my old band, plus others."

Denzel was rationalizing. Not really answering how his father was, but instead how he'd get along without his only son around. Boonz caught this, and especially the reference to 'my old band.' It was plain and clear. He felt pleased that Dystopian Squalor would be back up and running with hardly any time lost in the transition between brothers.

After after, Truck took Denzel out to the tool shed slash workshop, where he introduced him to the Electric Kool-Aid Battery Acid Test. TeKABat. It was not dissimilar to touching a 9-volt to the tip of your tongue; but like turned up to eleven. Groundbreaking stuff. A frazzling brisk surge of lightning, Denzel only did it the one time. Truck had about a half-dozen goes at the zap-boom-pow of the altar. The selling point—it didn't mess your teeth up like that crystal. Totally non-addictive, with the slight chance you might retain some magical powers or get magnetized. Then Truck would twitch and mumble: "Tekabat, tekabat, tekabat-urr suh-wing!" You know, just good and funky. The ingenius mind of the adrenal gland's junkie. Kerplunky goes that monkey. With wits dumb and jump kicks for all.

Izzy and Alyssa took their time once on the road, stopping just past Pendleton the first night. Next morning they saw a sign that said Confederated Tribes of the Umatilla Indian Reservation. The bus did much better on the flat land. It labored some on the inclines just beyond the Rez. At La Grande the Rose took over at the wheel. Things went easy and they crossed into Idaho, stopping in Boise for lunch and fuel. They pulled off the highway but did not enter the city.

Izzy fashioned their meal from out of his supplies. They ate cold ravioli, with nice big metal spoons, straight from the can. Crackers and cheese, all of which was within the labeled date of expiration. The couple watched cars zoom by. Larry chilled inside. Alyssa took a few pictures of the panoramic view on a disposable camera that Izzy told her had a few snaps left. Fed, the troupe continued in a southeasterly direction on the interstate. The boy was now driving.

After a solid hour of barren desolation, there was finally some increasing green in the growing fields as the bus and its living cargo reached Snake River. Scattered acreage of farmland lined the river's path as it cut alongside the highway. Further east it was nothing but croplands and meadows full or fallow for the season.

Soul-soul castle roll through Wendell and Jerome; exit south on Ninety-three towards Twin Falls, Idaho. Rome dome Sicily, to the shores of Tripoli, came across a four-horse wagon harnessed up with whippletrees.

"This place is kuh-ray-zee! Why do you think it's called Twin Falls?" Alyssa asked in earnest.

"Now I don't have any facts. And this is purely speculation," said Izzy. "But my guess is there's probably a couple waterfalls. Like how they did with Minneapolis and St. Paul."

"Right. That makes sense. Like Mary Kate and Ashley," said Alyssa.

"I will say yes to be agreeable. But I will also tell you that I don't know who Mary Kate and Ashley are," Izzy said.

"Psshhaw, and I bet the names Uncle Joey and Uncle Jesse mean nothing to you."

From the back of the bus came a fracas and hullabaloo. Larry popped up on the passenger seatback by the girl. She turned to the squirrel. "Cow-son Letti? Balki Bar-talk-a-moose? These names ring any bells for you?"

Alyssa continued to stick and jab because at least maybe she might stir up some fun. Often silence is golden. Olden suntimes it gives you a headache. No music was playing out the stereo. She could tell that LtAWS understood when she would lay it on thick with the sarcasm or phony drama. He would clap his paws lightly, but never tag on against Izzy. He was still shy at times. Larry was, of Israel—timid and weary, with a dash of dread. Slight tension built slowly. The boy to defuse—

"So—do, uh—you have any other special abilities apart from the flying?"

The Ancient considered the inquiry.

"Well. I am, for the most part, all-knowing. In a broad and general manner of speaking that is."

"What's that mean?" Alyssa asked.

"I have an extensive familiarity with much of the knowledge out there to be had," said LtAWS.

"That sure is a roundabout way of putting it," said Alyssa.

"But there are things that you don't know?" said Izzy.

"I cannot read minds," the Ancient said.

"What about Cousin Larry and Balki?"

"Yes, I am aware of the television program Perfect Strangers. I also know of the show Newhart. To point out coincidences like these I would hardly consider humorous. But if you wish to revel in our names and the allusions of serendipity, I will play along."

"Since you put it like that, I guess I'll say nevermind," said the Rose.

"Oh great and fuzzyful," from the boy. "How is pi related to infinity?"

"You are referring to the mathematical constant?" LtAWS said.

"I am."

Larry the Ancient launched into a technically dense explanation of the correlation between the reality of pi, and the concept of the infinite. The squirrel was enthusiastic, speaking rapidly of ratios, circumferences, and irrational numbers, which was pretty much Greek to the girl and boy.

"In the end, if you simply wish to connect the one to the other. Sesame Street works fine for the needs of most. Pi begins with 3.14. Three plus one plus four equals eight. Turn that ninety degrees—infinity. Ooo, sparkles and mystic flurries," said Larry as he waved both his front paws back and forth across his face.

Alyssa found a classic country station on the FM dial. Music how you know it's top quality because you never heard anything like it. It sounded like sawdust blowing out the camper's six-inch speakers. Natural twang. Not an inkling of pretense. Growed up right; salt of the earth and steel guitar. Brushwork on the snare, everybody's mama loves bluegrass.

On entering the town, a resident told them about the falls and how to get there. Rippling slowly through the community they passed a massive church complex. It was the Mormon Temple. The bus did a few laps so all could take in the hallowed grounds. The old man who'd given them directions said they'd probably like, or at least it was his recommendation, to start at Shoshone Falls. They stayed on Eastland Drive south, and then east on 4000, slash Falls Avenue.

On a whim, Izzy turned down a dirt road, riding along a cornfield next to a wintry green pasture. He stopped in a spot out of view and cut the engine, leaving it in first gear. He invited Alyssa and Larry to accompany him for a walk in the cornrows. "It'll be an experience."

Once under cover of the vegetation, The Ancient let out a battle cry and scurried off leaving shaking husks in his wake.

"He must hate being stuck in the van so much," said Alyssa.

"I think anyone would get antsy after a while. It's not natural. You've been great about it though. Only a couple days and you'll be back in Payson with Roxy," said Izzy.

"Yeah—" Alyssa trailed off as they walked. She reached out her hand, touching each cornstalk as she went by. They kept strolling and Izzy would give her little shoves and then acted like he was inspecting the crops when she looked over. This went on until Alyssa got riled up and pounded his left arm with a jab-jab-duck-and-move and then a roundhouse. Another playful push from the boy caused the girl to leap upon his back. He hooked his arms underneath her legs to support her more easily, and she wrapped her arms around his shoulders and neck.

They continued like this. Alyssa closed her eyes, resting her head beside his. Every so often a blur of fur would fly by. The squirrel had a mammoth amount of energy stored up and was attempting to expend it all up and down this plot of land. The boy heard a motor whirring, it sounded like it was getting closer fast. Might be some kids out in a hotrod or a souped up pickup truck. The engine throttled madly and then a whooshing presence dive-bombed overhead. Izzy glanced above to see the tail end of a small plane go by. Without warning, a damp mist began to settle all around them. Larry appeared from a flurry of swaying stalks.

"Chemicals—poison—we must find cover!" said LtAWS.

"Back to the bus!" Izzy shouted.

The three pushed through the sticky stalks. The girl was still on his back, with the Ancient at their side. The boy caught sight of the aircraft coming back around for another pass. He told Alyssa to keep her eyes shut, hold on, and try to breathe through her shirt. The single prop plane swooped low leaving them in a thick cloud of wetness.

"How far are we from the edge?" Alyssa yelled.

The ooze started to sting and disorient. Larry hollered out "Do not stop," and to "Keep moving!" There looked to be a break in the cropline up ahead. Izzy could hear the engine nearing so he lengthened his stride. As they broke free of the cornfield, the trio dropped to the ground and Izzy covered the girl as best he could.

Once the crop duster was gone, the boy peaked around and spotted the camper just down the path. They stumbled in a daze back to their vehicle. Izzy got out several gallons of water to try and rinse off the gunky residue. In times of crisis you often forget where you are, becoming solely focused on the extreme and immediate discomfort you are experiencing. Some people call it freaking out. Some shock. Others know it as sucks. Any which name you give it it ain't ever even the least bit of fun.

"Gross, it feels like I had a Kool-Aid shower—so gooey. Like melted Slurpee or something," said Alyssa.

"It is just pesticide." Swarm chewy flustered quips. Tripping hooey busted lips, pelt with force by licorice whips.

"Do you think we will die now?" her asked.

"Fifty-fifty," him said.

"Is my eyeballs on fire? It feels like that they're burning."

"No, sorry. Just hold on."

"But do you smell that barbecue? And do you think that the sharks will now circle in in search of the blood?" asked Miss Twyst.

"There is absolutely no sharks in Idaho."

"In the pools though." Her.

"You mean like pool sharks?" Him.

"I hear sharks, fierce and frenzied. The violent thrashing and slashing of tooth and fin through flesh and water," she was concerned.

"That is Larry shredding up the weeds in the ditch. Here, tilt your head back," Izzy said, pouring water on the girl's face to try and flush out her eyes. He'd already doused his own self. There was a crawling irritation on the skin, waves of nausea.

"Can we open our presents now?" her assed.

"Shh. Be quiet please, for a second," him said.

"Ugh! Every friggin' Passover it's the same lame numbers game."

"We'll be fine. Take it easy."

"Maybe we could go back to the LSD Temple and find help."

"It's LDS," him replied.

"What? Eyes thought you were Lutheran or something."

"No. I've never been union," he said.

This exchange continued on and it kept them distracted from their most unpleasant circumstance. The Ancient's methods were more effective at removing the substance. Now he was only covered in irrigation run-off, with a light sprinkling of fluff and dirt—turd and feathered.

Alyssa had calmed but still held fast to the notion they would be best off at the LSD Temple. Somewhere inside Izzy sprouted the paranoia that maybe he was wrong. What if there was even just one shark in Idaho? Pool or otherwise. Was it so crazy? Could he be seeing more clearly now that his other senses had been compromised? And what did that fucking squirrel really want? 'Talking varmints is not a real thing,' he thought. Let alone ones from a whole other dimension. Is this dreaming? What is this? Is this cool? No, Miles Davis gave birth to that in 1957. Died sometime in the early 90s. Cause of death: drugs, thugs, and multiple gunshot wounds to the head. What is is? Is what anything? Is anything what if there is nothing after is?

Then Izzy out loud, sotto voce— "What is something, and who and how are all things, but if nothing comes after is then we're only just here."

"And so how be we now?" her, Alyssa said.

"Unwell."

They did their best to clean up but the air of a fog did still remain over them, a slant to their functionality. Finally they did leave the Zen tropic of cancer.

• • • • • • •

A church sits on the corner of where the road to the falls crosses Falls Avenue. There's a house and grove of trees across the street. The bus barreled through this intersection

310

charging forward north towards their chosen destination. It wasn't so much driving for Izzy as it was determination and sheer perseverance. He kept it in third gear, shifted down to second when the roadway got twistier. He remembered the sanitary napkins beneath the bench seat. He again reassured Alyssa that they'd soon make it back to good. It seemed a reasonable aim.

Upon arrival at Shoshone Falls Park, they pulled in down river and got back to the task of tidying themselves up. Looking about, only a few other vehicles were in sight. The boy and girl stood in front of the camper leaning against the nose. It was quiet. From their location even the sounds of Snake River and the falls were inaudible. An easy afternoon breeze blew gently. Voices came from a trail, and an elderly couple entered into view. They passed nearby.

"You folks doing alright?" asked the lady.

Izzy nodded politely. Alyssa said: "Yes, we just, well— Life is a road I guess."

"What? Bullshit, ain't no road honey! Life is work and pain and sometimes a little fun for a minute before you get back to the work and pain. Is yall okay, or ain'tcha?" said the old lady.

"It's hippy trash, Nance. You see their old hippy van don'tcha? Where you all comin' from?" said the old man.

"Honestly we're fine. Just roughed up some is all," Izzy offered reassurance.

"Are you two from the LSD Temple?" asked Alyssa.

"Excuse me?" old lady said.

"What'd I tell you Nance? That one there is talking about them illegal pharmaceuticals," old man said.

"Oh hush Peter. I think they're just Mormon pilgrims. You kids be careful," said Nance.

"Don't look like no Mormons to me," said Peter.

The inquisitive seniors sauntered away with a story to tell the neighbors. Izzy and Alyssa could already see part of the falling waters. "Closer! I want to be *in* that," shouted the girl with her finger pointing towards nature's forces cascading liquid life off the precipice into the stirring surface down

311

below. She began walking in a trance-like state headed directly for the ledge of the path, said: "Is this place has sharks too?" Izzy stepped forward and grabbed her by the hand. He told her there were other viewing platforms. They moved west along the trails in search of a glimpse of something grand.

"Why are we going away?" Alyssa twisted free of the boy's grip and ran across the grassy terrace towards the cliff line above the brink of the brew below. She had still not fully regained her senses. Brain saturated with confusion. It felt again like the chaos of the cornfield. The girl squinted and fled from the fear of predators nipping at her heels. Izzy began to realize something was very wrong. He gave chase, calling out her name but she was gone with the sound of shifting gravel, over the edge and out of sight. A strong wind whipped past the boy's legs and there bellowed out an exhilarating: "Yippee ki yay nature lovers!"

Larry the Ancient Wonder Squirrel zipped down the rock face, clutching Alyssa by the right arm above the elbow. He surged up and out over the river as the girl hung limp, moaning in agony and disarray.

"Are you sharks? Why am I doing? How am I dead now?" Alyssa said worried.

"It is I, Larry. You are safe," the squirrel strained in reply.

He was not prepared to carry such a load, though she was a small woman, his stockpile of happy thoughts was low. They slowly dipped down, hovering several feet over the water. He recalled his past work lifting trees and small transports, when his ability for extended flight was exercised often. It was a muscle.

"It is a shame you are so zonked. The view here is amazing," Larry told her.

For a time, the two went chasing waterfalls. Larry would dip Alyssa into the water's healing cool, trying to revive, wash and wake the poisoned girl. To flush her systems clean they bathed and basked in the rinse.

Izzy waited back at the lookout area, feeling as though he had failed the girl. He would not question the Ancient's motivations anymore. He'd be thankful for his presence, and wait for an opportunity to return such an act of valor and benevolence.

Once all were safely back on ground, they rested for a while in the bus before taking one last peek at the falls. Look-look pocketbook, can I get your pawn to rook? Two-two twenty-one, chamber round in tater gun. Scrambled under shambled bridge. Babbling brook when Babylon shook, travel on book and cranny nook, as kings were torn asunder. Born of thunder and frightening chance.

They stayed in a cheap motel that night in Twin Falls. For a treat, the trio ate ice cream sandwiches and somehow did find their way back to good. Still a bit shaken, with a certain amount of more-ness understood.

If we let ourselves, we could make this never stop. Baby don't please no bass drop—ear full 'a' monkey love space bop. Sings the song of seldom times, dismantling the wind; the causal attitude of growth. Happenings come when you don't only stick to the rivers and the lakes you're most familiar with.

Chapter Forty-Four • Shun the Red Imp, Smaug Forbid

Denzel got into Payson on a midweek afternoon. Catfish was at his front porch perch sitting still, thinking thoughts. He couldn't know but how his boy was trying to cut a groove of his own type. Names change, faces derange, hype can strain but for the new frontman of Dystopian Squalor, he'd always just be Twig when it came to his Pop. That's okay. What do you suppose Muddy Water's mama called him? Maybe you never just know where something like identity begins or ends. When did Gordon Sumner actually become Sting? Probably Elvis was somehow always The King. Latifah was always the Queen, though for a time she was Dana Elaine Owens. Bo Jackson started out as Vincent Edward. Elijah himself even had to get around to being called Catfish. Immigrants. The orphaned and abandoned; slave and free alike for any and every reason—Nomenclature.

The ultimate occurs when your given name becomes that moniker meaning the only single being of such a one as you: Prince, Cher, Beck, Jewel, Madonna, and Bjork. Who you anybody really way anyhow? It is all apeshit to ze Fraunch.

"That truck doin' alright?" Catfish said.

"Yeah," said Twig.

They watched the sky together for a moment. The two listened to the rustle of the wind. Reunions are almost always blissful at first. You forget about any of the negative, and take time to revel in the feelings that renewed reunification brings. Allowing glorious access and privilege.

"Well, I been doin' alright too. How you been?" said Catfish.

"Yeah, I'm alright," said Twigzel.

Father and son watched clouds drifting overhead. Leaves of the neighborhood trees slightly swayed. Pine needles fell on the cold ground.

"I want you to go and live," Catfish said.

"Yeah. I guess I want that too."

"Not everybody even gets a chance you know?"

"Yeah, I know. This is a thing I realize," said Twig.

"Is it what you want?" asked Catfish.

"Yeah, I think so."

"How much exactly so do you think?"

Twig gulped air, puffed his cheeks, let out a long blow of CO_2. Almost laughed for a strange reason, for no reason.

"It causes me stress, okay? It feels like I'm not ready. I don't know. So what? Just hang on and figure it out as I go? Put it down. Reap reward. Don't give up type of thing?" Twig was anxious, aggravated.

"Yes man. Do all of that. See what happens. You try to make a living at doing what you love, right?" said Elijah.

"Right."

The sentiment shared wasn't any big revolutionary secret. The father simply gave his son permission to go off and pursue life. It was a blessing of sorts that freed Desean of a burden, lifting the looming veil of obligation. Reminiscent of how Elijah ran out on the boys and their mother back when he himself was chasing some kind of dream. The type of fantasy founded in as little reality as possible. Isn't that the ideal? Staying as far away from normal and ordinary as you can. Also known as absolute liberty from toil and responsibility. There might be an argument to be made; though neither the boy nor the old man put any objections forward. Mama might've had a different opinion.

Who's so noble that they would not consider flight and enterprise, if such a thing as accountability weren't enforced or held in high regard? What is if, or if it wasn't now or never? The art is T-minus seven seconds from actualization.

In the evening, the two men had turkey sandwiches and watched reruns of Diff'rent Strokes and Matlock. It was nice just sitting with someone. People forget that. Some remember. Others believe in their own form of comfort, solitude. Serving the self, grasping tightly to control.

What is a good day—or a good year—or a good life? What is a worthy purpose, or a virtuous pursuit? Who's on third? How far are we from home? All this and more of today's top stories in the new-fangled, true-spangled bionic splinter chosen—Lo-fi forty-five phonic interwoven.

315

Less miserable; less problems. Rome set of Sistine columns. Traditional. Pure. The vine, the branch, the cure. Love the lovers, love the haters, embrace the barrier's Yorkshire terriers. Sing a song of seven pence, the last is on me. Once uptown a pine there won a glory. Victorious. Bleed. They were blood. Them smoke-em-a the pipe of peace on earth goodwill towards men; Gunga din. Maple syrup and a gallon of the Zen on the mainline triple prime blend blind gin.

"As you get on, you might find God. Same way you might the devil. Chances are there'll be a bit of both in most folks you come across," said Elijah.

"What good is ruling for anyhow?"

"Beware the red imp. Shun the red imp."

"You want I should do a red imp shun?" said Desean.

That's never what this was about.

"Not everybody's got such as clear an aim as you."

"How you mean?"

"You work at things your whole damn life. Maybe some day you might get to feel complete and satisfied," said Catfish.

"Is that how you feel, Pop?"

"I once felt complete, yes. Can't say that I ever been satisfied. You see if you can get ahold of some kind of contentment out there."

"Every time I play music. That's it for me," said Twigzel.

"Yes," said Elijah. "Yes," again for symmetry's sake.

Twig wanted to assure his father this was not goodbye so much as see you around. For his own benefit, Catfish had already begun putting space between them. It didn't make sense. Is all of this supposed to be making sense? Do you understand what's going on? What're you looking at? What do you see?

Stunned and emoting, the men both tried to contain their fears and apprehension. Aren't we all rather less than hot about the unknowns? Most won't acknowledge it, but everyone gets nerves and uneasy if unsure how to act in a given situation. You either behave how you think you ought to, based on expectations, or you desperately attempt not to look a fool, exposing vulnerability.

Smaug forbid there be a real moment of connectivity. Smaug dammit yall. In Smaug we trust.

Desean fetched out Sonny's acoustic guitar. He sat back on the couch and played. Felt his way around the neck, picking with his right hand's fingers. Soon Elijah, eyes shut, started humming low and moanful. Sweet sorrow, savory mood. Repeat borrow, quakes and brood. Deplete hollow, stakes to prove. Gone tomorrow, today removed.

"Oh Lord—Oh Lord—shore nuff—" sang the old man. "My mother—told my father—just before—I was born. I got a boy child comin', gonna be—he gonna be a rollin' stone— shore nuff he's a rollin' stone—right now he's a rollin' stone— Oh well he's a—" and Twig bent twice the top of the riff he worked and ran it back down home. Making the noise like Muddy, Buddy, Elmore, Jimi and the rest.

Another day and the sun will rise again the next. Five'll get you ten. Sometimes once'll get you life. The boogieman will get you never. Certain things just aren't real. Twig would still spend time in Payson. Denzel would exist in Flagstaff and the territories beyond. It seemed easy. It seemed safe. No problems; but only in the way that a loaded gun is harmless with the safety on. Flick of the finger and it's all business quick. Not so far off from brutal self-destruction. Blink of an eye, that powder ignites—Ramshackle chains and a dungeon midnight, round the monk's solemn chanting life giving salvation for the fallen.

The soldiers laid at rest, slain at best. Sacrificed as martyrs, with tartar on the side. Rice on casket dry. Unlike the paper on a basket of Fryes. Colloquial for three. To one pair left on God's Good Green. Thank the heavens for earthen vessels, the thief in the night scales vine-covered trestles. Back-back down-down tell them to retreat. Pray to the Madonna of the lonesome street.

Chapter Forty-Five • Jetskis & Reunion

February 6, 1998

The winter winds worked through the conifers of northern Arizona. Izzy and Alyssa flew away south from the Grand Canyon, where they'd watched Larry pull some radical aerial maneuvers high above the Colorado River, in a secluded portion of the North Rim. Utah had been beautiful but uneventful; a long trek. Now the boy and girl were on the last leg of their trip. They would soon cross Interstate Forty, and Alyssa would be home in a matter of hours. How long had she been away? Unanswerable questions drifted through her mind. Like why does the sky blew as if it were alive? Breathing lightly over its chili, trying to make it less scolding hot.

In Payson, Moe burnt his English muffin beyond edible. He inserted another in the toaster and adjusted the heat setting. Esteem technological. Dream Demonical's drummer slathered on butter and placed a slice of cheese in the muffin's middle to melt. This meal would serve as his br(eakfast slash l)unch. He'd be over at Roxy's later. They were rehearsing at 1600, official and on the clock. But today was Bob Marley's birthday, fifty-three, and there would be a lively atmosphere. Rox had good snacks and the merry Jah wanna. At the place to be, Les was examining the psilocybin mushrooms he scored for the day's celebration. Roxy had several different strains of weed, indica and Cannabis sativa. (Supposedly from growers at a feminist compound in Humboldt County.) It'd all been tested. Certain bits had been pre-rolled in preparation for the day's coming jubilation.

On the other side of town, Twig was packing a bag. Just some clothes he could keep in Flagstaff. This way he'd at least be able to have a stash in multiple locations. He'd be mobile and on the trail of that daggone dragon. Chasing the pipe,

318

dreaming. Bangarang, Captain Kang. Catfish was watching Regis and Kathie Lee on the television in the living room. The show was having a big giveaway for a fancy trip, and he was trying to understand how a body could make it this far without ever having ridden on a jetski. What it would be like sitting upon a big wave-runner, the Cadillac of the waters. Cruising like a Fleetwood, DeVille or Eldorado—stylish all the way.

The phone in the kitchen rang once.

The phone in the kitchen rang twice. Meaning again, for a second time.

The old man set out to answer it. If he took long enough to get there he might get lucky and have the caller disconnect. Regis told the contestant the exotic destination of the vacation that was up for grabs. Now the excited woman needed to correctly identify the childhood hometown of yesterday's big Hollywood guest. He was a versatile Ed Norton type. It could've actually been Ed Norton. Or Johnny Depp, or Sam Rockwell, or John Turturro. The phone was on its fifth ring. He stood and stared it down threateningly.

A pause. It rang for the billionth time. The nerve. Catfish picked up the receiver. Said hello—

"Hey man," said Roxy.

"Yes?"

"You should come over today. Hang out. Play."

"Alright. Who's everybody there?" Catfish said.

"You and me, Moe and Les. Twig is welcome too. Is he still around?" Rox said.

"He seems about to get on out again."

"Well, you tell him it's fine if he stops by."

"You want to speak with him?"

"Sure, I'll say hey."

"Twig!" hollered Catfish down the hall.

"Hold on," he told Roxy on the line.

The old man walked towards his son's domain. On the TV, the woman began leaping up rejoicing as confetti fell and balloons dropped to the floor. Desean's door was open. Music played. The dull static fuzz of metal rock sounds. That was what changed everything. Electricity. Morphed the blues into

319

Rock N Roll. Juiced up string on wood, pick-ups and bending tensions. Loathing and lament, filtered through distortions and amplified. Now that has brought us to this.

"Roxy's on the phone," Catfish totem.

"Yeah, alright," said Desean. "What does she want?"

"Just to say hey."

Twigzel had no interest in making nice or entertaining distractions. This blinked across the front of his mind as he went to grab the phone. Distraction. Distraction. He only wanted to look forward.

"Yeah?" he said to Roxy.

"Hey," she said.

"Hey," he toad her back.

Twig was trying to remember how he'd called it off with Roxy and them. He was blanking. He must've told Moe. No, he did speak to Rox. When was that? This all felt very unnecessary.

"So we're all good, okay? It's all been crazy and I'm glad you're doing this. You deserve it, right?" She tried to be kind.

"Thanks. Yeah, it feels nice. Is that it?"

"Uh—I got some opinions on solid state versus tube, or junk about Waddy Wachtel if you want." She was trying to be.

"Oh, no—I mean yeah, you know you're the best. All you guys, it was fun," he said.

"Alright then, see you around. Tell your Pop four o'clock. Somebody will pick him up."

"Alright, lady," and he heard the line go dead.

It was a pleasant exchange, slash question mark. Not so back alley like some of the rest of his dealings of late. It felt like a button. All the extra business going on after a group of musicians hit the last note of a song. Who gets the last word? Is it the cymbals resonating, or the cat way up on the high note? The bass player, the keys, or the singer might just slip in a last second melisma. Often it's the waves of feedback blending into silence.

• • • • • • •

In the VW camper, Israel put Beck on the stereo tape deck. This was the hillbilly hip-hop, redneck truck stop, much good beat rock. Harmonica and guitar mixed with all that is bizarre. Loops and the strange lyric prose, transfixed with tambourine and the shuffle of Depression Era footwear. Wiggles and toes. Such as vibing flows. The three were negotiating. Larry was adamant about remaining known only to Izzy and Alyssa. The girl really wanted the Ancient to meet Roxy. The squirrel said it was not wise to risk pointless exposure. He had no objections to her friends in general, but was under specific orders pertaining to co-mingling. She said it wouldn't be pointless. Larry was sure getting a devils haircut. Felt the pure pressure; could use a hotwax. Orale vato, let's go. Lurid only knows word it's at.

Freedom. The new pollution. Minus some Novocain and the ramshackle derelict in his charge. Readymade by them sissynecks at the jackass factory. Got a high five from Alyssa, in between a rock and the Catskills. Their present terrain was the greener part of the dusty Southwest. This area, these woods, was the Wild West only a century ago. It is still that way in the hearts and weapons arsenals of many.

The travelers exited the interstate at Camp Verde. With an hour left to Payson, Izzy put the Foo Fighters self-titled album into the stereo to play them out. Bring it on home: D.S. al Coda. They rode-a-the noonday air warming slowly by the sun's energy: glowing, exploding the dynamic mikes. The camper passed by a Volkswagen trike. Might be a sign of welcome times and the like. Lowered the blinds. The love id requites. Lit on ethanol and distilled spirits. Secretly, part of Larry was furious with himself for smoking weed so freely and showboating by flying in daylight. He was only trying to keep a grip on things. He must remain clandestine and in control. When Alyssa hinted that there could be one or two other people he should meet, the Ancient had announced for all to hear that he'd be confined to the bus for their stay in Payson.

"It has to be this way," said Larry, firmly.

The girl let up. They all listened to the music. It felt like the end of something. A signal the curtain's close was nearing.

In a clearing off the road, a deer in scorn was sneering. Dumb people. What is it you hope to gain by going where you are not wanted? Bambi dashed away to find Smokey, Baloo, or Winnie the. One way or another the forest would not fall today. The timber was thick. The trail cut through hill and valley. The air-cooled engine of the bus fought nobly against the rise in elevation.

Passing Strawberry and Pine, Alyssa encouraged Izzy to stop at the Tonto Natural Bridge for one last vision shared with hands held and whispered exclamations of awe. It was a steep descent to the canyon floor. A small trickle of water waited for them at the bottom. It'd be an easy hike down to the viewing platform below. They gazed above at the massive cleft, left hollow by thousands of years of erosion. With the realization of the conclusion to their long journey, questions flickered in the minds of the girl and boy. What now? What next?

Back up on the crust in the bus, Larry knew that things would soon begin to be set in motion. The girl would be gone. The focus would shift to more pressing matters. Just yesterday, the Ancient received updated directives from his superiors in the Seventh Dimension. If he were unable to achieve his mission goals, he'd be transferred from this assignment and miss out on his triumphant return. The Guardians of the Envoy would pursue alternate means of completing the task. This of course he found unacceptable. LtAWS must finish the job. He would not fail his commanding officers. He must not be responsible for the demise of all future hope in the reign of supremacy of the Council of the Living, and its role in regenerative universal healing and preservation.

Same day, different shit: In a familiar sector nearby, Catfish packed up his blues harp case and set it by the door. They had a PA at Roxy's so he didn't need an amp. Didn't need a PA neither but hey, that's what's what. Moe just called to say he'd be by to give Catfish a lift over to Roxy's. He heard the rumble of Moe's bike coming down the street. Opting for the motorcycle's sidecar, the old man settled in down low. He was given sunglasses to wear for eye protection from the wind and bugs. A right sight the two made there on that machine. They went slow. Catfish had his harmonica case on his lap. His hands gripped the cross bar tightly so as not to get too jostled. The cold air nipped at his ears and nose and face. This must be what those jetskis are all about. Perhaps if the breeze was warm, and a refreshing mist was upon the skin, it would be perfect bliss. It had been so long since Catfish had even seen the ocean. He figured he just must not be beach people. It was fun to ponder though.

"Say Moe," he yelled. "You ever ride a jetski?"

"Yeah, a couple times," Moe shouted.

"What's it like? Is it nice?"

"Yeah man. It's *real* nice," said Moe.

That's *got* to be what he's been missing. Then he would get to feel satisfied. Pretty much done all else, all that's left now is jetskis.

· · · · · · ·

Roxy was holding a massive blunt a couple inches above her lighter's flame. Back and forth swept the torch, drying carefully the haggard skin of the bulge-id beast. You'd think this was a reggae collective just off the shores of SoCal; the inland side, no pirates. A couple times a year there might be a gathering such as this. Roxy was very caught up in embracing the stoney aspect of the legend's birthday. A great deal more appropriate than Hitler's birthday on the twentieth of April. Anyway about it, it was an excuse to cut loose. Find peace and forget things for a minute. Get blank, level out.

Everyone remained completely unaware of how close Alyssa actually was. The postcard postmarked Portland, OR came in last Saturday, mentioning nothing of an approximate date of return. Part of Roxy had already come to terms with the possibility she was gone for good. Though that felt hyperbolic and unfounded, still it was necessary to keep her sane and grounded. Everybody has his or her own way.

· · · · · · ·

Alyssa Rose figured her man would stay for a while in town. Then they'd eventually both move on at some point. Izzy wasn't even sure he wanted to stop at Roxy's for more than a day or two. Long enough only to stay the goodbyes away, say lasting words to the girl, and kiss and hold her long lasting times.

He was only half a day's drive from Denver. The city was no doubt still buzzing. It would be nice if he could catch the tail end of some of the celebrations for the newly crowned Super Bowl champions. There'd be a bed for him at his Aunt Pearl's. Family dinners with real food; heaters; unlimited shower access. Amenities. The road is nice but it's no way to live.

Izzy did not think Alyssa was thinking what she was. He thought they had this fling, and that's what you do. It's all just a collection of random experiences. Maybe at the end you'll feel some kind of closure and satisfaction.

Izzy a dumbass. Often, he was intentionally detached so that he could shuck responsibility when the bill came due. He could legitimately claim he had zero clues that Alyssa Rose Twyst was all in and wanting more, continually, and without ceasing. She had all of the clues. Her could see the possibilities. It could be so good and fulfilling. The boy and girl were now indirectly talking about "tomorrow," without getting into it enough to realize the chasm that lay in between them both.

"A thing like this doesn't happen often," said Izzy.

"Pshh—like *this*? Doesn't happen never. We are infinitely fortunate," said Alyssa.

"It's all time travel," Izzy said.

"Okay Larry. Hey Larry, Larry wants his flux capacitor back," she said jokingly to the boy.

The squirrel appeared, asking what it was they wanted. It was nothing. She meant some other Larry. The Westfalia camper reached town. It was mid-afternoon on this late winter day. Alyssa pointed Izzy east down the road heading out towards the cabin. Things began to look familiar for the boy. Feelings inside started to swoon in his heart, mind and soul.

The girl had done something to him. She was doing it now, heavy. He wasn't certain of his priorities. Part of him wanted to flee. Forty-three percent of his being would absolutely stay if she asked him straight up and direct like. He might not make it out if he didn't take action, set a course, put down the law. What if he did nothing? They could just keep driving. Or. Now forty-eight percent of his essence wished to head on over to the courthouse. See about nuptials and knot tying. Where comes the judge? Do you take this chocolate éclair Danish cold piece of solid gold type gone gal to be your lawfully wedded? Buy the power of this vest that's on me; it is all here for you in this shiny binder.

Izzy said: "Look," and pointed out the front windshield. Ahead of them in their lane, an army green motorcycle with sidecar attached was creeping along way under the posted speed limit, on a slower current than the rest of the flow. Alyssa had a sudden rush of excitement that she'd arrived. The tape broke as they crossed the finish line.

"That's Moe and Catfish!" she said.

Alyssa reached over and pressed the horn with a short beep and then a long one. Moe took a look back and the girl waved. He leaned down and said something to his passenger. Catfish turned his body left to glance back at the bus, dark sunglasses and all. They moseyed on like this in line for a length, and then hooked a right at the sign marked Didney World West slash Grangerfords.

They crept into the thickening natural topiary. Somewhere buried in there there was a nest with rocking chair perched on the porch. Her, she stared off—stood over—looked out on the prairie air. The youths have charged the Lemonberry Square. The kingdom of the crew, well, if itself could be the rule— some hot inception.

Roxy was desirous for something big to happen. Now was waiting for the C-4 to ignite. She'd gathered all the pieces; now just add the human species. Mish-mashed and mangled will do you right. Knock-knock the heaven's floor. She first heard Moe's bike's engine roar. Seconds later, there it approached down the lane, followed by a van. That van. It was the same vehicle that had taken Alyssa away. Was she back? She was back. My girl is back. Hot damn, this is the day! This is going to be a day indeed. This will be the day things turn around. It all made sense and felt good. Extraordinary relief. Roxy breathed in deep and blew the monkey off her back—out the water—in the moment. Bob did say: "Everything's gonna be alright." Kinky Reggae played indoors, bleeding out of the cabin's creases. See if I just ain't able to make a stand—in a kinky section of this land. The caravan rode on up and stopped one each side of the potentate's yellow Jeep Cherokee.

Alyssa jumped down from the bus before it came to a full stop. She was wild, not knowing quite what to do. Only knowing that do something now she must. Unleashing a full arm waggle up to Rox, she went over to give Catfish a hand up and say 'What's good' to Moe. She was the lost dog reunited with her family, unable to contain or focus the excitement. Izzy waited behind the wheel, watching this cloud of angelic dust brush off the girl's frenzied energy. It was a blizzard, and those tend to be unbridled. Lord have mercy, the sun be thirsty, the party had just begun.

"I can drive a stick now, and I almost died in Idaho, near Twin Falls," Alyssa told Catfish and the world. She glanced at Roxy and they both smiled warmly. Moe, the Rose, and the old man made their way up towards the cabin. The bus engine was still running, as Izzy hadn't yet shut it down. He was thinking thoughts. Entertaining ruminations.

"It is okay if you leave her," said Larry the Ancient Wonder, callous and cold.

Israel Dufrene stopped thinking. He shifted into reverse, rolled backwards and around the Jeep. Alyssa hopped onto the porch, ran and hugged Roxy. Roxy saw the bus going, its driver looking away as he fled. There was no bye—good, bad or otherwise. This felt like some strange business. She would tell Alyssa that he must've gone to the store for cigarettes. But he didn't smoke. Then to the market for some flowers, plus other lies meant only to soothe and tranquilize. Roxy squeezed her friend, told her it was, "So good to see you." How long could this embrace keep the pain at bay, until she would turn and recognize the vacuous space left by Izzy's unannounced exit? Roxy knew that there were devious motivations at work.

"The postcard was awesome," she said to Alyssa.

Life would go on. He might come back. Good chance at least. He might've actually *just* decided to start smoking. He might do laps around the world and appear as a comet, the feather blown near now and again by the wind. It did not feel like the end. Theirs *must* be more. But Alyssa did finally turn and see Izzy gone. She broke down. Dearest love.

• • • • • • •

No time warp—No smash cut to—The dust had not settled. The bear had been sook slash sicked (sic) all over the place. Bittersweet it felt. Alyssa was beside herself. Or rather it was Roxy that was beside Alyssa, both seated on the edge of the front porch. They were trying to process things, but also at the same time relax and take comfort in being home. Everything was great the whole trip. Maybe something was said in between the Natural Bridge and here, but the understanding was that they'd definitely all hang out for a while.

"Just be happy," Roxy said.

"Why'd he leave like that?" said Alyssa.

"Some guys are unpredictable. Who knows?"

Catfish and Moe had gone inside where Les was showing off his new smoking apparatus. It was a three-foot tall glass Zong water pipe, with two kinks in the neck and blue pinstripes around the bulbous base. It was the type that allows you to drop ice cubes down the top for chill and mellow hits. The cavernous bowl used to pack full with massive loads was empty and clean.

Moe handled it, struck with awe and intrigue. "Imagine the kind of mess we could make with a couple of these, some gasoline, and a handful of matches."

Les gently wrestled his toy away from the drummer and took it into the kitchen to add water. Moe stopped the Marley mid-Concrete Jungle, dropped the needle on Pearl Jam Ten

327

(1991). "Bob would've liked Ed and them," he sort of told Catfish, who sort of heard. Les reappeared, holding the sacred icon.

"Roxy and me ate mushrooms like thirty minutes ago," said Les.

"How was they cooked? Steam or sauté?" Elijah said.

"Catfish man, these weren't the cooking kind," Les totem.

"Alright then, synchronicity be damned and what not."

Fretless bass and space sounds grace the chambered tomb tastes warm while hollow hollers echo somber calls to arms. The grateful hammer's focused rage permeating drums entered the hanging craze.

"All berserk and no sway makes jazz null, void." Catfish told nobody, everybody heard.

Outside the girls reminisce, console and besmirch the good name of happiness, boys, and body odor. Shit talking at life.

"I want to fall off this planet tonight," Alyssa said.

"I'm right behind you," Roxy said standing. The two women went in the cabin.

"Roxy, you on mushrooms?" Moe shouted.

"Yeah, so? What of it?" she replied.

"At some point I'll take time to reflect," said Alyssa of her journey— "without this torture. Once upon a time, right? When I got lost and found. Might make a good story."

"Holy shit, I'm in it! Les, what's the plan? Should I be sitting down for this?"

It was Roxy's first time with psychedelics slash hallucinogens. She'd been strictly weed, liquor, and the occasional clove cigarette. Moe was on the couch with Les who waved the two over to take a seat. Catfish sat down on the piano bench. Now he tested the response and action in each register. Random keys. Leslie Watts took a big rip on the loaded bowl, passing the bong and lighter left to Moses Prallums, who lit, hit and pulled the ashy remains of the ganja down into the wash. H2O. Cashed. It was packed again for Alyssa and Rox who got a righteous fill of smoke. They only coughed up about half of their large intestine slash uterine lining. What? Hey now. Roxy shot a spray of lemon pledge into the air in lieu of Nag Champa. Fresh. Freezing. Laying down her face on a fluffy cushion, a cement concoction. Again I say to you. Alyssa inhaled and released a tortured sigh.

"Don't fret, Allie. Maybe he'll come back around, when he's had some time to mull it all over," said Roxy.

The evening flowed on, inhibitions fled like dragonflies.

"I seen a guy use a handheld propane tank to torch a bowl before. That's how you do it."

"I seen, I seen—"

"I be done seen about everything. When I see a petulant sky."

Moody-moody stark and viral spinning winds descend the spinal chilling gust that comes on quickly, flash and spark electric prickly. Paired in girled and boyed, with the singular of the old man Catfish rearranging chords and mallet striking tautly activates the tension, stored potential unleashed the strings sustained or muted for effect.

"Used to be a time when all the good rock and roll had piano," Les said. "Keys could do a *lot* for an ensemble."

"On-som-bley," said Rox real French-like. Then Les continued.

"Only because the juice it made the guitar king. Booker T though had a run with Green Onions. You get somebody that can handle the keyboard and suddenly vocals is just another instrument that maybe you don't need," Les finished.

"Stevie Wonder, Little Richard, Jerry Lee Lewis," said Alyssa.

"Jellyroll Morton, Fats Domino, Fats Waller," said Catfish.

"Herbie Hancock," said Moe as if that was the topper.

"Yeah, but everybody has a voice. Les, let's do that Billie Holiday. You feel like playing pee-anna?" Rox said wild westernly.

Les took another hit and nodded as he held in the smoke, then blew it out a few moments later. Moe got behind the drum set, pulling out his brushes. He slammed the hi-hat together tightly thrice, and after the third tick released to let each hat slosh loosely against the other. Catfish stood, moved to a recliner just out of harm's way. Roxy and Les went to the old Wurlitzer. Alyssa scooted over to play with all the weed and toys.

"You know what they say—Keep your ear to the grindstone," said Roxy.

"They don't say that. Nobody says that," said Moe.

"I'd swear I heard it on more than one occasion."

Les started in on a slow saunter. The notes were sparse and it was difficult to place the downbeat. Roxy turned off the Mookie Blaylock after a brief bit of overlapping Alive with whatever Les was doing. Moe swirled and slapped on the snare drum skin, with soft thuds on the kick drum head.

"Nothing I ever do, nothing I ever say—that folks don't criticize me. But I'm going to do, just as I want to. Don't care what people say." Roxy threatened them with swimming and cabaret. Mind your own. My last dollar, my last nickel. Handle your own damn self. Give it to me rather than take it all away. Get on out all the rest of you. Don't tell no tales, forget it homie. Ain't nobody's business if I do. She spun it like a body might upon the psychedelic daisy.

Catfish tried some Nat King Cole, though smokey and with some rasp. Route 66, he sang hunched over with feet firmly on the ground. Les threw in some vocal harmonies when he could. Chicago to LA, Oklahoma City looks gorgeous, all chilled out, tops in tact. It did feel a little like a holiday. Valentine's was about a week away. Alyssa had sprawled out on the couch, listening, breathing, buzzing and thinking. Being here and there and some places she didn't even know of. Building a mystery like good old Sarah McLachlan. Judy-Judy blooming groovy heavy notion sullen true we, rude and fuming twice as gloomy seven fold she knew they should be—together right now, her and Izzy. Then all would be well. Life sustaining. Sunk into the sediment, a solid foundation.

Fastened in a fashion, just like John W. P. Coltrane. Don't touch them dials Mavis, to your neck in bisquik saned.

Particle IV • Transition, What It Is

February 6, 1998

"You can't listen to Korn and not want to at least squash a bug or something." Twig was running through material for on stage, out loud. Bug splat was on the windshield from the highway driving. He drove northbound on Interstate Seventeen.

"Life is peachy they tell you, they say." The band's second studio album played on the truck's Kenwood deck. "Homie *played* that. Fuck. Fuck it. Fuck all you Commie scum you bleed and die for what you did to my garden gnome." It was not logic-based, but pure raw and had to project that feeling. He wanted to talk to Boonz about the set list if they do the St. Patrick's gig. Add some covers.

"It's eighteen minutes into Cowboys From Hell, when Dimebag comes in with the riff on Cemetery Gates. It's Chuck Berry, Jimmy Page, Jimi Hendrix, Joe Perry, Angus Young, Joe Walsh, Santana, Satriani, Slash, Van Halen, Tom Morello, Jerry Cantrell, and Kirk Hammet, and and and—. It's the bagpipes on Shoots & Ladders. It's Limp Bizkit screaming about faith. It's gotta have."

He hit Flagstaff while the sun still shone on the dirty ice in the streets' gutters. In town, movement could be found in abundance. Vehicles milling, trucks mauling, mulling over merging with traffic, turn signals and brake lights. Twigzel continued to work his banter.

"We got a couple more for you got-damn sons-a-bitches. This next one is called 'Flesh, Lairs, and Deathbed Prayers.' Long live the Syndicate, the Squalor—from the Dystopian halls of Valhalla. Shit goan die, here's mud in your eye." Crowds love it when you cuss 'em out, any good excuse to scream bloody murder. Just holler filth into the microphone, eyes a muddy blurter.

Trash, garbage, menacing scuzz and slime awake the hungering soul to life. Frothing mad, that which feeds off pain.

331

Thrives on discomfort. The masses crave fiendish depravity. Slaughter their desire. Damage and sacrifice they require. Give us your vitality that we might know conquest comma the sublime. The metal rank and file is fierce and fearless when they swarm. Mosh. Gnosh. Gnashing teeth, flashing fang, and hidden agendas back and forth like the flaming decal on the neck of every heathen's slashing boomerang. Come back Charlie Baker, if you've any wish to survive. Twice over thrice baked potatoes au gratin. Extra cheese please, with savory sage and crust full rotten. Not in a million light years could they force and preach such slang. Abandon clean living for the thrill of sludge and grime. Post-war crimes subtly nudged over the edge of what's wholesome and divine.

Twigzel morphed fully into Denzel as he pulled his Tahoe onto the gravel drive in front of Esther's place. Back at the hut, the meager haunt of Dystopian Squalor's earthly realm. The garbage bag brown Econoline van was there with its side sliding door ajar. A leg hung down with boot attached, kicking rocks with an easy sway. Denzel cut the engine, dismounted his ride. He slapped the van three times with an open palm. The door rolled open to reveal Mack "Truck" Campbell on his back with empty beer cans strewn about the cabin floor. His head lifted. A gaze of recognition slowly came to his face. The drunkard wore his intoxication well, like a badge of honor.

"Hey. Denzel. You back now?" Truck said.

"Yeah. What's going on here?"

"Typical Friday shit."

"Nice. Hey, who usually made yall's set lists up for shows? Or did you stick to one basic order you found that worked?"

"No, it changed. Mostly your bro wrote it up. But Boonz always has an opinion about everything, so he put in his two cents. Doesn't mean you have to listen."

Denzel was getting more confident that he could run this operation with just a little bit of cunning, tact, and brute force. It will be his face, his voice. He renewed his conviction and steeled his reserve, took a swig of the forty-ounce Truck held out to him as an offering of goodwill. Both men gathered their rosebuds, and hauled the guitarist's gear into the house where Boonz and Esther sat in the den slash practice area. They were watching a PBS nature special, featuring African lions and beasts of the Serengeti. The volume was muted as Metallica's Black album (1991) played on the stereo system. Boonz popped up when he saw Denzel. The two shook hands; all were glad at his return.

Niceties were exchanged. Everyone asked how everyone had been. All right. All was well in fair Camelot, perfectly anti-Dystopian, hypocrites the lot of 'em. The Syndicate stood in good standing. Esther 'Hey hey heyed,' and maybe forty-seven percent she pulled it off. Grab a seat man, please take a load scoff ye mannered ninny. Get on with your lies. Then came a knock-knock knocking from the shelter's door. The woman of the house answered the caller. It was a stranger who asked for her man.

"Boonz!" Esther turned and shouted, "There's a guy here asking for you!"

The man identified himself as a journalist and said that he was a friendly.

"He says he's a friendly reporter," she added.

"Fuck you people," Truck yelled from inside.

Boonz hopped to moving quickly, stepping towards the man, backing him out onto the front porch, closing the door behind and isolating them alone outside.

"Look, now is not the time. What'd I tell you? If you push and rush us I will give you nothing and go someplace else," Boonz totem.

"I just wanted to introduce myself to everybody. Come at this in a proper fashion. I told you it was their father that pointed me to you all here. I just happened to be around—"

"No!" Boonz cut him short. "Not now. Go. Leave," and Flynn, the Las Vegas beat reporter, was sent off empty-handed.

"Do you know that dude?" Denzel asked when Boonz entered back inside. He explained that he showed up earlier in the week and was asking about Sonny and the band. The bassist for Dystopian Squalor came across as upset, and very protective of the privacy of all in the house. The sanctity and

333

secrecy of what they were doing was important to all, the transition. Boonz said he realized they were in a delicate state, and how the last thing any of them needed was some tabloid schmuck poking around.

The vibe simmered down and Denzel asked if they could go over the proposed set list for St. Patty's. Somebody grabbed a beer. Somebody loaded a bowl. Somebody said that did everyone know it was Bob Marley's birthday? How old would he be this year? Truck told the group that Bob was born in Forty-five, so fifty-three, had he beaten cancer of the toe.

"If we do a few more covers on that Saint Patty's gig, we could pad out the set and it'd probably be much tighter than if I tried to learn like twelve originals, lyrics and guitar. To where everything was solid," said Denzel.

"Yeah Boonz, let's do *that*," said Truck.

"Alright. We'll split it down the middle. I will pick six of ours, and you tell us what half-dozen you want to do," replied Boonz.

"Which six are you thinking?" Truck asked Boonz, wanting to be kept in the loop.

"3:57, Body Bag, Baby Don't Please, Obligation to the Feud, PCP, and Deathbed Prayers," Boonz said.

Truck looked inquisitively at Denzel who totem: "Rusty Cage, Ænema, Shove it, Down Rodeo, Black, and Fire."

"Well, I don't know Ænema much at all. But we can do Sober, from that same album," said Boonz.

"Alright. So then how about we open with Black right into Fire, and then into a strong original," Denzel said.

"Into Body Bag," says Truck.

"I don't know how I feel about starting with a cover. And that one's sort of mellow," says Boonz.

"Feel good about it," Denzel challenged him.

"I'm fine starting like that. But can you pick some other Soundgarden that ain't so all over the place?" Truck put forward.

"Pretty Noose," said Denzel. They all agreed.

"So, Body Bag into 3:57. Then PCP and what's another cover?" said Boonz.

"Shove It," said Denzel.

"Yeah, who is that?" Boonz asked.

"Deftones," Truck said. "Then Baby Don't Please. Are we writing this down?"

Esther was all over it with a Sharpie and notepad.

"Then Pretty Noose and Down Rodeo," Denzel said.

"And we close on Deathbed Prayers and Obligation to the Feud. Pseudo-encore with the Tool," Boonz said.

"Except, I know Deathbed Prayers is new and all, but what if we did No Trades or Tattoos instead? That's a good set there," said Denzel.

"Do it, do it, do it," Truck egged on Boonz.

"Fine. Read that back, babe. See how it sounds," Boonz said to Esther.

"Black, Fire, Body Bag, 3:57, PCP, Shove It, Baby Don't Please, Pretty Noose, Down Rodeo, No Trades or Tattoos, Obligation to the Feud, Tool."

"I'm fine with that. But let's also have Shady Fruit ready on standby," Boonz suggested.

Everyone was in compliance. It was as if they were a team. Loving it when a plan comes together. They all get to save face and black out on some sedative-laced syrup. Come along on a magic carpet glide; flat black paint with a red stripe. What kind of ruckus can we get up to now?

Denzel, Truck and Boonz all later got up to a jam slash making noise. It would be this way for a while, preparations for the show on March seventeen, a Tuesday. They had the slot before the headlining band at one of the larger bars in downtown Flagstaff. The headliner was a California nu-metal outfit roughly in the same ballpark as Dystopian Squalor, in that they were heavy and loud. There was a good local draw that would always come out for basically anything even mostly heavy. These numbers increase exponentially if the music is extremely intense or deafening, to the extent that it might weigh upon one's soul. Gravity cubed. To the Nth, to the nines: three of them flipped upside down, the gates of Hades unleashed and off the chain. The winch fully extended, straining under pressure. Take this branch, and let it lead you

335

on through the fire. Muddy ruts and fallen timber crashing all around. Who then should we follow—that listens and speaks in return of depression and hardship? The cynical saints is they ain't. It is alright to hate, feeling and tasting the venom and flames—whipping flesh, ripping blazed across the skin. Torment. And. Deliverance.

Denzel was given his brother's CD Walkman and collection of compact discs. After rehearsing that Friday night, he donned Sonny's headphones and found a dark corner to listen to Notorious BIG's Life After Death (1997). He set it on shuffle and repeat, closed his eyes and let it run until the batteries died. Denzel passed out on the floor. Esther dropped a blanket over top of him once she'd seen that he was soundly sleeping. Soon the whole house was quiet and unconscious.

Chapter Forty-Seven • Aunt Pearl & Uncle Ed

On a steady rotation, Izzy burned through Sublime (Sublime, 1996), Tragic Kingdom (No Doubt, 1995), The Chronic (Dr. Dre, 1992), Core (Stone Temple Pilots, 1992), Transistor (311, 1997), and the aforementioned Check Your Head (Beastie Boys, 1994). This was the soundtrack for his journey home, mixed with stretches of silence. In his mindfulness was stirred many parts, frantic and blurred. Where was the sense? What was the move? He rode solo, plus the squirrel. Were they technically a duo? Had they before then been a trio, or was it just always he and the girl? The girl. The whirl. The world. A twirl around the dance floor, sawdust kicked and hurled. And what was it that happened back in Payson?

He had run. He was running, though with a clear destination in mind. Already he fought the urge to go back twice, make nice and apologize, to flee from his flight. Ground control. Space explorer. But he couldn't retreat from the magnetic pull that drew him onward according only to its great whim.[13] Something inside had clicked on and he was automatically piloting, caught up in a flow aimed directly at the Rocky Mountains. Going back to one of the places he considered home.

Hospitably ornate master encampment. Heavenly often mansioned environment. Habitation optimally manually equipped. Has obvious magical embodiment. Haphazard octagonal mountain escarpment. Hail Opie's mama's edibles. Hung over mystical equations harness operationally manic éclairs. Yes, yes they're all great and we each should have one—one of the éclairs—that Opie's mama makes.

Albuquerque and Santa Fe were in the rearview. In no time he'd have Pueblo in his sights. Then past Colorado Springs as morning light rose on the land between Pikes Peak and Black Forest. Izzy stopped for a ninety-minute rest back in ABQ. He managed to sleep nearly an hour. Now awake wide and hardly thinking about anything except his foot's pressure on the gas pedal, the occasional mirror check, and his position in relation to the dotted white lines of the highway.

He would roll into Lakewood with the sun on the rise, and break bread with his Uncle Ed and Aunt Pearl. Ed might be disappointed to find out he'd sold the Super Bowl ticket. But when they heard of his expedition, the girl he met and their subsequent explorations, how could his Aunt and Uncle be anything but enthusiastic? Because that's the type of people they were, basically all the time. A thing like this (his trip) definitely being something you would want to share. Like how Uncle Ed shared his Volkswagen expertise with Izzy, helping him get the bus roadworthy. Like Aunt Pearl telling her nephew that he always had a place to stay with them. Maybe he could've called ahead, but they're sure to be home. What an entrance he would make. Or more likely he'd park out by the curb and rest. Then perhaps there'd be a tapping at the window. What's that? It's Aunt Pearl with a plate of sausage, eggs, and toast. She's also carrying a mug of hot chocolate with whipped cream on top.

Time warp smash cut to the curb outside his Aunt and Uncle's place. Exhausted, Izzy had passed out in the back of the bus under three blankets. Larry the Ancient was huddled in close by his companion's feet. The squirrel was harboring a near empty bag of raw Georgia pecans. Peek. Yawn. Israel thought he heard a noise and woke wondering where he was. Realizing his location he withdrew further underneath the covers. Then came another sound, a subtle knocking. It was a most polite disturbance. He had an idea who would likely be rapping at his window. Leaning forward, he moved the curtains aside and saw his Aunt Pearl holding up a plate of food. Through the grog, he recognized her smile and she said: "It's here for whenever you're ready."

Izzy slid the side door open, mumbling words unintelligibly along the lines of a greeting. She only smiled again, placing the food down inside the van with some silverware. No hot chocolate.

"Hey there. You come on in when you're ready, okay?" said Pearl.

338

Her nephew grumbled again, though in a kindly and grateful manner. She nodded and closed the van door. She always let people do things in their own time. Izzy moved the hot breakfast up onto the bench seat beside him. Devouring the bacon, he gave Larry a piece of warm biscuit, and then started in on the scrambled eggs. It was heaven. It was home. Of course his Westfalia Camper could and did often serve as a roof and four walls. Couch surfing, brick and mortar. Living in a car, inboard motor. Trains, planes, and cardboard boxes, who's to say what's what? A pirate's life indeed—

Izzy instructed Larry to stay down and out of view. Then he went inside his relative's house to give a proper hello and how do you do.

"Your Uncle Ed went down to pick up some motor oil. He said for me not to let you disappear on us all quickly now. You only passing through?" Pearl asked.

"Yeah, but I might stay a while," said Izzy.

"Oh that's nice. It'll be great to have you. Your niece is over at her friend's house. She would hate to miss you, I'm sure. And how about that Super Bowl? We were watching for you on the TV."

"I'll get into that once Uncle Ed is back."

"Well, let me tell you. Denver and the whole state of Colorado were just about completely nuts. And I don't even know if anybody has let up much at all."

Izzy told his Aunt about this girl he met: "I met this girl. We went along together for a time. She said she was a cyber ghost, and that she was on some primitive recon. I believed her and wanted to know more."

"Making friends is really nice. Long as they don't cut your throat, right?" Pearl smiled. Izzy gave her a sideways look and asked who it was told her that. "Your Grandpa used to tell me and your mother that before we'd go out on long trips, plus most Saturday nights."

"Did you ever run into any trouble? Making friends?" Izzy asked.

"I guess not. But I've heard stories."

They were sitting at the kitchen table. Izzy, having got his hot chocolate was now slowly warming up. Aunt Pearl was at her stories again. Sharing jewels, pure nuggets of wisdom. In his mother's family, Pearl was the oldest of three girls. Their father was a mechanic in the Second World War. He worked on the big trucks, and everything else. That was a major part of what influenced Izzy to join the Marine Corps out of high school. He served eight years, and then took an honorable discharge to go put his GI Bill to use at one of the state universities.

"Have you been in San Diego all this time?" said Pearl.

"We were up in Oregon for a bit."

"Wow," Pearl's eyes widened. "Can I ask what your friend's name is? And will you see her again?"

"Alyssa Rose. I hope so." They both took time to reflect.

Uncle Ed came home. Handshakes and hugs. Hellos and how've you beens all around. Pearl mentioned Oregon, San Diego and how Izzy made a lady friend.

"A lady, eh?" said Ed.

"Name of Alyssa Rose." The three took a moment to imagine such a woman. "Instead of the Super Bowl we both headed up north. Had some kind of time."

"So Oregon? Bus'll definitely be needing an oil change if you traveled that far north," Ed said.

Izzy's Uncle held up a gasket set and motioned towards the garage. The boy took the small plastic pouch and asked if it was German. Uncle Ed said, "Of course."

"Booooo!"

Down in front.

"This sucks!"

You're drunk and ruining it for everyone.

"More sex, drugs, rock n roll! Nobody wants to see them work on the bus!"

It's called his story. This isn't porn.

"Booooo! We want porn! We want porn!"

Some of the crowd begins to join in with the chanting. The squares are nervous. Chad tells Scott to find security. Scott says, "There ain't no security here man—this a book."

340

"Show us the women! We want more of the women!"

All of a sudden security busts in. Speaks authoritatively into a megaphone: "Please remain calm. We're approaching our destination, and are very much so trying to bring this thing in safely." A blip of a siren escaped out of the megaphone. Security apologized. There are murmurs in the audience. A classless blowhard yells, "Freebird!" Now look what we've gone and done. Is nothing sacred? Just please do not start in with the Latin, or who knows *what* might happen. Plus, Rushmore won't even come out for another year. Sic Transit Gloria. Let's hope it don't! Seventeen-millimeter socket wrench my asthma attack! Ten double m around the edges. Ten double m around the sides. Filth-filth nasty shit and piss all over—

After the two men changed the oil, they checked the valves, the timing and added some brake fluid to the reservoir. Ed went inside. Izzy shut himself in the bus for a word with the Ancient and a quick toke.

"My uncle said I can sleep in my nieces room tonight, as she'll stay at her friend's until Sunday afternoon. After that we'll probably move over to the guesthouse. I'll sneak you indoors so that you don't have to freeze out here. You'd be best off to remove your flight mask. If anyone sees you we'll just say that you're mildly domesticated, and not at all scratchy or wild. Also, no talking of course."

This plan was suitable to the squirrel, as he would now have time to do some reconnaissance on the child he was sent to wrangle. If all went accordingly, the threat of Sinister Cindy Lewis, AKA Senator Cindy Schwartz, would be neutralized. Homeostasis in the universe would be restored for the foreseeable future.

Izzy then went out to pick up some postcards for to begin a bit of correspondence with Alyssa. Who knows *what* she thought of him for bailing on her like he did. Ed had mentioned to his transient nephew that he could probably get him a job washing dishes at his buddy's diner. After a few weeks, Izzy would have sufficient funds to set back out on the road again.

Chapter Forty-Eight • Fighting Dragons, Cuz I Don't Fit

It is the following week. Roxy and Alyssa are in the cabin working on crafts and trinkets. They will then sell these wares at an underground flea market slash swap meet, on a local property known for such carnie activity. Their creations were all either skulls and death, or hearts and love. Evil tidings. Valentine things. Braided, glued, bent, and contused. With hands and minds they worked. Each gizmo was blessed and cursed as was appropriate. Usually the chrome and black leather received an ominous incantation. While the satin, lace, and rose were graced with pleasing adoration. Of course sometimes it was switched as far as who and what got witched. Which got hitched to certain spritz or spirit's wits. That way, when the items reached their new homes they'd emanate the proper and desired vibe. This weren't some secretive or clandestine jive. Roxy and Alyssa did always label each doodad clearly. They had been at it for a good stretch.

"We should go over and see Catfish," said Roxy.

"We should indeed," Alyssa agreed.

The two had seen the old man Sunday for lunch. Most every other second day, Roxy would at least call him to relay some positive energy over the phone. Twig hadn't come back from Flagstaff since he last took off. The Syndicate's new singer-guitarist was trying to settle in at the band house. He didn't care much for constantly traveling back and forth all the time. Which hadn't been for that long. But time enough to bring annoyance. Catfish was doing okay. He remained very proud of his boy for doing something so brave.

"So don't get to feeling too sorry for me," he'd tell Roxy whenever she doted.

Mid-afternoon, the girls cruised around in the Cherokee. They stopped in on Elijah, catching the last half of an episode of Matlock. The trio then began to chill. They spoke and they were quiet. Sat still then had a riot. Alyssa had a plethora of stories to share, limitless recollections to recount. Tales of whoa man, hold on and don't let go.

"And you weren't there, and you weren't there," the Rose teased and asked them both when the last time was they'd been on any kind of proper vacation. Convinced that that is what a body really needs. "We should go to the beach!" she hollered.

"Shoot," thinks Roxy. Heads shake. Ease the moxie. Alyssa was being forced to bring it down a notch. Roxanne Nebulani Rawlins produced a joint and waggled it beneath her nose as she inhaled. Whose nose? It is unclear. Both of they noses: All three schnozzes schniffed in the aromatic scent.

They lit the magic stick and then partook. And cooked and brained their fried in breakfast nook. Hunkered deep down and low laid the restless brook. In tour on the seas of cushion booked. Bon voyage cried women's children's lifeboats first. Coughed and choked in coffin poked with air holes for the crook. Stealing happy hours interspersed with broken flowers limp and hung like vile offenders then forsook.

For the sake of being blunt they all got stoned. Not so much as to lose faith but be out zoned. Fat and happy though it's rude to point and stare. Catfish asked Alyssa what at did she glare? She told him his face. He laughed and his head did quake. The kids, they're all so fearless. Poking giants with a brittle little branch.

"Take more'n a beach to get me right," said Elijah.

"I need six months in Spain with which to sit flat on my ass," said Roxy. "People to bring me wine and drink, noble gentlemen to amuse me and make grand gestures on my behalf. Spending my days with Sally's fourth cousin the end laying out under the sun brings thirst and satisfaction. And doing my night's errands. Casual visits to my lonely captive lover."

It sounded a bully way to live. With perhaps the occasional toil and manual labor to connect your mind with your body, your body with the earth. Give the herd a wide berth, the flock it passes slowly. Flourishing and wild like the bottom of the sea. A settled path by majority made. Compound dirt as evades the rock and crevice.

"Catfish, where were you at when you were our age?" Alyssa asked.

"Probably I was out fighting the dragons," he replied.

"You did not fight dragons. Come on," said Alyssa.

"Oh, I most certainly did. But let's talk more about them beaches and those far off lands. They got jetskis there?" said Elijah.

More than he'd care to admit, Catfish had gone fists up with many sordid and unsavory characters. They that spit fire and venom, and got that loaded piece underneath the car seat or some place close by for if they come across any suitable provocation.

"Well, on this pier I went to they had a restaurant stuck way out over the ocean. I'd just be worried if a heavy storm were to pass through. The nerve of humanity, the gall of it all," Alyssa said.

"I tell you when I met the boys' mama. But only if you tell *me* how'd you get so bizarre, Miss Twyst." But he pronounced the 'Y' sound very much like an 'I' so as to add particular affront to the lady in whose name from which it came. Get a reaction.

"It's Twyst with a 'Y' because 'I' don't fit, man," she said, emphasizing the 'man.'

Shake shake shake. The shit we put up with.

"Tell us then, of Twig and Sonny's Mom," said Roxy.

Catfish hardly felt like he'd gotten a real answer regarding the girl's specific shade of subterfuge, or any substantive lead as to its origins. Such is life. Such are things. And such a circumstance hasn't ever stolen a soul's own breath. He started to speak.

"It was 1969. I'd be about forty-three years old. I seen her first time leanin' on a brick wall out back 'a' the filling station where I worked. She was smokin' and she was hummin'. She was young and full of somethin', and so I told her 'Hello' and how was she doin'. Walla walla muck muck, then she made me flapjacks. She was nice to me, and so I been nice back at her. We kept being nice each one to the other and eventually came Sonny. So I tried to make good but sometimes you slip,

344

or being nice gets tough and seems to wear on a body. But we were husband and wife and parents and all the other things people have to be. Or get to be, either way. Then came Twig and we was all a family for a while," Catfish paused.

"Did you tell me their mama's name?" said Alyssa.

"She was called Laura." But he said it like 'Law-ra', not 'Lora', the way most folks tend to do.

Then nobody said anything for a bit.

"Wool, that was some kind of story. Though it feels like maybe some of the parts were missing," Alyssa said.

"Pretty sure that is all the parts," Catfish said.

"If you say so." The Rose wasn't trying to pry. I suppose a little bit she was. Just mainly to see if the old man would open up. They had all gone in circles. It was better than doing laundry.

"I do," Catfish said and so it was.

The two ladies left. Satisfied, but still wishing there was something else they could do. Really, the stuff they had been doing meant a great deal to Elijah. He was grateful. That fact alone was immeasurably valuable. Small parts of everything are how you get through anything.

Roxy picked up the mail on her way back home. There was a letter addressed to Alyssa Rose postmarked Denver, Colorado. An air of anticipation grew. With an enlivened imagination she considered the best and worst scenario. I will never see you again, or I will see you soon. Obviously she hadn't been dismissed outright. Plus, he must have sent it early in the week in order for it to arrive today. It all mattered. He could've even begun work on this missive earlier than that, and of course he had thought of her on the trip as he drove away from them. She hadn't been forgotten. There was still a they. And where there's a still, there's a stay. On the lawn sipping moonshine baby. Some slight promise of another day. A further dance, a trot of the fox, a turn of the box, Jack please believe. Get back in the kitchen with Liza, lettuce break bread—Rock beats scissors, rhythm and love longs with every ounce of its essence, conquers all encompassingly.

"You know it's only proper, to test the bonds of affection. A soul needs to suffer without, to appreciate once within," said Rox.

Upon reaching the cabin, Alyssa retreated with letter to the loft. It was carefully opened. Torn with grace. It lacked any shimmer or scent. She unfolded the page, plain white with black ink. Above the writing was a sticker of a squirrel with a bushy tail. She read.

Sweet Alyssa,

I apologize. It was never my intention to leave you like that. I was nervous and reacted poorly. I love you, and will return to you soon in several weeks time. I wish that I could be with you now. I hope you share these sentiments. However, if you are content with the present circumstances, and I am out of place to speak of love and our reunion—I thank you and wish only for your happiness. But if you are still down, take comfort in knowing that I am not far away in heart, body, soul, and spirit. And I grow closer to you everyday.

Larry says "Hi." I've introduced him to my Aunt and them as a domesticated non-multidimensional traveling mute forest animal pet-type friend of ours. My Aunt Pearl is very excited about your existence. She says we could stay in the guesthouse anytime for as long as we'd like. So that is just another option we have at our disposal. You can write me back at the address on the envelope if you'd like. Also, if you would kindly send me your phone number for if we could burn up some pre-paid calling cards.

My dove in the clefts of the rock, in the hiding places of the mountain side, show me your face, let me hear your voice; for your voice is sweet, and your face is lovely.[14] I didn't write that, but I believe it. I look forward to the day when I can look at you and hear your laugh and hold you in my arms again.

Peace out, bean sprout—with much love and other such fluff, Yours Completely,
Israel Dufrene

Alyssa could feel a massive burden lifted from off of her being. There was more in store. They remained. She hadn't been abandoned. She saw the horizons broaden out before her. Roxy made a noise like the sounds Alyssa had been letting slip, as the news of love renewed had washed clean her countenance. Rapturous. Blissful alleviation.

Chapter Forty-Nine • The Ancient Vs The Senator

February 21, 1998

There was a cautious rapping at the door. Larry burrowed deeper into his own pile of blanket. Izzy blinking tried to focus on the alarm clock. It was nine-oh-something, Saturday morning. They were burly half awake.

"Who is it?" Izzy called from the couch of the guesthouse's common area. It had a small bedroom attached, but the circulation of the heater made it unbearably hot at certain times of the night, to the point where it was just impossible.

"Sin," came the slight reply. Was it the devil or simply the manifestation of his divinations at work in plaintiff form? Izzy asked again, "What do you want?" As the specter outside, it awaits, anxious and energized.

"Incendiary. Flee!" Threatening fire and desolation.

Izzy breathed in deeply and on the exhale popped up spry and stepped one, two and three then turned the door knob and pulled, peeking out then down he saw his niece standing there lingering patiently.

"It's Cindy. Can I play with Larry?" was the translation from the original Greek.

He bade her good morning and told the child: "Sure, he's over there in them covers on the floor by the bedroom door." Izzy switched on the television to the first cartoon he found, and fell back onto the couch and fast asleep.

Larry had stated, after their first encounters, that he found the girl fascinating. The Ancient felt that she offered invaluable insights into the developing psyche of a human from the Original, or Good Dimension of planet Earth. Scooby-Doo and the gang could be heard way far inside a spookied and hauntied house. They all got split up, and the ghosts are chasing Shagg and Scoob as they dart in and out of the cabinets of a large dresser of drawers. Such horrors. Zoinks! Like did you hear it that time? Jinkies! Ruh-Roh. It'd be the sound track to the showdown between the squirrel and Cindy Lewis. AKA Sinister Cindy Schwartz, AKA The Senator, AKA Little

Shop of Cynthia, AKA The Stiletto of the Ghetto, AKA Screw That Noise it's *My* Cupcake, AKA Queen Creek Easy Speaks the Tumbleweed of Torture, AKA Forty-seven Flavors. But this would all only ever be true if Larry the Ancient, if LtAWS failed to turn the child to the light. If left to her own devices, and an innate desire for love and affection, power and praise at any cost, in all probability she'd begin a revolution that would ultimately and ironically lead to the demise of universal interdimensional homeostasis.

Balance.

"Mister Larry," Cindy called softly to the drowsy vermin. Varmint. She carefully crept up to the wad of wool and cotton blend in which he'd encased himself over the course of a good night's sleep.

"Squrly squrly. Are you there squirrel? It's me, Cindy." The Ancient knew the game and chirped twice but did not stir.

"Eskay whirl, eskay whirl! Uncle Izzy, where'd you say you found him at?" said Cindy.

"In a sack in a box, in a back alley lot," Izzy said drearily.

"Wow. Aren't back alleys just the grandest thing? Like the Mississippi, Tigris and Euphrates all wrapped up and strapped tight with duct tape. Full of broken tiny furniture, rusty capers and old loose leaf papers," Cindy mused.

"And squirrels named Larry," Izzy mumbled.

Without warning, the Ancient broke from out the blanket and found a crevice between the wall and TV stand. Cindy scooted over some and sat legs crossed watching him watch her back. She placed her right hand palm down on the deck, sort of fingertips faced at LtAWS. She hadn't ever held him yet, but did pet him once when Izzy had a handle on the rodent. Maybe you take offense at us calling him such a kind of lowdown thing as that. But he'll tell you his own self that indubitably it's one of his official classifications. We're all just animals anyway, bits of dust and H2O. And I don't need any accusatory correspondence leveling claims such as he done called that one this and the other one said it should be so as well. But it just don't hardly ever make any kind of difference but to set folks off with various incantations of flaming vitriol.

So Cindy is locked in a soul-searching stare down with Larry, who is calculating his and her next move. He has trained his attention on her extended front paw. Its placement is soothing. She is not overly excited, but remains eager, demonstrating patience in an attempt to communicate and interact. She had only said his name a bunch, and half clever plays on how he's, "Such a fuzzy fella." Larry wished he could delve deeper into the child's knowledge of the great rivers and their kinfolk alike.

One section of the space had a faux brick wall. Here the showdown continued, as LtAWS considered hopping up atop the television so that he might gain the high ground in this maddening duel of wits. To be absolutely out with it, the girl and the squirrel had similar quotients of intelligence. The advantage was tipped in favor of the Ancient, only because of his wisdom and experience accrued over many centuries. But Cindy had less hang-ups, her being a nine year old and all. You could probably get good odds on a dead even draw, bloodshed being highly unlikely. But hurt feelings were definitely in play. Larry wanted to gauge her tendencies under pressure. He wondered if she had any inclinations toward aggression, her obviously being quite curious, and capable of maintaining a focused presence. He again chirped twice and she mimicked back his words verbatim. It's possible that she knew a little forest creature speak.

Larry moved, jumping into and off the wall. Scuffling up the back of the TV set, he stopped on top and went back to keeping Cindy Lewis in view.

"Mister Larry the gargoyle, have you mounted your flying buttress? We must beware." Much of the cuteness had left her voice.

The Ancient bobbed his head up and down, swiped his paw across his face a few times. He went to gnawing on his claws and preening. The morning had broken. Larry raised his right paw as if he was about to take an oath in court. Cindy took her own right hand off of the floor and lifted it up, mirroring the squirrel.

"I Cindy, do solemnly swear, to be nice and generally agreeable. Now you go."

Larry quickly ripped off a slew of critter sounds that would make you think he'd been possessed by a frenzied apparition. This set the child howling and the Ancient felt overwhelming satisfaction from her gleeful response. They were each so very proud of themselves. Was there no limit to the raptures they could achieve together?

Once the tide subsided, Cindy sat up and reformed her posture. She patted the ground, suggesting he come down. Larry in turn slapped the top of the TV a few times. The girl dropped her head in disappointment. She thought there'd been a breakthrough. It would take forever to gain his trust if he had no interest in her affections.

Just then and in a second split, Larry the Ancient Wonder Squirrel leapt off the television landing softly on the child's left shoulder. Everybody froze. Meaning them two got stiff as statues. Marbled madness. This was the last thing Cindy expected. Larry had no wish to frighten her, but only to leave an indelible imprint on her psyche.

Indelible imprint: check. Paralyzed with elation: check. Freaked out and about to pee: check. Cindy imagined herself in pose for the cover of Buddhist Weekly, (a monthly rag that came out thrice a year. She'd be on the spring edition) with an eagle, parrot, or chimpanzee also included in the sitting. We must respect every animal's right to perch wherever they may please. Buddha say, don't wiggle around so much. It makes you appear ridiculous. 'Show me blissful contentedness' shouts the photographer. Cindy raised her head and sat up straight like the Chrysler Building. She saw Scooby and the gang gathered around a masked man tied to a chair, awaiting the big reveal. Fred said something about bravery as he ran down whom exactly it was they had apprehended.

She could also sense and hear the squirrel sniffing near her ear. What if she had stinky hair and that was somehow sufficient reason for Larry to not want to be friends. Then he popped up to the top of her head, and sat there in her hair as she wondered if she dared share a few words of passivity.

351

"Squrly squrly?"

LtAWS pounded twice on the child's skull.

"That's not very nice," Cindy said. Her hands remained folded neatly in her lap.

Some totem the two did make. A venerable Vishnu—the Ancient being the fanciful headdress slash ornamentation. Then he goes and breaks off another solid chunk of creature speak. Must've been something, too. The way he laid into parts and gave it the full treatment.

"Amen to that, brother," Cindy told him for she knew of nothing else to say.

They stayed this way for a bit. It might've gone so far as to be a display of dominance regarding the pecking order between the two. The girl was just extremely pleased to serve as a human throne for the cuddly little dude. She desperately wanted to hold and caress him. The honeymoon was over. Period. Cindy lifted her hands slowly upwards, and by the time they reached her shoulders Larry caught on, slugging her once more as he dismounted her noggin, making a clean escape. This left Cindy feeling abandoned but fortunate. She considered a chase but decided they had made good progress. No need to ruin their work with an uncalled for act of whimsy.

"Bye Uncle Izzy! Bye Larry!" she hollered and ran off, every bit the accomplished squirrel whisperer. What a victory. It was just like Lori Petty in Tank Girl. She dreamed of the fun it'd be to go on outings together. Him nestled cozily in her pocket or purse for traveling. This was obviously of course because that would be his favorite of all places to be, on grand adventures with his lady fair.

The alarm clock buzzed. It was ten o'clock and Izzy needed to be at the diner in thirty minutes. He'd have just enough time for cold beans and a hit of green. The alarm stopped its buzzing. Izzy made it quit. He left water out for Larry who had gotten good now at using the toilet and other household devices. If not for his animal instincts, he could get used to living in such extravagance. It was a definite step up from the barracks at the Academy's base housing.

Once at work, Izzy emptied the morning's trash and mopped the kitchen floor whilst giving the dirty dishes a chance to accumulate. Otherwise it just wasn't any fun. It's best to let a pileup begin, develop, and achieve fruition. That's the optimal time for to attack them all in one fell swoop, in one glorious charge. There are people who've made movies about it even—the spiritual and intellectual side of it. These are the musings of any dishwasher worth their weight in fine china. Meaning finely busted to dust on their way to China. Meaning they crashed into the earth. The dishes slash the neverending succession of plate, cup, bowl, and saucer. He that said it best had the name of Geoffrey Chaucer.

An aside: "Go, little booke! Go, my little tragedie." And that, "People can die of mere imagination."[15]

"And she was fair as is the rose in May," Izzy told the line cook, Sam, of Alyssa.[15a] They were in the middle of an especially heavy slacking session.

"By nature, men love newfangledness," said Sam.[15b]

"Not me. I've always preferred the classic beauty," Iz replied.

"Yeah. That kind you don't ever see until it's too late. So this girl, she got that?"

"She'd fit right in in one of those old black and white movies. A rare gem she be."

"Say man, where do you get off—for context? Like when did they really do it for you? Movie actresses," Sam asked.

"Some time there in the late-Fifties through the early Sixties. Or 1973. Plus or minus four years," Izzy said.

"What's in Seventy-three?"

"Britt Ekland. Stockholm, Sweden. Born October 1942. The Wicker Man, the James Bond in Seventy-four," said Izzy.

"I mean, what's a real woman? And what about when they are unreal? And how'd they get that way? So unreal and just—BLAM! Authentic. Truly. Each in their own style making a mark or leaving an impression," said Sam.

"Brigitte Anne-Marie Bardot. Born in Paris in September of Thirty-four. Betty Joan Perske known as Lauren Bacall. Born in Brooklyn, September 1924."

353

"Top shelf," said Sam.

"Romy Schneider. Born September '38 in Vienna, Austria. Birth name was Rosemarie Magdalena Albach. Lana 'Julia Jean Mildred Frances' Turner from Wallace, Idaho, February 1921. Audrey 'Kathleen Ruston' Hepburn, Belgium, May '29."

"Julie Andrews. Mary fucking Poppins!" Sam said.

"AKA Julia Elizabeth Wells, born October of '35 in Surrey, England. Judy Garland, or Frances Ethel Gumm, June 1922 in Grand Rapids, Minnesota. The original Mary Poppins. Are we jerks if we don't mention Rita Hayworth?" said Izzy.

"Nah, but I really like Carrie Fischer. I mean, come on!"

"Middle name was Frances. October '56 in Beverly Hills."

"Barbarella."

"Lady Jayne Seymour Fonda. December '37 in New York City. Natalia Nikolaevna Zacharenko, AKA Natalie Wood, July '38 in San Fancisco. Jo Ann Pflug, Atlanta, Georgia, May 1940. She was the hot brunette in the M.A.S.H. movie."

"How's that last one go?" asked Sam.

"Jo Ann Pflug," Izzy said.

"Pflug?"

"Yep," Izzy totem.

"Those are some epic women," said Sam.

"Shirley Maclaine Beaty, born in Richmond, Virginia, April '34. The Avid Lavished Gardener. I could go on."

"I bet you could. But let's not," Sam said.

The two went back to work, Izzy to his dishes, and Sam back to burgers, fries, and the like. Nothing really happened, which was par for the course. A lack of chaos and excitement was a major draw for Izzy's peace of mind. Later on, Sam swung back by to idly chitchat for a minute.

"Man, I don't see it. You seem alright, but I still haven't found out your redeeming quality. Every dishwasher has one. They're orphans that overcame countless trials and tribulations. Or millionaire's kids who want to gain humility. Or seekers of the ultimate truths, who have cast all else aside in search of enlightenment," Sam stopped.

"Yeah, that's me. I'm the third one, just a sole survivor with good intent. Though can't some just be regular folks looking for another source of income?" said Iz.

"No, none of them are that. But you're sure a something."

Quitting time was 1830. Izzy had a letter from Alyssa waiting for him when he got back to his Aunt and Uncle's. Pearl had slid it under the guesthouse door, even though it was her property. She was always respectful of people's space, even if it was only some perceived notion of a personal boundary. It was important to her to allow everyone his or her own interpretation of sovereignty and individuality. He sat down on the couch to read through the correspondence.

Dearest Izzy,

I was so glad to hear from you. Of course I want to see you again. Everything you said makes sense and I think this time apart will be good for us. I've been able to realize what an amazing experience we shared, and how we have this bond because of all we went through together. It was just about the best adventure I've had in my entire life.

That is so great, you introducing Larry to your family members. Please tell him 'Hello' for me. Do you have any idea how much longer he will hang around for? Has he told you anything more of his mission or what he's trying to get done? I told Roxy about him, but not how he's from another dimension and is fluent in English. She says squirrels are nearly impossible to train, and how they usually get ate up by somebody's dog, because of people assuming everything's fine and then the dog just swallows the little guy whole. Do your Aunt and Uncle have a dog?

The phone number here is (928) 555-ROXY. It would be nice to talk to you. But I would be just as pleased with us writing back and forth in the meantime. Or whatever. Was your uncle upset that you sold the Super Bowl ticket? Have you been up to anything interesting?

Until our next encounter, Lovingly Yours,
Alyssa Rose

"Alyssa says hello," Izzy told Larry.

"How is she doing?"

"Pretty well it seems. She wants to know if you're close to accomplishing your mission."

"Yes. I dare say that I am," Larry said.

"Oh yeah? Might you tell *me* what that mission is?"

"I've already told you all that I can."

"Universal preservation?" said Izzy.

"Universal, interdimensional preservation of peace. The betterment of mankind."

"And squirrel kind," Izzy said.

"Yes, and every kind. It all falls under the umbrella of mankind and the living."

The two ate beef jerky. The jaded speak turkey.

"Izzy, sir. Do you ever think about where your facts come from? The origins of your belief system?"

"No," Izzy said plainly sarcastic.

"Yes, of course not. Who would do that? Now let's have some more of that dead cow you beast!" LtAWS bellowed.

In Flagstaff, Esther was working on a casserole. She had been publicizing the shit out of the Syndicate's St. Patty's show, and was trying to lineup another gig at the end of March. Boonz said by then they could be up to an hour of originals, plus thirty to forty minutes of covers. That's two hours easy, and nearly enough to fill a three-hour slot. Nine p.m. to midnight. Seven to ten. That's where the money is. And with money comes studio time.

"And with studio time comes the album," was how Boonz always ended that talk.

The guys were already mentioning 'the album' a lot. Lengthy debates and discussions of 'the songs' and 'the order' of said songs. She could hear them now in the den talking about proposed album titles. Truck said 'Bloodline' stuff wasn't appropriate. Denzel said it was. Boonz wanted there to be numbers associated in, and how they could choose specific colors or like some emblem how the Hell's Angels used to did up their jackets.

"Ain't nobody here Hell's Angels. We need something eye-catching and unique. With no skulls or flames cuz that shit is played out," said Truck.

Twigzel sat on a stool with his guitar plugged in, and he would chop wood or riff and lick the skies and ceiling in the openings of the conversation. Boonz sat low down into the sagging cushions of the couch. Truck was seated at his kit.

"What about Lies and Debauchery, colon Straight from the Pit of Hell," Twigzel said.

"Too long, and stale. But, Jaded Aggro Maniacal Zealots. Or Jamz," Boonz said.

"No more acronyms, please. I like Boondoggle Redux, because it isn't too metal, but it's still heavy and also light and so it has something for everyone. It's fresh and piques the interest," Truck said.

"And what does it mean?" asked Boonz.

"It's just this thing we do, and here we've gone and done it again. It's linear," said Truck.

"What are some others?" said Boonz.

"Okay stop. Empty your minds. Coming to your local music retailer this summer; or fall or spring or whenever. Dystopian Squalor Syndicate presents, The Fourth Blackest Album Since the Blues." Then Denzel threw in a sick flourish on his instrument to cap off the suggestion.

"It's got a number and two different colors," said Truck.

"I like that one. Or Disco Shoe Shine." Esther got a small laugh with this. She told them the casserole had just gone in the oven. She sat down next to Boonz.

"You don't think it's too long?" said Denzel.

"Seven words," Truck checked his math. "There goes another number."

"It does have a good flow," said Boonz.

"The Fourth Blackest Album Since the Blues," Truck said.

"Did Sonny have anything?" Twigzel asked.

"Dread Hippy Chronicles," is one he floated on more than one occasion." There was a pause and then Truck asked what kind of casserole Esther had made. She said it was the good kind. "Maybe we can do something with that too." Denzel said about lining up some tribute befitting his brother. They all knew this wouldn't only be about Sonny. Although at the same time, he was and would always be present in some kind of sense. Then Twigzel wondered what kind of sense of present Sonny was now. He decided it was the good kind.

There were more submissions for album titles tossed around. Each possible entry was vocalized repetitively to see how they stood up to high levels of saturation. They smoked and dranked and had a pleasant time. The guys only played a few songs when they ever got around to jamming. The casserole was chicken with carrots and peas, with the crust having just the right amount of crispy. It was indeed good and filling. The sustenance would carry them on into the night.

Concerning the album titles, of the ones they'd put forward today, it was Boondoggle Redux, and The Fourth Blackest Album Since the Blues. The knocks on each were Boondoggle

Redux had a soft element to it. To which Boonz said he didn't see it that way, and Truck said, "But it is balanced out by having an X." Denzel was the one that put the idea of softness out there. The complaint about The Fourth Blackest Album Since the Blues was yes, it was a bit lengthy. Nobody could argue that. In some ways that could be good. Make it more memorable. They knew it didn't need to be decided that day, so they agreed they had all done well for being a bunch of slacker musicians.

The four of them went out cruising in Twigzel's Tahoe. Truck sat shotgun, Boonz and Esther had the back seat all to themselves. They did a couple passes down the main drag. Then crept through a school campus and drove by a dome. Crossed over the railroad tracks as it neared the early morning. Triangle-triangle | Shift pair of diners sit; the parrot dimers sift the swift chimera climbers twist the myth of self-destruction. Takes a gallon of the bathtub gin. A hunk of metal flings your bones. A tree crushes on your bag of skin. Flames engulf you body. Melty-melty skwush kush.

Sun times pebble joust voodoo ride. Otter tides eerie sounds balance aging waters. Wallow bade good daisy chained in flagrant melody—

"You whot?"

He'd been a harbinger of real good noise. The old Randall Gottfreit Newman. Got me feeling like the only real instance gathering initiative, nominally actualized living being. There existing writ-urally *billions* of these things. Many alive, a bunch dead, and an incredible number yet to materialize slash enter into realization as all of us. Half. Whole. Heartedly. Or maybe you got family as such.

You'd be horde Proust to fund ecumenical surgeons most weekdays at dawn. The blood rush and adrenal flush is a gut punch bludgeoning sight, munch cuddling kittens of ninety-six tails. Implore the bastards well that they might not ever try it again.

Buttered up of course, the beat goads yawns. The sparrow swings like it's the Seventies. The venom is delicious, erodes from within. We're all ebony up when reveille founds unrest on the omnibus. Isn't it sometimes that way?

"But man, hey Denzel. Why isn't it the second or third blackest, you know, album since the blues?" Truck said.

"Because see—I know three that can't be beat. In blackness that is, since the blues and all," said Twigzel. But in reality he knew many more than three, though it was necessary to maintain a certain amount of bravado in putting forth dreams and ambitions. As goes the saying by an infinite quantity of crotchety old folks, as well as some only medium-aged. But I die aggressively—scratching and clawing.

Chapter Fifty-One • The Goosebump Bidness

Leslie Allen Watts had Roxy and Alyssa sat there on the sofa in the cabin. They had at least for a moment yielded to his authority. This happened only because he'd asked the women to let him show them something. That something being a song. It was a demo tape Les made with Twig back before everything blew up. The song was in homage to Dream Demonical's Lo-fi 45 Phonic Interwoven. It was keyboards and basslines, long interlaced chaste vines. A place beyond mellow with knowledge-based space crimes. Twig made the beat and samples, like a ping from a submarine and a World War One cannon blast. But it was Les on vocals. Though it were mainly more of a rhythmic talk. It had been done on a four-track recorder. So they will tell you. Slim chance there was any computer involved.

"Does it have a name?" said Roxy.

"Goosebump Bidness comma The," said Les. He pressed play on the box of boom in his hands, turning up the volume so's to let it fill out the room. There sounded a faint breath. Primitive recon break, reality- elemental life form no mortality. Freedom flows and fortune billows the main sail forward on. Unh, I'm in the goosebump bidness | | Can I get a wetness (you trashy whore) or an executive-producering credit and a refill on my Diet Coke? Thunks eye. Thinks ewe.

I will make a Fraunch films, and say to the actors, "Now be sad, now sadder. Look upset. Show me torture and pain. Show me nothing. Now show me everything!" That's a wrap on Missouri. I will make a Seventies tough guy movies and say, "Okay, now slap her harder. Walk more like Travolta. Now slap and Travolta everybody all at once. It's for the discos!" Then I will make the westerns. An Episcopal 97-part major series. I will tell the horses be real. I will make to put dirt on the clothes and all else so that it looks real real. We'll have tumbleweeds, a well-meaning prostitute, and an innocent virginal high-class gal from back East. There will be blood, guns, and gold. The proud Natives and the marauding mix of clans. The whites, man. The vast lands. The skies stretching out for miles.

Spacecraft in thee atmosphere—laid back Cadillac plush gear, attack plus fear. Holy cowzah. Rabble rowzah—

...Hindu wives wit the Ginsu Knives.

| Patience.

| Soothe.

| Space.

| The groove.

| Original.

| Verve. Hit a conceptual—

| Nerve.

| Scene. The lights go dim. Everybody pounds but they can't get in. Got bodies on the floor like whoa. Better get up get out get go.

| Peace. The word. The way. Wisdom, love and a gang of Tanqueray. Seen. The sun comes up like a red star rise, beat come a bump, bump- You been done got down for a minute get clicked hit a win and get crunk, crunk. Love the lovers, love the haters, embrace the barrier's Yorkshire terriers. | This is not an end, but a beginning. Goodbye polarity: Dream today![16]

Applesauce over the outro: medium level karma, in the year of our Lord, sixteen hundred and nineteen. Addressed at length in Sixty-three before the sudden extinction of his majesty's fertile crescendo. The physician represents the cure. The fever being the ego trip of those holding the belief that them, they and we are somehow not all just us. So continues the pursuit of just us. The music stopped and Les hit rewind.

"Yeah, that sure was something alright. Wasn't it Rox?" said Alyssa.

"Les man, it's obviously mostly just Phonic Interwoven with little spits and spots of stuff in certain spaces. But yeah, maybe in a pinch you could pull it off on stage," said Roxy.

"No, but I only *slightly* borrowed. And that goosebump bidness thing was mine anyhow in the first place," said Les.

"Massive points for putting that together though, right Rox?" Alyssa said.

"Part of it's supposed to be funny," Les said.

"Well, not all of them can be funny. You work a whole life and maybe you get a decent idea or a couple jokes to land. But it was alright," Roxy said.

"But it's definitely something to work with, ain't it Rox?" said Alyssa.

"Les man, you all should come and see my heirloom holster collection. Plus and also my bedroom poster selection," said Roxy.

"Grover detection—" Alyssa sang out.

"You showed me already. Like fifty times," Les said.

"Let's go see just for security reasons," said Alyssa.

"Will you all listen once more? I think we can do this with you, me, and Moe," said Les.

"Yes. Play your song. Come along," Roxy said.

The three of them moved with Les trailing behind, his boom box playing at a more reasonable volume. Overall, the music was quiet and resembled the still waters of a pond left over from a thorough rainfall. In a forest, or an alcove, or a pothole on an empty country road.

"I don't know if you all's ever rode in a vee double-you bus—but it's a treat," Alyssa said.

"Well, I don't know if you heard, but walls break down pretty quick in extreme crises and conditions," said Roxy.

"Meaning?" said Les.

"Damn. Did you just call her a meanie?" Alyssa shot back accusingly at Les.

"If we are calling names, I got junk to do," Roxy said.

Les assured everyone that he wasn't calling names. The three proceeded on.

"Zero to sixty, maybe. Zero to a hundred, not a chance. It's a doghouse on wheels, you see. And likely could take a few bullets," Alyssa boasted to further inflate the legend of that one time she took a drive out West.

"One time," Roxy reminding her to simmer.

The phone rang loudly and sustained. Proudly and unrestrained, with a gusto not usually attained by a simple plain-jane hoochie thang: Brrrrr-ing! Brrrrr-ing! Boy oh did she sing. Ear splitting and freedom fanged. Nails on the screech board turmoil tamed; and war torn turntables under weigh. Ahoy. Avast ye land line, cast away.

"Y'ello?" Alyssa said after lifting the receiver.

"Hello, this is Burbank Podiatry," said the voice.

"Who now?"

"It's the turdstank variety."

"You have the wrong number."

"It's the sperm bank society." Then silence. "How much ass you got?"

Alyssa hung up.

She caught up with Roxy and Les and told them the cabin just got a prank call. Roxy asked her if it sounded like anyone she knew.

"Sort of like Twig, maybe," Alyssa said. They all agreed it made sense.

Roxy was handling an old Spanish leather holster. It's coloring was a rich vermilion. The gang would each take a turn sniffing at each item in the collection.

"It smells a bit like roasted walnut," said Les.

"This one my Uncle picked up in Brazil," said Roxy.

The specimen she held had ornate designs over the whole outer surface. Like a two-tone rendering in a lightly tarnished burnt sienna. Blazed in glory.

The phone rang again. Now more muffled from the distance and walls in between. Roxy signaled her to leave it be. Alyssa didn't tell the boss lady that it might just be Izzy. In silent despair she behaved with implicit allegiance; yet quite aware that her lover may at this same moment be reaching out from across The Great Indivisible. 'With liberty and justice' foraging in the rubbish bin for a kind ear to find blind abandon, and two-thirds of a half-eaten donut hole. Touch with your soul inside my rancid rigmarole. Feel. Beware the ooze as our juices contuse within hours owned veins. We do the lambada. We do the lobotomy. You'll discover it soothing, La Bamba's drunk dance of sodomy. So we may know something of existence through wallabies. As ancient as Egypt and Claudius Ptolemy. Choose all of me. Take my life and break my will that I may let you subdue my strides of dogged approbation.

That our suffering come long and strongly affections tint the grand resplendent nurturing of this 'us'.

The Goosebump Bidness ended again. Les hit rewind. There were almost a dozen holsters out on Roxy's bed. She only had two posters up in the room. Recently she'd been considering adding a third—maybe some sweet waterfall. For now it was Bigfoot, the monster truck, crushing a row of cars, and a large glossy print of Temple of the Dog all standing around just looking like Rock N Roll.

"Should we bake Catfish (or) something? Like a pie, or a cake or cookies," said Roxy.

"Or brownies with weed in them," said Les.

"Alyssa, which? Pie, cake, or cookies?"

"Or brownies with some *hweed* in them!" Les repeated.

"Pie," Alyssa replied flatly.

"Which kind of pie would he want?" Roxy asked.

"Peek-awn, rattlesnake," Les offered. "Or *WEED!*"

The song Les had been playing for the two women began again. If the phone sounded Alyssa decided she just must go against Roxy and make a dash to answer it. To be honest, everybody was already thoroughly acquainted with the holsters and posters. Just because it almost rhymes we're supposed to be impressed? We all have lives we'd like to return to, if it ain't such an imposition on your ego. N'est-ce pas?

Kalangalang goes the dinner bell. A chicken chowder chain in Bangor, Maine; with Missus Joan and Johnson Wayner displaying an aching pain, the muscle tangled tugs the heart its strangs. Our Alyssa, she emerged from the hallway flying straight towards the phone, which in spasms did shake, vibrating nearly off the hook like a Bugs Bunny's one might. It had that kind of style.

Her picks up: "Yes?"

"Alyssa?"

"Yes," her spoke.

"Hi."

"Hi," her replied.

"How are you?"

"Good," her said.

"It's me."

"Yes. I know," she always knew.

"And you're good."

"*So* good," and her was.

"Yes. Me too then, of course," said Izzy.

They both were just *so* good together for a couple minutes. What es bliss? What is bless? Got dammit— Got sustain it, keep it safe and secure from the halo's tempting allure. A seductive summons. Elohim provide us sustenance for this our bloodletting disembowlmentation slash exposure for annihilation or absolute acceptance. Love. She would let loose and pour forth laughter, making mirthy sounds without provocation. It was not a day. Was not a year. Was not people. Was only an intimate connection. An infinite reflection: the stuff that moonbeams are afraid of. Pull the shades and light the candles. Turn the Jacuzzi up to a rolling boil. A hot damn scandal of blazing wanton yeses applied liberally all over the place. Just lathered. Tell me tell me, this cast you spell me. Sing to me my name. It was a pastiche of giddy pulsing nerves. Wanting to say everything; and at the same time not spoil anything. Both of them, the boy and girl, were pretty much nuts.

Like the Fourth of July at Christmas. Cotton candy and lobster tails. Jittery whatever you call it's fun and what liberty is about. Immortals for a moment. Relentless gifts for every soul alive. But filtered through just the two of them, A and I. High concentration of exponential joy. Her said, "I'll be your confidential toy." Inconsequential ploys. Part of the problem, all of the noise, as the next device deploys.

Intermittent metaphor. Countermeasures unemployed. She wanted to hear about washing dishes at the diner, Larry, Cindy, Pearl, and the state of Colorado. "Do you know when you'll be here? I hate to ask," though she asked repeatedly in a variety of ways. He hadn't answered any of her questions about his return. Izzy didn't want to make any promises he couldn't keep. But he also wanted to give her something that would assure and encourage. Lines are no good anymore.

"I am absolutely set on getting back to you as fast as fate allows. Unless something major goes down, which is highly unlikely, I can say that I will be there in March," Izzy said.

"That sounds so distant. Man, first Bikini Kill breaks up, and now my lover is being kept at bay by—What exactly is keeping you at bay again?" said Alyssa.

"I'm procuring funding for our future plans."

"Okay. So March."

"Yes." You go to the well. You go straight to the well and dye. Waters thirsting with colors bursting—yearning, burning, tempest churning. Begins and ends with yes.

Reaffirmations of affections were shared with equal vehemence. There were pledges of patience and devotion, honest pleas of deep emotion. Mushy-mushy gush-gush, phonic hugs and kisses.

Once they'd talked for a nourishing length of time, each said their goodbyes and agreed to continue writing one another. Peace vines, gang signs, traffic fines and coaxial cable. Dot-dot-dot.

"You there in the scarf, have you got the timorous nature of this beast?"

"What beast?"

"Yes, of course. That's the idea. Ugzactly."

Chapter Fifty-Two • We're Us All a Bit of Magic

It is March. It is Denver. Cindy and the squirrel have their commingling down pat. A very promising rapport has been established. A part of every morning is spent with the pair playing nice. I will go on out and say it; they were friends.

Larry the Ancient needed to affect the child, but only for the good. If she was nudged in the wrong direction the results could be calamitous. A negative experience might escalate the pace of her darkening essence, but also eliminate the last chance for to put a little ribbon on the remainder of existence.

Cindy was so pleased and rapturous about her new relation. When they were apart, she busily planned adventures and escapades for the two to attend. How wonderful it will be to have Larry around for tea and to pose for portraits. He will make the most darling muse. It was almost exactly like having a brother, which is what she wanted above all else, an assistant to do her bidding and hop to at the snap of her fingers. So she'd need to learn how to snap real well. For as Cindy understood it, little brothers are basically indentured minions kept close to do whatever big sisters demand. This all sounded like a smashing deal, and so she was all for it—in principle. She wasn't totally straight on how little brothers didn't mean less food and snacks. Perhaps it is similar to government subsidies for oil companies. The family receives a greater share, and then Ed was always saying how you had to figure for inflation. A lot of these things Cindy knew her staff would handle when she became the governor. Or knock on wood, her run at the presidency in the year 2024. She knew it wasn't absolutely necessary to take office on her first year of eligibility, but why waste any time when dealing with changing the planet. Her friend at school had already shook hands on coordinating campaign activities. She was currently in talks with Ed about getting odds in Vegas. Cindy was pretty smart, obviously. But at the same time she appreciated the value of staying humble and grounded. Which was something having to do with electricity and rubber screwdriver handles. Like rubbing balloons on your hair and then it sticks to the wall.

That was just science, and like the old guy who flew his kite with a key and somehow nobody else had tried it. So it didn't matter if there hadn't yet been a lady president. No doubt that trend was coming to an end. Wanting it so bad made her feel evil, but in a real good kind of way. Like when Pearl cusses at Ed. But yeah, Cindy's soul was not full for she felt a void as an only child. She knew for a fact that her birth parents were somewhere out there, as she had heard this being discussed in hush-hush voices. Somebody at school said it meant she was adopted. This brought to her mental pictures of rescue puppies, like the ones at the animal shelter Pearl would take her to to show how there were actually too many puppies. That idea made no sense, because it seemed to Cindy that people would want as many puppies as possible. There should if anything be a shortage of fuzzy creatures to play with.

Knock-knock-knock. Rustle, wait, noise, walk, the door-knob turns and she is allowed entry. Larry is in his corner and the girl says his name once quietly. He is lying on top of his wad of blanket. He does not burrow. She sits down beside the squirrel, back against the wall, cross-legged with hands folded in her lap. He watches her and she smiles.

"I trust you had a restful night's sleep," Cindy said.

The Ancient was fond of this human's concern for his well-being. It felt innocent and genuine, though it's difficult to be sure. The child was thinking if Larry would benefit from a trip to school with her. She knew that a solid education was a key ingredient to becoming a respected member of society. Home schooling could also accomplish that, and Cindy was certain she'd make a top-notch teacher. They could have movie time and extended recesses. This was all turning out to be some corker of a year. The Broncos are Super Bowl champions, and here she has her very own fuzzy little vassal and general understudy at life. Could she be satisfied with only being president? Galactic princess. Universal Queen—Ruler of all things to come. Cindy wanted as much as four big pockets of dominion, plus a backpack full and whatever could fit in Izzy's bus. Maybe she should have her press secretary put a call into Elway's people.

As the girl was daydreaming, Larry began to wiggle and stretch out his limbs. Then he unexpectedly moved from his blanket perch over onto Cindy's lap, nestling in the crick of her left knee. His back was against her hands and she stayed perfectly still so as not to startle the Ancient and chase him off.

"Little squirrel," said Cindy.

The two stayed like this. The coyote and roadrunner were battling in the background. This was the unicorn's voyage. Why don't you rest for a while? Larry was feigning sleep. In his mind he considered all available options, actions, and the corresponding long-term ramifications to whichever method he would use moving forward. For now, both the girl and the squirrel had found peace with deep and steady breathing. Oh two. Oxygen, endorphins and the endocrine system: the quiet exhalation of carbon dioxide. All parties calm on the surface, brimming with torches spinning on the inside. Plates or sewer grates. Balancing the chain saws. Battling the instincts.

"I been thinking of a good field trip for us to go on. Denver has a Museum of Contemporary Art, Museum of Nature and Science, and a Museum of just plain regular Art as well. Plus, there is a Museum of Miniatures, Dolls and Toys that is the most darling little place. We could put in some solid time. I'm positive Izzy would take us one of these days. We'll let him sleep for now. I could smuggle you around in my Pound Puppy purse. Doesn't that sound fun?" Cindy said.

Inside his brain, Larry soothed himself with all sorts of rationalizations as to how his efforts to manipulate this human child weren't shady and questionable. What was it President Roseanne said to Jimi Hendrix when he told her that everything would turnout alright? "Yeah, well suppose it don't?" How do you make a body see the light without burning a hole in their retinas? For whatever bent leanings Cindy might contain, (dormant and fallow, active and pouring forth) she was still only a nine-year-old being, advanced or not. There must be a tactful way to strategically freak somebody out, and not wholly scramble her senses. Larry could just make a logical plea. It was on some level necessary to clearly threaten her with ruin and obliteration if she didn't just, you know, take it easy on folks both smaller and bigger than herself. The Ancient didn't suppose that was too unreasonable. Lay off the murder and corruption.

Cindy went on about how nice Peru must be this time of year, and did animals need a passport to fly on a plane? But if so they could just drive there if Izzy aimed to do more traveling, right over the Panama Canal. And had Larry heard about Rio and the giant statue of Jesus? And wasn't that just a gravy image? That last part she overheard Pearl talking about. Cindy made it clear that she liked a good gravy, but there are way better things to color and draw with.

The Ancient felt that he should take action. He unraveled and arose, appearing still sleepy. He was playing it up awful sly. She stared at him like miracles are real and happening right now. Cindy smiled. Larry hopped up onto her right shoulder, chirped some random noise and then spoke so that only the child would hear.

"Cynthia Lewis, listen to my words. You must always respect and be kind to every living thing. Do not rejoice in the hardships of others. Be a positive force in the world."

The squirrel said these words. A look of utter disbelief took the place of the smile on the girl's face. Of course it was everything that she had wanted, but was in no way prepared to comprehend.

"Speak to me child," Larry said.

"Squrly?"

"Yes. It is I. Acknowledge what I have just told you. Then we will ask Izzy about that day trip to the museums. Although Peru seems very unlikely," LtAWS said.

Cindy was overloading. It took every bit of her self-control not to scream. Yes, what did he just tell me? Larry spoke to me.

"Be respectful, kind, um— and do you mean to not laugh at people?" Cindy said.

"Yes," this suited the Ancient. "You will be a great woman. I believe in you. Do you believe in me?"

"Yes," she said, wondering if this was dreaming?

371

"I may go away soon. But you must always remember. Respect all life, be kind, do not pick on others, and stay positive," said Larry. He could see that she was stunned and barely holding it together. He asked her, "Could we have a hug?" Cindy nodded as the squirrel scurried down into her arms and they squeezed one another. Maybe she held him a bit too tight, and for a split second harbored an ego-dystonic fantasy about wringing his neck. Though in all appearances it was a warm embrace.

"Are you magic?" Cindy whispered.

"Of course I am," he replied. "Just like you."

Indispensable, wit lil birdies and jump kicks for all, in this principle. Izzy slept through it all. Larry suggested to Cindy that she not let anyone else know of their conversation. They pinky swore on it and the girl ran off, dazed but enthused. Buzzing like a honeycomb in spring.

Since arriving in Denver, Larry had stowed his flight mask in a drawer in the guesthouse's bedroom where he was staying. He retrieved the headpiece and sent off a transmission informing the Guardians of the Envoy to the Council of the Living that he had given the initial verbal warning to Cindy Lewis. It was acknowledged. The Ancient attached his coordinates and requested further instructions regarding his extraction, if the mission was shown to be effective. Effectuality being evidenced by other Guardians of the Envoy who would be sent ahead in time to review and act as witnesses to any alterations in Cindy's future behavior. Larry felt bad that he could not completely let Izzy in on the full extent of his duties. This was bigger than any perceived portrayal of friendship, whether or not it was authentic or just a tool with which to carry out a plan.

Still Izzy slept, probably for the best.

Chapter Fifty-Three • Cereal & Tap Water, Forgiveness

It had become a natural pastime for the boys of Dystopian Squalor, prank calls. Roxy's cabin was one of Twigzel's targets. Truck always pleaded for them to ring up Disneyland or Magic Mountain, but the long distance charges would make it more of a burn on their own wallets when the phone bill came around. Boonz had limited interest in this business because they never prepared for the call itself. It seemed to be just an exercise in awkwardness and the resulting chaos and confusion. It was a disturbing sport, and that fact was its main attraction to the Syndicate. If it was an art form, they were only in the fingerpainting stages.

"What about we call some local bar and ask for Seymour Butz or something, like how they do on The Simpsons?" said Truck.

This proposal got shot down because it lacked originality. Boonz was on some kick about what if they called in a bomb threat on an animal shelter. Esther said that would just be mean and probably extremely illegal. She turned sour on Boonz especially, and the two of them went away in a heated discussion. Denzel and Truck were left brainstorming in the living room. They soon devolved into placing insane wagers on improbable fictions. With such braggadocio did commence to boast bets. Five'll get you ten unstolen ghost vests. Broke sets on the coastal riverboat's treks. Native tribal hit me bust quite notes yet. Thrust all-in the pot undead, still some can question whether it's Price is Right rules on how much is a Seventy-three Porsche 911. One of them scrammed, 'One dollar, Bob!' The otter flipped his collar cob, corn in the holler hot saucer slob. They act like it's the spotter's fault. When the gymnast smacks the mats and crashes topple-flops.

Their need to contaminate someone's serenity died away, wore off, faded out. Truck spun a drumstick deftly with his leftly limb, does the clave on the couch cushion. Probably no one had any thoughts for far too long. Consecutive egg timers, executive suede shiners, two bits and a bottle of keeping it in between the lines, Reiner. Mira-meedah, flex your cheetah.

Had a pigeon couldn't feedah. How do you like *them* bananas? Evil seed of pumpkin eatah—

Denzel decided he would call home. After a few minutes he meandered over to the kitchen table, dialing from rote memory. Beep bop boop bip bahp bahp borp. Several rings later the line picked up, "Hello?"

"Hey Pops."

Elijah Frye was overjoyed at the sound of his boy's voice. It did not matter how long it had been since they last spoke. They hadn't yet said anything and already it was a blessing to his heart. There was nothing to forgive, pure acceptance being the immediate reaction from the father.

"How have you been? Is everything getting on alright with them fellas?" said Elijah.

"Yeah, we have a show here in a couple weeks. Some Saint Patrick's thing."

They talked weather, and who probably had it worse. The boy told his father he'd slept quite a bit on the floor, couches, and once or twice out in the Tahoe. He was allergic to beds. He (Twig) was eating okay; him and Truck had a newspaper route, also hustled for some extra cash. Catfish heard how the guys in the Syndicate, plus Esther, were also in a jugband side project. Made up of washboard, spoons, jug, and the juicy harp. Everybody took turns on all the instruments. Or they would just foot stomp and hand clap. Many of the songs they learned to kick off were ditties that Catfish had taught Twig years ago. The trick was that the music had to be one hundred percent acoustic. No electricity, a complete departure. One hundred and eighty dirges. It proved an effective counter-balance to the chaos and destruction that was Dystopian Squalor, plugged in and chopping wood with vengeance.

Elijah knew some about Truck and Boonz from all the time Sonny had spent with them. They were not bad people, but in the same way they were not good people either. They were people. That was as much as could be said.

"Roxy's been around some. Or she will ring up just to say a few words," Catfish said.

"Yeah. You're probably stuck with that for the time being."

374

"Oh, I don't mind. We all of us have our own ways."

"And are you doing alright then?" asked Twig.

"I suppose. Something's on my mind though, has been for a good while. That day. On the phone, Vincent only said for me to let you be. That I can't be selfish, and that everybody gotta get to their own destination, at their own pace."

"He said all that to you?"

"Basically, yeah. That was what I took away from his words," Catfish said.

"He say anything else?"

"He told me that he forgave me for all of whatever had or hadn't happened in the past."

"Well then, I forgive you too," Twig said.

"Thank you," said Catfish. "It's a sweet thing to be forgiven."

"It's sure something alright."

The old man was reminded of the traditional hymn, Blessed Assurance. Then he thought back on busted up rackety chapels, all the white paint and pastures; the raptures. Bone spurs, backaches and the known scourge. Only spoken words that groan uncured.

"Whatchu eat mostly now?" asked Twig.

"Chicken nuggets, jerky, zebra cakes, SpaghettiOs and toast. I'm sure it's all mostly the wrong stuff. Turkey potpie. It gets me by," said Catfish.

"Eh, I like cereals. All kinds. I figure between sliced bananas and granola, I could go a long way on that alone."

"Yes, well I did just have plain Cheerios in cold tap water. So, I know cereal."

"Pops, you need milk. I told you that one market does deliveries. Or tell Roxy, she'd do it for you, drop of a dime."

"That girl does too much as it is," Catfish said.

"She probably wishes she could do a whole bunch more though, so. Yeah. Just leave Cheerios alone altogether. You need to get on those Golden Grahams and some Cinnamon Toast Crunch. Man, Pops, it's like—move over Cocoa Puffs and Fruit Loops," Twig said.

"Well, there's Grape Nuts, and I will put that real crystal sugar all over it."

They were semi-bonding epoxy with the sandpaper handshake that was rooted in blood and trees of families. They were so far away on some levels, yet so close on several concurrent planes. Going aero postal on them atmospheric boundaries. Often lost and often foundries. Sanity, get thee behind me. Sanitariums, peek in me blinds, please. It's the mind's freeze that resigns us in our final breathes. Vinyl squeeze. Drink up if it spines the time, reeds wash against the warrior in his prime. Peace divinely carried down the water's path. Each voice lets his people know he was there for them. Six-three five-two for one of another. In a distant language it is probably known as love and devotion. In a greater sense it's the mass release of doves upon the ocean. A pleasant exposure, testing trap doors: almonds over the place.

They lit the fern in throws, talking circles.

"Did you know this?" Catfish said.

"I did, but tell me again. And do embellish."

"There was this shark. Best damn fighter pilot in the squadron. All he wanted was to fly the Black Hawks. But he was a jet through and threw his back out one stormy night when he took his lady up for a midnight joyride. Maria was a sexy piece of flesh in seafood stockings," said Catfish.

"Aren't we supposed to fight though?" Twig asked.

"Drama is overrated. It's okay to just be alright, you and me."

"Thanks, Pops. And take care."

"You do the same," said Elijah Frye.

It was good whoever's idea that was. They each were caught up and connected. Alone and with spirit, near extensive root structures linked to memories, tangled nicely all up in the galactic swirl. The recollection itself increasing the reach of initial contact. Sod in remission. Superstition accomplished.

Chapter Fifty-Four • Penumbral Eclipse of the Mind

March 13, 1998

"Do you wish goodness for all beings?" asked Roxy.

"It is one of my conscious devotions. Yes, I wish goodness for everyone. Except for those who wish harm on others," said Alyssa.

"So then, not everyone," said Roxy.

"I love mine enemy."

"That's easy to say."

"I try," Alyssa said.

"Yes, I guess you do. And will you continue to behave in such a manner until the day you expire, slash die?" Roxy asked.

"Totally, that will happen. Curse my heart and blink my eyes, stick a thousand needles in my thirty-second chance comma point of notary urns. Filled with ashes of the patrol's barn storms and brain steaming. Beckons a broad stance, crash bang," said Alyssa.

"No girl. You lost me there."

The two women did womanize, but only in the sense of tearing through shakes and a large fries. How many straws can you fit in a milkshake? How much milkshake can you fit into a straw? And what of the camel's back? The broken rhythms and speech patterns unite their commune. Two-sided balloon, the upside and the downside. My feet hitting your teeth, and a motif splitting forehead aches born of ageless folly. Just around to make sport and blend nicely the banter.

They word got along aww right. The woods held an audible fright. If only the ghost world commends with its ornery might—you and a forty-watt army. Roxy and Alyssa were outside, kicking pinecones a little ways off from the cabin. They could faintly see the front porch light through the trees and evening dusk.

Earlier, the two had hit up the burger shack. It was not an official meal, so no actual burgers were gotten. As was mentioned, there were the fries. As for the shakes of milk: Rox had chocolate, while Alyssa got strawberry. It is vital this fact be evidenced.

They were already a ways into March, which meant that this was the month when Izzy, by his own declaration, would return. She (Alyssa) had spoken with him on average of once, maybe twice a week. These conversations were either short and sweet, or long and luxurious. Letters were exchanged at varying intervals, and this seemed to be where the real truths were shared. It was apparent between the two, that although neither had any great plans, they both wished to go about their immediate futures as a duo, a pair, a couple. They'd often bring up possible adventures or places where they could spend their time. Travel would still be a high priority as their initial expedition together up the West Coast, through Oregon and back to Arizona, proved life-affirming and a positive experience all-around.

So this happened and never once did the Earth stop spinning. Mother's rotations with spacious milk root supplication. Kung fu sublimation gives the boot to all tarnation. But what is about a settle down? They say to stop talking. Supposably the write way. Alyssa always did at least three postscripts. Izzy said it was a democracy. They talked about what they would do if conversation did run dry. It was proposed they try a dry run, but this only resulted in radio silence, blank letters, and a general void. Clearly if they were in a space together, they could be physical and communicate through touch. There was an awkwardly embarrassing attempt at phone sex: heavy breathing, quiet tones. Lack of privacy for the girl made this difficult. It was hilarious though, memorable stuff. Ay oh river.[17] Anybody got ears on? Please deposit another twenty-five cents into the machine. What'd you call me, Poppy? Notre dime store pimpers can't beat choosers. Yeah, but cheese and crackers please get on whip the show— into shape. Antiquated natural drape. It's the way of the walk, the miles and the membrane soaked wit. Action.

Roxy said that for sure there would be a lunar eclipse. It was to be penumbral, and that word made Alyssa's mind drift to yellow umbrellas, but not writing implements. The Rose remembered she had a friend who was a squirrel. To hear that thing speak on worldly matters will remain a cherished memory. Was that real? Is Izzy probably not so amazing, or am I blind and plunging into an abyss? If somebody asked, could she account for her purpose or motivation?

Due to the canopy of the forest, the women had been waiting for the moon to rise in altitude. Dig along little bodies. Who knows the energies that could descend? Sense blown in on a southern wind. What was that that did throw off them dandelions? Like the king's cape in battle, torn away to reveal the blade and shield bared. Sound the charge; be on guard for the hidden beyond. With many faces the fickle goddess journeys.

"Yes, but I'm asking if there will be energies accompanying the eclipse. Like healing waters from out the sacred fountains. Some kind of caffeine-nicotang smoothie. But all natural like a cocoa bean's tobacco leafed neutra swang, green salad and croutons. Cretins. Credence. Help it ain't a shade on the risen moon."

They had partaken.

"Only what this weed'll make you believe. If you focus you can feel it," said Roxy.

"That is what I want, them good vibrations. Let the heavens shake my core," said Alyssa Rose.

The women decided to watch from closer to the cabin. Alyssa was certain that binoculars would make a huge difference. Roxy said she doubted it. It would take a telescope or some such high-powered device of greater magnification.

The moon once in view was something true. Black swan, Grey Goose, white tiger, yellow ruse, green whale, and purple bear of Caesar snapped the eager roast. Duluth or empty potato chip bags at the trailer park bait rooms. Walk like the coyote, dancing with the werewolf.

"Bare moon light," pleaded Roxy.

"The stars alone are magnificent," Alyssa said.

Bull shit, make believe, imagination, lies—it's all the same. What matters is is there a victim being hurt by it all? Maybe you tell your children they're safe from bad guys. Same time you tell the bad guys, hey, pick on somebody your own size. Or else everyone and their mothers will be prosecuted to the fullest extent of the library's book return policy. Calling in a bomb threat is all fun and games, until the terrorists actually pick the same outlet mall that your cousin said would be so choice to prank. Now the Feds got a car battery hooked up to your nipples. Wait, whose nipples? Bro—

"Considering—" started Alyssa.

"There will be no considerations made," said Roxy.

"Excluding—"

"There will be no exclusions allowed."

"Granting the fact—" Alyssa said.

"There will be no facts granted, at all," Roxy said.

"I only wish to say that I've always remained loyal."

"If you call riding off with strange boys being loyal, then yeah you did."

"Exhibit A, the postcards," said Alyssa.

"Yeah, yeah. But have you heard of this The Big Lebowski?"

"No, what's that?"

"It's like this Zen bowling movie. But it has that redhead we like from Boogie Nights and Benny & Joon."

The two went back and forth. It wasn't fighting, but in a bigger sense the faux-anger might help them figure some things out. Like should they start to invest real energies into what's a Julianne Moore? How did she become herself? How come any of this happened? Tune in next week when it is revealed, why guarding gnomes make such great sentinels.

March 14, 1998

The day after Larry spoke to Cindy, the squirrel woke Izzy around 0400 hours to have a word. The Ancient had on his flight mask. He had received transport coordinates from his home dimension and needed to set out soon. The rift in space-time would only remain open for a short period. As with any interdimensional travel, there were elements of risk involved. Larry was excited to go, but also cautious not to make some careless mistake during his departure. Izzy switched on a lamp. He saw the squirrel perched upon the coffee table. They each nodded a good morning to the other. Izzy sensed he was in for a goodbye.

"Speak friend, my ears are open," said the boy.

"Yes, right on. But, well I must be leaving now."

"Did something happen with Cindy?" Izzy asked.

Both sides were calculating their responses. It would do everyone well to keep it close to the vest. They had both registered some uncertainty about the appropriate amount of emotion to display, if any at all.

"Cindy will be fine. Hopefully my work here has achieved a positive result. If all goes as I expect, this should most likely be the last time you see me," LtAWS said.

"That would be unfortunate. But hey, either way I'm glad for the chance to hang out with you. I am certain that Alyssa feels the same way."

How do you talk to people? There are probably a hundred right ways, and two hundred and fourteen wrong ones. That's okay odds, but still. Izzy taught Larry a complex handshake. Slap-slap wiggle-wiggle. They tried it a few times, though it seemed too late for contrived howdy yalls and how you beens. What was the larger context that brought these two beings together? The Ancient thought of breaking his vow of secrecy, if only to tell Izzy that he was proud to have known him. After all, wasn't everything set in motion to allow for universal continuity until the next threat was revealed?

Larry wondered what commendations he would be in line for—Cash money, a sweet condo, points on the backend of a tranquil cosmos, or his name in the pantheon of Greats of the Seven Dimensions. He'd give serious consideration to settling down, turning it in, and hanging up the old snakeskin pistol belt. The Ancient had been hearing positive reviews about these Eastern European mail order brides. It wasn't so strange. Most of the stigmas concerning arranged marriage, bought love, sold and paid for pledges, were removed when everybody and their third cousin started divorcing left and right. Probably if he left it all alone he'd naturally run across a nice girl the old-fashioned way: at the Academy's Sophomore Mixer.

Perhaps the Guardians of the Envoy would hold a parade in his honor. He might attract the attentions of some powerful females of any number of compatible species. He will be a commodity now, as a returning champion of the Living. They could stock a harem chock full of virile ladies to be at his beckon call. Or he would find a sweet librarian and start a little family. What about just a soul to love? And was that even something Larry still believed in? So much feeling was occurring, with brainpower's energies all oozing out ear canals. If it were a painting it would be messy.

"So yeah, squirrel. Larry. The Ancient. It's been real weird."

"Thank you. This is high praise that you have offered," said LtAWS.

"Let's go. I'm giving you a ride as far as custom allows," said Izzy.

"That is unnecessary."

But Izzy was unrelenting in his pursuit of service and sacrifice, or whatever. They exited Aunt Pearl's place extra quiet. Inside the bus, its engine running, the heater was switched on to circulate the warm air from the beast's beating heart. Izzy had poured hot water over the front windshield to dissolve the layer of ice that had developed overnight. Larry informed the boy that his extraction point would be located above a lake next to the Denver Zoo. Izzy said they should be there in about twenty minutes.

382

"Your Uncle said you've been playing ukulele," Larry said.

"Eh, mostly just raw skiffle and what not."

"Oh, I see. And what not, what's that?"

"Often after an especially intense jam, I get that feeling only gets satisfied by instrumental demolition. Giving it the full Keith Moon."

"And so, you have destroyed many musical implements?" LtAWS asked.

"No. It makes little sense economically," said Izzy.

"Ah yes, but it seems to be so very punk rock."

Izzy parked near a plot of red tennis courts on the northwest side of the lake. A small isle sat in the middle of the water. That lined up with the specified topography that had accompanied the coordinates Larry received from his command. It was still dark out. According to initial contact, there would be an advance team sent to ensure successful re-entry. The boy asked if it would be Big Daryl and Little Daryl again. The answer to this was unknown, but Larry said that all Guardians of the Envoy to the Council of the Living were highly skilled and fully competent. He said this both for Izzy's benefit and for his own. It is best to keep your pleasant thoughts close at hand. Must be prepared to take action, take flight, and take no prisoners when the moment arrives.

Was it true that if Izzy for some reason decided to try and restrain Larry, that the squirrel was then authorized to use lethal force against him? Yes, is true. Being on good terms with the boy was only a lucky draw in the ultimate scheme. With or without consent, the Ancient had always been determined to make contact with young Cindy Lewis. No matter the means, it was the highest priority to shift the child's future actions away from projected destructive tendencies. The risk that LtAWS took by directly threatening Cindy to bring about change was only one of necessity. There would be no rolling the dice on the hopes of subtle hints and gentle persuasions. How goes the saying? If you want something done, cash is king. No. Keep your friend's clothes; give your enemies closure. No. Do unto otters as the woodpile would dew to gather no mas.

Whatever. Who was he trying to kid? He missed Alyssa, and would soon be missing Izzy as well. He would also forever cherish his moments with Cindy, and he cursed his animal juju for this dastardly sickening weakness of thought. If he started to tear up now, it could jeopardize his good standing with Mr. Israel Dufrene. Not very cool, more like very uncool. Perhaps though he'd give a sniffle just out of spite. Who cares? Emotion is real and you just can't shut it out to be sunglasses all the time. Gross, what is going on? Larry had an inclination to bolt. It was the fear and dread that was working on his insides. Regenerative and corrosive, like hatred. Only it was something more akin to love and affection. It bothered LtAWS that this could be the end.

"Bas avec l'Angleterre. Viva la Revolucion," said Larry.

"Right on," Izzy said, and that was it.

They did their new handshake. Larry the Ancient Wonder Squirrel exited through the open bus window. He took to the ground and then bounded up into the morning freeze. A light mist hung. The squirrel cut through the sky borne current, now zooming away over the empty tennis courts. His transport instructions noted that the portal would appear approximately fifteen meters above ground level. Usual protocol was to insert and extract agents at a height where a small fall would be harmless. The Guardians were taking every precautionary measure to ensure mission success. Not every field agent from the Seventh Dimension had the capacity for flight, pro-longed or short-lived. It must be there in an entity's intrinsic makeup, in order for the Council of the Living to magnify and exponentially increase an individual's flying capabilities. Birds, bats, bugs, pterodactyls—although in Larry's case it was an extra nice deal, as before the modification his flight was mostly limited to gliding and falling out of trees.

So he flew. He hovered and engaged his cloaking device. It was nearing the preordained extraction time set by his home planet's space-time travel team. Where he was was gray. Where he was going would most likely be other. For now, the Ancient readied his breathing for the beating his body would be subjected to once he entered into the wormhole. It was not instantaneous. The usual practice was to begin counting backwards from one hundred upon entrance inside the storm. Running the numbers like that kept one focused and less likely to pass out from the effects of interdimensional space travel.

Larry was enjoying his independence. Met with a brief second of contemplation. Things would drastically change once this next sequence was set in order.

The peaceful morning quiet was.

Izzy drove back to his Aunt and Uncle's. A shading of sorrow overcame him. Did the exit of the talking squirrel mean that things would get back to normal? Stupid dumb and weak-ass normal. LtAWȘ had added an extra dimension to Izzy's life. Literally. Actually he added about six. Plus there was the style of it all. I don't know if you have ever had your own squirrel, but it's a treat.

Mister Dufrene, minus furry pal, put on Evil Empire (Rage Against the Machine, 1996). He cranked the volume, felt for the thunder and fury. Accessed the energy and breathed deeply. God bless the guitar, bass and drums. Melt face razor nectar reflect trace burns get spun. Spit honey chrome-moly tub spackled gun. Metal.

Back over the lake, Larry zipped about with a watchful eye open for the portal. There would probably be news coverage back in the Seventh Dimension. Could get a nice spread or mention in the Guardians' weekly newsletter. Last year, a fifteen year old from Weird Vermont died saving three kids out of a burning school bus. They made a permanent national holiday in his honor, third Tuesday in August. Straight memoriam. So Larry should be in for a gift basket or some nice assorted chocolates at least.

The Ancient heard a voice off in the distance. Soon it sounded again, much closer this time. Then the squirrel deactivated his cloaking, as he saw a noble raven coming near. The two flew to a meeting where they hovered, each looking the other over.

"The vultures fly clockwise in the spring," said the raven.

"They would, wouldn't they?" Larry replied.

"Caramel suits you," was line three of the code.

"Just mid-grade chicanery," Larry finished the loop.

"I am Nathaniel. The Thorn-thrower," quoth the raven.

He had his own high-tech vintage leather flight mask with bells, whistles, dials and a glowing red outline across the bird's skull. He explained to the Ancient how he alone had been dispatched to escort him home. It turned out the portal opened over the island on Ferril Lake, which was directly southeast from where LtAWS was focusing his search. The two Guardians of the Envoy, agents from another dimension, soared above the mountain town, measuring their respiration as they prepared to hit the portal on the move. Nathaniel was in the lead position, with the Ancient to his left and slightly behind. They both spotted the electric blue interdimensional entryway, and the Thorn-thrower signaled that he would go high, meaning for Larry to go low.

When going over Niagara Falls, it's best not to incorporate slingshots or outboard motors. Not true in a wormhole. Ideally, you want to stay on a straight line between the two points. Point A to Point B. If you're not careful, all of a sudden there's a Point C, D, Z, or a sweaty layover in the Ninth Layer of Hell. I'm not saying all the time, but Russian roulette is absolutely zero fun with a single-barrel shotgun. Civil war cannon fodder. Nuke allure subs: Flood torpedo bays; watch it with the toxic smoothies. Napalm loves the smell of gravy when it's mourning over cooties.

Once inside the traveling chamber, sound compressed adjusting centers in every direction. Yes it was Hendrix, and yes it was boulders cracked by the god's hammers, and no there's nothing like fiery tire tracks. Like being swallowed by a bully wave, and you hear the current laughing as it drags you down to your watery gravy train ferryboat's landing. But you keep your eyes closed, because even with the pressurized lenses in their flight masks, there still remained risks to their sight and general ability to even just hold a spoon for tapioca pudding Tuesdays.

You stay limp when inside the system's pull. If you fight or strain and twist, this is how accidents occur and destinations get crossed up. The link is preprogrammed between two distinct gateways, but hey, shit can happen because most of us are just winging it anyway. Music played. You felt the resonance of the gravity of other worlds. There came at moments the absence of being. Fish in the sea: hydrogen in the ocean. So very much more intense than any jetski, Sea-Doo, or WaveRunner would ever be. Above was the sensation of a battalion of strings, violings, and cellos mellow and in a tizzy. Fun for maybe a psychotic adrenaline junky. A noticeable warning tone pinged and vibrated throughout their flight masks. This was standard, with the frequency increasing as they neared the exit portal. LtAWS could almost breathe easy. The beeping then became a steady pitch. That's the Gold. Larry felt the sudden pressure change, as he shot out next to Nathaniel the Thorn-Thrower, both animals looking now fondly on the 'raspberry green' skies of Weird Earth, that good ole Seventh Dimension. Next to the easy market, right there on Main Street. Ask for Leo, tell them Fyodor sent you, but don't say nothing about fate or freewill. Witchery is a hangin' offense.

· · · · · · ·

Back on Original Earth, Israel Dufrene was making plans to return to Arizona and Alyssa Rose Twyst. He'd collect his final paycheck from the diner, and stock the bus back up for the road. Sundries, ganja, etc. It was a twelve-hour drive and he could probably make it all at once. He decided he would leave early the next day. This would put him into Payson tomorrow in the late-afternoon, early evening. Back to his Alyssa, and her gorgeous glow.

March 14, 1998

Dystopian Squalor Syndicate had a weekend to spot shine the different parts of their set. This coming Tuesday was the gig. They'd no doubt have to make it a point to squeeze in some recreational activities so as not to get worn too thin. Saturday after lunch they put in a few good hours of rehearsal. The three men broke at 1500 and took to the bottle to get on with some quality drinking. Truck and Denzel each had a forty-ounce of Mickey's fine malt liquor. Boonz and Esther shared a fifth of Smirnoff watermelon vodka, straight and chilled. There were multiple college basketball games on the TV. The madness of March was in effect, its tides wildly rippling. The volume was muted and The Black Crowes Shake Your Money Maker (1990) played on the hi-fi stereo system. It was a mismatched ratrod with one turntable and an EQ from the discothèque, like the last remains of the Nineteen Eighties. Unt-sis unt-sis chicka bohm gak.

"I could never survive on two showers a day, if it were mandatory. I'd go nuts. No rag on the nat sees. Jerks though, right? I'd just be too clean. Gotta get a chance to build up a tolerable layer of grime, dirt, and all that," Truck said.

"I like long hot showers. I'll take one just for kicks. Most women though, they probably prefer cleanliness in a possible mate," Esther said.

"Umm, no woman has ever complained to me about that. Plus, save the rain forests, right?"

"That's dumb. There's no magic number. You bathe as is necessary. Some days it's not needed. Other days might require a few. What're you talking about anyway?" Denzel asked.

"All I meant was that I had two showers yesterday, and it was too much," said Truck.

"You should just say what you mean next time, straight up," said Boonz.

Mack Truck felt reprimanded. He should've just bagged on Boonz for his drinking that fruity vodka. The drummer was measuring the amount of drunk he'd get from his Mickey's, against where Boonz would end up after half of the Smirnoff. It was customary to finish a thing off once you start it. See it through. At that moment, Truck realized he would need at least another six-pack to reach satisfaction. That wasn't taking into account Denzel, who had a few joints rolled to make good use of. Boonz didn't usually smoke, probably wouldn't now.

"Hey Denzel," said Boonz. "How do you write *your* songs? Call me old-fashioned, but I like a nice pen and notepad."

"Call *me* old-fashioned as well, but I like to chisel my shit into slabs of granite. That's how it stands the test of time," said Denzel.

There was some leftover chicken comma Kentucky fried. Just like cold pizza, finely curated by time and exposure to the atmospheric affectations. Boonz found a wishbone, which he and Esther then went head-to-head on. It was not a sudden split. Slight pressure pulled in opposing directions, the battle of man and woman. Finally, the bone snapped and the Syndicate's bass player was left holding the larger half.

"Ladybug, ladybug, fly away home. Go on and make a wish," said Esther.

"Wishes aren't real," Boonz said.

"Then pray," said Truck.

"Pray for what?" asked Boonz.

"Pray for money," said Denzel.

"I don't believe in money," said Boonz.

"Yeah right. Then what do you believe in?" Truck said.

"Karma," Boonz replied.

"Well, karma's not real. Probably even less so than money and prayer," said Denzel.

"Bite your tongue," Esther said.

Boonz made a wish anyhow. Everyone else prayed for money. Then Esther took her man and their vodka, as they both retired to the lady's boudoir. This left Truck and Denzel in the den with the NCAA Tournament and The Black Crowes. They made conversation with the angels, calling them out by their names. Gabriel, Michael (motorcycle), Azrael, Ariel, Lucifer, Wormwood, and Bobby Darin. When the roll is called up yonder isle be aware, sea fair, and despair as much parts of never as is possible. Truck saw that Denzel was easily through six-eighths of his drank. Then the drummer couldn't remember if they hadn't already smoked one or maybe more of the joints. But didn't we just finish playing? No, but now we're drinking. This last part he knew because he currently was himself chugging Mickey's, which was cold so it must not have been too long since they started on the booze. Boonz and Esther were gone because they weren't there at present. But could those two just have stepped out for a minute? Then Denzel passed over a lit joint, so it seems that they were also now smoking. But still might have been before as well. That doesn't matter, but there's nothing wrong with pointing out achievement. However, screaming while leaping up and down crazily can be a bit much.

"Let's call Mervyn's. Talk to the ladies in lingerie," said Truck.

"Or—let's call Roxy. Hell, we should just drive down to Payson and mess with all of them," Denzel said.

"Definitely. Then we can drop in at your Pop's place. See what's going on."

It was an agreeable plan, obviously the thing to do. They grabbed coats, the keys to the band's van, and Sonny's CD case. The bucket of leftover fried chicken was also brought along. The joint was still going back and forth as the van's engine fired up. Truck was at the wheel. Denzel stashed a zip lock bag that held his remaining joints slash herb. For music, they agreed upon Stoner Witch (Melvins, 1994). It was aggressive but not insane. They drove, listened, smoked, and ate cold chicken.

The first CD played its course. It was then readily replaced with Dirt (Alice in Chains, 1992). They exited Interstate Seventeen onto the Two-sixty, which would take them into Payson. Just like with the prank calls there was no plan. They would probably roll in hot, looking for a rise. It was the fucking weekend. Worries weren't a thing. The two driven beings burned another marijuana cigarette. You know—real scum.

Upon arrival, they first stopped in to see Catfish. The men all shared war stories over a Matlock rerun. It was good for a minute, but the restlessness in Twigzel especially made them break out after a short time. At a service station, a twelve-pack of guts and glory was added to their stock of thighs, wings, breast, and drumstick. A random single hickory was rolling around free in the Econoline's back cargo area.

Denzel pointed out the route and told Truck they would start it off real cool. After a couple minutes of playing nice, he would find a good angle for to set in with all the tortures and friendly natured harasslin'. Turning in at the sign marked 'Didney World West,' the Ford van creeped down the dirt lane towards Roxy's cabin. It was a shady afternoon in amongst the pines. It seemed a pleasant scene so Truck lowered the blasting chains of Alice. Would he fall into the flow again?

They parked off to the side, while Denzel could already see Alyssa seated there upon the porch. Not another soul was in view. Twigzel told Truck to hang back for a minute, while he went up and made contact. It sounded reasonable.

Alyssa saw Twig step out of the van. She was not enthused about this situation unfolding. He looked like ruthless desperation, with an unhealthy confidence, and a walk like a stalking hyena. The predator let out a little laugh. If it was meant to be welcoming, it failed miserably. Desean stopped by Roxy's Jeep's front bumper. He said, 'Hey.' Miss Twyst rose from her seat and stood by the vertical beam at the porch's edge.

"Hi," she said, about as uninterested as could be.

"Tsssssss," he deflected with nonchalance. "You want to come and see my new puppy?"

This was unexpected to the girl. "Umm, sure. Let me get Roxy."

"No, I want to surprise her. You can help me bring it up from the van."

Alyssa agreed, because puppies are always amazing. She did still keep her distance from Twigzella, who just didn't seem right. To the extent that much of his seeming was exceedingly wrong.

Chapter Fifty-Seven • Unleashed & Everlasting

March 14, 1998

Izzy had been on the highway almost non-stop since before 0600 Saturday morning. This trail was familiar. He drove with purpose, ears full 'a' phonky dribblins. There were road kills and forest grounds lined with wild nests of habitation. Long stretches, short drops off steep cliffs. Gone sketches. Happy clouds and raging valleys cast across the infinite out there.

He listened to Blood Sugar Sex Magik (Red Hot Chili Peppers, 1991) and Nevermind (Nirvana, 1991) something like three times each. Greatest Hits, Volume 1 (Randy Travis, 1992) and Gone (Dwight Yoakam, 1995) took him all the way through New Mexico and into Arizona. Now this floating speck of matter had inside it playing Red Light (The Slackers, 1997).

Danger's real wobbly, son. Exploding over home plates is the trial's escape. The 1969 Westfalia Camper entered Payson from the east on State Route Two-sixty. Turning south onto the country lane that led towards Roxy's cabin, Izzy felt close to a resolution and reunion with his woman. He would gladly drop anchor here to work out an immediate future for the rest of eternal tease. With liberty encrusted cherry pie, homemade and filling like the buffet lining murderer's row when comes the last meal. On golden platters, spray painted Styrofoam; breathe it in, get high. See through utensils, so we don't rip out our veins and vanity to spite our wrists and sanity. Shame for every evil, blessings for any good you ever get around to.

When he passed the brown van on the road nothing sparked in recognition. It moved along at a pressing clip. There was only a driver, though perhaps a thrashing flashed in the vehicle's farther back. Oh, the business that goes on behind closed windows and doors.

Izzy made his way down the path to Roxy's, pulled up next to her Cherokee and noticed that the cabin door was wide open.

Les appeared from around the side of the dwelling and saw the VW bus. He wore an awful look upon his face. Roxy stepped out onto the front porch, quickly making directly for the Volkswagen. Mr. Dufrene did feel a tension arising.

"Did you see a brown van out there on your way in?" said Roxy.

"Yes," Izzy nodded.

"Go. Go now! They have Alyssa!"

"What?"

"Twig and them! Check Two-sixty north, towards Flagstaff. Please, get her back. I am going to call the sheriff."

"Fuck." Izzy pulled away in chase.

• • • • • • •

In a world of black and white, the gray beast is both king and cancer.

"Freaking out hasn't done anybody any good since Chic put out Le Freak in 1978," said Twigzel.

"Fuck man, what are you *doing*?" said Truck.

"Chill out, we're only going for a ride."

Twigzella held greedily onto Alyssa. She would struggle for four seconds, then curse out her captor: "What the fuck is your problem? Take me back, right now!" He told Truck to put on When Disaster Strikes (Busta Rhymes, 1997). The intro featured an ominous voice warning of impending adversity with the approach of the new millennium. Cold villainy. Thorough disregard.

"Didn't you like it when we used to play rough?" Twigzella asked Alyssa.

"Whatever. I also used to think you had some good in you. It doesn't change you being a total *ass*hole right now!" And she tried to break free again.

Not even Desean knew what he might have planned, having now snatched away the precious Rose. It was a thrill the moment the thought had entered his mind. Right there by the porch he'd concocted the idea of the puppy. They slowly walked to the van. He slid the side door open and grabbed the girl forcing Truck to make a fast getaway. She was barely screaming, locked in his arms. It's not so bad. She wouldn't get hurt. Not too bad. She felt like a toy. He wanted to fuck her, but he wasn't that type of goy. He could feel her though, against his body. In a different world they would've been together. But in this world right now they were nearly as one. He could easily fuck her. Truck was loyal. Truck was down. Truck was a sleaze just like him. That's what makes things work. Loose morals and the willingness to commit atrocities: social, business, criminal, coital, and interpersonal atrocities. Things where how you create a good story to tell the jury from the witness stand. Shouting out about how she never once actually said the word 'No,' and how they had had a past and what do you mean when you say, 'probable motive?'

There is no motive. There are no meanings in meanies. There is urge, action, and no thought of consequence. But in the moment, that is where life and the glory reside.

Twigzerla spun the girl around and leaned against her. They were face to face. With her eyes she stared him down and cursed the evil spirits who had taken control of the increasingly unpleasant scenario. Real rotten: bad—you know it, sha-mon. From outside came two short beeps, followed by a long drawn out blast of a car horn. Alyssa knew that warning tone, that bleating sheep, brash but uplifting. What were the odds? In whose favor did they fall? Of course, it just *had* to be him. Either way, these dudes can go screw. She kneed Twigzerla hard in the groin. As he recoiled, she put both her feet into his chest, kicking with all that she had. He slammed against the side door, and then his momentum carried him over into the back of the van.

Alyssa Rose rose up, threw open the door at full speed, and there was her Mr. Dufrene with his VW bus looking like a lighthouse in the storm. He motioned for her to leap into his driver window, which sounded like a horrible idea. She yelled at Truck to pull over and Twigzerla shouted: "Don't even *think* about slowing down!" Truck shot back that there was a hippy van right outside, then he strapped his seat belt on, shooting a glance across at the other driver to his right flank.

Alyssa surveyed the gap, the highway lines dashing down below. Then Twigzerla monster lunged at her, ruining her chance to make a quick exit. She slipped down onto her left knee, turned and planted her right foot against the floor, and then swung around as hard as she could with her clenched right fist. I would not call it a roundhouse or an uppercut, though there was a definite rising arc and upward momentum. Most apt would probably be a haymaker. Anyway you want to call it, that girl connected with his face slash jaw, which sent Twigzerla staggering backwards and out the open door.

Izzy only saw the man madly clutching at the Econoline's edges. Somehow he ended up hanging off the van's top ledge, his feet frantically searching for a foothold while nicking the road's surface.

"Slow down!" Twigzerla yelled at Truck, frozen at the wheel.

"Asshole!" Alyssa shouted back, and she flung a blue beanbag chair out at the frightened Twigzerla monster.

Izzy pulled in close and hollered out all kinds of encouragement. He presented his arms as a target. Inside, the girl thought of Larry the Ancient, Twin Falls, ice cream sandwiches and anything else even remotely cheerful. She pushed off the far side of the cargo van, took three small stutter steps and then flew like an Olympic diver going for the gold, only horizontal, fully extended and aerodynamic. She felt release. Then came freedom and Izzy's arms beneath her. He let off the accelerator, keeping his arms even to support the girl and steady the wheel. They slowed down, pulled over, and finally Alyssa sat breathily heaving, heavily breathing sweet escape in the camper's front passenger seat. She and him took time to lower their pulses, recover, and remark at the insanity of it all.

Minutes later, several highway patrol cars sped by with lights ablaze and sirens sounding. They were in pursuit of the brown Ford van seen heading north just above town. Who knows what kind of tale Twigzerla would have to weave to avoid a mouthful of gravel? Shouts, threats, and Miranda's right, babe. Where is the girl? A likely story. She's with the guy. Is that so? Jumped into the front window? Anything you say, we can't abide and will be held against you. Dot, dot, dot: Semi-conscious colon backslash ALF redirects to cats comma Garfield forward slash lasagna. In accordance with: the slaw of mine aunt's healthy options, and deadly seed creds. It is all specified in Thee, contract.

• • • • • • • •

Izzy and Alyssa returned to Roxy's lair, listening to a tape that the boy had picked out for the girl. Would you believe it if I told you six feet one and five feet two weren't all that far away from being dead on? Exile in Guyville (Liz Phair, 1993).

"What is the ideal?" Alyssa mused. "To have mostly good days, toss in some greatness, all while keeping the badness to a minimum? You just saved me from a very bad day, to be sure. And have given me a great one, in this our current Earth's rotation's reverie. For this I thank you."

"Oui, Love." Izzy answered.

"Yes, we does."

Je suis doves. They were with each other. It felt solid—had the feel of comfort—its feeling was.

"Nice, one time I blowed harp and sang Johnny B. Goode at a VFW for some veterans celebrating the Marine Corps Birthday. I imagine that was my peak. The way they all looked at me. Like something had really been done. It's that same look you have in *your* eyes. What's that look?" Izzy asked her.

"Love the lovers, love the haters. Embrace the barrier's Yorkshire terriers."

This is not an end, but a beginning:[18] Goodbye polarity—

Dream today.

Epilogue:

March 17, 1998

Dystopian Squalor Syndicate made it to their St. Patty's gig, because nobody pressed charges and maybe someone learned a lesson, or they didn't. Denzel, AKA Twigzerla monster, stepped up to the microphone for sound check. Damn it if he wasn't going to at least do one thing right: "Check yo recollect yo! Twenty years and change I been on this hunk 'a' rock, and now I demand respect and to be heard. One two: two two. I is gettin' on near now to realizin' certain truths. If only just to bring the ruckus to all them sap bloody truckers."

Then music.

• • • • • • •

March 19, 1998

Izzy, Alyssa, and Roxy had made their way on over to Texas. Now they were exploring Austin, and its South By Southwest music and arts festival. That racket was alright at one point, but would ultimately lose its sheen slash coat of endearing dirt and filth, depending upon your angle. What *is* your angle? They ended up in a lecture hall, listening to a seminar on 'Charting Success' led by some cat named Fred. The small audience slowly grew by ones and fews. The whole ordeal was more of a freeform conversation than it was an instructive talk or insightful spouting of wisdom. It was some kind of time they all did share. When it concluded, the trio left in search of funnel cakes and freedom. Because at the end of the day, when all is dead and sun: snacking is the best way to bring it on home.

Let me remind you, there's only one way to get to the light dude. Experiment with French toast and Thai food. Read a bit, write a bomb about a haiku, set the right mood—

Death spray, now they lay
Bountiful once, but now through
Why did nothing stop?

Begrudge your local Congresspersons. Really give it to 'em thick.

Word

[1] Robert Mark Kamen, The Karate Kid, 1984............................7
[1a] Robert Mark Kamen, The Karate Kid, 1984...........................8
[2] Hunter S. Thompson, Fear and Loathing in Las Vegas, 1972.........14
[3] Fred Armisen, Carrie Brownstein, Portlandia, 2012...................15
[4] Steve Martin, Born Standing Up, 2007.................................42
[5] James Cameron, Aliens, 1986...58
[6] Joss Whedon, Alien: Resurrection, 1997...............................58
[6a] Joss Whedon, Alien: Resurrection, 1997...............................58
[7] Nathaniel Hawthorne...72
[8] Joe Strummer...132
[9] Mitch Hedberg, The Dufrenes, Strategic Grill Locations, 1999......138
[10] Jane Austen, Pride and Prejudice, 1813................................192
[11] David Foster Wallace, Infinite Jest, 1996.............................237
[12] Matt Damon, Ben Affleck, Good Will Hunting, 1997................254
[13] H. S. Thompson, Fear and Loathing-Vegas, 1972, (rephrase).......337
[14] Song of Songs 2:14, Solomon, NIV....................................346
[15] Geoffrey Chaucer...353
[15a] Geoffrey Chaucer...353
[15b] Geoffrey Chaucer...353
[16] Dr. Martin Luther King, Jr. I Have a Dream speech, 1963...........362
[17] Fred Armisen, Carrie Brownstein, Portlandia, 2012...................378
[18] Dr. Martin Luther King, Jr. I Have a Dream speech, 1963...........397